To
Dad. (Col

Happy birthday
30th May 1998.

From your loving daughter and
son in law Gina and Mark

Wishing you a very happy 56
birthday and wish you every success
in your ambition to become a Pilot.
Its a beautiful world of peace
and serenity up there in the clouds.

With Best Wishes
From.

Charles Faulkner BSc.
(Ex Royal Air Force Cranwell)
4th OCTOBER 1997

THE YOUNG FIGHTER PILOT

THE YOUNG
FIGHTER PILOT

Charles Faulkner

The Book Guild Ltd
Sussex, England

The Book Guild Ltd
25 High Street
Lewes, Sussex

First published 1997
© Charles Faulkner 1997
Set in Baskerville
Typesetting by Southern Reproductions (Sussex)
Crowborough, Sussex

Printed in Great Britain by
Antony Rowe Ltd,
Chippenham, Wiltshire

A catalogue record for this book is
available from the British Library

ISBN 1 85776 186 3

The greatest fighter deserves the most beautiful woman
Adolf Hitler

To Sarah – with love, affection and understanding

ACKNOWLEDGEMENTS

The author would like to thank the undermentioned people for their support, contribution, expertise and technical information, in the preparation of this story. Without them, this story would not have come to fruition.

Special thanks go to my secretarial team. Without their grammatical and secretarial skills this book would not have been to the publisher's specification in order to be considered for publication. The persons whose recognition should be commended are Mrs June Redfern MBE, the late Miss Linda Beverly LLB, who gave up so much of their time to proof read my original script, and to Mrs Barbara Morgan, who I am indebted to for reading the final script. Her proof reading skills were beyond excellence, for which I am truly grateful. My sincere thanks go to Mr Peter Bourne MCSD, Managing Director of Quadraphic Design Consultants, whose brilliant design in the cover of the book is to be commended. I owe him a deep sense of gratitude for producing such an attractive cover.

This story is in remembrance of the front-line pilots of the Allied Air Forces who were attached to the Air Defence of Great Britain (ADGB) during the period of Hitler's Vengeance Weapon attack from June 1944 to March 1945.

My gratitude also goes to my secretary at my place of employment, who gave up so much of her time to type the first half of this book. Secondly, to Miss Barbara Devereaux (her name has been changed to protect her identity) who is one of the main characters of the book. Without her permission, this story could not have been told. So I am indeed very grateful to her that she has given her consent to be mentioned in this story. She represented the wives, girlfriends and families whose love, affection and loyalty gave the pilots attached to the ADGB an anchor to display their courage, flying skills and unparalleled determination to prevent Adolf Hitler's final attempt to annihilate the population and cities of the United Kingdom. To those loved ones the Nation owes a deep debt of gratitude which throughout the annals of history is often forgotten.

There were many people from all walks of life who offered their characteristics, mannerisms and habits for me to make up true characters to play the parts of people who appear in this narrative. I thank them.

Throughout the writing of this story I had to tap people's knowledge, both technical, geographical and historical. I list them below:

The Air Historical Branch of Defence in London, two names in particular: Air Commodore (Retired) Henry Probert and Mr Eric Munday
Mr Michael Cooper, ex-Royal Air Force
Mrs Jan Buckberry ALA, Librarian at Royal Air Force College, Cranwell
Mr Eric Badby, ex-Royal Air Force
Mr Paul Bamford
Mr Ian Boulter
Mr Paul Danby
The late Trevor Brown
Lieutenant Colonel Anthony Mather OBE, Central Chancery of the Orders of Knighthood
Mr Jack Glover – I am indebted to him for helping me finalise the script – ex-Royal Air Force

Flight Lieutenant B. Wildin GD/N RAF (Ret'd)
Squadron Leader (Retired) Ray Harle, Director of the
South West Area of the Royal Air Forces Association
Mrs Lorna Hood. Without her post editing skills, I could
not have completed the final checking of the edited
manuscript in time. To the many hours she contributed,
I owe her a deep sense of gratitude.
Mrs Evelyn Hill
Mrs Susie Hewitt, Librarian at Okehampton Library
Mrs Sue Jones
Mr Jim Negus
Dr L. Palmer MBCHB, Diploma in Anaesthetics
Flight Lieutenant (Retired) Donald Rankin GD/P
Miss Caroline Redfern
Mr Adrian Peter Redfern
Mr Anthony George Fletcher
Mr Michael Snell, ex-Royal Air Force
Mr Simon Twigg, Manager of Waterstone, Exeter
To Mr Howard Lewis and his office staff at the Watford
Branch of my employer, for all their support in the
preparation of this novel.
Dover District Council, Tourism Department for their
help in assisting in the material for the cover of this
book.
Mrs Paula Mardo BA, Assistant Reference Librarian at
Exeter Central Library
Dr Sylvia Rosevear MBCHB, MD, MRCOG, FRNZCOG.

Finally I must thank my devoted wife for her undivided
support. Her help in the research was immense, and a great
asset to me. To the many hundreds of hours in which I had to
research this intriguing challenge, she spent many hours
alone for which I am truly grateful.

PREFACE

The characters, events and the formation of this special squadron of Spitfires to counter attack Hitler's secret weapon, namely, the Vergeltungswaffe Eins (the V1 or Reprisal Weapon One) are entirely fictitious.

However, there was a war and pilots like Pilot Officer Hamilton were engaged to shoot down this lethal weapon which Hitler's scientists first designed in the early part of 1942.

Due to the success and accuracy of bombing the assembly plants and launching sites by the Allied Air Forces, Hitler's plans for preventing the Normandy landings were thwarted.

This story is a tribute to the gallantry, courage and fortitude of those small bands of pilots, many of whom gave their lives for the freedom of this land which at that time was threatened.

1

In the early evening of 3 April 1944 Barry and I were anxiously waiting on the cold, dirty, crowded platform of Stafford Station for our train to take us south, to the bombarded city of London.

For both of us it had been a day of momentous events. That morning we had successfully passed our advanced pilots' training course at No. 61 Operational Training Unit, Royal Air Force, Rednal in Shropshire. The day had been tiring and hard due to the discipline we had both endured throughout the passing out parade. It was a significant day in our lives as the climax of two years' hard work of intensive pilot training had come to an end. Although excited about the excellent turnout our passing out entry had achieved in front of the Reviewing Officer, Major General Sir George Stobbart KCB DSO MC, we also felt sadness at leaving the comradeship, enjoyment and fulfilment we had known for the past two years. At this time the Second World War was entering a new phase, a phase of attack rather than defence which we had experienced since that fateful day on 3 September 1939 when we declared war on Germany.

British and Allied Forces under the Supreme Allied Commander, General Dwight D. Eisenhower, were preparing the largest armada of armed forces ever to be undertaken in the D-Day landings. We, as new recruits, were going to play some part in the new phase of the war. What this would be, however, we would not know until we arrived at our new squadrons; Barry to No. 41 Squadron stationed at Hornchurch, Essex, while I was being posted to the Home

Defensive System, namely 629 Squadron at Hambridge in Kent.

The train eventually arrived on Platform 1 some 20 minutes late with all the coaches except the first-class compartment at the front full to capacity. We decided on the spur of the moment to jump at the chance of a seat in the first-class carriage as we had been up since 0500 hours that morning and our bodies were desperately tired by the time the train arrived. The Army and the Navy seemed well represented on the train with a handful of civilians seated here and there. Both of us instantly decided to risk the fine imposed on people travelling in a first-class compartment with a second-class ticket. We made for the first coach which had a few vacant seats, stored our cases as best we could and sat down on the seats opposite two women in the Armed Forces. A card-cum-dining table separated them from us. The top of the table, which was brown in colour, had seen better days. The women were both officers, one in khaki uniform with three pips on her shoulder, young and attractive, the other dressed in the uniform of the WAAF and looking much older than we two, holding the rank of Flight Officer.

The steam train, belching smoke into our carriage, eventually pulled out slowly from Stafford Station, the engine puffing and straining as it gained speed. We thought we would reach London in good time to be able to have a drink together before finally parting to join our respective squadrons. However, that was not to be. Due to excess weight, the train laboriously puffed and panted its way to London. It seemed that the final hours of this important day were going to be tedious and frustrating but all this was changed by the voice of the elder officer who leaned over towards us and said, 'Have you just passed out from Rednal or Shawbury today?'

'Yes, Ma'am,' I replied, smiling with apprehension and wondering how she knew.

'There were two passing out parades in Shropshire today,' she said, 'and by your appearance you seem to have just left one of them.'

She glanced at my new cap which was sitting on the table.

'Yes, we completed our OTU course at Rednal and are now on our way to our squadrons.'

'Oh, I see,' she said as she leant back into her comfortable seat.

Before she could pick up her magazine I leaned over and pointing to Barry whispered, 'This is Pilot Officer Barry Sargent and I'm Donald Hamilton.'

'Pleased to meet you both,' she replied. 'I'm Flight Officer Jean Hampshire, a doctor from Wroughton Hospital and this is Captain Elizabeth Horton from the Royal Military Hospital at Aldershot, who is a senior sister. We have both been attending a burns course at a hospital in Crewe.' She put her magazine down and prepared herself for further conversation. 'You both look tired. Completing courses is very tiring, isn't it?'

'Yes, ma'am,' I replied.

Barry got into a conversation with the nursing sister and I was glad that I no longer had the job of stimulating the conversation between the two sexes.

'Your mother must be proud of you,' Flight Officer Hampshire said in a pleasant voice as she leaned over once again and looked straight into my eyes.

'I expect so,' I said, 'but my brother has just been awarded the Distinguished Service Medal for gallantry in the Aegean Sea so I expect her thoughts were on him rather than me today.'

'Your parents must be very proud of you both since qualifying for those coveted wings is no mean achievement, especially these days when we're desperately short of pilots.'

'Yes,' I said, and with that I picked up my paper. I didn't want to get involved since she seemed to have a bossy manner and was senior in rank to me. Meanwhile Barry was deep in conversation with Elizabeth, and being a Mancunian he was a good talker. Jean got up out of her seat and made for the carriage door to open the window, letting in even more smoke from the hard-pressed, noisy steam engine up front. My thoughts instantly turned to the excitement of seeing my fiancée that evening in her home in New Malden, Surrey. We had met two years previously on my first leave as an Officer Cadet. It was one of those opportunistic meetings when one goes dancing on Saturday nights at the local dance hall. We took a liking to each other at the first instant as we had various interests in common which brought us together, mainly dancing, swimming, badminton and walking. Undoubtedly the Officer Cadet uniform helped. It was quite distinctive from other uniforms in that we had to wear white bands around our hats and white tabs on our lapels.

As the train jostled towards London, so my thoughts turned towards the future, to joining my new squadron in south-east England and to my love for Barbara Anne Devereaux, whom I had proposed to the previous December while on Christmas leave. Also I was conscious of the dangers which would be present when as a second-line pilot I would fly Spitfires with the Home Defence System. Barry on the other hand was going to pilot Spitfires with an offensive role with 41 Squadron. We were relieved that the Battle of Britain was over. The density of enemy aircraft attacking Britain was now decreasing because the Luftwaffe had sustained heavy losses and the Allied bombing offensive, both day and night, was taking a heavy toll on Hitler's factories in the Ruhr. Our role was going to be completely new since, instead of being on the defensive as we had been since 1939, we were now on the attack.

The train eventually arrived one hour late at Euston Station in the heart of London. We said goodbye to the two senior female officers before alighting from the train. Barry's departure was a sentimental moment for me because we had been great friends throughout our pilot training. He wasn't too good at the academics of flying but he was a truly magnificent pilot. From the start he was a natural-born flier whereas I just scraped through every test.

We finally said goodbye to each other outside the platform gates at Euston Station. I made my way down the escalator to catch the tube for Waterloo Station and on to New Malden.

As the train approached the somewhat dimly-lit station at New Malden a feeling of excitement came over me as the road leading to Barbara's suburban house came into view from the dirty window of the train. Although exhausted from the long arduous day, I decided to walk the mile or so, since the air was fresh and my luggage light. A few people were pottering here and there but generally the streets were empty, an air raid being in progress at the time.

I hadn't gone far along the road when my thoughts were distracted by the drone of a heavy enemy bomber, probably a Ju 88 high above me in the darkened sky. Suddenly the night sky was lit up with an array of searchlights which scanned the horizon from left to right looking for the intruder which was probably on its way to bomb London. The lights momentarily caught the outline of the German bomber but as the pilot took evasive action so the lights lost their target and had to repeat their process of scanning the sky. A few moments went by, then the lights focused on the aeroplane and locked on to their target. Instantaneously the ack-ack guns opened fire from behind me. They seemed jolly close, too close for my liking; the recoil blast of the shells projecting out into the sky battered my ear drums. As I reached Barbara's road, I was glad to escape those frightening ack-ack shells and fragments which were falling nearby. Suddenly there was an almighty explosion in the illuminated sky. The aeroplane became a ball of orange fire, spiralling to the ground with increasing speed in the direction of Kingston. The dull thud of impact could be heard for miles around as it hit the ground, accompanied by a sheet of flame which reflected in the night sky.

I was sincerely relieved when I reached the door of Barbara's house. The cold sweat on my brow had stuck to my cap. Pausing momentarily to take a deep breath to relieve my tension, I rang the doorbell. The house was in darkness because of the air raid and looked deserted and cold. Then the door opened cautiously, and a figure stood in the doorway. There was an embarrassed silence as we gazed at each other. The large, solid mahogany door, with its stained-glass window, could be seen from the light in the hall. It opened wider and as I stepped forward to greet her she looked tense and nervous in the shadow of the hall light. She was so relieved when she eventually recognised me as I crossed the threshold and embraced her, kissing her tenderly on the lips.

She stood motionless, gathering her thoughts, then she said, 'You might have telephoned either at Stafford or Euston to let me know what time you would be arriving and whether you wanted a meal.'

'I do apologise, darling, for not phoning but both at Stafford and Euston Station the queues for the telephone were long and time-consuming. Also the train was an hour late arriving in London, I suppose because of the excessive load it was carrying.'

With this the tension between us faded away. She took my hand and led me into the drawing-room which was warm and dimly lit. It was heated by a lovely, glowing coal fire, its red-hot ashes surrounded by a marble fireplace. Coal fires always attracted my attention since all my life both at school, at home and in the services I had been surrounded by radiators which lacked the glowing feeling when you entered a room.

The wall lights were dimmed because of reduced voltage. Barbara took another step forward into the light and I could see her face was pale with black circles under her eyes. She looked tired, nervous and positively jaded. She certainly appeared to have changed both emotionally and in appearance since we last met.

'Can I get you a drink, Pilot Officer Hamilton?' she said formally, turning towards an expensive antique cocktail cabinet that had been well used over the years.

'Please, the usual if you have any in stock,' I replied since she knew I liked a drop of Scotch. She brought over two large whiskies with ice and led me to the costly, brown, velvet-covered sofa, where we sat down.

'Cheers, it's lovely to have you home again,' she said affectionately as she touched her glass to mine and then continued to explain why she was hesitant at the front door: because she could only see an outline of a man and my new uniform and cap had thrown her, plus she was disturbed by the local artillery which had been firing at the enemy plane.

'Probably it was my fault,' I said, 'I should have telephoned.'

'That's OK now,' she said in a more relaxed voice, and looked at me for a long time, refilling our glasses with more of her father's whisky from a beautiful cut-glass decanter. She leaned forward supporting herself on my arm and said sweetly, 'It's wonderful to see you. I do love you,' she went on, kissing me on the cheek. 'I miss you so, especially at weekends when Mummy and Daddy are away with the band. Four months seems a long time since we met, doesn't it?' She held my hands tightly.

'Yes, darling, a lot's happened since we last met and it's good to be home with you, even though we only have this evening together.'

I kissed her on the cheek as she pressed her lips against my face and said, 'That uniform of yours suits you. I like your pilot's wings. He must be a good tailor you have at Rednal. It's a pity you can't stay for a few days, but I suppose we're lucky you're home for this one night.'

I looked straight into her sparkling eyes and said, 'We've both been through a hard time of our lives. Your work at the bank and the extra burden of your exams must have been stressful for you. For me, the sheer concentration of learning to fly and the high standard required for passing to get these full wings has left me shattered.'

She interrupted my thoughts and said, 'I'm sorry I couldn't be at your passing out parade today, but with staff shortages at work I daren't ask the boss for a day off.'

She came closer to me. 'That's all right, darling. It would have been difficult until after the parade to see you and anyway it wasn't your cup of tea with all those strangers about.'

She met my gaze and let me look her up and down. Her eyes scanned my face and uniform and she said, 'That uniform makes you rather attractive, you know. You'll have to

7

keep all those WAAFs at bay, otherwise I'll be jealous.' She smiled, putting her arms around my neck.

'Don't worry,' I said, as I kissed her lips to reassure her. She was dressed in a very expensive, dark grey two-piece suit with matching blouse. The jacket seemed to fit her squarely across the shoulders although, unfortunately, it hid her lovely figure. A pocket handkerchief in her breast pocket gave her a professional look and her black, pointed high-heeled shoes with ankle straps completed her appearance of elegance and beauty. She was really a lovely girl and I admired her immensely.

After a light meal and some more whisky we chatted about the progress of the war, the frequent air raids, her father's participation in the local band and the future we hoped for ourselves. Communication in the past between us had been meagre and erratic, with only a trickle of letters being exchanged since neither of us liked putting pen to paper – we found the telephone much more to our liking when we could get a line.

One of the many tragedies of war was the disintegration of engagements and marriages through separation. For some the time lapse was weeks, for some months, and for many, years, so that the bond of love and friendship had to be strong to overcome the pain of loneliness.

I leaned over the sofa and kissed her soft red mouth. She wasn't a bit surprised and closed her eyes as I brushed my lips against her cheek. 'Well,' I said, 'we've both had a long day and if you don't mind, my bed is calling me.'

With that she got up from the sofa, put the guard against the fire and led me upstairs to the guest room above the garage. After switching the bedroom light off and drawing the heavy, gold velvet curtains, I opened the window and inhaled the cold, fresh air. The activity we had heard earlier had now died down and it was peaceful once again. The events of the day had drained my strength and taxed my nervous system so I was glad to get into bed and relax among the soft bedclothes.

Although it seemed a long time, it was only a few moments later that I heard Barbara's footsteps tiptoeing towards my door. She opened it slowly and whispered, 'Are you asleep?'

I replied, 'Of course not; I've been waiting for you,' and with that, dressed in a light, embroidered nightgown, she jumped in beside me sending me further down into the bed.

We talked for quite a while about personal matters, such as our future, where I was going and whether her father would be promoted in the band. We both agreed to marry at a later date in order to get over my first set of operations. It was a sound and wise decision because the death toll of pilots in the Royal Air Force was still heavy, even though the Luftwaffe had turned its main interests to the Eastern Front rather than on us.

As we lay side by side our thoughts turned from the present to the past. The one night we could never forget was the night in December 1943 when we had got engaged at the Dorchester Hotel. It had been a wonderful night for both of us. The food, wine and service were excellent, as expected from this luxurious hotel. The champagne, at her father's expense, flowed freely and the orchestra played romantic songs of the present decade.

We had both felt a sense of elation. Her father kindly gave us permission to return home on our own using his black Sunbeam Talbot saloon. It was our first night together when Barbara wasn't chaperoned on her return journey from London at night. In the past, one of her family had met her in the City to escort her home. We said goodbye to our respective parents and called the porter to collect her father's car from the car park.

Barbara had looked radiant in her long, red evening dress which was buttoned up to the neck. She wore earrings and shoes to match her colourful gown. The engagement ring of sapphires and diamonds, which I had bought earlier in the day from a jeweller in Hatton Gardens, glittered on her left hand. As we had approached the revolving doors of the hotel to make our exit, I reached for my wallet to give the porter a tip. He had brushed aside my token of appreciation and said, 'Have it on me, guv,' in his cockney accent and beckoned us on to our awaiting car.

We had made our way south through the darkened streets of Knightsbridge, Hammersmith, Chiswick and Kew where the famous Royal Botanic Gardens are sited by the River Thames. The weather was appalling for driving with heavy rain falling in bucket loads and my poor windscreen wipers couldn't match the force of the rain. Several times I had had to stop to let the windscreen clear.

It was just past midnight when we had decided to pull up alongside the river in Petersham Meadows. We waited a little while cuddling each other, then when the rain eased off we went for a walk along the towpath towards Richmond. It had been quiet and peaceful and there was not a soul in sight. We had put our arms around each other and I put my coat over her evening dress. We had watched the strong current ebb out to sea – water for me is marvellously relaxing – and had strolled along the towpath until our clothes were quite damp, when we had decided to return to the car for shelter.

'What shall we do now?' Barbara had said as the night was still young.

'Don't really know,' I had replied, as I dried her hair and face with my service issue handkerchief. 'We could sleep in the car if you like or go to a hotel in Richmond,' hoping her reply would be positive.

She had laughed quietly and replied, 'Daddy wouldn't like that at all. I promised him we'd go straight home.'

'Well, that's that then,' and I had started the car.

In a whispering voice she had said, 'We could stay here a while if you like,' and switched off the engine with the ignition key. Turning towards me she had moved as close as the gearstick would allow.

We had held each other affectionately and made love until the dawn chorus of the birds had told us it was time to return home.

It was at this moment that we both awakened to our present thoughts. She was lying very close to me in a bed made for one and the warmth of her body radiated against mine as we lay side by side in the darkness under the bedclothes. She rolled onto her right side and kissed my lips with her surprisingly soft mouth. Taking my right arm towards her she laid the palm of my hand on her firm, round breasts and rotated my fingers in a circular motion. Her breasts were now rising and falling in exultation. With her other hand she pulled the bow of the cord of her nightdress which opened immediately and her full young breasts popped free against my naked chest. They were warm and smooth as I fondled them making her nipples rise to hardness. She liked what I was doing and pressed closer to me, her bare body interlocking with mine. We kissed again and again, our lips opened and I could feel her tongue sending tingling sensations down my spine which excited me.

The room was dark and peaceful, the bed warm and comfortable. Barbara then rolled on top of me, pressing her shapely figure against me, sinking me further and further into the soft feather mattress. I probed her slowly inside, feeling her inward sensations. The frequency of body motions increased until she let out a profound sigh, her whole body relaxing with satisfaction. She kissed me again, clinging to me with a joy and passion which I had never felt before, and we fell asleep in each other's arms, cherishing the moments the war had just given us.

I was awakened by Barbara's father with a cup of tea. 'Glad to have you home, son,' he said, and disappeared downstairs.

Luckily for both Barbara and me she had crept back to her own bedroom while I was asleep, otherwise it would have been an embarrassing situation. Mrs Devereaux greeted me warmly as I came down the long, narrow, thickly carpeted stairs. With her usual speed and expertise she prepared a huge breakfast which smelt wonderful as I went into the dining room. Barbara, on the other hand, was coming and going, first upstairs, then downstairs, in a bright blue towelling

11

dressing gown, which made her face look whiter than normal. She eventually came into the dining room while I was enjoying my breakfast, kissed me good morning and said, 'Did you sleep well, darling?'

'Yes, thank you, dear; just like a log.'

I wondered what her mother and father would have thought if they knew that half the night we were making love to each other. In Barbara's hand was a lovely, single red rose. She leaned over the breakfast table and waved it to and fro in front of my face, saying, 'Now whenever you go up there in your flying machine, I want you to put a rose like this in your cockpit.' With that, she handed it to me as a sign of remembrance and affection and I carefully tucked it away in my left breast pocket.

Saying farewell to all of them on the doorstep of their lovely detached house I made my way on foot to the railway station at New Malden. On the way, however, the bus driver of a number 213 kindly took pity on seeing me walking and offered me a lift. The train from Surbiton was somewhat late but eventually it arrived with only four coaches, which at the time seemed to me to be a very small train indeed for such a busy line. This meant standing room only so I read the morning newspaper leaning up against the fire extinguisher on the carriage wall. It was so crowded that when the train braked you could not fall over anyway. Eventually we arrived at Waterloo and I changed platforms for my connection to Dover having failed to find a porter to carry my suitcase. Luckily, at Dover Station there was a three-ton truck waiting to collect the daily mail so after chatting the driver up and giving him a Mars bar, I cadged a lift to my appointed station, RAF Hambridge.

On arrival and with a sore backside, since the truck had seen better days, I reported first to the Guardroom and secondly to the Station Adjutant, Flt Lt James (Jim) McTaggert. He received me with caution and, in his broad Scottish accent, gave me instructions on how to book in to the station. After checking my identity card and looking up his daily file of new recruits, he gave me a blue card which required numerous

12

signatures from various departments on the station, including the Pay Office, Sick Bay and the Guardroom. Eventually I arrived at the Squadron Office which was in No. 3 Hangar opposite the control tower.

2

A gentle, warm sun shone down on No. 3 Hangar as I entered
the Squadron Office on this day in April 1944. Three WAAF
clerks were busily filing and typing in their shirtsleeves, the
first I had seen this spring and I made for the attractive, dark-
haired one who sat nearest the Commanding Officer's door,
hoping that she was his secretary.

'Good morning,' I said, lowering my head to attract her
attention.

'Good morning, sir,' she replied, giving a broad smile
across her very attractive face.

'Could I see Squadron Leader Mitchell, please?'

'Have you an appointment?' she replied, with a tone of
voice like a sergeant major.

'No, I'm afraid I haven't,' I said, thinking the conversation
was getting a bit formal.

'I'm afraid you'll have to wait then because he has a
disciplinary matter to attend to in a few minutes.'

'Oh, I see.'

She waved her hand in the direction of the vacant seat
opposite her where I could see her nicely shaped legs. I could
see the Squadron noticeboard and was able to read the short
history of the Squadron and how it was formed in January
1944 for special duties with the Free French Air Force.
However due to an administration error at the Air Ministry it
had become a Royal Air Force squadron attached to the
Home Defence System.

The door suddenly opened and a tall, dark-haired,
immaculately dressed Battle of Britain pilot stood in the

14

doorway, and said to the WAAF at the desk who I had been talking to, 'Has Pilot Officer Donald Hamilton arrived yet? He should have been here by now.' With that I stood up, saluted and introduced myself.

The girl looked absolutely flabbergasted and said, 'Why the hell didn't you say, sir,' as she lowered her head towards her antiquated typewriter.

'Come on in, Pilot Officer Hamilton, and take a seat.'

He sat down rather quickly at his metal desk and pulled out a file amongst many on his desk. 'Did you have a good journey from Rednal?' he asked, as he examined my file closely.

'Yes, thank you, sir,' I replied as I looked at the DFC ribbon below his pilot wings.

'Are the trees on the approach road to the Officers' Mess in blossom yet?' I knew that he had been one of the first pilots to receive advanced training at No. 61 OTU Rednal.

'No, not quite, sir,' I replied courteously, knowing full well I hadn't noticed whether they were in blossom or not.

'I see you come from Richmond, Surrey, and attended the Grammar School at East Sheen.'

'That's correct, sir.'

'I come from Twickenham, across the bridge you know, not far from you.'

'Oh do you, sir? Anywhere near the Green?'

'As a matter of fact my parents' house is right on the Green. They own the bus company, Fountain Coaches.'

'Yes, I know them very well; my father used to do some work for them. I believe he still does.'

'How many hours on Spits, Hamilton? It doesn't seem to say on your file.'

'Thirty-six hours on the Mark Five, a few hours on the Mark One, sir,' I replied positively.

'Well, that's more than the average we're getting into the Squadron from the Flying Training School at present.'

He took a cigarette from his silver cigarette case and lit it with an old petrol lighter, then said, 'Flying requires maximum concentration throughout your sorties. Something is going on all the time up there and you must learn to

15

concentrate instinctively. This squadron is new and we're learning by teamwork all the time. You must check and recheck both at briefings and in your cockpit drill. We're here at Hambridge to do a special job, which you will be told about later. This job is vitally important to the defence of these islands. It requires new flying skills and techniques which you will have to learn and you'll have to be quick and accurate. If you don't concentrate you're a dead airman as far as I am concerned. I am allocating you to Red Section in 'A' flight under Flight Lieutenant Murphy. He's an exceptional leader and when I'm in the air he's my Number Two. He'll teach you all you need to know. All you have to do is to be as good as he is and you'll be fine. Well then, Pilot Officer Hamilton, we shall have to see what they taught you at Rednal,' and with that he picked up his flying helmet and parachute and said, 'follow me.'

I stood up, saluted and followed him out of his office. My interview with him gave me the impression that he was well organised, a natural, born leader, extremely efficient who knew exactly where he was going, and how he was going to get the best out of his men. I was extremely impressed and with that I closed his office door and accompanied him to the pilots' locker room. I collected my flying helmet and parachute from the locker room and followed him to the dispersal where there were 12 Spitfire Mark Nines refuelled, re-armed and ready to go on the next alert.

'You take the end one, Hamilton, NG Five-Six-Oh and keep on my port wing just behind me. We shall climb to ten thousand feet and level off. I don't want to see any flashes of genius, just conventional flying,' he said as he turned and went in the direction of his awaiting aircraft which was nearest the dispersal hut.

Buckling my parachute I climbed onto the port wing of my allocated Spitfire, and hauled myself up to the narrow cockpit. Having adjusted my safety harness I closed the small hatch which had to be bolted on the inside before starting the engine. On completing the thirty-five point cockpit drill which I had memorized on Advanced Training, I primed the engine, switched on and with the aid of the trolley accumulator which supplied the 24 volts, pressed the starter button. The Rolls Royce Merlin engine burst into life. The instruments monitoring engine performance and pneumatics registered satisfactorily. Indicating all was well on my instrument panel, I waved to the ground crew to pull the chocks away and gently pushed the engine throttle to get NG 560 underway towards the take-off point. My Squadron Commander was already there when I arrived with my perspex canopy closed and my brakes in the locked position.

The signal to take off came over the R/T. We took off into the wind and settled into a maximum rate of climb to 'Angels One Zero' when we levelled off. With my oxygen supply now switched on, drying my throat in the process, I closed in on my CO at a steady speed of 300 miles per hour. Over the R/T came the voice of Squadron Leader Mitchell (Mitch to us later) with specific instructions to stay in formation and to keep a lookout. We were to fly straight ahead. I could see the Channel which had a slight swell due to the light breeze blowing. Orders came over the R/T to break formation and try a few manoeuvres endeavouring to co-ordinate the controls to give me properly balanced turns. As I opened the throttle, I felt the tremendous power of the 1,515 hp Merlin 61 engine and the significant characteristic of all Spitfires, the aircraft's response to the lightest of touches. She was positive both at low speeds and in the turn which was another splendid example of the work of the designer, Reginald J. Mitchell, who unfortunately died in June 1937.

The next moment my heart sank to my knees and my pulse rate leapt to unhealthy heights because as I searched the horizon from side to side I couldn't see my leader. I scanned the sky until my eyes and neck ached with fatigue and then suddenly over the R/T came a simulated noise of machine-gun fire and a voice yelling 'You're as good as dead, young Hamilton.' I knew somewhere in the clouds he was with me, but where at that moment in time remained a mystery. I couldn't see whether he was behind me due to the sun's reflection in my rear-view mirror, when suddenly, almost instantaneously, he flew past me at great speed, his slipstream shaking my cockpit as he yawed and rolled in front of me. It was certainly a great relief to my mind and heart to see him again. Over the R/T came the instruction to carry out a simulated dogfight in which he was the enemy. In doing so I pitched, yawed, rolled, dived and did high 'G' turns which made my knees and legs ache, to escape from his firing range.

Eventually, after climbing to 18,000 feet, I managed to lose him. My main concern now was to hide from him which I did successfully due to the impressive performance of this newly improved Mark IX Spitfire over the Mark V I had flown at Rednal during my advanced flying training. Finally over the R/T came the soft voice, 'Land now, Hamilton. I'll stay a thousand feet above you to monitor your approach.'

Returning to the airfield I joined the circuit on the dead side letting down to 1,000 feet. I noted the limp orange windsock as I turned on to the downwind leg and ran through my landing checks. There was a slight thump as the undercarriage locked down. There were no other aircraft ahead of me, and after conferring with 'LOCAL' for permission to land, I chose a landing run which gave me the least amount of taxiing back to the dispersal where I could see the other ten aircraft of my squadron still sitting motionless. I turned finally, lowered the flaps, throttled back and smiled with satisfaction as we landed with barely a screech on the short grass. As I opened the canopy to cool down, since on landing it got very hot in there from the bright sun, I noticed the ever-vigilant Corporal Jackson, my fitter, waiting on the Squadron pan for our return. On alighting from the cockpit and jumping down off the port wing, my Squadron Commander came over to me with rather a favourable smile on his face.

'Young Hamilton,' he said, 'that final approach and landing was far better than your Rednal Report suggests. I wished all my introductory flights with new members of the squadron could be like that. A splendid show that, Hamilton,' as though I had just completed my stage act at the Lyric Theatre. 'The

18

only serious comment I can make is that you must watch your bloody mirror all the time,' emphasising the 'all' bit. 'I can't afford the loss of this Spitfire or you,' he said as he was pointing to my aeroplane. He shook my hand strongly and made his way back to his Spitfire where he completed his visual checks on the airframe and controls.

As I sat on the starboard wing, sighing with relief and wiping the sweat off my forehead, a voice behind me said with a Geordie accent, 'A fine landing that, sir, if I may say so.' It was Corporal Jackson who was checking the tyres. As he faced me he said, 'They usually bump on the ground or balloon rather than float. How long have you been on Spits then, sir?'

'About four months altogether, Corporal,' I replied as I sensed an interest in my airmanship.

'That's longer than some who come here from the Flying Schools,' he stated knowledgeably. 'The Governor was pleased with you. I could see it in the expression on his face when he landed. Usually he is cursing and swearing and muttering "What bloody idiots they're sending me!" But with you there wasn't a murmur.'

'Thanks, Corporal. See you tomorrow,' I said as I made my way jubilantly towards the flying locker room and then on to the Mess where I knew I could get a cup of tea.

3

The Officers' Mess at RAF Hambridge was one of the largest
domestic buildings on the station. It was situated in beautiful
surroundings with high, immaculately-trimmed hedges
giving it an air of seclusion and privacy. On the whole the
aerodrome, even in wartime, was kept tidy, the grass verges
cut with meticulous care.

The entrance to my new home was similar to that of Rednal,
since the planners and architects at the Air Ministry seemed to
keep a uniform pattern of bricks and mortar for their
buildings. I was greeted with a pleasant smile from the WAAF
corporal as I booked in. The receptionist, small in stature but
extremely pretty, opened the conversation by saying, 'You
must be Pilot Officer Hamilton of 629 Squadron.'

'Yes, that's correct, Corporal. How did you guess?' I said,
looking casually at her.

'You're the only new member not accounted for on my list,
sir,' she replied as she raised the typed list of incoming
officers.

'Is my room ready, Corporal?' I asked quietly.

'Yes, sir. I've given you one at the rear where a couple of
your Squadron pilots are accommodated. Room One-Two-
Eight on the first floor.'

'Thanks, Corporal,' I replied as I took the room keys from
her.

The foyer, which was thickly carpeted and well furnished,
gave the first-time visitor a feeling of warmth and comfort.
Many pictures of famous Royal Air Force leaders decorated
the walls. The huge lounge on my left was furnished in soft

green fabrics which blended magnificently with the dark brown carpet. Members of the Mess who represented numerous occupations such as aircrew, accountants, technicians and controllers, were sitting like stuffed dummies reading their daily newspapers or writing to their loved ones on tables dotted here and there.

Not an eye was turned or a murmur uttered as I entered the room. Not a greeting of any kind was echoed in the silent room. I left the unwelcoming scene with a feeling of despondency and depression. Nothing like this happened at Rednal, I thought, as I skirted round the corner into the bar, where the atmosphere was just the opposite. Jolly faces confronted each other at the long brass-surfaced bar. Two aircraftsmen were busy pulling pints of wartime beer for their thirsty customers and the odd hello and warm smile greeted me as I meandered between the officers on my way out of the most popular room in the Mess.

Continuing down several corridors as carpets gave way to cold looking linoleum one got the feeling that the grandeur of the entrance was only superficial and didn't really represent the average conditions of the Mess. On several walls were the usual communication boards, such items as PORs, duty rosters, local information were displayed in an irregular manner. The mail board, which was the main attraction, was littered with uncollected mail. If your name began with an 'S' the task of retrieving your letters was a laborious one as many were regretfully still awaiting their rightful owner. As I stood gazing at the slotted mail board so the voice of a tall, blonde, slim-looking WAAF wearing the insignia of a LACW interrupted my thoughts.

'Are you looking for your mail, sir?' she said softly.

'No, just gazing. In fact, I'm on my way down to room One-Two-Eight,' I replied, turning to face her with my case in one hand. 'Is it in this direction?' I asked, pointing in the direction of the rear of the Mess.

'I'll show you if you like, sir,' she said putting down her tea tray and leading off down the poorly illuminated corridor, her shapely hips swinging from side to side.

21

'You must be the new pilot for Six-Two-Nine Squadron we've been expecting?' she said with an informative voice.

'Yes, that's right. One of the "Green Chaps" just out of training school.'

'Was that Cranwell, sir?' she asked looking at me with interest.

'No, I'm afraid not. Just Number Sixty-One OTU Rednal,' I replied.

'You'll find it a bit different here from Rednal,' she said as she opened my door cautiously. 'Here you are, sir; Room One-Two-Eight. Quite a nice room really. Has a nice view over the rear gardens. You'll be quiet here. Pilot Officer Cooper liked it very much. He slept over there.' She pointed her slim finger to the other available bed.

'Where is Mr Cooper now?' I asked as I stepped nearer the window.

'Went missing yesterday. Pity really, I rather liked him. A jolly fellow from Dublin. Could never get him up in the morning, though.'

'That will be all, miss,' I said, opening the door for her so that she could return to her tea tray.

'LACW Juliet Walters is the name, sir.'

'Thank you for showing me the way, Miss Walters.'

'That's a pleasure, sir. Hope you enjoy your stay with us. Don't forget to put your shoes out for cleaning tonight,' she said smiling.

'I'll see you in the morning with tea at Oh-Five-Thirty hours,' and with that she gently closed my door.

The room was small in size with two single beds positioned up against the outside walls. Standard Air Ministry horsehair mattresses covered the tensioned steel springs. The walls were covered in the usual cream paint and the doors that sickly bright green which met you everywhere throughout the Service. It seemed they had endless gallons of the stuff. Still, it was my room and possibly my home for the next few weeks or months. The green metal bedstead and the hard mattress to suit any back sufferer greeted my tired body as I lay down and had an afternoon nap.

22

A thunderous knock at my door awoke me from my deep sleep. The door then opened and in came this tall Flight Lieutenant holding a large tot of whisky in a thick-rimmed glass. He had a bull neck, a round face and a tough look about him; his hair was blond with natural curls and he wore the mauve and silver ribbon of the Distinguished Flying Cross under his coveted wings.

'I'm Spud Murphy, your Red Section Leader from the Squadron,' he announced as he trundled into my room, a bit unsteady on his feet. Looking out of the window he said, 'A nice view you have here, Hamilton. The daffodils are so lovely this time of year.'

'Yes, sir,' I replied, as I stretched my tired body from head to toe.

'Thought you might like a drink before dinner, Pilot Officer Hamilton.'

'Is it dinner time already, sir?' I asked my superior as I wiped my eyes and sat upright on the bed.

'Yes, I'm afraid it is, young Hamilton. Undoubtedly you've had a long day travelling. Rednal wasn't it?'

'Yes, sir,' I replied as I got to my feet.

'Good-looking wench, that,' he said as he picked up Barbara's photograph and examined it closely. 'Wife or fiancée?'

'Fiancée,' I replied, taking the silver-framed picture from him and putting it down on my metal bedside locker.

'You'll have no time for women in this game, Hamilton. Just seduce them and leave them, that's the best bet these days,' he said, with a slight grin across his wrinkled, well tanned face. 'See you in ten minutes at the bar,' he said as he turned towards the open door and departed down the quiet corridor.

I quickly washed and shaved and made my way down endless corridors to the bar at the front of the building. It was crowded from wall to wall with officers from various parts of the Commonwealth and occupied Europe and there was no space to be seen. Smoke seemed to linger from floor to ceiling with the density of a small bonfire which reminded me of a

23

dingy Soho nightclub I had once visited soon after leaving school.

'Come in, Hamilton,' said my new Squadron Commander, who was surrounded by some very young men like myself. 'What will you have to drink?' He reached his right arm for the white order pad situated between several empty glasses.

'A pint of Watney's, if they've got it, sir.'

'A pint of the best,' the Squadron Leader said to the aircraftsman behind the bar. 'While we're waiting for your drink, let me introduce you to some of the lads from the Squadron.'

He turned me first in one direction, then in the other, introducing me to several pilots whose age ranges differed very little from one to another; some wore decorations of gallantry, some didn't. In a few minutes, over a pint of watery, wartime beer, the feeling of being a complete stranger had been transformed into a feeling of belonging and friendship.

It wasn't long before a stocky, overweight Flight Sergeant shouted at the top of his voice that dinner was being served. At first nobody took any notice until our Squadron Commander clapped his hands and bawled out at the top of his voice that the last in the dining room would be paying for the first round after dinner. Suddenly there was a mad rush of bodies for the exit. My CO beckoned me to walk along with him. The corridor approaching the dining room was very impressive, reminding me of the loyalty, tradition and chivalry this young service represented. Illuminated a few feet above me hung several portraits of famous Royal Air Force leaders such as Trenchard, Portal, Dowding and Sholto-Douglas.

The dining room, which was huge in size, was similarly decorated with illuminated portraits. This time, they were Air-Aces of the First and Second World War. Dimly lit, the room seated several hundred hungry men. As we sat down at the large, highly-polished mahogany tables, decorated with expensive silver tableware, I sensed a feeling of security and attachment. The huge tables measured some ten feet by four and when full seated ten members of the Mess. If you could hear what the opposite fellow was saying, you were lucky. If the person occupying the top seat wanted the salt, and you were down the other end, you didn't pass the condiment but slid it along the highly-polished surface like they do Rye bottles in American westerns.

Overcoming the disadvantage of distance I had a very interesting conversation with my new flying partner of Red Section, Flying Officer Gordon Grant. Gordon, a fellow Scot, obtained his wings through Cambridge University Air Squadron. He was young, heavily built, with brown hair and wide, grey eyes, and he came from the small village of Glenliver which nestled in the Cairngorms. The place was well known to whisky drinkers since it was here they produce one of the finest malt whiskies in the world. His great grandfather came from a famous Scottish singing family and on one occasion had been presented to the Royal Family. He was certainly a connoisseur of food and wine, but unfortunately shy of women.

After dinner we both sought the friendship of our flying colleagues in the bar. It didn't take long to discover their weaknesses and their strengths for they were an average bunch of men who drank a lot and sang a lot when the chance was given them. They never knew from one day to another whether this pint or that song would be their last and one thing they all had in common was this polite but vigorous potential about them. After a skinful of watery beer Gordon and I retired to bed leaving the hard campaigners still propping up the bar.

4

The morning was sunny and bright and there was plenty of activity going on when I reached the dispersal. Spitfires were being re-armed and refuelled. The ground crew were milling around their aircraft carrying out pre-flight checks under the supervision of Flight Sergeant Bill Devlin, who came from Saxmundham in Suffolk. Bill was a veteran of the First World War and he knew with expertise and management skills how to handle his men and machines. He was great to talk to when he had the time. A rigger by trade, he spent a lot of time examining and re-examining the fabric of the aircraft which was the most vulnerable part under attack from enemy fighters and guns.

Spud and Gordon were sitting in their deckchairs reading and chatting to each other like old comrades. Tattered magazines were scattered everywhere. The squadron contained sixteen Mark IX Spitfires of which twelve were out on the pan and the remaining four were under repair in the hangars. Initially the Royal Air Force was equipped in 1938 with the Mark I Spitfire whose break horse power was 990, but since then the engine power had been improved to 1,740 horse power. This was to match the speed and thrust of the Messerschmitt B109E. Our Spitfires had been produced at Castle Bromwich under the guidance of Chicago Clark who had constructed elaborate jigs at great cost to enable the Supermarine Spitfire to be manufactured in large quantities. The Royal Air Force and the Air Ministry were continually putting new demands on Rolls Royce who made the engines and Vickers who made the aeroplane in order to match the manoeuvrability and power of our German adversary.

The Squadron Commander arrived and at once approached Red Section as we sat together on our dilapidated deckchairs by the dispersal hut. He looked fresh and clean. 'Low level cross-country run today, chaps, with gunnery practice air-to-ground at Aberporth,' he said pointing to our Section Leader, Flight Lieutenant Murphy. 'Take off Oh-Eight-Thirty hours,' and he turned towards the dispersal hut with a pile of maps under his left arm.

Red Section took off precisely on time into the wind which was light and moderate. Our Squadron code name over the R/T was Bronco, with our Leader at Number 1, Gordon as starboard wingman Number 2 and I was at Number 3. With my propeller in fine pitch and the engine at full throttle I could hear the characteristic sound of the Spitfire from its exhausts as Red Section gained height. You could feel the willingness of this beautifully engineered machine to fly like a bird, its graceful sense of manoeuvrability and thin wings glided unsurpassingly across the azure sky. With my left hand pulling back on the throttle and my foot applying pressure to the left rudder, I made a tight climbing turn to port as instructed over the R/T.

Flying in 'V' formation we flew in patchy white cloud at 3,000 feet. Our flight plan took us over Ashford, Chippenham and over the Severn Estuary which widened considerably at Bristol. Climbing to 10,000 feet the oxygen supply was switched on and the flow meter checked for a suitable reading. There seemed to be plenty of activity below us on the Brecon Beacons although we were too high to identify the vehicles or troops below. Making for the small Welsh town of Cardigan we dived in formation to 2,000 feet as a practice 'shoot-up' before levelling off above the River Teifi which looked serene as it flowed out to sea. The white troughs of the sea could be seen as we flew over the coastline northwards towards Aberporth where the target range was situated a few miles out to sea. Over the R/T came the voice of Bronco 1, 'Number Three, attack target at four hundred feet using cannon only and then climb to vector Zero Nine Four to three thousand feet.'

'OK Bronco One,' I said as I could see my leader hugging the Welsh coast firing his shells directly into a derelict fishing boat. With my air speed indicator reading 260 miles per hour and my artificial horizon, I adjusted with apprehension the two horizontal lines of my reflector gunsight to the width of the target. Holding the aircraft straight and level I approached the target. With my eyes adjusted a few inches away from the reflector sight it came within the two boundary lines and I pressed the cannon firing button on my control column. The 20 mm shells shot like fireworks from both wings and shook my bones so that they rattled as the recoil wave passed through me. The shells splintered the target with such ferocity and power that hundreds of seabirds coalescing nearby took off in fright. My feeling was one of elation as the target was hit although I felt some sympathy for the seabirds who had lost their home temporarily.

Joining my two colleagues from Red Section over Aberystwyth we turned east towards Kidderminster and then on to Oxford and home. We yawed, rolled and practised in turn engine switch-off and switch-on to break the monotony on our way home. We flew low over Folkestone passing the two green mounds of soil which became our landmark on the downwind leg of the approach to the airfield. I could hear the Air Traffic Control Officer, Flight Lieutenant Moore, asking me to change to local frequency for landing which I did without hesitation. After receiving the green light from the control wagon at the end of the runway I lowered my flaps, locked my undercarriage and noticed three greens so turned to port to make a three-point landing on the short grass at Royal Air Force, Hambridge. All three aircraft of Red Section returned safely, led by Flight Lieutenant Spud Murphy. The flight had been quiet but interesting and my aircraft NG 560 had handled lightly and positively. Our leader showed airmanship of a high standard. The CO was right – he was a fine leader and a good pilot who seemed to fear no one except tall girls wearing thick-rimmed glasses. On taxiing to the dispersal I was glad my canopy was open as my body was hot and clammy.

Corporal Jackson waved us in and the throttle lever was pulled back and the switches turned off. The Spitfire's toughness seemed remarkable when you analyse how frail it looked. 'Everything all right, sir?' Jackson shouted, as I unclipped my harness.

'Yes thank you, Corporal. See she's refuelled and rearmed straight away and check the outlet of the port wing cannon, will you, there might be some damage done to the aperture while firing at Aberporth.' I climbed off the starboard wing.

'Do it straight away, sir,' replied Jackson.

'Tell the Chief, will you, and record it on the seven hundred.'

'Will do,' said Corporal Jackson.

I went off to the Officers' Mess and met up with Spud and Gordon swilling their mouths with good old Watney's beer. After reporting to the Intelligence Officer, Flight Lieutenant Armstrong, all of us including the IO left the dispersal and made directly for the Officers' Mess. We were all pleased by the accuracy of the gunnery report which had been received at the Operations Room during our flight home.

The Squadron Commander came over to the bar and said, 'Jolly good show at Aberporth this morning! Tony's just told me you gained the highest number of hits this week so I expect you will be in the running for that grubby old cup which has seen better days. The only trouble is, Spud, you'll have to pay to fill it up.'

'I disagree, sir, since it's your Squadron and you earn the most money round here.' The CO gently picked up his stick and cap and made for the bar door.

Gordon said, 'I told you, Donald, you wouldn't get an ounce of liquid off the old miser, since for every round he purchased ten other people would have to do the same – no wonder he's got clean underpants and shirts on every day because he's the only one who can afford it. He's renowned in the Mess to be a tight-fisted skinflint.' With that we relaxed at the bar drinking as many beers as we could blackmail off the bar steward.

It was late afternoon when I was awakened from my afternoon nap by a lovely young WAAF with a cup of tea in her hand. 'I thought you might like a cup of tea, sir, as I was making one next door in the kitchen.'

'That's very nice of you, Miss Walters,' I said looking at her figure inside her uniform. 'I thought you were having the day off today.'

'I was, but LACW Wagstaff had a date so I offered to stand in for her this afternoon.'

'Oh that's good of you. She's quite attractive isn't she, Miss Walters?'

'If you think so then I suppose she is; you young pilots are all the same. All you think about is bed and sex,' she said with a hoarse voice as though she'd drunk half a bottle of Bell's whisky. 'Do you find me attractive, Pilot Officer Hamilton?' she said coming close to my bed.

'Yes, I do. I think you're a very nice young lady.'

'What's the young bit, I'm older than you,' she said lifting up her skirt to her knees.

'What are you doing on Sunday afternoon, Miss Walters?' I said with the experience of a womaniser.

'Oh, nothing much really. I'm off all day, might do a bit of washing and ironing, although I don't feel like doing that.'

'Good then, we can go for a cycle ride and enjoy ourselves in this lovely English weather.'

'Who sir, you and me, and in uniform? You'll get us both into trouble.'

'I'm always in trouble so why can't you for a few hours? There won't be a problem because you're going to put your old casuals on and I'll hide my uniform with one of your white jumpers.'

'What about your bike?' she said enquiringly.

'Oh, I hadn't thought of that.'

'Don't worry, sir, I can borrow one for Sunday. I'll leave it by the back door.'

'Where shall we meet?' I said excitedly as my adrenalin got going.

'The airmen's pub is about two miles from here. You just

turn left outside the main gate and you can't miss it. See you on Sunday at thirteen hundred hours, and don't be late otherwise all the food will have gone.' And with that she departed down the corridor swinging her hips and singing the lyric 'I'm in the mood for love'.

5

The next morning I was awakened by the LACW orderly knocking on my door and shouting in a deep voice, 'Oh-five-hundred hours, sir.' The room was dark and cold.

I wrestled with my slim body for a few moments until all my senses revived and then looked for my cup of tea which Juliet usually brought in at the crack of dawn. Unfortunately she couldn't have been on duty this morning since there was no sign of it. My mouth and throat were extremely dry from the heavy drinking of the night before.

After washing and shaving, I dressed in my Irwin trousers, white sweater which had been knitted by my mother and leather flying boots. After breakfast I collected my Irwin flying jacket and headed towards the locker room. There I collected my parachute, flying helmet and gloves, and made my way to my Spitfire at the dispersal. Corporal Jackson and LAC Ronald Sinclair were busy refuelling her and checking the levels on the respective fuel gauges. These two ground crew, under the supervision of Flight Sergeant Bill Devlin, were extremely conscientious and loved working on Spitfires. They worked as a team which was good to observe, with no dividing line between their menial daily tasks of refuelling, re-arming and checking the electric circuits or radio. On or off duty, they both kept very much to themselves and shared common interests such as tennis and fishing. They often spoke about setting up a small garage business after the war if they had enough capital behind them.

'Good morning, sir,' said Corporal Jackson cordially.

'Good morning, Corporal,' I replied, yawning my head off

as I spoke. 'What's the weather going to be like today?' I asked him as I followed him round to the other side of the aircraft.

'Fair, I believe, sir, with a moderate wind.' We both looked up at the morning sky. 'Shall I put your parachute, helmet and gloves in the cockpit, sir?' A few minutes earlier I had put them on the port wing.

'Yes please, Corporal.'

'Going to be another busy day for you, isn't it, sir?' said LAC Sinclair as he stepped out of the cockpit.

'Guess so from the latest intelligence reports,' I replied holding out my hand to give him support as he jumped down off the wing. 'Is the seven hundred ready for signing in the Chief's office?' I asked the Corporal.

'In a minute, sir,' Corporal Jackson replied as he was just finishing cleaning the canopy. 'Just a few more checks to do, sir, then she'll be ready.'

'OK,' and with that I returned to the dilapidated dispersal hut where other members of the Squadron were preparing themselves for take-off. There I found Gordon engrossed in a game of dominoes with Flt Lt Hugh Edwards, the Flight Commander of Blue Section. How on earth they could concentrate mind and body on that sort of game at the crack of dawn puzzled even the intellectuals amongst us. Blue Section Leader was a small chap with a great sense of humour and had joined 629 Squadron at the request of our Squadron Commander in early January 1944. He was a pilot of great skill and tenacity with five Huns to his credit. We did hear that the CO had put forward to Group a recommendation for a bravery award when he pulled a young Sergeant pilot out of his burning aircraft at our satellite airfield the week before I arrived.

Flight Lieutenant 'Spud' Murphy was fast asleep in his deckchair catching up on his night's sleep. The few strands of canvas holding his overweight body seemed imminently about to snap under the tension. Squadron Leader James Mitchell who always looked impeccably dressed night or day was busy writing reports when suddenly the quiet surroundings we were sitting in erupted into turmoil and confusion at the shrill ring of the dispersal's telephone

'Scramble, Bronco Squadron,' shouted the telephone orderly. Tables, chairs and dominoes shot at random into the air. Pilots and ground crew ran in all direction as a red Very cartridge exploded high above the Control Tower. Gordon bolted like an athlete to his waiting Spitfire and by the time my short legs got me to my aircraft he was halfway to the take-off point.

Over the R/T came the familiar voice of our Squadron Commander as I started my engine. 'Bandits, thirty-plus approaching Dover at Angels Two-One at four o'clock.'

After rapidly completing my cockpit checks and bumping erratically over the long grass I trailed my Section Leader into the air with Gordon on his starboard side. Over the R/T came his southern accent. 'Bronco Three, this is Bronco One. Make sure your oxygen supply rate is set for a fast climb.' He knew I always forgot to set my oxygen supply until the last minute.

'Bronco Three to Bronco One. Roger.' I lowered my seat and adjusted the throttle control to keep up with my Section Leader.

As we headed south-east towards the enemy I felt unnerved flying in close formation for it demanded a great deal of skill and concentration due to the turbulence of the other aircraft and the short distance between wing tips. The slipstream made you frog about in all directions like a weathervane pivoting on a church spire in a strong wind. Three sections were flying today, Red, Yellow and Blue with Green on standby at base to defend the airfield in case Jerry came over in his Stukas.

'Hello Broncos from Bronco Leader,' came the voice in my earphones, 'Bandits at Angels "G" for George. Turn to starboard on vector one-four-oh and maintain course. Out.' Fumbling for the code card in my left boot to find out what height 'G' represented, an unmistakable shriek came down my earpiece as my wing tip came very close to my Section Leader's, but luckily for both of us my reaction was quick enough to avoid a collision. Mutterings from 'Spud' were still coming over the headphones as I corrected my position.

By this time we were in a 'V' formation heading out over the Channel. The wind was cold and biting, the sun hazy and the clouds patchy. The combined smell of 100-octane fuel and burning exhaust gases was enough to sicken the fittest of men. As I scanned the horizon, first to port and then to starboard, so the thought of having to ditch in the glass-like sea below due to engine or fuel failure sent shivers down my spine. We had been told frequently at Training School that the chances of survival in deep water in this small, slimline monoplane were pretty slim. Many an air ace of the Battle of Britain lost his life due to the inability of the Spitfire to float on open water. I forced myself to concentrate on flying, my instruments and our objective to engage the Hun. Several times Gordon and I came too close for comfort due to buffeting from the slipstream. It had taken me a long time at the Advanced Training School to master close formation flying as it wasn't at all easy, but you had to accept that this was the best method for attracting the enemy in large numbers. We, as a squadron, had to match his tenacity, strength and flying skill in order to survive.

Watching my ASI register 320 miles per hour, Bronco Leader came over the R/T a little distorted due to interference, saying, 'Bandits two miles on starboard side.'

Sure enough, below us several black specks appeared above the thin, white cloud. Black smoke poured from my Merlin exhausts as I moved my left hand forward to full throttle. 'Bronco Leader calling. Form formation line astern. Keep tight. Act independently when we dive. Out.'

His voice gave me confidence as I checked and rechecked my instrument panel from engine revolutions to fuel gauges and prepared for battle switching my firing button to 'fire'. The Squadron closed in to about a mile when we could see a much clearer view of the opposition, a formation of Heinkel 111s heavily escorted by a large number of Messerschmitt 109s.

'Bronco Squadron, this is Bronco Leader calling. Attack bombers first. Out.'

Flight Lieutenant Murphy peeled away from the formation. Kicking hard with my right foot on the rudder and my joystick hard over in the same direction, I made a tight turn to starboard and headed in the direction of one of the bombers which had a fighter escort sticking to it like a bee to a queen. My earphones were filled with voices shouting all at once and the sky became a mêlée of swirling fighters and bombers. Whichever way you looked, the hunter was being hunted. I braced my whole body with my feet on the footplate ready for the kill, both hands on the control column as I approached my target. To my surprise it was a Messerschmitt 109G equipped with two large auxiliary fuel tanks under its wings, camouflaged in colours of pale grey above the fuselage and wings, sky blue below them.

At last he saw me but was slow to turn. As his wingspan came within the two horizontal lines of my reflector gunsite I opened fire. Pieces of canopy and fuselage flew off like fragments of an exploding shell and white smoke trailed from the engine. Momentarily he took evasive action by diving vertically downwards but within seconds he was engulfed in a ball of burning wreckage. Absolutely fascinated by my first victory, I followed him down. He hit the sea with a huge splash of white foam, the spot quickly marked by a circular patch of murky oil in the grey sea below. I felt elated and thought how easy it was to take both human life and machine. In training we never experienced the true feeling of an executioner because we only shot at dummy targets. I almost felt sorry for my opponent as the sky unbelievably transformed in a few moments from the confused hurly-burly of a dogfight to one of solitude and apparent emptiness.

All of a sudden, as I momentarily lost concentration, a voice shrieked over the R/T saying, 'Get the hell out of there, Bronco Three.' Almost instantaneously, as the voice died away, my Spitfire reverberated as streams of tracer flew over me. Taking a deep breath and with all the force I could muster I swung the control column to the left and kicked hard on the left rudder to make a steep turn to port, hoping that my sudden evasive action would shake off my pursuer, but how

36

wrong I was. More tracer smashed into my fuselage and tail, missing my frail body by inches. The armoured plate which shielded my back was at that instant my protector as more bullets scorched past me and my starboard wing. I couldn't see my opponent, but I could certainly feel the effect of his fire. Oh God, did I pray, as I swayed from side to side, searching the sky for him in my rear-view mirror. I jinked up and down, banked and turned repeatedly. There was no alternative but to dive and skim the surface of the sea. I glared at my altimeter and engine revolutions counter and my engine howled as I tried to make my escape. The inside of my helmet became saturated with sweat. With my engine at full boost and my fuel low, I made for the white cliffs of Dover. Plucking up enough courage I looked behind me, and there, to my astonishment, was Flying Officer Grant, all guns blazing away at the yellow-nosed Messerschmitt on my tail. A yellow ball of flame appeared in my mirror as my attacker fell into the sea. Gordon flew beside me raising his hand in victory and flipping his wings from side to side. I felt stunned but greatly relieved. My blood circulated in my veins once more as my pulse rate returned to normal.

With my flaps and undercarriage down I flew low over the airfield before settling down on the long grass near our dispersal, mighty glad to be on earth once again. As I opened my canopy the cold, fresh air revived my spirits and after switching off the engine, my elation turned to remorse. Corporal Jackson informed me that Flight Lieutenant 'Spud' Murphy, my Section Leader, tutor and friend, had been killed in the dogfight. On hearing the news I just sat bewildered in the warmth of the cockpit. The ground crew stood solemn and motionless on either side of my aircraft – they too were stunned by his loss.

On landing, Gordon came straight over to me, and we shared our grief together. We had both lost an amiable mentor. He was undoubtedly a master tactician, a brilliant leader and an ace in the skies who would be difficult to replace at this stage of the war. We reported solemnly to the Intelligence Officer to record our kills which had been confirmed by 11 Group. We made our way to the locker room to discharge our flying gear and then set off for the bar at the Officers' Mess. It had been one hell of a morning.

The bar for this time of day was unusually crowded and unbearably smoky. Many of them, like us, had seen aerial combat that morning and maybe lost their leader or friends. A stimulant of alcohol was called for to soothe our shattered nerves and rekindle our confidence as front-line fighter pilots. After drowning our sorrows with as much wartime beer as our stomachs could consume, we left the bar and made our way to our respective rooms. On passing 'Spud' Murphy's room I could see a hive of activity through the open door. The President of the Mess Committee and an appointed officer were busily compiling an inventory of his personal belongings. His letters, photographs and wallet were all sealed in envelopes. The appointed 'mini' committee's task was both nauseating and sombre but it was an essential duty of the administrators to return the missing or dead pilot's effects to the next of kin. Until his property was packed up and sent to the central authority dealing with such matters, his room would be sealed and locked.

As I was approaching my room I heard the distant echo of my Squadron Commander calling out to me from a few doors back. 'Have you got a minute, Donald?'

Turning slowly so that I kept my balance and obtained the necessary delay to clear my fuzzy head, I entered his room which looked south over the beautifully kept gardens of the entrance to the Mess.

'Sit down. Would you like a drink?'

'No thank you, sir. I'm afraid I've been propping up the bar too long as it is.'

In front of him on his small writing table was an unfinished letter to 'Spud' Murphy's parents in Twickenham, Middlesex.

'Nasty business this, aye, young Hamilton,' he said as he picked up the hand-written letter and then put it down.

'Yes, sir, I'm afraid it is. He'll be sadly missed by us all.' I

38

fidgeted about on his uncomfortable seat.

'Did he have a girlfriend at all?'

'I don't actually know. All I do know, if it's of any help, is that he liked one-night stands. To me he was against regular relationships.'

Turning to his incomplete letter he finally said, 'Difficult, these letters, you know.'

Then with the confidence of a schoolmaster addressing his pupils I said, 'I am sure that with your vocabulary and professional tact you'll be sending his parents a nice one.'

'Difficult, my boy. An unenviable task, this,' he replied as he swung athletically towards his desk. 'See you in the morning, young Hamilton.'

'Yes, sir,' and with that I left him with his innermost thoughts.

To my surprise, as I opened my door, LACW Juliet Walters was busily tidying my bed.

'Oh, hello, sir. I thought I'd just give your room a tidy up. I thought you wouldn't be in yet.'

'Carry on, Miss Walters. You're doing a fine job,' I said as I closed the distance between us to admire her slim, well shaped body. 'Any chance of a cup of tea? I'm dying of thirst.'

'Yes, I suppose so, if you'll give me a minute.'

'Fine,' I said as she went out of the room swinging those flirtatious hips from side to side.

She returned a few minutes later with a mug of piping hot tea and an arrowroot biscuit which I ate reluctantly. Crouching beside the bed I was lying on, she said, 'I've taken Flying Officer Grant one as well. He was busy dabbling with his paint brush on that garden scene of his. The trees are absolutely to perfection. He's a jolly good painter, isn't he?'

'Yes, he's good with those natural scenes and seems to have a gift for drawing trees. He goes everywhere sketching them on his notepad.'

'Women as well!'

'How do you know that?'

'He often leaves his notepad on the side of his bed with his female drawings in it.'

39

'And you have a good peep at them, do you, Juliet?'

'Just a peep, sir. I admire his work both in the air and on the ground,' she said smilingly as her strong scent whiffed past my nose. 'Don't forget next Sunday. I have your bicycle arranged. Don't be late, will you?' and with that she squeezed my hand and left. In a matter of minutes I was fast asleep.

That evening Gordon and I spent a pleasant few hours visiting various hotels in the town of Folkestone which we flew low over nearly every morning. Gordon was good to be with, not only for his friendliness, but also for his wealth of knowledge of food and wine and his instinctive knack of selecting the right menus in restaurants and hotels. As the hour approached midnight and with our stomachs full to capacity, we staggered back to camp under a moonlit sky wondering what the next morning would bring.

6

The next day Gordon Grant and I were summoned to the Squadron Commander's office in Number 3 hangar. The WAAFs in the adjoining office were busy with their daily administration when we arrived on this warm and sunny late April morning.

'Hello,' I said to LACW Cynthia Woodhams whom I had embarrassed the day I arrived.

'Good morning, sir,' she replied, turning her radiant blue eyes and shapely legs towards me with the aid of the swivel action on her chair. 'Sorry to hear about Flight Lieutenant Murphy yesterday.'

'Yes, Miss Woodhams, we shall miss him badly,' I said with a lump in my throat.

'Even the Governor looks sad and dejected this morning,' she replied as she guided yet another piece of foolscap paper into her outmoded Air Ministry issue typewriter. 'He won't keep you long, sir. He's interviewing a new sergeant pilot who arrived late last night from Number One Squadron. I'd guess from his voice that he's either an Australian or a New Zealander; I can never tell who's from where.'

'Is he good-looking like me, Cynthia?' I asked, looking directly at her affectionately.

'Yes, I suppose he is in a modish sort of way,' she replied, looking up from her desk which was littered with notes from the CO waiting to be typed.

'Not as good-looking as yours truly, eh, Miss Woodhams?' said Gordon, breaking the silence with his broad but pleasant Scottish accent.

'You're very attractive for a Scotsman,' Cynthia conceded as she rose from her desk and stepped closer to Gordon.

'Doing anything tonight, Cynthia?' he asked loud enough for ACW Rosemary Stannard to hear clearly.

'Nothing much tonight, sir. I may stop in and do a bit of washing but I could be persuaded to do it another night,' she said in her lovely voice.

'How about seeing Errol Flynn at the station cinema?'

'That would be marvellous,' she replied, deepening her voice.

'See you at nineteen-thirty outside "B" Block, and don't be late.' Gordon concluded the conversation.

With that Squadron Leader Mitchell's door opened and he beckoned us in. We both saluted simultaneously and sat down on the two vacant seats beside the new pilot he had just interviewed.

'Two things, gentlemen, this morning,' he said as he sat down with practised care. 'First, the formalities, this is Sergeant Andrew Matthews, with two Ts, from Number One Squadron, Eleven Group. He will complete Red Section's complement. Gordon, you will lead the Section for the time being.'

'Yes, sir.' Gordon stood up, saluted and then sat down again as though he were practising for an investiture at Buckingham Palace before a member of the Royal Family. After completing the round of handshakes and welcoming compliments, we all sat down. The CO then informed us of the experience Sergeant Matthews had gained with Number 1 Squadron including three victories, two probables and one shared, to his credit. The CO continued, 'Sergeant Matthews will not fly today; I will show him around and get him settled in. Second, Grant and Hamilton, you'll fly a "Rhubarb" this morning to northern France. Take-off oh-eight-thirty. You're to report to OC Flying who will give you all the details. Flight Sergeant Devlin is now fitting a high-speed camera to your aircraft, NG Five-Five-Nine, Gordon. You'd better check with him that the installation is completed on your way to the Ops Room. That will be all, gentlemen, and good luck,' he concluded as he got up from his well-worn seat and showed us out.

Sergeant Matthews was slightly older than us. In his middle twenties, he had been with No. 1 Squadron for several months after joining them from the Operational Training Unit, Hawarden. Both Gordon and I thought that considering his combat experience he should be our new Section Leader, but obviously due to his present rank this would be impossible. We both felt novices compared to his flying skills and victories. He had crinkly black hair and dark, bushy eyebrows and he was thickly set, jaunty and the right height for comfort in a Spitfire. Born in Whangarei in the North Island of New Zealand, he had volunteered for active service as a pilot at the outbreak of war but had been turned down. Eventually, after much persuasion from his family and friends, he successfully found his way to No. 15 SFTS at Chipping Norton. Many of the sergeant pilots, who formed the backbone of our air defence system, had refused commissions to officer rank. They preferred to fly without the burden of administration and responsibility which was associated with being commissioned and preferred the social life of the Sergeants' Mess to that of the Officers' Mess, where it was much cheaper too. To the front-line Squadrons, sergeant pilots were the salt of the earth and many of them were decorated for valour like Andrew Matthews.

We parted company, Sergeant Matthews to the Station Adjutant's office, the two of us to the Operations Room for a briefing from OC Flying, Wing Commander Ian Thraves DSO DFC and Bar. He was an ex-Battle of Britain pilot who lost his left arm in a tussle with a Messerschmitt 110 while the British Expeditionary Force were evacuating from Dunkirk in 1940.

'Good morning, boys,' he said as we approached him and saluted.

'Good morning, sir,' we replied courteously.

Before the war this tall, senior officer had been a schoolmaster at Oundle School near Peterborough. With an air of authority, he always treated us like his pupils in the classroom – we were always 'his boys'. Pointing to a large map

43

on his desk which was littered with the latest weather reports, photographs and maps, he said, with a hint of a Leicestershire accent, 'This Rhubarb you're going on this morning, intelligence reports inform us that Jerry is up to something between Dieppe and Neufchatel in northern France.'

Indicating with his right hand at the distinct targets of St Agathe and Croixdalle, he continued giving us large photo reconnaissance pictures of the area.

'I want you to take a close look at these photographs. You'll see amongst the cluster of trees several small buildings well camouflaged from the air. You'll also see if you examine them closely that at the junction of two concrete roads there lies an elevated ramp supported on a number of concrete blocks. What is significant to us is that these elevated ramps, which we think are made of metal, are pointing in the same direction, towards England, of course. I want you two to go in at low level, take some pictures, Grant, make merry hell and get your arses out of there before Jerry pounces. Is that understood?' he stated firmly.

'Yes, sir,' we replied as we handed the pictures back to him.

'A word of caution before you go, boys,' he said in his schoolmaster's manner. 'Jerry is very sensitive in this area. These sites are heavily guarded with enemy guns and planes. Be careful – I want you both back in one piece. Any questions, gentlemen?'

'No, sir,' we replied nonchalantly, and with that we made a few notes on the sites, weather forecast and the position of flak batteries, and planned our route with the operations staff. With our preparations completed we went to the dispersal picking up our flying gear on the way. At the pan Flight Sergeant Devlin was busily finalising the rearming and refuelling of our Spitfires. I clambered into my cockpit with the help of the ground crew. Plugging in my R/T, I switched over to the local frequency and heard the Control Tower giving instructions to some incoming aircraft on finals. After priming my engine one of the ground staff opened the flap on the side of the nose and plugged in the end of the trolley ACC to provide starting power. Switching and pressing the starter button, there was a loud cough and a splutter followed by an explosion which engulfed my cockpit in a cloud of clear blue smoke. My Merlin engine was running sweetly, an engine it was unanimously agreed throughout the Royal Air Force was one of the most efficient ever produced by Rolls Royce.

With my chocks away I released the handbrake on the central stick, gave my aircraft a little throttle and NG 560 was on its way to the take-off point. Flying Officer Grant, acting Red Section Leader, was just in front of me zig-zagging. This was general practice with the Spitfire because, due to the long nose, you couldn't see the ground in front of you. Checking to see my fuel tanks, engine revolutions, temperature and all other instruments were satisfactory, I confirmed with Gordon and with the local controller that I was ready for take-off.

The pair of us took off into the wind, pumping our undercarriages until we heard the thump and the red light came on. Throttling back to cruising speed I closed the hood and set course for Dieppe. Switching on my gunsight, the red circle and dot appeared simultaneously on the bulletproof glass in front of the windshield. Still at a height of 300 feet, the earphones in my helmet crackled with the voice of Gordon over the R/T.

'Bronco Three, this is Bronco Two. Set engine speed for three-fifty at present height.'

'Affirmative, Bronco Two,' I replied, adjusting my engine accordingly. The Rolls Royce Merlin engine purred serenely across the sky. The weather was beautiful for flying: bright and sunny with patches of white cloud above us in case of need. As we flew low over the English Channel with the huge, empty sky ahead of us, I had the daunting feeling of gremlins rumbling in the pit of my stomach. It was general throughout the Royal Air Force that pilots had a feeling of awe when alone in the sky approaching the enemy coast. Some of us had hallucinations, some had numbness in the legs, others had nausea, headaches and backache. One had to control one's feelings, but it was difficult to forget them. It was better to talk to oneself and tell the gremlins, fears and anxiety to go to hell.

The French coast loomed up ahead, the clouds seeming thicker as we approached Dieppe.

Looking down at the German-occupied sandy coastline I couldn't help but picture the 250,000 German troops of the Wehrmacht Hitler had stood in readiness on these shores for operation 'Sea Lion' in September 1940. It was a frightening notion although many in England never knew. The thought of all these troops and associated equipment just 60 miles or so from our peaceful shores was quickly forgotten as there was a burst of machine-gun fire and red Very lights began to explode around us – the German Observer Corps had recognised us as hostiles. Quickly I hauled the control column back a little to gain precious height from the ground fire which splattered into my fuselage, one bullet whistling past my right leg as I yawed and rolled forward.

Out of range of enemy fire we dropped to treetop height to evade the intercepting radar until we reached our target area. The main road linking Dieppe and Neufchatel could be clearly seen. Suddenly a large enemy convoy of trucks appeared ahead and before I could say 'Jack Robinson' Gordon was diving down towards them, strafing them with his 20 mm cannon and 0.303 machine-guns. I followed suit through a curtain of small-arms fire from the German troops who were being ferried towards Dieppe. Short bursts from my machine-guns riddled the forward trucks and a mighty explosion followed as I circled to attack again. I must have hit a fuel tanker since sheets of yellow flame gutted the whole length of the vehicle as it split in two. A column of thick black smoke rose into the sky and German soldiers scattered in all directions to escape the heat of the blaze. Many of those escaping were trapped on the road as I pressed my firing button and confusion at the scene was indescribable. I joined Gordon on vector zero-five-eight at 200 feet. Looking at the map references, which I had stuffed into my left flying boot, we set course for destinations St Agathe and Croixdalle respectively.

On arrival over St Agathe I flew above Gordon in search of enemy fighters while Gordon carried out his PR work with his newly acquired high-speed camera built into the nose of his Spitfire. The sky was peaceful, free from interference by the enemy. I scanned the horizon for our adversaries but there were none. As I circled the yellow and green fields a hive of activity attracted my attention to the port side. There, at a junction of two small concrete roads and surrounded by trees which gave excellent camouflage, were a number of small prefabricated buildings, about six in all. At one of the road junctions my eyes focused on a long, metal elevated ramp which pointed towards the sky, and was supported on concrete blocks. I completed another circuit and out of the woods came flashes of enemy fire. In seconds the sky was filled with puffs of black smoke and thunderous noises. German tracer flashed over my head. I kicked my starboard rudder pedal as hard as I could and brought my Spitfire round to face the flak emplacement. A long burst from my cannon silenced these guns but ominous streams of tracer from the opposite side of the village thudded into my port wing damaging my port aileron. Luckily it was still serviceable. Instantly, Gordon called up on the R/T saying, 'Get the hell out of here.'

I turned sharply for home. As I did so I caught a glimpse of a swarm of ME 109s a few thousand feet above us under the cloud formation.

'Bandits zero-eight-five at Angels Four One,' I shouted into my microphone.

'Roger, Bronco Three. Out,' Gordon replied.

I could see him plunging headlong into the enemy fighters, disregarding his own personal safety and the odds against us. Climbing upwards towards the cloud base to guard Gordon's tail I could see three short bursts of fire from Gordon's speeding Spitfire send the enemy tail-ender spiralling in flames towards the ground. Saying to myself, 'Kill or be killed,' I waded into the attack. A German Me 109E appeared in my gunsight and I instantly pressed the firing button. Bullets streaked unerringly into it from nose to fuselage and a trail of black smoke billowed from its Daimler-Benz engine. The enemy machine – nicknamed 'Emil' after Willy Emil

Messerschmitt, the creator of Germany's foremost single-engined fighter, lost height quickly as I followed him down. The yellow nose was now blackened by the hot vapour escaping from its engine. I could see the pilot struggling to get out but he failed to do so as it hit the ground and burst into flames.

I climbed back into the dogfight. This time I engaged a Me 109E which had the distinctive marking of a yellow rose painted on an unusual black nose. I recognised my adversary at once for it belonged to a famous German air ace who only a few weeks ago, in March 1944, had received the Knight's Cross with Oak Leaves from the Führer himself in Berlin. His name was Major Hans-Karl Hoffmann of Jagdeschwader 31, attached to Luftflotte 2, and he had received from the Third Reich Leader one of Germany's highest decorations for valour, being credited with two hundred victories.

I thumbed my firing button. A streak of cannon emitted from my guns. Blast, I'd missed him. He disappeared into the thick patchy cloud. German pilots had very high scores throughout the war, some with hundreds being credited to their name, many of which were from the Russian front. This seemed hard to believe but it was true. They flew unlimited sorties, some doing over a thousand, until they were killed, maimed or captured. There were no magic number of sorties for them as there were for Allied airmen.

Once again the mêlée of battle died down and I was left alone in the blue sky – this feeling of solitude spelt instant danger to those who flew. I scanned the sky for my acting Red Section Leader, but there was only cloud which was thickening as I crossed the enemy coast. I said to myself, 'I'm still alive.' A few seconds passed, then a low, husky voice came over the R/T. 'This is Bronco Two calling, vector one-five-eight at Angels Nine. Cockpit full of smoke. I can't see.'

The R/T then went silent. Pulling the stick back I climbed immediately to the given vector and there, in a break in the cloud just below me, I could see a Spitfire NG 559. Gordon was struggling to open his canopy as clouds of smoke engulfed him. I closed up on him and could see that by now his hood was fully opened. Shouting over the R/T while I watched the smoke increase in density I said, 'Bale out, Bronco Two.'

By this time we were a few miles into the English Channel. I switched over to the emergency frequency on my radio and gave Base a fix so that the RAF's Air Sea Rescue from Folkestone could pick him up. The engine of Spitfire NG 559 was now a ball of flames and I lost track for a second as to whether Gordon had baled out or not. Just then, as my mind raced, he flipped his Spitfire over onto its back and fell free, plummeting into the cold, grey, choppy sea of the English Channel. His chute remained unopened.

Circling the spot I called, 'Mayday, Mayday,' and repeated our position to Base but there was no sign of life — I had lost to the sea my friend and my mentor. His burning Spitfire had crashed less than 100 yards from where he was drowned.

I returned to Base full of gloom and despondency. My legs and shoulders ached and my mind was confused at the morning's events. Flying Officer Gordon Grant from Glenlivet, Scotland was posted missing, presumed killed, on active service.

That evening, our Squadron Commander James Mitchell asked me to notify his parents of his failure to return from our daily 'Rhubarb', which I agreed to do. Already the telegram to Glenlivet had left the station post office.

Cynthia remained calm and resolute but excelled herself typing at her desk to escape the reality of death of someone she knew and possibly loved. Tears fell down onto her typewriter as her nimble fingers thumped the keys. Cowardly, I withdrew and left her to her inner thoughts. I just walked and walked the perimeter track of the airfield until all my physical energy had been consumed. I felt so bitter about the loss of my two friends from Red Section who had both died like so many before them to keep our shores free from the common foe. The day's results had been one of failure – we even lost the vital camera to the muddy sea of the English Channel. It had been another miserable day as the sun began to disappear below the horizon.

On entering the Mess I made directly for the telephone kiosk and broke the news to Gordon's devoted parents as my

CO had asked. He was their only son. Later that evening I learned that our Squadron Commander had recommended to Group Headquarters the posthumous award of the Distinguished Flying Cross to Flying Officer Gordon Grant for valuable services in the air. A well-deserved award, I thought, as I made my way to my room, confused and exhausted by the exploits of the day.

As I lay on my hard mattress reliving the events of that day, I decided to turn my thoughts and emotions to joy and think about my impending cycle ride with LACW Juliet Walters the following Sunday. Wishing Sunday would be peaceful and warm, I gradually fell asleep to distant noises of friendly aircraft droning their way eastwards to bomb targets in enemy-occupied Europe.

7

At first, when I sat on the saddle, I did feel a twinge of anxiety and guilt about meeting Juliet. However, as the wheels of my borrowed bicycle gained momentum towards Paddlesworth, my doubts quickly receded.

When I arrived, she was sitting down on the grass verge outside the local public house called The Airman. She looked absolutely radiant in her casual clothes of green and white, very different from her daily service uniform, her shining blonde hair blowing across her face giving her femininity as she waved.

'Hello,' she said, 'ETA normal,' and she smiled as I approached her.

'You know what pilots are like for timekeeping. We work like clockwork. Would you like a drink before we go?' I hoped she would agree to my suggestion.

'Yes, please,' she replied demurely.

With that, we entered the small public house situated at the junction of two country lanes. There were two small bars, one Private, the other Public and we chose the Private one, hoping to get a bit of privacy. As we entered the room, it was full of lunchtime drinkers representing mainly the Army and Air Force, although thinly scattered amongst them were a few of the locals. The pub itself was very old and on ordering our drinks from the licensee I learned that it was about 600 years old. Around the walls of the bar were reminders of the pilots of RAF Hambridge who had fought in the Battle of Britain and due citation framed on the wall caught my eye. It was about a local lad who became a hero in the skies defending his airfield from the German invaders. During our drink we decided our destination for the afternoon ride would be the picturesque bay of St Margaret's, almost 14 miles away. On leaving the pub we cycled along the muddy, narrow country lane linking the public house with the village of Hambridge. From there, we ascended the hill keeping the airfield perimeter to our right.

I soon began to realise the stamina Juliet possessed as I began to trail her, feet first, then yards, until she stopped on a plateau overlooking Folkestone. The view from this spot was really panoramic as you looked down over the town and the coastal waters nearby.

'Do you still want to go on, sir?' she said with not a sign of breathlessness in her lungs after climbing the hill.

'Yes, I do,' I said emphatically and with that she mounted her bicycle, smiled and cycled swiftly away.

We were still on the same high plateau when we reached the main Folkestone to Dover road. Turning left onto the main road, I felt much happier since I could ride parallel to her although she still kept up a good pace. Approaching Dover, nicknamed 'Hellfire Corner', due to the hammering it received from the Luftwaffe in 1940, we went downhill to the centre of the town. Since there were no signs about we took the Castle road which was extremely steep so we both simultaneously dismounted from our bicycles and walked the remaining gradient. On reaching the top, the view of the harbour was magnificent. Several ships were being attended to, possibly bringing in supplies of food and equipment for the war effort. A couple of miles on we could see the splendour of the Castle which housed several units of the Army and the Observer Corps.

We eventually turned off the main road to our right leading to St Margaret's Bay. The road was narrow and the gradient steep, which frequently caused us to get off our bicycles and walk. At last we came to the small Kent village of St Margaret's with its usual facilities of church, public house and a scattering of shops. We headed in the direction of the bay which was close by, finally coming down a very steep hill which terminated at the beach. Juliet looked as fresh as a daisy as we stacked our bicycles against the base of the cliff. As for me, I was exhausted.

'How are you feeling, sir?' she asked without a sign of tiredness in her voice.

'I wish you wouldn't keep calling me "sir", Juliet. My name's Donald.'

'Yes, I know,' she replied, laughing.

'How do you know?'

'I looked up your mess hall number H twenty-four and from the Purser's file I obtained your full name, home address and next of kin.'

'Oh, did you now?' I smiled into her sparkling hazel eyes and put my hand on her shoulder. 'Shall we walk, you naughty girl?' and with that we held hands and made our way towards the white caps of the sea.

After walking along the seafront which was barricaded with coils of barbed wire, girders and concrete palings, we lay down on the shingle beach side by side. The beauty and serenity of this lovely bay enclosed by towering white cliffs was now ruined by the excreta of war. In peacetime the bay had been used annually by the courageous swimmers who tried to beat the existing record to cross the Channel to Calais. Juliet lay flat on her back stretching out her legs. Her white shorts and ankle socks matched the green of her open cotton blouse. Her breasts were small and succulent as she breathed lightly. Her nipples protruded majestically giving a seductive invitation to caress them. Suddenly she rolled towards me putting her head across my chest and said, 'Isn't it peaceful here? You wouldn't think there was a war on, would you?'

'No,' I replied. 'If Jerry comes over now or those long-range guns at Calais open up on us, we'd better scarper into those caves over there.'

As she pressed her body against mine with tenderness and passion I could hear in the background behind me feet approaching over the shingle. As they drew near I could feel my emotions being threatened and looking up I saw a tall man in uniform coming closer and closer. When he reached us he said, 'Good afternoon, sir,' his voice echoing against the base of the cliff.

'Good afternoon, sir,' I replied politely.

Tentatively we both stood up to face our visitor who wore a blue beret and around his neck a pair of expensive Zeiss binoculars.

'Could you tell me what you're doing here in this Prohibited Area?'

'Just resting. We've cycled from Hambridge and are just about to have our tea before we return.'

'Oh, I see,' said the elderly man who was heavily built and had a red complexion. 'Did you not see the red sign at the top of the hill warning you that this area is mined?'

'Mined?' I shouted in alarm.

'Yes, mined,' he said in earnest.

'Well I'll be damned.' Turning to Juliet who was by now hiding behind me, I asked, 'Did you see that sign, Juliet?'

'I'm afraid not, Donald. I was concentrating on going down that steep hill to the bay.'

He turned us in the direction of the coils of barbed wire which stretched the length of the beach and said, 'There are two channels of mines, one either side of the wire. They're about thirty feet apart so don't go anywhere near the wire, especially this side.' With that, he turned towards us and said, 'Well, I'll be off then. Have a nice day, but don't stay too long. Jerry will be over soon. He always comes about this time.'

We both thanked him for his kindness and consideration and he departed in the direction he had come from. When he was out of sight, Juliet said, 'Who the hell was that?'

'That,' I said, 'is a member of the Observer Corps posted, I expect, at Dover Castle.'

'Do you think he will report us, Donald?'

'I doubt it. He doesn't know who we are.'

We then both turned to face each other and I embraced her, kissing her on the left cheek. She squeezed her shapely body against mine and I could feel her passion transmitting through to me. She lowered her head and kissed me on the forehead saying, 'I like you, Pilot Officer Donald.'

54

'I like you too, Juliet,' and with that we collected our bicycles and walked up the very steep hill towards the village en route home to Hambridge.

8

It was now the first week of May 1944. I had now been with Number 629 Squadron attached to the Air Defence of Great Britain long enough to form ebullient relationships with my flying colleagues and ground crew, and had begun to learn the shortcuts of Royal Air Force red tape to obtain such luxuries as a whole bar of soap or a tin of Nestlé's milk. I rather liked the station and the *esprit de corps* associated with it, the main subject for discussion being the imminent invasion of Europe. Parts of southern England swarmed with men of all nationalities from the British Empire, United States of America and other European countries including the Free French, Dutch, Belgian and Polish forces.

However, lurking in the background to these unparalleled preparations to land in France lay the fears of Hitler's new secret weapons which once again endangered our shores. Reports were constantly coming in from the British Intelligence Service, Allied agents and spies that Hitler was preparing to launch a devastating weapon in the form of a rocket or pilotless plane. It had been known for some time, as early as 1943, that trials on a propelled rocket had been carried out at Swinemunde and Peenemunde. What form of rocket, how it was propelled and what warhead it would carry puzzled both the British Chiefs of Staff and the scientists engaged in finding the answers to these searching questions. It was not just an idle rumour but was a very real threat which the nation took seriously.

Evidence supporting a secret weapon came from many sources including the Royal Air Force's own Photographic

Reconnaissance Units. The conclusions drawn from aerial photographs taken over a number of months suggested that on scattered sites in enemy-occupied Europe a long object resembling the shape of a rocket, whose dimensions were in the order of forty feet long and seven feet wide, had been seen. These sites appeared as far north as the north of Holland and as far south as Cherbourg, and on them could be seen rectangular concrete ramps pointing all in the same direction – the City of London. In fact it was this information that Gordon Grant and I sought to confirm at St Agathe and Croixdalle on our first Rhubarb before he was killed.

What puzzled the scientists was how these huge rockets could be propelled. Had the Germans invented a new form of fuel of at least twice the calorific value of cordite? Whether you were in a local public house, in a communal gathering or in shop talk in the Officers' Mess, the subject for discussion was the trepidation of this unknown weapon. It was on this very subject that 629 Squadron, and other neighbouring squadrons based on the south-east coast, were going to be employed specifically on 'Operation Crossbow', whose objective was to destroy these indistinguishable and scattered launch sites, code-named 'No-ball'. These launching stations were originally ski-sites, however, they were later transformed into 'Modified Sites' because the majority of the original ski-sites were bombed by Allied fighters and bombers.

The 'Modified Sites', consisting of prefabricated buildings and a launch pad, were transportable. They were erected generally in orchards or wooded farms by the Flakregiment, a special unit attached to the Wehrmacht, which made it difficult to spot them from the air as Gordon and I had found out on our last Rhubarb. With clear visibility, a wood was easily identifiable from the air. The main problem was how to escape the numerous flak batteries guarding these sites when flying at very low altitude, and it became paramount that you planned your route meticulously to avoid being shot down.

After a thorough briefing from the Wing Commander Flying and Squadron Leader Mitchell, Sergeant Matthews and myself took off early one morning on a Rhubarb sortie. Our target was a 'No-ball' site situated inland between Dieppe and Mesnil-Val in northern France. It was a glorious May morning as we flew over the sea, fully armed and refreshed from the alcohol of the night before. A whiff of oxygen was always an expedient remedy for the lingering hangover. The sun shone into my cockpit making my eyes squint due to its reflection in my rear-view mirror. Below us were 60 miles of unguarded green-blue sea. The endless expanse of water and the feeling of immobility heightened one's sense of awareness as one flew over it.

I checked my directional gyro once more against the compass and monitored my engine revolutions and temperature gauges as my Merlin 61 roared noisily across the colourful blue sky. My exhaust stacks on either side of the engine belched a thin stream of pale blue smoke. Minutes passed, then we could see the enemy coast ahead. Nothing from this range signified that the land below was occupied by the Germans.

'Bronco Two from Bronco Three,' I intoned into my microphone. 'Enemy coast ahead. R/T silence. Out,' and I switched it off. Matthews did not reply but just waggled his wings and flew on slightly behind me.

Scattered flak started to appear on the horizon. In seconds the peaceful sky was transformed into a yellow and black mass of exploding shells and puffs of smoke. My concentration weakened as I tensed at the sight of the frightening flak. We both pulled hard on our control columns and climbed steeply a few thousand feet more to evade the shells directly beneath us. On clearing the flak we dived immediately to treetop height to escape early detection. Our target was at Bailly-en-Campaigne, just north of Londinieres.

Out of the corner of my eye I was attracted by a slow-moving German train as it made its exit from a railway tunnel on my port side, its probable destination was Dieppe with troop reinforcements and equipment to strengthen their defences prior to the imminent invasion. Calling up Sergeant Matthews on the R/T I broke radio silence. 'Attacking train below Bronco Two. Cover me. Out.'

I peeled hard to port and swung my Spitfire round in line astern to the train. I was cautious at this point since many of these trains were mobile flak batteries which were to be avoided at all times, so I decided to circle it once more before attacking. The old, black engine was puffing and blowing white clouds of smoke as it jogged its way through the yellow and green fields below. Several coaches contained steel-helmeted German troops. With the devil in me, I attacked, plastering the engine and leading coaches with cannon and machine-gun fire. A few seconds passed and as metal hit metal the engine and adjoining coaches were engulfed in clouds of steam and ascending smoke. The train came to a sudden halt. Matthews came up behind me as I climbed away and his machine-guns fuelled the already burning wreckage. All hell let loose below as exploding shells went off in all directions. Several German soldiers could be seen leaping for safety, some of them with their uniforms on fire, while clouds of yellow smoke were silhouetted against the bright blue sky. We flew away from the scene knowing that a lot of troops were not going to join their new regiment. The German High Command were very sensitive about their troop trains — top priority was always given for them to Russia and the West.

We continued on our mission at low level hoping the activity of the train did not arouse the Luftflotte 2 airfields at Abbeville and Merville under the command of Field Marshal Albert Kesselring. At Wanchielle we turned east so that we approached the target through an area of low flak concentration. But how wrong we were when we eventually arrived! At the perimeter of the No-ball site we encountered a heavy barrage of guns and machine-gun fire coming up at us from the weapons manned by the Regiment 155W, commonly known as the Flakgruppe Creil.

Calling up Matt over the R/T, I suggested he attack first while I drew the enemy artillery fire off him. As he went in to the attack he was greeted with long streams of tracer and dozens of exploding shells. The site seemed heavily guarded and we were both under constant fire from the flak emplacements. The sound of gunfire and our low sweeps alerted the neighbouring guns at Fresnoy and Puisenval which trebled the intensity of enemy fire. The flak positions were so well camouflaged it was hard to identify them straight away. At one point the edge of the forest was a fountain of orange tracer –very unpleasant to say the least. As Matthews ended his run I dived to treetop height to attack the target. As I approached I weaved and waggled my way over open fields and through the enemy gunfire, praying that my life and machine would be spared. Then all of a sudden, just as I thought I was in hell, peace prevailed due to Matt flying around strafing the ominous 20 mm Flakvierling 38-gun batteries. As the prefabricated buildings came into view I pressed my firing buttons, unleashing cannon and machine-gun fire into them. There followed a loud explosion and black smoke billowed up into the sky like an inflated mushroom. Even the adjacent trees began to burn with the intensity of the fire. I must have hit the fuel depot close to the launching platform. You could see soldiers of the Flakregiment running in all directions to control the fire as sheets of flame mixed with the exploding ammunition to make the whole scene hazardous both for the enemy and ourselves. We climbed steeply away knowing full well that this site temporarily was another unoperative statistic for the German High Command.

My hands loosened on the control stick. What happened a few moments ago lay behind me as my mind and body relaxed – the tension had been unbelievable. My engine was firing sweetly and my gauges looking good as we both sought refuge at altitude and headed for home in the direction of Tocqueville, nicknamed Mosquito-Ville due to the continuous sorties flown over it. Suddenly out of the blue came a gaggle of Focke-Wulf 190s attacking our stern. The R/T chatter changed abruptly from the weather to 'Red Section Break. Bandits six o'clock', from Sergeant Matthews. In a few seconds, the peace and tranquillity of the air became a confusion of inter-weaving attackers and defenders.

A Focke-Wulf 190 with a yellow nose and three-bladed propeller glistening in the sun flew in front of me. It seemed as though he must have misjudged either the distance interval or his speed to be in that position. I peeled hard to port and attacked him at a range of 200 yards from his tail which was covered with a large swastika. No favours, I thought, at this stage of the game, with such high stakes as one's life. I pressed my firing buttons with ease, hoping and praying there was enough ammunition left in my wing. A short burst blew his tail completely off. Helplessly out of control, this masterpiece of warplane design began to spin towards the ground. A black speck appeared from the cockpit followed by a parachute blooming uncontrollably in the warm air. The Luftwaffe pilot had baled out within sight of the French coast.

Over the R/T came a muffled voice, 'Two one-nineties closing in on your tail, Bronco Three.'

'Roger, Bronco Two. Out.'

I weaved, turned and dived as tracer whipped past me with incessant regularity. A wave of nausea came over me and sweat poured down my brow, arms and legs. I couldn't see them and I couldn't shake them off. Then, as one passed me, I felt a shudder in the cockpit from the impact of his tracer hitting my Merlin engine. As my attacker drifted into my gunsight I pressed my firing buttons. Blast! All I could hear was the unbelievable hiss which I had always dreamt about – I was out of ammunition. However, that was not all. My engine began to lose power as the revolutions counter began to record a significant drop. A knocking noise could be heard unmistakably in my cockpit. The engine temperature rose alarmingly and thick black smoke began to pour out of the engine stacks. Hot oil and glycol sprayed like a fountain around me restricting my view.

I called Sergeant Matthews on the R/T. 'On fire, Bronco Two. Losing height. Baling out.' Quickly looking around me, I couldn't see either my adversaries or Matthews – I was all alone in my burning Spitfire as I felt myself passing out with trepidation and exhaustion. 'Don't panic,' I repeatedly kept saying to myself. 'Do things systematically and calmly.'

I slid open the canopy, rolled my aeroplane on her back, unfastened my harness and fell out, keeping my knees bent and close to my chest. Closing my eyes, I just prayed that my parachute would open and I would fall free from the wings, tail and fuselage. Feeling weightlessness and an awesome silence was indeed frightening as I cleared the Spitfire. I was spinning downwards towards the blue-green sea like a child's top on a school playground as the surface of the sea rotated around me.

Without looking, I hastily pulled the ripcord and waited for the notorious jerk. It seemed an age before the recoil action buffeted my shoulders but my chute opened. Holding on to the straps with both hands for stability I began to float down at the speed of gravitation in a controlled manner.

The sea became my environment for I was in it and my parachute pulled me along the surface of the water at an alarming rate. My flying boots instantly filled with cold water, weighing me down even further, although surprisingly the water wasn't too cold. My body kept bobbing up and down, first in the water, then out, my legs and arms going like pistons to keep me buoyant in the water.

Quickly I turned the wheel on the parachute release box and banged as hard as I could to release the straps around me. Luckily they opened at the first attempt, entangling my legs amongst them. During the struggle I swallowed a large amount of sea water which restricted my breathing and so each time I surfaced I took deep breaths of fresh air to regain the energy that I had lost during the battle for the straps. At last I was free from them. They were always a nightmare for ditching pilots, but eventually my parachute floated away.

In training the Royal Air Force never told you how exhausting this exercise is. Every muscle in my body ached. My flying clothing restricted my movements and my legs felt as though they had been replaced by tubes of lead. I lay on my back and floated, not having the energy to even wipe the sea water away from my burning face.

After a few minutes floating and with my energy partially restored, I released the dinghy which was attached to my Mae West. Gently, so as not to overinflate it, I filled it with compressed air. With the dinghy fully inflated, I placed the rope ladder in position to board her. At the training school we had just one lesson at Oxford Swimming Baths on how to perform this trick of getting into a floating dinghy successfully – no mean task at the best of times. I found it extremely difficult because as soon as you put your first foot on the bottom of the ladder your body weight just pulled the dinghy right over on top of you. Twice in as many minutes I tried to board my floating home and twice I failed, by which time the sea felt painfully cold. My lungs felt constricted and I began to feel numb in several parts of my body. In order to rest between attempts I hung on to the side of the dinghy with both hands.

At long last I managed to haul my heavy, saturated human frame into the dinghy. I was completely drained of all energy and just lay there sheltering my face from the bracing wind and burning sun. After a rest I began to gather my thoughts. Where was I? Where was Sergeant Matthews? Did he see me enter the water? In which direction should I be going? Was I going up or down the Channel, east or west? All these searching questions drifted through my mind without answers. Meanwhile I felt my past catching up on me, and the guilty feeling of not doing all the things I should have done began to circulate through my brain. Had I been fair to my parents for the lack of communication between us? Was it right that I should flirt with LACW Juliet Walters while being engaged to Barbara? While these thoughts impinged on my conscience I wondered how the present seemingly insur-mountable problems were going to be solved, if neither friend nor foe rescued me from the Channel. What made matters worse was the real possibility that nobody on either side of the English Channel knew I was there. This thought was reinforced because I hadn't sent a May Day signal prior to baling out and was at the mercy of the Earth's elements of wind, weather, temperature and tides.

As I lay in my small dinghy my sensitised ears, which earlier had filled with sea water, suddenly detected a distant droning noise high above me. As the seconds passed so the noise became louder and louder, closely followed by a black speck

63

in the sky which grew larger and larger until its shape resembled an aeroplane. It was difficult to recognise whose side it was on due to the colour reflection of the sea in the sky. My immediate reaction was to stand up in the dinghy, which I found difficult to do, and wave my hands frantically in the air to attract attention, at the same time yelling directly at the plane, eventually causing my throat to be hoarse and sore. As my eyes focused on the aircraft I could see I was alone with the enemy. The plane was a single-engined Messerschmitt 109E, possibly from 1 Staffel of Jagdgeschwader 78 based at Saint Omer. Built at the German factory in Augsburg, it would have been one of 35,000 produced during the war.

My adversary flew very low over me, waggling his wings as a sign of recognition, and made a wide circle around me. I was praying that his firing button was switched to the 'off' position since I was a sitting duck. He then flew off in the direction from whence he came. As his image receded on the horizon I decided he was returning to his base in northern France so, hesitantly, I changed course since now I had a fix on my position. The possibility that this decision might deposit me in friendly waters was still debatable due to the increase in wind and tide. The thought of how far I was from the enemy coast sent shivers down my spine while the danger of being taken prisoner worried me unceasingly.

I drifted for several hours and was beginning to get hungry, glad I had in my flying suit a small silver brandy flask which went with me everywhere, whether I was flying or on the golf course. As I gazed into the brilliant blue sky my thoughts turned to what preparations I should make if I wasn't picked up by nightfall. Then suddenly, on the horizon, my eyes were attracted by a dark shadow silhouetted against the now grey-green background of sea and sky. The object began to increase in size. My eyes gazed at it.

Minutes ticked by until the shadow became visible to the naked eye – it was the bow of a ship steaming towards me. My heartbeat fluttered; sweat poured from my brow. Would the captain and crew see me in the water? The chances of the ship being a friendly one were good since there were more Allied ships in the Channel than German. My fears and doubts turned to elation as a voice over the megaphone echoed 'Man on starboard side' as the merchant vessel, which was part of a British convoy, slowed to a crawl. My mind and body relaxed into Utopia as ropes from all directions came spiralling at me, one of which knocked me clean over in the dinghy. At last I managed to scoop one up out of the water and pull myself onto the vertical rope ladder with the help of two seamen – I was safe from the dangerous elements of the sea.

As time passed, so other ships appeared on the horizon. They were escorts to the convoy. Some were corvettes, some were frigates. The convoy was travelling westbound and I found out later their destination was Southampton. Seeing about a dozen British ships raised my spirits of recovery.

I rejoined 629 Squadron the next day, after enjoying the ship's hospitality – the food was good, the rum exquisite.

9

The next day I arrived back at RAF Hambridge unscathed from my ordeal in the English Channel except for a sunburned face and neck. Many of the Squadron's personnel were there when I arrived at our old dilapidated dispersal hut. As soon as they saw me they congregated round me and before I could avoid this unexpected reception, I was lifted into the air on the shoulders of my comrades like the captain of a football team which had just won the FA Cup. When they eventually put me down on the green grass of Kent, I had to answer a series of questions about my experiences in the cold water separating England from France. Specifically, they wanted to know about my escape from the Spitfire and the problems of boarding a dinghy. Leaving some of their questions unanswered, I was eventually relieved from my ordeal by the familiar shout from the Squadron Commander. After a series of professional questions about the technicalities of escape, I offered to give my fellow pilots, at a later date, a demonstration of 'How not to get into an inflated dinghy'.

Flight Sergeant Bill Devlin appeared with a crate of beer bottles and some enamel mugs which were soon filled to the brim. The celebration was soon saddened by the news that Flight Lieutenant Hugh Edwards, Blue Section Leader, had been reported missing, presumed killed. The gathering of experienced and inexperienced pilots raised their mugs in salute to the memory of a very fine officer and a courageous flier.

Flight Lieutenant Neil McKinnon, Yellow Section Leader, the pilots off duty and myself continued our celebration in a quieter atmosphere in the bar at the Officers' Mess. With a stomach full of alcohol and my brain losing control, Neil and I were discreetly interrupted by the presence of a small, rather attractive WAAF Pilot Officer who was a complete stranger to both of us. 'Are you Pilot Officer Hamilton of 629 Squadron?' she asked softly, so as not to attract attention from the assembled officers.

'I'm afraid he is,' said Neil in a broad Scottish accent. 'I suppose you're from the Publicity Unit seeking information on this gallant officer's escape from the English Channel today,' and he put his left arm around her narrow shoulders and squeezed her tightly.

'I'm sorry to disappoint you, sir,' she said, 'but I'm the Station Commander's new Personnel Assistant.'

'Are you, be damned?' said Neil, swallowing his words apologetically and removing his arm swiftly but politely from her upper body.

'Could I have a word with you privately, sir?' she said to me as she turned away from Neil.

'Of course you may. Be my guest,' I replied and with that I led the slim brunette with tiny hands to a quieter part of the room.

'My name is Louisa Jefferson, and if you're going to the bar, I'd like a Bristol Cream Sherry.'

'Of course,' and with that I trotted off dutifully to the bar. On my return she had luckily found an empty table in the adjoining room where several pilots from 629 Squadron were engaged in a quieter evening playing cards and Monopoly.

'Group Captain Walker wishes to see you at oh-eight-thirty hours tomorrow at Station HQ,' she said after sipping her sherry in a thick whisky glass.

'Any idea what the "Old Man" wants me for, Miss Jefferson?' I said, turning on my stool so that my sore neck was more comfortable.

'No, I'm afraid I haven't a clue. However, I can say that it's not a disciplinary matter otherwise the Station Adjutant would be sitting here right now.'

'Well, that's a blessing,' I said as my tension relaxed to near normal. 'I don't like going up to HQ at the best of times unless it's about my pay,' and I drew my old leather stool closer to her. 'I cannot recall in either my sober or intoxicated state where we've met before, Miss Jefferson.'

'I'm sorry to disappoint you this time, sir, but we haven't,' she said as she raised her glass once more to her bright red lips. 'I've only been here a week so it's been pretty hectic trying to learn all the new procedures laid down by the Station Commander.'

'All work and no play makes Miss Jefferson a dull girl,' I said, holding her slim, white manicured hands. 'We shall have to bring some joy and pleasure into your life here, Miss Jefferson.'

'It's Louisa, Donald Hamilton,' she replied and we both smiled at each other as we finished our drinks.

'How did you know my christian name was Donald?'

'I spoke to your mother on the telephone yesterday. She seemed very cool under the circumstances when you were posted missing. All she wanted to know was whether you'd been burnt or not!'

'How morbid. Glad she knows that I'm safe now. I'll have to telephone her later.'

'You do that, Donald,' she said, emphasising the importance of making contact with home.

'Louisa's a lovely name, isn't it?' I replied, trying to change the subject. She smiled radiantly and we held hands loosely. 'Where d'you come from with that unrecognisable accent?' I said as I squeezed her hand tightly.

'Barnack in Lincolnshire,' she answered spontaneously.

'That's near RAF Wittering, isn't it?'

'Yes,' she said positively. 'How did you know?'

'Well, to cut a long story short, my father used to call in at Stamford to collect his favourite pork pies from a shop in the High Street on our way south from Grantham; but one day, we got ourselves lost in a dense autumn fog and found ourselves passing through Barnack and Ufford en route to Peterborough.'

'You must have come off the A1,' she replied teasingly and

68

let go of my hands.

'I don't want to sound rude, Miss Jefferson, but aren't you a bit young to be the Station Commander's PA?'

'No, not really,' she replied passively. 'I'm nineteen years old, height five feet nothing, matriculated from Stamford High School for Girls and still a virgin.'

The occupants of the next table seemed dumbfounded as they heard the state of her sex life. My blood pressure rose threefold as my face turned from white to red. I became uneasy as the neighbouring boys in blue all stared at us but Louisa just sat motionless on her seat and smiled politely. You could have heard a pin drop in our corner of the room. One of the officers on the adjacent table remarked, 'Aye, lads, we've a right one here,' as he raised his lukewarm wartime beer to his lips.

I decided to change our surroundings and suggested we take a stroll down to 629 Squadron's dispersal to see my new Spitfire number 565. She agreed unhesitatingly and we left the aircrews at the next table in their humorous mood.

As we walked along by the well-trimmed hedges and lawns surrounding the Officers' Mess we discussed common interests such as photography, films and music. We both agreed Esther Williams was a fabulous actress and a starlet of Hollywood. Louisa was enchanted by David Niven and Errol Flynn and being a prodigy from an upper-class school she was well read in Shakespeare, Jane Austen and George Eliot. My academic achievement was no match for her brilliant schooling as we walked hand in hand on this pleasant early evening stroll towards the airfield. When we reached the dispersal the earlier frivolities had now died down and crews were resting before night patrols began. Corporal Jackson and LAC O'Flanagan, the new Armourer, were preparing the evening cup of tea. Flight Sergeant Bill Devlin, who seemed to be constantly at work, was busily writing up technical data on the aircraft servicing sheets. Quietly I drew Bill's attention to the possibility of showing Louisa my new Spitfire. 'Of course, sir,' he replied, and stood up when he saw her in view.

Collecting the Form 700 from his littered desk, we strolled

casually over to my new fighting machine which had been wheeled out from the hangar after a major overhaul. It looked frail and beautiful in the evening sunlight. Due to her tight-fitting skirt, we had trouble getting Louisa onto the port wing, but once she was in position to enter the cockpit she had no difficulty in cradling her slim body into the pilot's seat. Her physical measurements matched the aircraft designer's cockpit to a tee. For several minutes she glared at the numerous dials and waved the control column erratically as though she was driving a dodgem car at Hampton Court Fair. Her only comment was the hardness of the seat since she was sitting on bare metal stiffened by the protective bulletproof shield.

While we walked back to the Mess in the twilight of the night sky, I frequently gazed at her round, radiant face. The slight breeze which was blowing was cool and pleasant. Her complexion was healthy and smooth, she had a combination of elegance and beauty rarely seen in WAAF officers and was well groomed. She walked in a straight line keeping her narrow hips firm as though to reduce her femininity. The curvature of her bust could clearly be seen by the correct tension of her belt pulling in her waistline.

As we approached the entrance to the Mess we could hear sounds of dance music bellowing through the open windows. We decided to join in the festivities and entered the smoky bar which was now crammed full of officers of all ages relaxing before their next flight in the sky alone. In one corner of the room was a group of 629 Squadron pilots playing silly buggers with glasses on the dusty floor. Others were trying to enjoy themselves, possibly their last night of freedom. Some, like myself, feared death so frequently that the best night was always the last night of living. A few were propping up the piano singing famous songs from the Welsh valleys.

We both decided not to join any of the groups and moved sensibly to the small, square not-so-polished dance floor where civilised couples were holding their partners to the music. We danced to tune after tune from the worn-out records until our feet became immobile and our bodies exhausted. By this time the evening had slipped into the early hours of the morning. We embraced each other fondly at our last dance together before retiring to our own quarters. The echoes of loud music could still be heard as I cuddled my hard service issue pillow around my head before going to sleep.

At 08.30 hours the following morning I reported as requested to the Station Commander's Office. The room was large and well furnished compared to others I had seen.

'Pleased to see you back all in one piece, Hamilton,' the Station Commander said soberly as he beckoned me to an unfurnished chair in front of his desk.

'Glad to be back, sir,' I replied swiftly.

The Group Captain was very tall and quite well built, somewhat overweight in parts, especially around the midrift: he still commanded an air of elegance and stature. His eyebrows were thick and unruly, his hair unevenly cut. Below his coveted wings were several rows of campaign medals and awards, one of which was the Distinguished Service Order which took pride of place near his left lapel. He ruled with an authoritarian power and firmness, but was a good leader and was well liked by those who served under him. Except for my personal file the only other item which lay before him on his highly polished mahogany table was a black leather blotting pad which had been passed down from one Station Commander to another. It was an unbelievable picture of tidiness even though the work of administration was horrendous and the associated paperwork cumbersome. High above him in the background hung three pictures of past Kings of England.

He opened my personal file and began reading the contents. Several papers were typed, others hand-written. The room remained silent until the quietness was broken when he politely coughed and said, 'Pleased to see you've fully recovered from the elements of the English Channel, Hamilton. How long were you in the water?'

'Not long, sir,' I replied nervously.

'Your mother has been on the telephone several times enquiring about your recovery. I was pleased to tell her you'd been picked up, reclothed and fed. She never mentioned your father. Is he still alive?'

'Yes, sir, he's retired.'

'Lucky chap,' the Commander replied as he flipped over several pages of my report. 'I was pleased about your combat report over Bailley-en-Campaigne. I am sure the Head of Air Ministry Scientific Intelligence would be interested in what you saw with Sergeant Matthews. Anything on the launch ramp as you flew over?'

'No, I'm afraid not, sir.'

'It was a good show. Well done.'

'Thank you, sir.'

'It's a pity Sergeant Matthews refuses to take a commission. He would make a fine officer and leader.'

'Yes, sir,' I replied guardedly.

'The Squadron Commander is extremely pleased with your flying skills in Red Section, Hamilton.'

'Pleased to hear that, sir.'

'You're doing a fine job, my boy. Keep up the good work. Your promotion to Flying Officer has been confirmed by Group.'

'Has it, sir?' I replied excitedly.

'Yes, it came through the other day.'

After a firm handshake, a salute and a smart about turn, I departed from the room of power and made my way back to the Squadron, jubilant about my early and unexpected promotion.

A few days later, as we approached the middle of May 1944, all pilots of Hambridge Wing assembled in the operations room to be addressed by our Air Officer Commanding Number 11 Group. Speculation had it that he was to expose the myth about Hitler's secret weapon which for weeks had been discussed and argued about over several pints of watery beer. Rumours about the nature of the weapon had ranged from an aerial torpedo to a pilotless gliding bomb. Even a large, high velocity shell, fired from the coast of Northern France, had been suggested on a number of occasions. What had added to the confusion was that both the Luftwaffe and the German Army had weapons with lethal potential directed at the heart of London.

After formal introductions had been completed by the Station Commander, the Air Marshal confirmed with certainty that the Hun was up to something in northern France. He continued by saying that a new phase of air warfare was about to begin. Rumours were rife at Group that a large, long-range rocket, alleged to carry several tons of high explosive, was being prepared in the Pas de Calais to Cherbourg region. The exact description of the rocket and how it was going to be propelled still remained a mystery to the British scientists and the Allied Chiefs of Staff. However it was envisaged that the three Squadrons at Hambridge were going to be in the firing line. In order that they stood some chance of retaliation, they were being equipped with the new Mark XIV Spitfire which had increased thrust and the new 'E' type wing. He concluded that all pilots would be given time for conversion plus a forty-eight hour pass before the month of May was out. We all stood up on his departure from the assembly; the meeting continued under the direction of our one-armed Wing Commander, Ian Thraves.

With several large drawings of the proposed new plane he began to characterise the Mark XIV Spitfire which had been in the Royal Air Force since January 1944. Basically the difference between the Mark IX and the new Mark XIV was the increase in maximum speed and its improved firepower. The former was obtained by the incorporation of a five-blade Rotol airscrew driven by a newly developed Griffon 65 engine, named after a mythical bird, which gave the pilot an increase of 9 per cent at the top end of the speed range. Firepower was boosted by fitting 0.5 inch Browning machine-guns into both wings instead of the old 0.303. The 'E' wing configuration was being adopted on the new machine so that the 20 mm cannon could be mounted in the outboard position. Furthermore the new aircraft's range was extended by the introduction of a 72-gallon fuel tank in the rear parts of the fuselage. The addition of black and white invasion stripes were being painted under the wings to increase identification over the expected high-density flying areas of Operation Overlord.

We were all delighted with the news of our new combat aircraft, especially in its characteristics of speed and firepower which had been lacking in the current Mark IX. However, suspicion still prevailed about the mystery of Hitler's secret weapon which was supposedly going to flatten such cities as London, Bristol, Southampton and Plymouth.

Back in No. 3 Hangar Sergeant Matthews and I were called into the Squadron Commander's office where LACW Cynthia Woodhams was busily making tea. She looked much more relaxed than of late following the loss of Gordon Grant and smiled at us as she closed the solid green door separating the two rooms.

'Sit down, both of you,' the Officer Commanding 629 Squadron said in his usual suave manner. 'I want you to meet our new Red Section Leader, Flight Lieutenant Christopher Rawlinson DFC and Bar.'

We both stood up and shook hands with our newly appointed Section Leader who was well built with a face that was lean and thickly wrinkled below his eyes, possibly due to the stress of war. His skin was nicely tanned by the burning Mediterranean sun while flying on his last overseas tour with 261 Squadron in Malta. His eyes seemed to seek new horizons while his dense curly hair was dark in colour.

At the end of a short introduction by the CO our new Section Leader and fighter ace turned abruptly towards us and said in a voice enriched by a deep Yorkshire accent, 'At the slightest excuse, I gamble, drink and seduce women but up in the sky I'm a disciplinarian like Hitler. That's why I've survived so far. If you two urchins want to see the last day of the war out with me you'd bloody well better do as you're told, right?'

Sergeant Matthews and myself stood motionless in amazement. The CO, sitting behind his desk, didn't know whether to put his hat on or spit in his bucket, but after a brief pause we both agreed to our master's wishes and we all left the CO's office. Luckily, the Squadron Adjutant kindly led Rawlinson away to complete his arrival procedures while Matthews and I stayed in the Squadron's office chatting up Cynthia and Rosemary over a pot of tea.

'Who's the new guy with the suntanned face?' Cynthia said questioningly as she stirred the teapot.

'Our new Red Section Leader from Two-Six-One Squadron in Malta,' I replied.

'I don't like him one little bit, Donald. He seems disillusioned and ill-mannered and was very rude to Rosemary because he had to wait to see the CO.'

'You shouldn't judge a man by your initial reactions, Cynthia, especially in these times of tragedy and war. You never know, he may have had a hard time out there in the Mediterranean.'

'Hard times or not, Donald, he shouldn't be rude to us.'

'Yes, I agree, Cynthia, there's no excuse for rudeness, but I expect as time goes by he'll settle in to our boss's ways and we'll be one happy family once again.'

'I don't know so much, Donald,' Cynthia said, 'he strikes me as a bit of a loner if you ask me.'

'Whether you hold a double Iron Cross or a double DFC, you shouldn't be so abrasive to people you've got to work with,' Rosemary said as she passed us our hot enamel mugs of tea.

'Well, let's give him the benefit of the doubt, eh lads and lasses?' I said as I concluded the conversation on our new leader.

A few minutes later, while the four of us were in conversation around the teapot, the outer door suddenly opened and the two WAAFs stood smartly to attention while Matt and I remained seated.

'Ah, there you are, Flying Officer Hamilton, I've been looking for you everywhere,' said Pilot Officer Jefferson as she entered the office. 'Can I see you for a moment in private?'

'Of course you can, ma'am,' I said as I escorted her out of the room.

'Would you like to come with me to Folkestone?' she said. 'I have to do a bit of shopping for the Station Commander who's kindly lent me his Hillman.'

'Sure thing, Miss Jefferson,' I replied excitedly as I hadn't anything better to do than accompany Sergeant Matthews back to the Mess.

'We shan't be long; be back for dinner,' she said turning towards me.

'OK by me, ma'am,' I replied and with that we sat in the Governor's blue Hillman Minx with black hoods over the headlights, and away we went to one of the nicest seaside towns on the south coast.

We arrived at Folkestone about an hour later after stopping a couple of times en route. The streets seemed exceptionally quiet for this time of day until we realised it was early closing day. After parking the car we wandered around the few shops which were open. Luckily the bank was open so we could get cash for the Station Commander's necessities.

'How about a spot of lunch, Louisa?' I said as we waited in the bank queue.

'That would be just fine, Donald. Where shall we go to eat?'

'I thought we might go up to the Royal Oak on the Folkestone-Dover Road. It'll be quiet there.'

Having done the Group Captain's shopping, we hopped into his car and gently made our way to the pub with Louisa driving. When we arrived the place seemed exceptionally busy with people from all walks of life seeming to fill both bars. The blue uniforms of the Royal Observer Corps were mingled with khaki uniforms of the Royal Artillery. However after a push here and a shove there we managed to get to the landlord and order a couple of pork pies and a round of drinks. Since there wasn't any room to sit we decided that as it was a lovely sunny day we would sit outside on the wings of the car, using the car bonnet as a beer table. The wind was light and the temperature warm but as we were in sight of the aerodrome we decided not to take our jackets off in case a senior officer passed by.

Refreshed, we decided to climb up onto the heathland overlooking the town of Folkestone. There we walked amongst the gorse which was in full bloom under a cloudless blue sky. It was one of those May days you always dream about when you feel on top of the world. A lone Spitfire interrupted the silence of our surroundings, perhaps on a test flight because it regularly followed the same aerial path. I doubted whether it was a pupil pilot since I thought we were too near the enemy for training to be allowed. The panoramic view of Folkestone left me breathless – these Kent seaside towns all along the coast offered wonderful scenic views from above. They nestled between the North Sea and green pastureland with such grace and beauty. All seemed impressively quiet as we scanned the horizon.

We walked for quite some time towards Capel le Ferne, the density of the trees and gorse giving us privacy as we held hands. On the outskirts of the village we lay down on a green patch of short grass to cool down. We just lay there looking up at the peaceful sky which four years ago was littered with aeroplanes from both sides of the Channel, and talked about many things although the main topic of conversation was about the progress of the war and the effect it had on our lives. We thought about the future. Would the war be over soon and when it was, what occupations would we follow? Louisa was quite determined to follow her father's footsteps and become a teacher. For me, the question was unanswerable – I couldn't accept the thought of living beyond the next raid, although I often thought if I survived the war I'd like to be a lawyer. Louisa explained the deep family roots her family had in decades of teaching in several well-known schools such as Oundle and King's, which bordered the Leicestershire and Lincolnshire counties.

Analysing my own thoughts as the wind cooled our bodies, I just wanted to see the end of hostilities. We fighter pilots lived from one scramble to another. It was too incomprehensible to think in terms of days or even weeks ahead. Our losses on 629 Squadron had been high these past few weeks due mainly to the increase in our activity over Northern France. There was hardly a day went by when one of the Squadron Commanders in the Wing did not have the unenviable task of informing the next of kin of their personal loss.

As we lay there in the setting sun, our bodies relaxed, I had a great desire to reach out and hold her tiny frame, but discretion got the better of me so I kept my hands to myself. Suddenly she sat up, raised her hands to her neck and removed her black tie. I thought as I gazed at her that her shoulders and upper slim body supported her head admirably. Her irrepressible blue eyes bubbled like chilled champagne as she lowered her head towards me and for a few seconds our bodies were locked in mutual affection. The warmth of her breasts transmitted through my shirt to my already warm chest.

'Are you married by any chance, Donald?' she said enquiringly as she compressed my body still further into the hard ground.

'No, I'm afraid not,' I replied as I held my arms around her. 'I've had neither the time nor the opportunity, although I'm engaged.'

'You are, are you, Donald? You never said.'

'You never asked, Miss Jefferson.'

'Is she very attractive?'

'Yes, she is, In fact she's very beautiful and comes from a very wealthy family in New Malden.'

'Where does she work, Donald? I'd love to meet her.'

'She works in a London bank, as a secretary.'

'You get on well with girls, don't you, Mr Hamilton?'

'Why do you say that?' I asked as she stretched her body to arm's length above my head.

'I was watching Sergeant Matthews and yourself chatting up two of my WAAFs prior to our meeting today.'

'Oh, were you now! Well, you've nothing to fear. I'm just a harmless young lad from Richmond,' and with that we both giggled with laughter as she fell flat on my chest, winding me in the process. She then put one arm around my neck and with the other reached into my shirt front. Her hand was warm, her motions sexual. Our eyes remained locked as we kissed momentarily and softly. I could feel her fragility and unmistakable tenderness. She took hold of my recalcitrant hand and guided it into her unopened shirt onto her small round breasts and then unbuttoned her shirt and bra so that the whole of one breast sank into the palm of my hand. She rhythmically moved her body into a cyclic path so that her breasts were caressed. We were both getting sexually excited. By now her neck and bosom and parts of her stomach were open to the evening sun. She made no further advances but moaned and groaned as I caressed the vital parts of her body. Then with a great sigh of relief she lay passive as though anaesthetised amongst the Kent gorse with her head resting on my shoulder. As we lay quietly watching the seagulls calling noisily above us the ferocity of war seemed far away.

Time being our enemy, we had to leave our peaceful surroundings to the butterflies and birds. It had been a surprisingly eventful day which both of us would remember as war dragged on both above and across the Channel.

10

Lloyds Bank, Cheapside in London was buzzing with lunchtime customers as I entered the building on the stroke of twelve-thirty. People of all nationalities and from all walks of life were queuing at the cash desks to be served. In the far corner at the enquiries desk stood a tall, willowy Royal Air Force officer with New Zealand flashes on his shoulders, quietly having an amusing conversation with the pretty, petite young female clerk who did not look old enough to have left school. As I made my way towards him, he suddenly turned to me and said, 'Good morning, home on a spot of leave?' in a soft broken voice which sounded more Australian than his native tongue. I just stood there motionless and embarrassed. Out of habit I almost shot my right arm up to salute him but at the last second remembered where I was.

'Good morning, sir,' I replied nervously. The embarrassment grew even worse when I looked at his uniform and noticed a silver rosette on each of his DSO and DFC ribbons. Gee, I thought, a fighter or bomber ace talking to me. I'd never met such a highly decorated officer in the flesh before. I'd read plenty of reports about them, but had never actually seen one. He seemed so shy in his mannerisms and appearance, it was no wonder the girl cashier blushed as he spoke to her. I guessed he must have been a regular customer at the bank.

When I stepped up to the counter after the distinguished officer had gone I asked the girl clerk who it was that she had served a few moments ago. 'Oh, him. I don't know really, but he comes in often on a Friday. He's very charming, isn't he?'

'Yes, I suppose he is,' I said trying to remember whether I'd seen a photograph of him in the papers. When I get back to base, I must ask the Squadron CO who he was. Visiting the bank regularly he must be pretty close to London, I thought, as I stared at the young girl with the sparkling blue eyes.

'Can I help you, sir?' she said enquiringly.

'Yes, you can. Could you tell Miss Barbara Devereaux that Flying Officer Hamilton has arrived.'

'Oh, so you're Donald Hamilton. We've heard a lot about you.'

'I hope some of it's good, what you've heard,' I said as I gazed at her freckled face.

'Oh, yes! Wow!' and she ran off up the stairs behind her and disappeared.

The reception area of the bank was densely crowded by this time. Young and efficient teller clerks flicked their fingers to and fro with effortless precision as they counted the notes. Even the coins were collected in pairs and picked up in straight lines for easy counting. It seemed a bit unfair of management to put so much pressure on these girls in one day, Friday. Why, I thought to myself, couldn't employees receive their pay cheques on other days? Why always Friday? It seemed a ludicrous system to me.

As the minutes ticked by my relaxed body began to give way to gremlins attacking the inner wall of my stomach which I so often experienced as I flew low over the French coast. Tension turned into anxiety as several people stared curiously at my uniform. I hoped Barbara wouldn't be long but, knowing women, they take ages in dressing rooms preparing their make-up before entering the arena. Happily the situation changed as Barbara came into view. I quickly waded through the crowd of onlookers who were watching our emotional meeting for we hadn't seen each other since I joined 629 Squadron in April 1944. As we got within arm's reach of one another there was this final spurt of speed which terminated in us embracing each other warmly and affectionately. A cheer of approval came not only from her working colleagues, but also from strangers in the crowd. Both our faces turned a bright red with embarrassment. A little old lady with a charming smile came over to us and said, 'I wish you luck,' and proceeded to hug both of us.

The Bank Manager, whose body was as thin as a broomstick, came over, shook my hand and gave Barbara an official white envelope. 'Off you go, you two. You're holding things up here. Have a good time,' and he kissed Barbara on the cheek as we turned to leave. We stood outside in the busy street for a few moments to catch our breath and look for a taxi. This gave me the opportunity to gaze at Barbara as she searched up and down the busy highway. Her dress was beautifully cut in pale blue cotton with white spots and her silk stockings were impeccably straight right down to her black patent shoes. Her pastel shade hat matched her dress to perfection. During these past months she had become a woman of great beauty and her figure was positively arousing. Eventually she hailed a taxi, although it was a hair-raising experience trying to attract the attention of the driver. Directing the driver to the Café de Paris, we sat back on the blue leather seat and looked into each other's eyes. She kissed me tenderly, squeezed my hands and said, 'It's lovely to have you home, darling.'

'Why don't you open the letter?' I asked pointing to the Manager's present.

'Oh! That's a good idea. In the excitement I'd forgotten all about it,' and with that she began to open the letter. In it was a cheque and a scribbled note which said, 'See you Monday. Have a meal on me,' signed by the Manager.

'That's a nice thought,' I said to Barbara.

'Yes, isn't it? Typical of him though. He's a very thoughtful man. Kind and considerate as well. He comes from Sunbury on Thames.'

'Oh, that's not far from you, is it?'

'No, not really,' Barbara said taking off her wide-brimmed hat and putting it on her lap.

From the taxi we heard the familiar sound of air-raid sirens wailing with their high resonating chorus and I felt as though I should be up there in the clouds rather than being driven around the crowded streets of the West End. Isolated bursts of gunfire could be heard close by and people in the street began to dart into nearby doorways as the firing increased. Our licensed cabby, with his green oval badge buttoned to his jacket, continued on his way as though he hadn't heard a thing. Through street after street he throttled and braked his blue taxi past the scars of war. Damage to some buildings was extensive with several bordering on complete destruction. The people of London, weary from the long bombardment since 1940, resolutely continued on with their way of life. Working with unparalleled devotion to duty, they supported their Leader with patriotism and courage, whilst in the evenings they relaxed in their favourite pub drinking the local beer and singing their favourite songs.

At last our London cabby turned his taxi sharply round a corner and stopped outside our destination. The door was quickly opened by a small, stubby, middle-aged doorman who looked like Mr Pickwick dressed in a smart red tunic embroidered with gold braid and brass buttons.

'Good afternoon, Sir and Madam. Welcome to the Café de Paris,' he said, holding Barbara's hand as she alighted. We were then ushered through the large swing door into a brilliant red foyer whose furnishings and fabrics must have cost the earth. The Head Waiter, immaculately dressed in black, confirmed our reservation and showed us to our table in the middle of a large dining room. As expected by the clientele, the room was tastefully furnished in blue and cream. The orchestra, dressed in red blazers to harmonise with the occasion, played soft wartime melodies on a raised platform. The dining room was full of women being wined and dined by rich men from the City. To us, this visit was the chance of a lifetime – to them, it was a daily ritual of eating exquisite food and drinking expensive wines.

Several waiters attended us politely and efficiently, always making sure our personal needs were met. Some offered us suggestions, others just stood there taking our orders. Soon, with the orchestra playing a selection of Glen Miller melodies, we tucked into a fabulous meal of hors d'oeuvres, fish, roast crown of lamb, washed down with a delightful bottle of Côtes du Rhône. Sweets, coffee and brandies concluded this prodigious meal.

It was with considerable regret that we had to leave but our stomachs were full and the Bank Manager's cheque well and truly spent. As we walked along the busy streets towards Regent's Park people took no notice of the current air raid – they just carried on in their unflappable way. Reminders of the war could be seen in large, humorous posters stuck on various billboards. One comical one showed four people travelling on the London tube talking to each other. At the bottom were the words 'Careless Talk Costs Lives'. Another, in red and black with a tall, white man holding an ARP shield said, 'Serve To Save'.

We made our way to a quiet part of the park opposite Bedford College where there were flowerbeds nestling amongst the green bushes and surrounding the whole area well-trimmed lawns. We sat down on one of them and relaxed. The aroma of nearby tulips hung in the air. People sat everywhere amongst the rolling lawns and flowers enjoying the tranquillity of this famous London scene. The air-raid sirens were now giving off a constant wail indicating that the enemy aircraft had left the badly bombarded city. We lay down side by side staring at the peaceful clouds which hardly moved across the sky when Barbara suddenly turned towards me and said, 'Oh, you've been promoted then,' whilst pointing to the thick stripe at the end of my sleeve.

'Yes, I'm sorry. I forgot to tell you on the telephone the other evening.'

'Does that mean you'll get more money?'

'Yes. You bankers are all the same. All you think about is hoarding your money away in small deposit boxes or large vaults.' I held her hands tightly and gave her an encouraging smile.

She grinned back, pleased and turned her shapely body towards me. Her hair was now cut short, her blue, glistening earrings matching the quality of her dress. 'How many aircraft have you shot down now, Donald?' she asked as she picked a blade of grass and twisted it close to my face.

'Why do you ask?' I replied trying to evade the question.

'Well, you're a fighter pilot and the girls in the office often ask me your score and I always tell them I don't know.'

'Well you can jolly well continue to give them the same answer,' I said, holding her face in my hands and giving her the usual grin. 'By the way, Barbara, they don't by any chance record the number of times they have intercourse a year, do they?' and I pulled her down on top of me with shouts of laughter.

She chuckled and said, 'Now you're getting very personal, young Flying Officer Hamilton,' and with that she kissed me sexually on the lips, almost stifling me. After withdrawing her red lips and wiping the lipstick off my mouth she whispered in my ear, 'How many Jerrys have you shot down?'

Pausing to reconsider my earlier decision I gazed at her beautiful face and replied, 'Four if you must know, but I don't want Tom, Dick or Harry to know,' and I hugged her curvaceous body.

'I promise to keep it to myself,' she said and with that she got up and straightened her dress. After brushing several blades of grass from her expensive looking dress we made our way home on the train to New Malden.

On arrival at her suburban home, I took the opportunity of telephoning my uncle at Cheam in Surrey while Barbara changed into something more casual. He lived with my grandmother in Wakefield Road, a delightful part of the town, and was a brilliant aeronautical engineer who had designed many mechanical components for the famous Hawker Hurricane under its Chief Designer, Sydney Camm. His main hobbies were gardening and tinkering about with mechanical gadgets but he also loved driving his Flying Standard Ten saloon which he had purchased for one hundred pounds in 1937. It had been a number of years since I had seen him and so we were both invited over for tea that afternoon.

After boarding the 213 bus to Sutton it seemed no time at all before we arrived at their lovely detached house built some twenty years earlier. My mother's relations greeted us warmly and my uncle was clearly impressed by Barbara as they chatted cordially about their work and hobbies. When the two ladies went into the house to prepare tea, my uncle led me away down to the bottom of the garden where his prefabricated garage stood. Inside one immediately became aware of a gleaming, unused maroon saloon car under discarded dust sheets.

Having lit up his usual cigarette – he was a heavy smoker – and wiping his dark, horn-rimmed glasses, he said quietly and quite out of the blue, 'How would you like to have this car, Donald?'

'Who me, Uncle?' I said in amazement, knowing this was the last thing he would want to give away. 'This vehicle's your pride and joy. I couldn't possibly accept it,' and I rubbed my hands over the dazzling chrome on the radiator.

'Yes, I know, Donald, but it hasn't been on the road since the outbreak of war and your grandmother and I decided that it would be much more beneficial to you and your needs than standing here gathering dust.'

'Yes, I know, Uncle, but this could be stored for many years.'

'Nevertheless, Donald, we want you to have it. You have the contacts and know how to have it licensed and get petrol coupons. Your need is much greater than ours.'

'Well, Uncle, I'm just overwhelmed. Oh, I don't know what to say.'

'Don't say anything. Just help me with the battery and tyres and you can take it away with you now. Your father will be able to fix your car licence up next week.'

We wheeled this beautiful specimen of British craftsmanship out of the garage and onto his gravel drive. When we wiped the dust off the paintwork the body shone from bumper to bumper, the chrome glistened in the evening sunlight and the inside upholstery, which had been cleaned with Mansion polish, looked unscathed.

After a delightful tea all four of us completed the necessary tasks to get the car on the road. Since it was untaxed I decided to use a Watney's beer label as a tax disc, which were displayed on many cars belonging to servicemen to keep the police at bay. After showing our appreciation for the tea and car, we said goodbye to our friendly hosts and made our way back to Barbara's home at New Malden.

It was while driving through Worcester Park that we decided to spend the weekend away rather than stay in New Malden. Barbara hastily packed an overnight bag and we speedily departed in our newly acquired car to the country lanes of west Hertfordshire. I knew of an excellent small hotel there which nestled amongst the beechwoods on the outskirts of Bovingdon, one which offered exquisite cuisine and a comfortable bed at a reasonable price. On approaching the sleepy village of Bovingdon, which lies on the edge of the green, chalk-flecked Chilterns, we came across the airfield which was used by the 92nd Bomber Group of the United States Eighth Air Force to train their wartime crews on Boeing B17 Flying Fortresses. As we passed the perimeter on the Chesham side of the airfield we could see these huge four-engined bombers taking off into the wind towards Hemel Hempstead. The noise at full revolutions was absolutely deafening, as their engines lifted them off the ground. They were a familiar sight to me since I had seen them often on their way to bomb targets in daylight over France and Germany whereas to Barbara they were not only unknown but a frightening spectacle as well.

Scattered amongst the stationary 'Flying Forts', as they were known, were a number of Dakotas, probably used to ferry personnel and cargo from neighbouring American bases. Bovingdon airfield was also widely used by officers of Air Rank as a stepping stone to the bright lights of London for a night out or an important meeting. General Eisenhower, the Supreme Allied Commander, whose headquarters were at Bushey Park, often kept his personal B17 here.

87

As we entered the side door of the Highcroft Hotel we were greeted warmly by a pleasant middle-aged lady who was busy totting up her daily balance sheet on several bits of paper.

'Good evening, sir,' she said with an enchanting smile.

'Good evening,' I replied in a timid London accent. 'Is there any possibility of a room either for the night or preferably for the weekend?'

'Yes, sir, you're in luck. Only a few moments ago I had a cancellation from an American couple who were unfortunately held up in London on family matters. The room's vacant until Monday.'

'I'll take it, if I may,' I replied eagerly. 'Has it a bathroom?'

'No, sir, I'm afraid it hasn't. In fact none of our rooms have bathrooms.' She extracted a flat cigarette from an expensive gold case. 'Do you still wish to take the room, sir?' she asked, puffing heavily on her lighted cigarette.

'Yes, please,' and I stepped forward apprehensively to sign the hotel register which was beautifully bound in real red leather.

On examining the open book I couldn't help but notice that the whole page consisted of American Air Force names and their families. I couldn't see one Smith, Brown or Jones anywhere. It looked on paper as though the hotel was used for accommodating American servicemen and their wives in transit. Boldly writing the name Flying Officer and Mrs Hamilton gave me a sense of elation at being British.

With the formalities completed, the receptionist led us up a very wide wooden staircase, richly carpeted in traditional blue. The double rooms were accommodated on the first floor. We passed several doors, all painted brown, two of which were the bathroom and toilet respectively. Our room was at the end of the wide, uncarpeted passageway for we had left the carpeted region way back on the stairway, but it was light, warm and airy, the light coming from two single-sash windows and the warmth from the kitchen below. One window looked out over the front car park and an old barn which housed the proprietor's black Austin 10 saloon car while the other overlooked a large garden mainly laid to lawn. Towards the horizon I could see the rural, unspoilt countryside of the Chilterns. This triangular belt of land, which crossed the counties of Hertfordshire, Buckinghamshire and Oxfordshire, comprised many fine acres of chalky grassland and glorious beechwoods rising high into the sky.

The scenic countryside which lay between Oxford and London offered the visitor peacefulness, beauty and unparalleled walks. One of these walks was the famous Ridgeway which offered the weekend walker a challenge not to be missed. The path crossed about 80 miles of some of the finest green chalky grassland unrivalled in England. The area was further improved by little villages hidden away amongst the green and yellow valleys which were dotted with wonderful open commons, coppices and obscure narrow footpaths leading to many a fine Elizabethan cottage, Tudor house or the ubiquitous country pub.

'What did you put in the register, darling?' Barbara asked, interrupting my thoughts on the green pastures outside.

'Oh, the register. Oh, that. Well, I put Flying Officer and Mrs Hamilton, Royal Air Force,' I replied as I stood by the window inhaling the cool, late spring air.

'You naughty boy,' Barbara replied as she came slowly towards me with a dress in one hand and a pair of pointed shoes in the other. Smiling with that inherent sparkle in her eyes, she said, 'I thought you'd do that somehow.'

'I had no choice, did I?' I wondered whether I'd made the right decision. Pausing to assess my guilty situation and to relax her I said with an amused smile, 'I'll have to buy you a wedding ring tomorrow. Until then, you could turn your engagement ring over tonight at dinner.'

'No need, Donald,' she replied triumphantly as she opened her handbag. 'I've brought my grandmother's wedding ring,' and in seconds she had taken off her engagement ring and put both rings on the third finger of her left hand. I held my arms out to her and we embraced each other tightly as I whispered into her ear, 'You are wonderful, darling,' and within seconds we were making love on the soft, wide, comfortable bed.

On hearing the evening dinner bell we made our way down to the foyer where several guests were gathered for pre-dinner drinks at the bar. The room, although small, catered comfortably for the hotel guests and local visitors. The majority of the guests were Americans, the men in uniform, the ladies in evening dress. A few patrons from the nearby village were scattered here and there. It seemed a very friendly atmosphere as people of mixed nationalities chatted amicably to one another over a glass of local beer and cigarette smoke filled the tiny bar. The foyer was interlinked with the lounge, dining room and bar by a series of interconnecting doors, in the centre of which stood the impeccably dressed head waiter with an unusually large menu under his arm. An Irishman, he was courteous, efficient and administered his waitresses with practised ease. All the ground floor rooms were tastefully furnished in blue and pink fabrics while the furniture, which was solid and modern, looked expensive. It was obvious from the first moment you stepped inside the building that the keynote of this hotel was one of comfort and tranquillity. After pre-dinner drinks we were ushered to our table by the polite head waiter who had been there a number of years and had seen new proprietors come and go. Since we had eaten earlier in the day at the Café de Paris, we both decided to have the fresh salmon salad from an appetizing list of specialities washed down by a chilled bottle of Moselle.

After a delightful meal we decided to exercise our legs and walk to the local village of Bovingdon which was about a mile away. The evening was beautiful and the peace of it all just perfect. The lane was narrow and undulating as it led us to the sleepy village which was typical of the kind you see in this part of the country. The red brick terraced houses built during the Recession rubbed shoulders with sunken cottages of a century before and dilapidated shop windows squatted aimlessly along one side of the high street. At the southern end of the village in memory of a past Member of Parliament stood a well which sixty years before had been the sole supply of water for the whole community. Today, it is just a reminder of days gone by. Like all rural communities, its activities centred on and around the local church, and here the church of St Lawrence, with its avenue of huge clipped yews, held the secrets of past religious and political sectarianism. The eerie silence of the surroundings on this beautiful late spring evening in 1944 was a pleasant contrast to the noise and bustle of London suburbia and the only sign of life was the occasional American car or the distant drone of B17s warming up in preparation for the next flight.

As the light faded we made our way back to the hotel where happy voices could be heard as we approached the front door. As the door slowly opened I hastily grabbed Barbara's arm and led her in the opposite direction to escape the jolly crowd in the bar and we retreated silently to our bedroom at the far end of the hotel via the unoccupied kitchen and the tradesmen's entrance to the first floor.

By the time I had refreshed my body Barbara was in bed. The room was dark and warm, the warmth due to the heat generated earlier by the kitchens below. Outside the still night air was undisturbed other than by the occasional faint echoes from the revellers below. As we lay side by side I could feel she wanted to make love. The fragrance of her body was from an expensive perfume she had put on earlier in the evening, perhaps Chanel No. 5. Gradually we interlocked our bodies with our arms and legs until we embraced totally. She did not resist as I pulled her thin cotton nightdress over her head and shoulders, leaving her shapely body naked on the sheets. She lay there motionless beside me, her long arms clinging tightly around my neck. My lips touched her large round breasts which hung exquisitely from her chest and I could feel her nipples extend outwards like thimbles as my hands roamed the full length of her soft body. With probing tongues circulating the inner walls of our mouths, the combination of love, passion and sexual desire began to excite us. My spine tingled as I blew warm air into her supple uterus so that her whole body writhed sensuously until suddenly she rose high towards me, clinging with her vibrant body to my arched back. Then she groaned in ecstasy as her body fell away towards the base of the bed and even her nipples sank back. I tried to move away from her but she tightened her grip around my neck murmuring drowsily, 'Don't go away, darling.' With renewed energy we made love once again before finally going off to sleep in each other's arms.

The next morning, after a hearty breakfast of bacon and eggs, we set off in our little car to explore the recommended beauty spots within a few miles of our hotel. We didn't have to go far before we came across the picturesque village of Aldbury. Here the whitewashed, timber-clad Tudor cottages gleamed brightly in the morning sun and the ducks in the village pond splashed majestically in the cloudy water. Overlooking the village under some tall trees stood a mid-Georgian mansion called Stocks House which once housed the famous Victorian romantic novelist, Mrs Humphrey Ward. A frequent guest in those days had been none other than George Bernard Shaw himself.

Leaving this scenic beauty spot, which could be seen on many a picture postcard, we motored north through some lovely woods until we came to a tall, Doric column, standing in open woodland on the edge of Ashridge Estate. This austere piece of architecture was built in memory of the so-called 'Father of Inland Navigation', the eccentric Third Duke of Bridgwater. With the help of a brilliant engineer who could neither read nor write he designed the famous Worsley to Manchester ship canal.

We couldn't resist the challenge to get to the top and after mastering the 170 spiral steps we arrived breathless at the top from where the view was breathtaking. You could see for many miles on a clear day.

Descending to the ground quicker than we ascended we made our way to Ashridge House. On entering the estate, which lies north-east of Berkhamsted, you could see why foreign diplomats and visitors included it in their itinerary. The estate housed some of the finest beechwoods and glades this side of Norfolk. The house, which is neo-Gothic, has been the home of many royal families including Henry VIII and Queen Elizabeth I. Now, in 1944, the house was being used as an emergency evacuation hospital for London's patients. Several people in their dressing gowns sat in antiquated deckchairs convalescing in the midday sun. Many waved as we toured the battlements and unguarded towers. The associated gardens gave the house a tranquil setting in the warm sunlight and the masses of azaleas and rhododendrons were a picturesque sight, once seen never forgotten.

Unfortunately we had to leave this magnificent place but we both promised each other we would one day bring our children to play in this peaceful haven on the edge of the Chilterns. Our final port of call was the climb to Ivinghoe Beacon, where we promised ourselves refreshments from the hotel picnic hamper. At the top of this 800-foot plateau we could see many fine acres of corn. Sleepy villages nestled amongst the hills together with the chimney stacks of the local cement works. Here, the Ridgeway continued on its way to Overton Hills in Wiltshire. Over the centuries countless heavy feet had trodden this path which in spring is edged with violets and where in summer the hills grow yellow with cowslips.

Reluctantly we left this undulating scene and made our way back to the hotel. After an appetizing evening dinner we retired to bed to the background noise of Flying Fortresses circling above us. Having been told at the bar that both Clark Gable and William Holden were stationed here Barbara kept praying that they would be in the hotel's breakfast room the next morning. Unfortunately, she was disappointed and we left after Sunday breakfast without seeing them. After saying my farewells to Barbara and her parents, I returned to RAF Hambridge to prepare for the Wing's meeting the next day.

11

The following morning pilots of Hambridge Wing were summoned into the compact Operations Room. In front of the formal gathering of battle weary pilots and new recruits were a number of senior officers of Air Rank from Group. Some were carrying large rolls of statistics and geographical maps, others, their battered, black briefcases. Amongst them was a civilian who we later learned was Doctor Trevor Brown, Head of Scientific Air Intelligence.

After an introductory talk by the Air Marshal on the latest news of Hitler's two new secret weapons, the A4 rocket or V2 and the 'Flying Bomb', code-named KIRSCHKERN (Cherrystone), the Air Officer Commanding handed over the lectern to the civilian who was seated next to our Wing Commander Flying. Dr Brown, BSc, Ph.D, FRS, was an Oxford Physicist before the war. Now he held the prestigious post of Scientific Adviser to the Prime Minister, Mr Winston Churchill. He was tall and gangly with a shining, bald head. He had a long, melancholy face, strong hands and well manicured fingernails and was dressed in a black pinstripe suit which seemed two sizes too small for him, especially round the shoulders and waist. Attached to his lower waistcoat button hung a very expensive looking gold watch chain.

He commenced his talk by saying that since the early part of 1943, his team of scientists had been monitoring the development of a pilotless missile whose physical size was half that of a Spitfire or Hurricane, but whose capability as a bomber was both lethal and destructive. It was jet-propelled by an unknown fuel and guided by an unknown control system. They also had reservations about it being radio-controlled from launch to target. He explained with sketches that the missile, which was painted black, was a mid-wing monoplane with typical fuselage, two wings and an unprecedented propulsion unit above the fuselage. It had no ailerons but incorporated a conventional tailplane with elevators set forward from a fin and rudder.

After lighting a cigarette, to the dismay of his hosts, he continued in a very explicit manner to give us some technical information about the Fieseler Fi103 or V1 Flying Bomb. Pointing to a scaled black and white drawing, he informed us that the fuselage was 25 feet long and 2 feet 8 inches wide. The front of the fuselage housed the 1-ton Amatol warhead which was a mixture of TNT and ammonium nitrate.

Turning to a colourful picture of the propulsion unit, which was exceptionally clear compared to the other drawings, he explained that the 'Argus Impulse Duct' engine developed the necessary thrust to drive the missile towards its target at very high velocity. Basically, the thermodynamic operation was both simple and economic. He continued his explanation by saying that an explosive mixture was pumped into a combustion chamber and ignited. Once ignited, the fuel was then cut off and the pulse jet continued to produce explosions in a welded mild steel tube to provide the continuous thrust.

Leaning against the lectern, as though he was bored by churning out the same old story over and over again, he paused to ask us if we had any questions. The gathering of experienced and untried fliers remained nonchalant and silent. Waiting patiently to see if there was any response from his audience he passed the time by rubbing his bald head with one hand and relighting another cigarette with the other. Since there was no one brave enough to ask any foolish questions he quietly continued to describe the inherent control mechanism of this unmanned flying bomb. Pointing to another detailed drawing he explained that before launching some of the automatic controls like range, height and bearing were preset. The remainder operated the control surfaces during flight to maintain the vengeance weapon on its current flight path to its target while a master compass kept the cigar-shaped aircraft exactly on course. With technical jargon still pouring from his lips and some of the audience nodding off, especially at the back, he paused again to answer any questions the pilots may have had. The Wing Commander Flying broke the silence by asking the boffin whether the missile had any feed-back system in its guidance mechanism. This question woke many of us up as we never thought our leader had it in him to ask such a knowledgeable question as that. The speaker quietly explained to those who were interested that the deviation from the mean flight path was controlled by two servo-motors which controlled the rudder and elevators to correct any error. The Wing Commander thanked him for his clear answer and the rest of us murmured our agreement.

Next, the professor pinned up on the operations wall some statistics which were most frightening and brought us all to our senses. Range of the missile from launch to target was in the region of 140 miles. Its operating height was between 1,000 and 4,000 feet. This had us all gasping, including the sleepers. Then he paused and said in a loud, humorous voice, 'Estimated speed across the English coast about three hundred and forty miles per hour.' To emphasise this figure he wrote in large numbers on the blackboard 340. The audience remained silent as he continued to explain that as the missile consumed fuel, the speed increased to in excess of 400 mph approaching its target.

At this statement the silence of the meeting erupted into commotion. Voices from flabbergasted pilots echoed above the moans of despair from the front benches.

Sergeant Matthews whispered in my ear, 'How the hell do we catch the bloody thing at that speed?'

A reply behind me said, 'With a ruddy butterfly net!' Roars of laughter came from the airmen seated behind me and there was so much noise the Station Commander had to call us to order.

Sergeant Matthews turned towards me and said, 'What the hell do we do, Donald?' I just raised my hands in total despair and said nothing.

Several murmurs of bewilderment spread around the room. I had seen frustration and dismay many times before but not on such a grand scale as this. Squadron Leader Mitchell sensed the feelings of his colleagues and tried to break the silence and introduce a bit of humour into the proceedings but he was politely silenced by the Station Commander.

Doctor Brown, at the request of the Air Marshal, continued by saying that this weapon was extremely fast and capable of destroying several streets in a city if it went off. Pausing to put his cigarette out he emphasised clearly to us all in the Hambridge Wing that this new weapon posed a serious threat to our nation and to the state of the war. Pointing to the large diagram of the missile he repeatedly assured his audience that this weapon, although simple to manufacture, was lethal. British scientists had nothing but praise for their German counterparts.

Referring to its speed he said the next problem for us pilots was the time taken for the weapon to reach the edge of the Southern Area gun belt from launching in northern France. This, he assured us, was approximately ten minutes which meant we had only five minutes to vector onto our target and shoot it down during its flight path in the 30-mile gun belt region. This meant if we had any chance at all of seeing it we had to be vectored onto it by the radar controller before it flashed past our gunsights.

Finally, drawing his stimulating lecture to a close, he professed that this black midget aeroplane with no pilot or propeller could, if the Germans were successful, change the course of the war. He then sat down amid an air of gloom and despondency. You could feel how once again we felt inadequate as our brothers did in 1940. Here we were in 1944, with the latest Spitfire Mark XIV with only a fractional margin of speed advantage over our adversary.

When question time came, our Wing Commander Flying

sensed the feelings running through his men so he called a halt to the meeting. He thanked the senior officers and Dr Brown for coming and giving up their valuable time to talk to the Wing and the party left the Operations Room with a number of problems unsolved.

We all continued to sit and discuss what had been said over a cup of NAAFI tea. Andrew Matthews, Christopher Rawlinson and I studied its range of speed and explosive warhead with dismay and trepidation and we all agreed its maximum airspeed across the coast in level flight posed serious combat problems. We also felt sympathy for those on the receiving end in towns and cities which were in range from this high-explosive bomb. It posed a serious threat to people and property on a much larger scale than had been anticipated so that interception would have to be effective in the early stages of flight if we were going to be successful in shooting it down, otherwise our own guns would be blasting at us and I didn't fancy that one little bit. The morning's meeting was brought to a close. Before the Wing Commander left us he promised further meetings to discuss methods of interception. A big cheer went up when he informed us that all leave was cancelled, all pilots would camp at the dispersal when 'Diver Patrols' started. Since we were the only Wing in the Group equipped with the latest Mark XIV Spitfires there was no doubt in anybody's mind that our squadrons were going to be the first line of defence against Hitler's latest weapon. As Red Section left the Operations Room, we decided to have a game of badminton in No. 1 Hangar before going off to lunch.

After a relaxed game of badminton and a pint or two over lunch, personnel of 629 Squadron assembled in the dispersal hut on the far side of the airfield where the main topic of conversation was poorly written on the Squadron Commander's blackboard as we took our seats. The prefabricated hut was full to capacity with even our latest engine fitter there.

98

Several drawings of the pilotless missile were pinned up on adjacent walls, the pictures of scantily clothed ladies having been removed and put on the table nearest the door. The topic of discussion was deciphered by one of the riggers as 'Diver Patrols' – we later learned that this was the code name for the interception of the crewless aeroplanes or V1.

Before commencing with air tactics, the Squadron Commander gave us a brief resumé of the plans the Station Commander had put into effect after this morning's visit by the top brass. Basically, as we had learned in the morning, all operational pilots at Hambridge would be accommodated in tents at the dispersal. The number of pilots per squadron would be increased to 30 and all ground crews would have to work round the clock to keep our newly acquired Spitfires in the air. It was anticipated that extreme pressure would fall on the engine fitters since it was assumed that the engines would be worked to their limits chasing the flying bombs. It was stressed again by our CO that our Spitfires had only a slight margin at maximum air speed over the missile.

The Squadron Leader then gave out menial tasks to all of us. Flight Sergeant Devlin had the important job of obtaining the tents and erecting them, the Squadron Adjutant, food supplies. Since the CO knew I had an electrical background I had the surprisingly simple task of supplying electricity to the tents. He gave me Andrew since he knew we worked well together. Our Flight Commander had to erect (with some airmen from the equipment section) temporary latrines, his face one of amazement when he learned of his new administrative role.

During a lull in the discussions Flight Lieutenant Charles Rankin asked what was going to happen to the WAAF clerks under the new arrangements. A prompt but humorous reply came back from the CO and our Green Section Leader said no more. Squadron Leader Mitchell, a keen bridge player, then turned to the topic of 'Air Interception'. He suggested that all ground crew could leave if they wanted to but nobody accepted his invitation and they all stayed.

In his astute manner he continued to tell us that the target was small, elusive and swept across the sky at high speed. There was no time to jiggle about or to scan the clouds for the enemy as we had done in the past with the Messerschmitts and Focke-Wulfs. Drawing a straight chalk line on the blackboard he emphasised that the enemy this time flew straight and level and did not weave, bob or turn like the yellow noses we had been used to. With hand movements to represent the missile he demonstrated the effects one would see if the rocket was interrupted either by a shortage of fuel or a faulty gyroscope – it would glide into the ground. The serious problems facing us all, he declared, were how we were going to sight the bomb and how we were going to destroy it knowing it had one ton of high explosive in its nose. Since nobody in ADGB had actually seen one in the air, it was difficult to imagine its behaviour in flight. On no account, he warned, would any pilot in the Squadron attack the bomb within 200 yards.

Flight Lieutenant Christopher Rawlinson interrupted the proceedings by rudely going up to the blackboard and explaining one method of attack: coming up behind the bomb and giving it short bursts. At this point the Wing Commander Flying applauded Rawlinson's suggestion but offered an alternative one – let the bomb fly along parallel with you and fire deflection bursts at it when it passed, being careful to be outside the 200 yard radii for protection. We all thought this was an excellent idea so long as the rocket's speed did not exceed our maximum boost speed.

However, I still had reservations about the size and speed of the target. Also uppermost in our minds was the serious problem of flying within range of our own 40 mm guns. Some sort of communication was necessary between the gunnery officer, radar controller and ourselves to prevent us being shot at by our own shells. Squadron Leader Mitchell explained that ADGB would be in communication with the Royal Observer Corps and General Pile's Anti-Aircraft Command about co-ordination, but he stressed that chasing the Fieseler Fi103 Bomb in the statutory gun belt would be putting our lives and machines at risk.

Another element of interception which was discussed in the

100

meeting was the new technique of attacking the enemy at low level and at high speed. The majority of us in the Squadron hadn't attacked the Hun at 400 miles per hour and we certainly needed some practice before the real thing. Accuracy of interception by the radar controller was absolutely essential if we were going to be successful.

We had been informed that the Overlord-Diver Defence Plan would provide front-line Spitfire, Tempest and Mustang Standing Patrols at 12,000 feet above the English Channel. The Mustang IIIs were being lent from 129 and 315 Squadrons from Brenzett Island. Also at the same height would be other patrols above the coast between Newhaven and Dover and inland between Ashford and Haywards Heath.

When the VI attacks were in progress it was suggested that fighters from various units on the south-east coast would be sent off to patrol a wide band of lanes at 6,000 feet. It was proposed by new Blue Section Leader Robert Hill that we flew to a neutral zone with Tempest Vs from Newchurch in order to gain some practice at low level and high speed. Wing Commander Flying Ian Thraves thought this was a good idea and said before leaving the discussion that he would get in touch with Royal Air Force Coningsby to see if they could accommodate us.

The Tempest, which reached 408 miles per hour in level flight at 2,000 feet, had, like the Mustang, only a small margin of speed in hand over the Fieseler Bomb and our own Spitfire Mark XIV would have to reply on sporadic bursts of maximum boost to gain any sort of ground over the new weapon. Finally, the assembly of well-experienced pilots, intermediaries and novices broke up in angry displeasure. Our new duties in the air weren't very popular with the majority of us, in fact, the more experienced pilots like our Squadron Commander thought the traditional aerobatic skills would now be replaced by monotonous straight flying. The fun of weaving, yawing and diving from a piloted yellownose plane would be sadly missed. Whether it was a Messerschmitt or a Focke-Wulf Fw 190 you were tangling with, pilots on both sides respected each other's skills and tenacity. In the new phase of this war all we had to do was to get in range of the pilotless plane, fire quick bursts with our cannon and escape the explosion. The human element now seemed to have disappeared.

Our new Red Section Leader summed up his thoughts to his section saying, 'We faced the bloody enemy in 1940 and we'll do it again in 1944, even if we do have to stretch our engines to the limit.'

My reply was silent. I preferred to pitch my aerobatic skills against conventional machines rather than uninteresting, black, crewless missiles. Andrew and I decided to offer our services to Flight Sergeant Devlin in pitching tents and scrounging whatever was going to make our stay at the dispersal a bit more comfortable.

The next day 629 Squadron took off to Royal Air Force Coningsby in Lincolnshire. Each squadron of the Wing would take it in turns to be away for a few days to practise low-level high-speed flying with Tempest Mark Vs. The days were long and arduous since our Commander kept us at it from morning to dusk, some of us extending our flying into the early evening. I soon found it was far more difficult to fly in the dark than I had first thought. What hit me most was the sense of loneliness. All I could see and hear was the dim lights of the instrument panel and the squeaky voice of the controller. At night they really were your compass and your eyes. Red Section were efficient as a team during the day but at night just a bunch of individual hawks. We soon discovered our inadequacies at night flying and were glad our key role was going to be by day rather than at night.

We found in practice that the Tempest had at least 30 miles per hour excess speed over our new Griffon-engined Spitfires in level flight. This made it difficult to catch them unless you were up above them and could gain extra airspeed by diving on to their tails. However we did find it fun firing at the drogue being towed by a Mosquito. The Section revelled in high-altitude flying, low-level combat and target practice but in spite of this we soon became bored with the straight level stuff and often did other things to break the monotony.

It was during our stay at Coningsby that we heard the long-awaited news that Operation Overlord had begun. The day was the 6 June 1944 and the place, Normandy, was quite a surprise for all of us as we had thought the Supreme Allied Commander would have gone farther north to prevent such a long sea crossing for the Expeditionary Force.

As the week drew to a close in this quiet part of England, where the cereal crops grew in abundance and the blackcurrants ripened in the hot summer sun, we flew south to our temporary accommodation at Hambridge. On arrival we found that Bill Devlin and his crew had done a splendid job in sighting and erecting the tents at the dispersal. We were all accommodated in sections with plenty of room between the canvases.

My first job was to acquire some 24-volt batteries and lamps and rig up a temporary lighting system. It's amazing in war what can be found stored away in discarded Nissen huts and salvage yards. After several night patrols around the airfield Andrew and I obtained enough equipment to provide adequate illumination for all concerned. The only thing was that switching off the supplies was crude due to the shortage of switches. Being an ex-Scout, I had the experience and inventiveness to cope with the inadequacies of camping, but for some their temporary accommodation seemed unbearable. Washing up was primitive due to there only being one tap in the vicinity, but after another nightly prowl around the equipment section Christopher and I came back with some collapsible canvas wash basins with wooden tripods. We also managed to acquire some canvas camp beds which, once erected, seemed quite comfortable after a busy day. One thought however could never escape our minds and that was the thin protection of canvas which stood between us and the attacking Hun if he decided to return to Hambridge on another strafing exercise. After a general meeting we all decided to put the shovels to work and dig trenches within running distance of our new camp.

The next morning all pilots were instructed by the CO to help the riggers remove the green and brown paintwork from the Spitfires' external framework and polish them instead in order to reduce drag and nominally increase our maximum speed. The latter was further increased by removing unnecessary fittings such as the rear-view mirror and replacing the fuel with a higher octane rating. After a day of stripping paintwork and polishing you could identify the unfit members of our Squadron. Several of the heavy smokers sighed with relief as three WAAFs constantly fed us with cold drinks to quench our thirst.

Eventually, after several days, all the external paintwork of our aircraft was removed leaving a highly polished surface glittering in the June sunshine. All we had to do now was to wait for Hitler's Retaliation Weapon to cross our shores.

12

When Operation Overlord commenced in the early hours of
that Tuesday morning, 6 June 1944, it became an historic day
in military history as the greatest seaborne invasion ever
carried out, got under way. In one single day some 175,000
men came ashore on the Normandy beaches between Le
Havre and Cherbourg. In fact the invasion under the
leadership of General Dwight D. Eisenhower was divided into
five different landing beaches along the Normandy coast. It
was the turning point of the war where the defence of the
United Kingdom was turned into the assault on enemy-
occupied Europe. It was a day that all of us who were involved
in Operation Overlord will never forget. For the Allied
Expeditionary Force it was a highly dangerous task and one
hell of a place to be in. The invasion force had to cross a grey,
choppy sea from the peace and tranquillity of their bases in
beautiful parts of south-west England. Their objective was to
establish a foothold against a well-trained, very experienced,
well-equipped and battle-hardened enemy. General
Eisenhower told them in no uncertain terms that their
mission would be extremely difficult since the Wehrmacht
fought savagely as shown on the Russian Front.

To confuse the enemy General Eisenhower and his
logistical team planned, hours prior to the main invasion, two
diversionary operations to throw the enemy and confuse him
as to where the main Allied Expeditionary Force was actually
going to land, and to boost the morale amongst our troops.
One was Operation Taxable which involved Lancasters from
617 Squadron and the Royal Navy making the Germans

believe that the invasion was going to land between Dieppe and Cap d'Antifer. The Royal Navy used 18 small vessels towing balloons to show up as large ships on the German radar screens while the Lancasters heavily bombed enemy installation.

The second one, code-named Operation Glimmer, was much more successful in persuading the German High Command that Boulogne was going to be the major landing site. It involved only six aircraft and a few boats but it brought out all the German defenders including night fighters and E-boats. Searchlights came on and heavy guns roared away into the night on a convoy that was not there as many high-ranking Germans thought this would be the battleground for the defence of Europe because of the narrow sea-crossing from Britain to France. Fighter Command, from November 1943 to October 1944, was renamed the Air Defence of Great Britain (ADGB). Our Squadron, 629, was part of this new Command, whose aim was not only to defend Great Britain but be flexible enough to move forward as the invasion of Normandy progressed.

Pilots would fly between two and four sorties a day although the norm was to be two per day. The fighters' aim was to maintain air supremacy, reconnoitre enemy positions and movements, disrupt communications and prevent a flow of supplies and reinforcements. Also they were to attack enemy shipping and give close support to the Allied Expeditionary Force. Our Squadron's main objective was still to search for and seek out V1 and V2 sites.

Early on 6 June 1944 Red Section of 629 Squadron were ordered to support the Allied Air Forces over the beaches of Utah and Omaha of Normandy. We flew in tight formation across the grey, choppy and unattractive Channel. The cloud base was about 2,000 feet and the visibility was about 5 miles which meant that there were far too many Allied planes concentrated in such small air space and certainly the added black and white stripes on our wings, fuselage and tail were going to be a blessing in disguise. Also efficient communication between squadrons was paramount in order to avoid mid-air collisions. Over the R/T we often heard friendly voices asking whether there was any traffic about, meaning the Hun, over the target area and frequently the answer came back, 'NOT A BLOODY THING', which was most unexpected. As we approached Le Havre the flak was heavy and got hotter as we neared our specific target beaches of Utah and Omaha.

Chris, our Section Leader, decided it was too hot to sit around, so we flew north to seek out the V1 and V2 launching sites between Rouen and Mouscron even though we were forced down to a low altitude by the persistent intermittent cloud. From intelligence reports we knew that the Wehrmacht were supplying the V1 bombs via a railway line from Rouen through Beaumont and Arras and terminating at Mouscron. The problem we found was not only the ferocious barrage of flak shaking our spines and feet, but also that parts of the line went along narrow river valleys, giving us a restricted view of the sites.

Since we were running short of fuel we decided to attack the very large marshalling yards at Mouscron with three-second bursts of cannon, take some photographs and head for home.

On our return to Royal Air Force Hambridge Andrew noticed how badly damaged my tail was. Luckily my elevators and rudder were not affected otherwise I would have had serious trouble getting home. We also noticed with regret that our Red Section Leader had not returned and sitting on empty orange boxes in the warm sun with a hot cup of tea, we waited earnestly for his return. We scanned the horizon for many hours and the CO took off to see if he could locate him but unfortunately he was unable to, so Flight Lieutenant Christopher Rawlinson DFC and Bar was later posted as missing.

After debriefing, with the Intelligence Officer sitting on an empty beer crate, the CO called me into his office and asked me if I would take over Red Section with immediate effect with the rank of Flight Lieutenant. I was overjoyed and asked him whether he would promote Sergeant Matthews to Flight Sergeant so that he could be my Number 2, and he agreed.

107

With the good news of our promotions but saddened by the loss of our dear friend, we both went off to the beer tent and filled our thirsty bellies with weak British beer. I soon telephoned Barbara at work and although her boss was reluctant to bring her to the telephone he eventually relented. She was elated with the news of my promotion to Flight Lieutenant and the award of the Distinguished Flying Cross which the CO had told me about at our briefing. She yelled with excitement down the phone and I could hear all the girls in the office shouting their heads off with joy before I was forced to ring off.

While Andy and I were having a drink at the bar a smart looking Pilot Officer was asking the Mess Steward for the whereabouts of the Officer Commanding 629 Squadron, so I immediately stepped forward and introduced myself to the new recruit. I asked what his name was and he said he was Pilot Officer Adrian Dalgleish and was posted to 629 Squadron. I invited him to a table and asked Andy to join us. We offered him a beer but he refused although he said he would like a cup of tea since he had been travelling all day from Number 41 Squadron based in East Anglia, so I called over the steward and ordered a pot of tea for three since Andy and I had another sortie to do later in the day.

We both asked him questions generally concerning his background before he joined Number 41 Squadron three months earlier. He was 5 ft 6 in. in height, weight a bit above average but was more mature than the average pilot joining us to make up for our heavy losses. He told us he had attended a public school at Denstone in Staffordshire and after leaving there he was selected at an interview in London to join 61 Operational Training Unit at Rednal. When I told him that was where I had done my basic training he seemed to relax. He said he had been born at Clayton in Staffordshire and was courting a girl from the same hamlet.

After drinking our tea I told Andy to get some sleep while I took Adrian over to see our Commanding Officer but as we were leaving the bar, the Officer Commanding Flying Wing, Wing Commander Thraves, confronted us. After returning salutes he congratulated me on my promotion to Flight Lieutenant and my award of the DFC, concluding by saying what a good job I was doing for the Hambridge Wing.

On our walk over to the CO's tent Pilot Officer Dalgleish told me that he would help anybody in need if he was asked politely to do so, but if strongly ordered he could be a bit abrasive. I warned him that the CO was a strict disciplinarian both on the ground and in the air but that we all admired him for his leadership and got on well with him because you knew where you stood with him and he gave credit or a reprimand whenever it was due. I told the new pilot the CO was a great leader both in the air and socially in the Mess.

I knocked on the tent door as best I could and introduced Pilot Officer Dalgleish who saluted very smartly and presented his posting papers to the CO who asked me to wait outside which gave me a chance to chat up the girls in the office. One of them congratulated me on my award and promotion and offered to sew my second bar and ribbon onto my battledress tunic and best blue, an offer I readily accepted as I hated sewing.

The door flew open and Pilot Officer Dalgleish appeared looking a little uneasy because he had been given a thorough briefing, or perhaps the idea of shooting down an enemy target without a pilot had shaken him somewhat.

The CO called me back in and asked me to sit down. He told me that the round-faced, chubby looking pilot with straight brown hair who smoked like a trouper had a satisfactory record at Rednal and the CO of 41 Squadron was sorry to lose him. He thought he was a bit abrasive in nature but that this might be due to his ex-public school days and not his natural behaviour. He said he would fly Red 3 in a couple of days. While on our sortie that afternoon commencing at 15.00 hours he would take him up locally to assess his flying skills and teach him the Squadron procedures. 'Be back at fifteen hundred hours, Flight Lieutenant Hamilton,' he said as I turned to leave. 'I have a nice job for you today taking pictures. By the way where's Andy?'

'I sent him off to sleep sir, an hour ago.' With that I

departed to my bed where Andy was snoring his head off and was soon asleep myself.

At 15.00 hours Andy and I reported to the Commanding Officer as requested earlier in the day. The girls in the office were still smiling as Andy put his hands around the bottom of the prettiest one. On the table in the CO's office was a large map of Northern France. He told us to forget the rumours that were floating about the Squadron that Hitler's new weapon could be objects from long-range shells fired from the French coast or missiles being projected from low flying enemy aircraft. The specially built planes, such as the new Me 262 turbo jet, which was the first jet fighter that Hitler had on the production line, was a great worry to us due to its high speed, maximum manoeuvrability and increased height far better than the Spitfire's specifications. These, if launched, could devastate our defences as their flying capabilities far outweighed those of the Spitfire XIV.

When I told him that we did not see one German aircraft that morning on patrol he was extremely worried. He put it down to two things: either they were gathering strength to defend the Reich, or there was to be a mass attack on our defences, although over the months immediately prior to the D-Day landings the American 8th Tactical Air Force had been hammering their airfields by day so they could have pulled back to the German or Dutch border.

Anyway our mission was to sweep the area of launching sites in the Pas de Calais area, take photographs of the airfields at Abbeville, Drucat and Merville and re-examine what was happening on the Rouen to Mouscron railway line. It was well known to us this was feeding the enemy with supplies of their new tactical weapons which by now we all thought would be the main threat to our defence of the United Kingdom.

Since my aircraft was not ready to fly the CO offered me the old battleaxe which was one of our spares. Luckily Flight Sergeant Devlin had painted the necessary stripes on the wings, fuselage and tail and wished me 'Bon voyage', laughing as he said it. With visibility vastly improved from the morning sortie and the clouds thinned out considerably, we took off at 15.35 hours heading west to our designated destination. In fact when we reached 6,000 feet the sky was quite cumulous and we could estimate visibility being at least 7-10 miles, much better than we flew through at low level earlier. At least it gave us a better chance against the ferocious flak the Werhmacht had thrown at us that morning. I did not fancy losing my tail like I nearly did then.

We decided that as soon as we crossed the French coast we would fly in close formation at about 1,500 feet to avoid the heavy flak of the big guns but chance light flak hitting us or possibly machine-gun fire if we came too low. But when we crossed the French coast all hell was let loose so we climbed to 10,000 feet and hoped for the best. The visibility was improving even though there was cloud about. We first flew to the airfields where the Luftwaffe were stationed and to our amazement there were groups of aircraft still on the ground so we decided to fly in, give them hell with bursts of cannon and machine-gun fire, take some photographs and get the hell out of it. Surprisingly we did not encounter one enemy plane.

We then flew to the suspected V1 sites from Rouen, Beaumont, Amiens and finally to Arras but decided to miss out Mouscron as we dared not push our luck twice in one day. The sites were well camouflaged, although there was even more activity than before, especially on the railway line, and there were stationary trucks everywhere. So we dived to 250 feet and gave them as much ammunition as possible before climbing back to 7,000 feet since the flak was too hot for comfort. One cheeky German gunner put a bullet right under my seat and I was pleased to discover that the sheet of armour that Flight Sergeant Devlin had fitted earlier saved me from injury.

I noticed smoke trailing from Andy's engine and he reported over the R/T that he was losing engine revolutions slowly so I told him to return directly to base and I would cover him from above. As we left the French coast I got him to fly just above the choppy sea keeping his revolutions as low as possible without stalling. With 5 miles to touchdown he was really losing oil, most of it splattering over his windscreen, restricting his view so that he was actually flying blind. I called out a May Day signal and kept a close eye on him. He seemed to keep the Spitfire steady in flight but I was worried because he was losing altitude too fast. Luckily we crossed the English coast and I told him to climb to a sensible height and bale out. I received a few unrepeatable words from him but a few seconds later he turned his aircraft over and fell out of the cockpit. I held my breath hoping his parachute would open at its first pull, which thankfully it did. Sweat was pouring down my face as I watched my friend floating down to the yellow cornfields of England.

He landed safely but lay flat on the ground and waved from this position so I guessed he must have damaged his legs. I circled fairly low over him twice and radioed Hambridge for help since I knew he needed medical attention quickly, so I gave the Hambridge Controller, Flight Lieutenant Michael Moore, the co-ordinates of his landing. When I returned to base I learnt he'd damaged his left knee and broken his left ankle.

I reported to the Intelligence Officer about our findings and he told me Andy had been taken to the local military hospital. After an open shower between the tents I dashed over to see him with some cigarettes and a couple of good old weak British beers which I had scrounged from the CO. I found him in the plaster room and as usual he was telling dirty jokes to the nurses.

Next day I learnt from the CO he had been awarded a Bar to his Distinguished Flying Medal.

13

The next morning, D-Day+1, I was awakened by a sharp nudge to my right shoulder as daylight began to break through the canvas of my tent. Standing over me was a young man in a short white coat with a tray in his hand. 'Who the hell are you?' I said abruptly while rubbing my eyes and trying to get my confused brain to function.

'I'm your new batman as from today, sir,' the airman said as he put a cup of hot tea on my bedside locker.

'Since when did this happen?' I said sharply.

'Yesterday, sir,' he said as he stood a couple of paces away from my bed. Before I could reply he continued, 'I'm AC2 Graham Wilson from Huddersfield, sir.'

'Oh, I see, Wilson,' and I sat up to drink my hot tea in a thick china mug which could have been cleaner!

'If you leave your leather flying boots and shoes out, sir, I'll clean them after I've completed my tea round.'

'Thank you, Wilson,' I replied as he about-faced and walked towards the tent flap.

'Oh, by the way, sir, Squadron Leader Mitchell wants you in his office at oh-seven-thirty hours.'

'Thank you, Wilson,' I replied surprised that the meeting was to be so late in the morning. Must be something different today, I thought to myself since we're usually airborne well before this time on a normal flying day during Rhubarb runs. Maybe I'm being rested, I thought hopefully, or perhaps he wants me to do some local flight testing after the ground staff have completed their servicing on damaged aircraft. Then as I thought Andrew would be passing at any minute, I realised

I'd completely forgotten about his accident the day before. He'd tricked his way into a nice soft bed with pretty nurses waiting on him hand and foot at the local hospital. I decided that since I had time to spare I would go out in the beautiful, refreshing June morning air and have a run around the perimeter track. There was still an ambient white mist lying over the airfield and as I passed the last tent in my row I heard a loud voice say, 'That crazy geezer Hamilton is at it again,' to his tent mates. This made me run even faster and inspired me to complete the circuit in record time. On my return I opened up the flap of the same noisy tent and pulled them both out of bed. 'Eh, you bloody idiot,' one said.

'What are you doing?' the other pilot added.

'Making sure you're at the meeting at ten hundred hours,' I shouted at them as they both climbed back into bed.

'Can't get any peace around here with that physical fanatic running about. No wonder he's like a beanpole,' one said as I left for the shower tent a few yards from the CO's office building.

At 0730 hours, while members of the Squadron were anxiously waiting outside on whatever seats they could find – empty orange boxes, old deckchairs, hand-made seats and rockers – I entered the Squadron Commander's office. Inside there were the other two Flight Commanders sitting patiently waiting for me.

'Good morning gentlemen,' the CO said as he sat down behind an old trestle table used prior to the war for pasting on wallpaper for those people who could afford it. On the table were a few neatly piled folders, some bits of paper, a large map rolled up and an old black telephone. 'You'll be pleased to know that we're standing down today for several reasons. One is a talk by Officer Commanding Wing at ten hundred hours in Hangar Three; secondly the ground staff need more time to repair the damaged aircraft; thirdly, Windross, another new recruit, arrived late last night while you were all sleeping. He's Flight Sergeant Paul Windross from ninety-one Squadron stationed at West Malling and he's to replace Flight Sergeant Andrew Matthews while he's grounded, and is a very

114

experienced pilot with plenty of hours on Spitfire XIIs and XIVs. By the way Chris Rawlinson is now missing, presumed killed, and his next of kin have been informed. Donald, you've been confirmed by Group to take over Red Section.'

There was a loud knock on the door, the CO stood up and walked over to open it. He spoke quietly to Cynthia Woodhams and then shut the door. 'That's all for now, gentlemen, I'll see you at the ten hundred hours meeting.' With that he sat down again and said, 'Can I have a word with you, Donald.'

'Yes, sir,' I replied and returned to my seat as the other Flight Commanders left.

The CO picked up the ugly black telephone and told one of the girls to send in Flight Sergeant Windross. The door opened, a tired-looking, mature NCO marched in, saluted smartly and stood to attention. The CO returned his salute and asked him to sit down next to me. Before doing so, he gave his posting orders to the Squadron Commander.

After a quick appraisal of his file, he closed it and said, 'Fine record you have, Windross. Very pleased to have you here. We could do with some combat experience with the job 629 Squadron has to do shortly.'

'What sort of job, sir?' the new pilot wearing the ribbon of the Distinguished Flying Medal under his coveted wings asked.

'Have you not been told anything, Windross, about what we're going to do?' the CO said sharply.

'No, sir,' he replied positively.

'By the way, Windross, this is Flight Lieutenant Donald Hamilton, your new Flight Commander. He leads Red Section and you will replace Matthews as his Number Two while the other new pilot we have, Pilot Officer Adrian Dalgleish, will be your Number Three.'

'Yes, sir,' he said and we both got up from our seats and shook hands.

'Incidentally, Windross, Hamilton is a very good mixer. He likes discipline in the air and on the ground, but he's not rank conscious and gets on well with the NCO pilots.'

'Pleased to hear that,' Paul Windross said as he sat down.

'I'll leave you two together now, Hamilton,' the CO said as he got up from his rickety old table. 'Brief him on our plans as soon as you can,' and then the CO departed leaving us sitting there together in his office. As soon as the CO left, I picked up Flight Sergeant Windross's file and had a brief look at his past record. I was very pleased with what I read. The CO of 91 Squadron regretted losing him due to orders from Group.

'You're very conversant then, Paul, with the Spitfire models XII and XIV?' I asked as I turned my seat to face him.

'Yes, sir,' he said. He was much more mature than the young pilots we had been getting from the Advanced Training Unit and had flown a number of low-flying sorties with 91 Squadron mainly attacking enemy troop trains and supply lines in Northern France. He'd been awarded his decoration for a daring low-flying, strafing raid on the marshalling yards north of Calais, he was 27 years of age and had attended South Hunsley Secondary School with a good report. After basic training he went to Number 5 Pilots' Advanced Training Flying Unit at Ternhill. On completing the course with flying colours he joined 91 Squadron at West Malling in Kent, soon became an accomplished pilot and was promoted to Flight Sergeant on the award of his DFM. I asked him how he liked 91 Squadron and he replied by saying that he liked it there and did not really want to leave his friends or squadron since it was a very happy one. He also had a wife and children living in a rented house near the airfield at West Malling. Separation from loved ones was a bitter pill to swallow in war.

I thought of Barbara at that moment and as I was letting my thoughts run away in her direction I quickly switched them off to pay attention to my Number 2. I told him that 629 Squadron was a special Squadron formed a little while ago to defend the south-east of England and the City of London from Adolf Hitler's so-called new secret vengeance weapons. He asked me what this new threat meant to pilots of 629 Squadron and I told him that I did not really know as we'd not

116

seen one as yet. We'd been briefed earlier by Dr Brown from London and knew what to expect but until we'd seen one it was anybody's guess. I told him that all we knew from the latest intelligence reports was that they were missiles of some kind, designed by the Luftwaffe at Upselan in Germany, were cigar-shaped and were catapulted into the air by a launching pad. The oddest thing about them was that all the launching pads faced towards London. The missiles flew through the air at very high speed approaching 400 miles per hour. They flew in a straight line and were half the size of a Spitfire. 'The main thing is, that it will not be the normal man-to-man flying combat of the past, as experienced in the Battle of Britain. This is why this Squadron has been formed and we've practised up in the North of England firing bursts of cannon and machine-gun fire at targets being towed by Mosquitoes. What we do know, Windross, is that they fly in a straight line.'

After my short briefing I told him he would learn more about the missile at the 1000 hours meeting in Hangar Number 3. His slim face was amazed at what I had said. As he leaned back comfortably in his seat he asked, 'Do you really think, sir, that these missiles are pilotless?'

'Yes, I do, Paul, and it means a complete new flying skill to catch these bastards.' I told him we belonged to the Air Defence of Great Britain Command, the old Fighter Command, to combat this new and serious threat to the freedom of our country. 'That's why we need the most experienced pilots we can get, Paul. It's not going to be easy because of their size and speed.' I concluded our conversation by telling him we really didn't know what was going to be thrown at us until we'd seen it, that several rumours were going around and suggested he wait like all of us until we'd actually seen one. With that I told him to go and have some breakfast and clean up. 'The office girls, especially Cynthia, will help you settle in. If you have any questions, Paul, please don't hesitate to ask me.'

With that I departed from the office leaving him chatting to Cynthia and was just passing some of the lads lounging about and eating on their mixture of seating when a huge cheer went up. This made me swing round and there was Andrew with his left leg in plaster being supported by two old wooden crutches which were the worse for wear. 'What the hell are you doing here?' I asked, smiling at him as he tried to salute with one crutch in his hand. 'You should be in hospital, Andrew.'

'No blinking fear,' he replied laughing, 'what with those bloody bedpans and urine bottles I decided to get the hell out of there. I told the doctor that I was desperately needed at 629 Squadron and they couldn't do without my knowledge, so he released me with regular monthly check-ups.'

'You cheeky devil, Andrew,' I said as I put my hand around his shoulders and guided him to the best seat available. 'The CO's going to have a bloody fit when he sees you here.'

We made him as comfortable as possible in his seat with a set of petrol cans to support his left leg. Smiling, he said, 'I can always help the girls in the office.'

'Yes, I bet you can,' I replied good-humouredly. 'I'll get you some breakfast, so stay there; possibly a flying breakfast if I can.' The steward was a bit reluctant to give Andrew a flying breakfast, but I told him to be a good boy and do what he could for our new hero.

After breakfast I returned to the office and there, waiting for the Squadron Commander, was a beautiful auburn-haired Flight Officer. 'Good morning,' I said with a charming smile.

'Are you Squadron Leader Mitchell?' she enquired with a cut-glass voice.

'No, I'm afraid I'm not,' I said as I approached the desk. 'I'm Flight Lieutenant Donald Hamilton, Red Section Leader with Six-Two-Nine Squadron. This is the Squadron office you're in. Can I help you?' I stared at her lovely hair, cut short under her cap. 'Please do take a seat,' I said and as she did so she took off her cap. 'What strikingly coloured hair you have,' I went on as I turned to face her directly.

'It's genuine you know. No tints or coloured dye. It's real,' she replied smiling. 'I'm Flight Officer Sue Shaw of Air Traffic Control under Flight Lieutenant Michael Moore.'

'Oh, are you,' I replied.'When did you arrive?' I began to sit down in the CO's chair.

'A couple of days ago, sir. I've just been booking in, such a bother isn't it, every time you arrive at a new station?'

'Yes,' I replied, 'but it has to be done for security reasons as well as knowing who's about and who isn't.'

'Yes, I suppose you're right, sir. The trouble is you can never find the places you have to go to except the Officers' Mess and the Guardroom,' she said in what sounded to me like a broad Devonshire accent.

I stared at her for quite some time and then said, 'Where were you born?'

'In Devon, sir, at a small dairy and arable farm in Spreyton, near Crediton.'

'I guess your parents are farmers then, doing a vital job in this war?'

'Yes,' she said, 'it's very hard work being farmers in the South-West.' She went on to say she had attended Exeter High School for Girls and joined the WAAFs two years ago, explaining that she wanted to be a ferry pilot but failed her basic flying training, so she chose to be an Air Traffic Controller because she wanted to be up front where the action was. 'I've been to Group but it was so boring I got posted here.'

I replied by saying, 'In the next few months life here at Royal Air Force Hambridge is going to be pretty hectic, so I should get your fun and sleep before the balloon bursts. By the way, what's the purpose of your visit, Sue?'

She looked surprised when I called her by her Christian name and then after taking a deep breath she replied, 'The Station Commander told me to become conversant with all the pilots of the Hambridge Wing so that's what I'm doing today.'

'Any chance of buying you a drink, Sue, later on this evening?' I stood up and put out my hand to greet her.

'Well, Flight Lieutenant Donald Hamilton, I may give that a bit of thought. I've been told you're one for the girls.'

'Who me? Never! Just a sociable but quite harmless chap,

you know. I'm engaged to be married so you're in safe hands with me.'

'What's she like, Donald?'

'She's beautiful and comes from a similar background to yourself except that her father's in big business in London.'

I opened the office door, we exchanged salutes with our caps on and off she went to the other two squadrons which formed the Hambridge Wing. The remarks I got from Cynthia and Rosemary could not be repeated! I replied to them on leaving, 'There are plenty of young men sitting on their backsides doing nothing. Get amongst them, you may get a free drink tonight.' On passing them I heard the retort from Rosemary, 'I'll be bloody lucky,' and I departed from the office to await the 1000 hours meeting at Hangar Number 3. My mental thoughts soon switched from the CO Wing's meeting to the delightful thoughts of having a drink with this new Flight Officer who was slimly built, had strikingly coloured hair and freckles on her lovely face. I thought about it with mounting excitement as I walked briskly in the warm June sunshine back towards my tent.

At 1000 hours, all air crews and associated personnel attended the Wing Commander's meeting in Hangar Number 3. At the top of the table was the Station Commander, who never flew although he was a battle-hardened pilot, the three Squadron Commanders and, of course, the main speaker, Wing Commander Ian Thraves, Officer Commanding the Hambridge Wing.

He commenced the lecture by saying this was going to be a long meeting and suggested we took notes on what he was about to say. He told us that the Luftwaffe had designed a new vengeance weapon in retaliation against Allied bombing on German cities and to regain the respect of Adolf Hitler after their defeat in the Battle of Britain. He went on to say that from the latest intelligence reports and from our own photographic reconnaissance Group Headquarters believed that this new aerial threat would be the V1 Flying Bomb or as the Germans called it the VERGELTUNGSWAFFE EINS or FIESELER Fi-103. On the screen behind him was a large diagram showing details of the V1 Flying Bomb, which later became known as the Doodlebug.

He continued, pointing his stick at the diagram to draw our attention, that this pilotless plane was small in design, about half the size of the Spitfire. It was fast with a maximum speed over the target area of approximately 400 miles per hour, taking off from its launching pad at a maximum of 300 miles per hour, whilst carrying approximately 1,870 lbs of high explosive in its nose. The most interesting characteristic of the Flying Bomb was the design of its power unit. He strongly emphasised in a loud voice that its engine was a 'pulse jet' which drove it forward by a series of explosions in a combustion chamber fitted above the fuselage. These engine explosions when heard from the ground gave it a distinctive audible sound which could be heard for miles around. He then put his stick down and poured himself a glass of water before handing over the lecture to our Squadron Commander, Squadron Leader Mitchell.

As the Wing Commander sat down so our CO took over the main role of speaker. His voice could be heard more distinctly, especially for those unlucky chaps at the back of the hangar. Squadron Leader Mitchell continued the lecture by saying that the Flying Bomb, which was shaped like a cigar, could not take off under its own power – it had to be attached to a separately powered catapult. He then proceeded to get out a detailed drawing of the launch pad and pinned it adjacent to Wing Commander Thraves's diagram of the Doodlebug. Pointing to the launch pad he said that the catapult was fuelled and ignited by an electric spark. Expanding gases drove the catapult up the launching ramp and this accelerated the pilotless plane to its take-off speed. He showed us on a slide the action he had just explained, with the catapult being dropped off after the cigar-shaped object left its launching pad. The plane's own engine then took over to a speed of around 300 miles per hour before it accelerated past the 350 m.p.h. mark and possibly up to 400 m.p.h. at the end of its flight.

With another drawing, which looked as though it had been roughly drawn by himself, he explained that the robot flew in a straight line at a height of approximately 2,500-3,000 feet. When the missile reached a predicted distance, a simple device in the missile cut off the fuel and it nosed down onto its target. He said that Doctor Brown, who had previously given us a lecture, calculated that once the fuel was cut off there would be, for the population below, twelve seconds of silence before the missile impacted resulting in death and injury and widespread destruction of buildings. Then on a blackboard he proceeded to give some vital statistics of Hitler's new vengeance weapon: range 150 miles, fuel capacity 180 gallons, overall length 25 feet 4½ inches, wing span with *no* ailerons 17 feet 6 inches; the wings were tapered in shape and covered in sheet steel; the fuselage had a smooth, contoured shape made out of plywood and sheet steel; the design of the Doodlebug was both economical and simple. He emphasised this was a lethal weapon, elusive in the sky due to its high speed and small size. It meant that pilot-to-pilot combat, which we had been used to in the Battle of Britain and the years following, was now obsolescent. A new approach to attack this pilotless plane, which flew fast and in a straight line, had to be planned and developed. He mentioned that 629 Squadron had already tried attacking windsocks being towed by Mosquitoes at 350 miles per hour with little success. The speed of the Luftwaffe's new weapon, the Fieseler Fi-103, was going to be the major factor in our success or failure.

With that he thanked us for listening so intently to his lecture and returned to his seat next to the Station Commander. The latter rose and thanked both lecturers for their excellent presentation and said the lecture would continue in one hour's time for question time from the bemused audience. We all stood to attention and the senior officers departed in single file. In the background, as pilots dispersed to their own squadrons, a lot of mumbling was going on between them. The expression on their faces showed bewilderment and amazement that Adolf Hitler could produce such a lethal weapon which was simple and economical to manufacture.

On resumption Squadron Leader Mitchell continued his lecture with sketches of the remaining parts of the vengeance weapon which the Germans had code-named Operation 'Kirschkern' or 'Cherry Stone'. What puzzled us the most was how the robot was guided without a pilot, but he soon answered our queries by introducing the actual guidance system of this mid-wing monoplane.

He explained simply and without too many technical terms, because he was both academically and technically unqualified to do so, how the guidance system functioned. By pointing his stick to the rear of the monoplane he tried to describe as best he could in layman's terms how it all worked, pointing out that the automatic pilot was driven by three air-driven gyroscopes controlling height and setting, plus a pneumatic servo-mechanism which operated the rudder and elevator. The supply of compressed air came from two spherical air bottles placed in the rear of the fuselage which controlled the autopilot, rudder and elevator. He told us that there were two classes of Doodlebug – those directed by a pre-set automatic pilot controlled by compressed air and individually launched from launching pads, and those attached to airborne aircraft, based mainly in Belgium, which were then released from their parent aircraft and steered by radio control onto the target.

He said that the other most important item to bring to our attention was that this combination of missile and monoplane was expendable once it left its launching pad or parent aircraft. He repeatedly emphasised that the guidance system was a combination of pre-set auto-pilot and elevator, controlled by gyroscopes supplied with compressed air. With that Squadron Leader Mitchell sipped some water out of a thick NAAFI mug and sat down while the Station Commander rose to his feet to take any sensible questions. There was utter silence from his audience. To break it I asked Doctor Brown how long the Flying Bomb would take from its

123

launching pad to reach its target supposing its destination was London. He stood up with his bald head shining and in his scruffy old black suit which had seen better days, and replied by saying it took 22 minutes at an average speed of 350 miles per hour.

I replied by saying, 'Sir, this doesn't give the fighters much time to attack the missile between the French coast and the gun-site belt.'

His reply was, 'I'm afraid you haven't much choice in the matter. If they're launched as we presume they are going to be, you have twenty miles of sea to attack them before the gun belt takes over and fires at them at will. This is under the orders of the Royal Observer Corps because they have orders to shoot on sight. The problem is the missile is fast and very small and gives attacking pilots a serious problem to engage in time to shoot them down.'

Flight Sergeant Windross asked the next question which was vital to the meeting. 'Sir,' directing his voice to Doctor Brown, 'how the hell do we shoot them down when they're flying in a straight line at three hundred and fifty miles per hour?'

Doctor Brown looked bewildered, scratched his bald head being partially amused by the question, and then said, 'I guess you should have put this vital and very important question to your Squadron Commander. Although I'm a scientist I have no knowledge at all and neither does the Ministry how you young pilots are going to plan your method of individual attacks. I personally feel the fighters will be our main line of defence.' He then took his seat and lit a cigarette which we could see annoyed the top brass. Squadron Leader Mitchell then went to the lectern and said that senior pilots of the Wing would meet at a later time that day to discuss methods of attack. With that he sat down after picking up his drawings and as he did so drank the last drop of water from his NAAFI mug.

The Station Commander rose to his feet, thanked our special guest Doctor Brown from the MOD for giving up his valuable time to be with us that morning and ended the meeting at twelve noon.

124

We all dispersed with bits of paper, notepads and drawings and departed from the meeting with mixed emotions about how on earth we were going to attack this Flying Bomb within 22 minutes from launch to target at a speed equal to or above our own maximum speed. A serious doubt crossed my mind that unless we got greater speed by diving onto the robot, we had no chance of shooting them down at all.

The only constructive thought I had at this time was that the Flying Bomb was vulnerable immediately after its launch, so the best bet was to attack it at its minimum speed of approximately 300 miles per hour. This seemed to be the best option but the chances of seeing the launch of a Doodlebug were quite remote so I dismissed the idea although I still thought about it deeply. It would be pure luck for any pilot to see one launch, never mind attack it at low speed.

With serious doubts still crossing my mind about the method of attack I entered the 629 Squadron Office where I got a negative reception from Cynthia and Rosemary. 'Had a good meeting, Donald?' Cynthia said in a low-key voice as I passed her desk.

'Very interesting,' I said, 'but I don't want you to discuss the meeting with pilots of Hambridge Wing since it's top secret.'

I leant over close to her face and she replied, 'We know more about the new vengeance weapon than you may think, Flight Lieutenant Hamilton.'

'Well if you do then damned well keep it secret and don't discuss it with anyone, even Rosemary sitting beside you.'

'Yes, sir,' she said adamantly as she returned to her office chair which either needed replacing or throwing out of the window to the pilots who sat around waiting to scramble.

With that Squadron Leader James Mitchell followed me into his office and told me to sit down. 'Want a cup of tea or coffee?' the CO said with a dry mouth after his mammoth lecture.

'Yes, please, sir,' I replied quickly. He picked up the black telephone which must have been donkey's years old and asked Cynthia, his secretary, to bring in two cups of strong coffee. While waiting for this he went over and brought out a bottle of brandy from his old storage cupboard.

'Donald,' he said, 'would you like a top-up with your coffee?' knowing I was a connoisseur of brandy.

'I would be delighted to join you in that luxury,' I replied, smiling.

'You know, Donald, the new vengeance weapon frightens the hell out of me. There are so many unknown factors about it. It's not like pilot-to-pilot combat of the old days. Here we are engaged in trying to shoot down a flying bomb travelling at our normal level flight maximum speed and we have the task of bringing the bloody thing down.' With that he sat down on his old swivel chair he'd brought from home and faced me with disillusionment. The silence was broken by Cynthia bringing in two NAAFI mugs of black coffee in which the CO put a large quantity of brandy. 'Cheers,' he laughed as he swivelled in his comfortable chair. 'Any thoughts yet on how we're going to attack this bomb in about thirteen minutes or less?'

'Well, sir, I haven't had much time to think about it, but if we could get the Doodlebug taking off from its launching pad at a speed of three hundred miles per hour or as close to the north French coast as possible, the better chance we have of shooting them down. The trouble is if we use twenty millimetre cannon within two hundred yards of the missile we're likely to get blown out of the sky or badly burned in the process, even our aircraft could be badly scorched from the explosion.'

'I hadn't thought of that aspect – a good point to raise with the Squadron. If we can't do that how on earth are we going to attack it as it flies slightly faster than our maximum speed?' With that, he sipped his coffee, gazing round the room like a young schoolboy at Eton who doesn't know what he's doing.

'Sir,' I replied, sipping my luxurious coffee, although it tasted awful. 'How about if we gain height above the Flying Bomb, say to six thousand feet, and then dive at it giving us the extra speed we need to catch it, or pass it, now that we have the high-octane fuel and the five-blade Griffin Sixty-Five engine?'

'Good idea, we'll have to work on that because at least with your idea we could catch the bloody thing even though we're too close to fire at it. The best bet would be for our pilots to practise this in pairs and allow the two hundred yards interval before the cannon is fired,' he yawned wearily before finishing his coffee. 'Donald,' the CO said, 'could we fly alongside it and tip one of its small wings so that we upset the compressed air driven auto-pilot or gyroscopes?'

'That's a jolly good idea, sir, but the problem with that is twofold. One, can we get up enough speed for this short period over the English Channel before the gun belt comes into range and two, we could damage our own wings by doing it as the monoplane wings are made of steel and stronger than our Spitfire wings,' I replied as I finished my lousy brandy-laced coffee.

'Well, it's something to think about, Donald,' the CO said as he looked out at the sunshine penetrating his window. 'Have a chat with the other Flight Commanders, including this new guy, Flight Sergeant Paul Windross. See if you can improve on this idea as I think it could work. If we can tip the auto-pilot or gyros, or both, we would disturb the darn thing, effective enough for the bloody thing to alter its course or even dive into the sea or ground. It's a nice idea but it's fraught with danger due to the high speed and small wingspan of the Flying Bomb.' With that he offered me more horrible coffee which I accepted before I went back to my tent to think over our discussion as there had to be an answer to this very difficult problem.

Only with someone in real combat with this pilotless plane would we know whether the idea of tipping would be successful. I was afraid that conventional shooting with 20 mm cannon could cause horrific damage to our pilots and aeroplanes because you had to get close to the new weapon in order to destroy it. If you flew within 200 yards of a robot carrying about a ton of high explosive the fireball the missile would make on exploding could set fire to the Spitfire. All of which was theory and we hadn't even seen, let alone tried to attack, a V1 bomb.

Later on that afternoon, after a good break from our long briefing all four Flight Commanders were summoned to the OC Wing's Headquarters which were luxuriously fitted out with carpets and chairs, in contrast to those of us in the front line who lived in tents with wet grass to walk on and beds which caused the fittest of pilots to have a bad back.

The OC Wing had on his blackboard several diagrams with a Spitfire attacking the Fi-103 pilotless plane, drawings which had been made by a professional draughtsman so that the details were clear and accurate.

The meeting was interrupted by a smartly-dressed Pilot Officer who introduced herself to new members of the Wing as Pilot Officer Louisa Jefferson, the OC Wing's and Station Commander's PA. She asked the OC Wing if I could be excused since I was wanted on the telephone and he agreed. I left the room following the young PA with the slim, attractive legs. Picking up the telephone I realised with amazement that it was Barbara on the line. 'How did you get this number?' I asked her rather bluntly, as we were on alert.

She replied by saying, 'My father has influential friends, including the Minister for Defence, so I prised out of him your Hambridge telephone number.' She went on, 'You haven't rung me today,' to which I replied that it was a rest day and that we had meeting after meeting. I told her that during the next few days life was going to be hectic and flying could be round the clock, but before the green flares were fired I'd try and ring her or get home to see her for a few hours. I suggested that I might fly to Biggin Hill and she meet me there in her father's black Riley. She said, 'I love you very much, Donald,' her voice started to waver and I could feel she was a little upset. 'Please do take care of yourself, I love you so much.'

'I must go, darling,' I said. 'I'm in a meeting with my Wing Commander. I love you very much, so take care of yourself and I'll see you very soon, bye for now.' I put the Station Commander's telephone down and hurried back to the meeting. The OC Wing asked if my telephone call was both urgent and interesting and I replied by saying it wasn't urgent but it was very interesting. At that he took a dim view of my leaving the meeting but after sitting down and trying to listen to what the Officer Commanding was saying my right ear began to burn. My thoughts immediately turned to Barbara's voice still ringing in my ears; I loved her very dearly and hoped that one day we would be married, have a couple of children and establish a long and happy marriage until death do us part. As the Second World War was entering its last phase and our Allied troops had established a foothold in Europe my thoughts about marriage seemed stronger and stronger. I then came to with the OC Wing with his diagrams uppermost in my thoughts since his subject of attacking the new pilotless Flying Bomb in aerial combat was vital to my Squadron. After his short briefing we departed back to the Officers' Mess to drink the usual weak Watneys wartime beer.

14

On 12 June 1944 we heard from Squadron Headquarters that the first V1 Flying Bomb had crossed the English coast. The first recorded Doodlebug we heard about landed at Swanscombe in Kent with no fatalities. The second however was much more devastating in both fatalities and destruction of property, falling on Bethnal Green in London.

The Commanding Officer of 629 Squadron ordered all flying personnel to the briefing room to give us the latest information. Diver Patrols would commence when ordered from Group and all personal communication, letters, phone calls etc. would now be strictly prohibited. He repeated by saying that this was Hitler's attempt to prevent more troops from landing in Normandy and to break the high morale of the British people. Operation 'Crossbow' was also officially launched with aircraft set to attack the launching pads at random in conjunction with other Allied Air Forces.

Squadron Leader Mitchell went over the final details of the monoplane-cum-missile. It was lethal, an expendable weapon, pilotless, and it flew at 350 miles per hour. The distance between launch site and target area would be in the region of 130 miles which meant that between the fighters, gun batteries and barrage balloons we had only 22 minutes to catch the bastards. The fighters had approximately 45 miles in distance from the French coast to the British gun batteries placed on the North Downs to attack the ugly, cigar-shaped Flying Bombs. The V1 launching was controlled by the Flak Regiment which was headed by Colonel Max Wachtel. Under his command he had 48 platoons in 13 batteries and around

3,500 to 4,500 engineers and technicians.

Since the Royal Air Force at West Malling was right in line between the launching pads and London it was decided by Group Headquarters that this would be the most appropriate controlling centre for Diver Patrols. This air lane was eventually called 'Doodlebug Alley' to aid air recognition between air to ground and ground to air communications.

With the Spitfire XIVs from 91 Squadron, 322 Squadron and 96 Squadron all stationed at West Malling, this formed the core of our defence against the Fieseler Fi-103 Flying Bombs reaching the English coast and the City of London. The Spitfire XIVs had the advantage over the Spitfire XII in that they had that extra speed enabling them to catch the high-speed missiles.

In support we had the new Tempest Vs of 150 Wing based at Newchurch. It was the fastest propelled aircraft attacking the V1 below 20,000 feet. Squadron Leader Mitchell's final word of warning was not to fire our 20 mm cannon within 200 yards of the target otherwise the aircraft would fly right through the fireball possibly killing the pilot and certainly severely damaging the aircraft. With that he called the meeting to a close and said that 629 Squadron would take off at 1130 hours on 16 June as we needed to train the new pilots to the technique of attacking the bomb and to give Flight Sergeant Devlin enough time to prepare all 16 aircraft for battle readiness.

At 1130 hours on 16 June we all reported to the briefing room where we were given the weather forecast and the latest positions of the launching sites since the Flak Regiment often moved them regularly from village to village in northern France because of the relentless daylight attacks by the Allied Air Forces based in Great Britain.

Intelligence had told us that one launching site was actually sited down the high street of a village in northern France. The Germans moved these launch pads for their Flying Bombs swiftly and efficiently which did not help pinpointing targets for the Allied Air Forces.

After the briefing we all scrambled to our aircraft. Corporal Jackson had my engine running and was ready to help strap me in to the tight Spitfire cockpit. Although I was only 5 feet 8½ inches in height I found the seating most uncomfortable. What amazed me was that there were taller chaps, much larger than me, who managed to get in them and not complain! Pilot Officer Dalgleish was on my port side and Flight Sergeant Windross on my starboard side as we took off into the wind. The grass was a bit bumpy but we were soon airborne over RAF Hambridge. The Officer Commanding Wing decided to stay behind and control the operation whilst Squadron Leader Mitchell led 629 Squadron. In support were 322 and 96 Squadrons from West Malling.

We climbed under the orders of the Commanding Officer at a slow rate of climb into a cloudless sky until we reached 6,000 feet over Folkestone. Below, the English Channel sparkled in an ultra blue, flecked with white caps. We levelled off at 6,000 feet with 20 aircraft in formation under the Master Controller at Biggin Hill. Over the R/T came the familiar voice of Squadron Leader Mitchell, 'This is code name Bronco. Everyone must reply to their coloured section and Bronco number.' Pilot Officer Dalgleish had already forgotten he was in Red Section and answered to Blue Section with code name Bronco 3. When Flight Sergeant Windross answered he had no hesitancy whatsoever in his identity or call sign.

The Squadron Leader said over the R/T, 'Keep your eyes peeled between two and a half and three thousand feet, and keep in formation. These bloody new weapons apparently go like hell in a straight line. Contact me if you see one or think you've seen one. You should know by now what they look like. You've all had enough briefings on this long fuselage, miniature wing, pilotless plane. Good hunting, everybody. Bronco One out.'

After a few minutes he came back over the R/T to say we would fly at Angels Six between the Pas de Calais and Caen and peel off in sections. 'It's up to the Flight Commanders then what action to take. But for Christ's sake keep a lookout,

132

both port and starboard.'

At 1202 hours Flight Sergeant Windross spotted his first cigar-shaped V1 Flying Bomb. Then more voices over the R/T warned of others launched by FlakGruppe Criel flying at high speed in a straight line towards their target – London, which had a German code name T42. The Master Controller at Biggin Hill said the main attack had started at 1118 hours and 55 FlakGruppe Criel sites had launched their lethal weapons. On average we counted a dozen Flying Bombs on target to London and the south-east coast, so I told Adrian and Paul to attack in their own time concentrating on one V1 Flying Bomb at a time. As I flew overhead of Windross I could see he was climbing to an altitude of Angels One Two and then diving down onto his target to gain enough speed to approach within the safety net distance. He opened fire with his 20 mm cannon and there was a devastating explosion in the air. A tremendous fireball erupted before the flying bomb disintegrated in the air and the remains of it fell into the sea. There was a cheer on the R/T so I had to tell them to keep quiet and silent forthwith and also to watch their fuel gauges as they had only 850 miles of maximum mileage capacity.

At long last at Angels Seven I spotted my first cigar-shaped black cross object flying starboard of me in a straight line, flame from its pulse jet making an obvious target. As I approached at Angels Three I thought I would have a good look round it before attacking this vengeance weapon, although I would have to be quick since I had only about 30 miles within which to attack before the United Kingdom gun batteries would open fire. The Flying Bomb as explained to us by Doctor Brown was like a black cross flying across the sky. The top half of the bomb was bronze in colour and the base was pale blue; the wings were small, square and stubby. It had a solid look about it which bore no resemblance to a conventional engined monoplane. The fuselage was slim, round and tapered with its nose pointed, the propulsion unit was at the rear end and it had two elevators on the tailplane like conventional aircraft.

Having taken some pictures and flown alongside it at high

speed, I was at a loss to know what to do due to its small size and high speed. I decided to withdraw from my first contact, climb to Angels One Two and dive on to it although I had only precious seconds left before the gun battery would take over through the Royal Observer Corps. Flying directly behind it and keeping my distance to well outside the danger limit I fired a short burst of cannon. Immediately the tail blew off and the Flying Bomb destined for England dived straight into the English Channel. Luckily for me it did not explode until it hit the choppy sea far below.

I was greatly relieved because ever since Doctor Brown's briefing I had had the fear of being burned by the explosion of nearly one ton of high explosive. Since I was now within range of the gun batteries I took evasive action to starboard and got out of their range before they had me for dinner! When I landed I was covered in sweat from head to foot and although I have never trembled before this time Corporal Jackson at dispersal noticed I was shaking like a leaf. Luckily he had a silver hip flask given to him by his grandfather and I was truly grateful for a sip of his brandy. He told me Adrian had not yet returned but Paul had landed a few minutes before with a V1 Flying Bomb to his credit. Corporal Jackson said, 'What motif are we going to paint on our fuselages for V1 victories? I'll have a chat with Flight Sergeant Devlin about that, sir, but I believe Group Headquarters are already considering the matter.'

'Let us know how you get on, Jackson, and thanks for the brandy.' God, I had a thirst as I jumped off the port wing! Then I said to him, 'Fill her up, Corporal, with fuel and ammo,' and I walked back with him to the dispersal area.

He asked me, 'What was it like, sir, seeing your first vengeance weapon?'

'Rather a surprise really, Jackson, bloody fast and by God don't they explode when you hit them! They're also very small like flying model aeroplanes in the sky; luckily for me mine exploded in the sea, but poor old Windross had his explode soon after he hit it.'

'I bet it shook him right down to his boots,' Corporal

Jackson said. Flight Sergeant Windross was OK, although a bit shaken by shock, but his rear fuselage and tail were severely burnt. Luckily for him his elevators and rudders worked satisfactorily, a bloody miracle, I thought, when I saw the damage. With that I reported to the Intelligence Office, had a chat to the Commanding Officer and went off to have a shower and write to Barbara before dinner even though I was not supposed to correspond with her.

A steward came in with a nice cup of tea and a hard looking piece of NAAFI fruit cake. Also on the plate was an official letter On His Majesty's Service – I thought at first I'd been posted to another squadron. I dreaded the thought since I was very happy here and got on well with the Squadron Commander and all the crews. Opening the letter it was an invitation from King George VI to attend an Investiture at Buckingham Palace on 20 June 1944 at 10.30 a.m. to receive from him the award of the Distinguished Flying Cross for meritorious work carrying out aerial reconnaissance over northern France. I was allowed two guests and no more to attend the ceremony.

Since I could not telephone Barbara I wrote a quick note with the approval of the Squadron Commander to tell her of this great event and to ask her to meet me outside Buckingham Palace at 0930 hours in her best bib and tucker, emphasising that a hat was necessary to complete the outfit.

After that events happened so quickly that I couldn't keep up with time and reality. I knew I had to take off later in the day for another Diver Patrol but at what time I did not know. I gave the steward my letter to Barbara and told him to get down to the post box immediately and if anybody stopped him tell them that this has priority from both the Station Commander and the Squadron Commander. What I did not know was that through normal Air Ministry procedures Barbara would receive her own personal invitation.

After the bit of NAAFI cake and what the steward had

scrounged from the Mess, I did not feel hungry because I was excited about going to Buckingham Palace with Barbara so unexpectedly and at the prospect of seeing her sweet smile and lovely figure. The Intelligence Officer popped in and said that between 0418 hours and 1400 hours today some 200 V1 Flying Bombs had been launched from 55 sites. Once he had told me I just could not take in the amount of pressure that this would put on our air defences in the South-East with the number of weapons available and especially the shortage of Spitfire XIVs. Still it left a bad feeling in one's mind about the devastation these vengeance weapons could cause in both the destruction of buildings and the large loss of life. It was even more important for our fighters, gun batteries and balloon teams to work efficiently and expediently in order to prevent too many Flying Bombs reaching their designated targets.

During the late afternoon I was awakened by Squadron Leader Mitchell sitting on my bed with a tray of biscuits and a cup of tea. 'Sorry to wake you, Donald, but we're taking off at nineteen hundred hours this evening to cover for Ninety-One Squadron,' and he told me the latest reports about the number of Flying Bombs crossing the English coast and the destruction they were causing to buildings and factories in and around London as well as their effect on the morale of the civilian population. He then showed me pictures of children being evacuated and some horrendous photographs of damaged buildings caused by the new Flying Bomb.

One glance at them was enough for me. 'Devastating, aren't they, Chris? Streets and streets of houses demolished. Talk about a lethal weapon – Hitler was no fool. He knew what he was doing all right.'

'I've heard this afternoon,' Chris said, 'that you're going to your Investiture at Buckingham Palace with Andrew Matthews and his pair of old rotten crutches on the twentieth. Since the Air Officer Commanding Group is also attending the Investiture he's agreed to take you both up in his staff car and will pick you up at oh-seven-hundred hours at the

Guardroom. That will give you plenty of time in case of mishaps.'

'Yes, sir,' I replied.

'I suggest,' Chris said, 'that you get your bloody hair cut before you go, since it's long both back and sides.'

'Yes, Chris, I'll do that later today as the barber's open at six this evening.'

Chris said, 'Would you also please check Andrew's appearance and dress when you go over and see him this evening at the hospital, and take over his best blue.'

'Yes, Chris, I'll do that – Cynthia Woodhams wants to come too so she can drive me.' He agreed, got off my untidy bed and picked up the silver-framed picture of Barbara on my bedside locker.

'A beautiful girl, Donald, you ought to marry her before some Yank from the Eighth American Air Force Bomber Group at Bushey grabs her,' he said as he returned the silver frame to my locker.

'I should have married her before coming to RAF Hambridge,' I said, 'but since things have been so hectic lately one doesn't get time to think about getting wed. Anyway I can't see you giving me a few days off to get married, Chris.'

'I think you're right there, Donald, I don't think I would. Don't forget we're on Red Alert.' He stood up and put my chair under the bedside locker.

'Good luck for this evening's flight,' and with that Chris left my tent. Typical officer, I thought under my breath, they always leave the damn flap open, so I had to get up and close it. But he re-opened it just as I got back into bed, and putting his head inside said, 'Pilot Officer Adrian Dalgleish was killed in action today. One of the pilots of Blue Section saw him fly straight into the rear of a Flying Bomb about five miles off Dover. The report describes the incident as a devastating explosion in which both aircraft disintegrated together. Quite a fireball, the other pilot reported. I've just written off to his next of kin.' With that he put my tent flap down and at last I got off to a well-earned sleep. Before doing so I considered what a nice chap Adrian had been but they come and go like chefs in restaurants. He was well liked by the ground crew and I recalled telling him, quite specifically, not to go too close to Doodlebugs when attacking them due to the enormous explosive power in the nose of the plane. But for the short while I'd known Adrian I knew he would not obey that instruction due to his attacking instinct. I would have to ring Group Headquarters later and get another replacement. Since our formation there was only Andrew, myself and the CO left from the original team.

Waking after a short sleep I decided to have my tea and sandwiches and reflect on how the war was going. We had beaten the Germans in the Battle of Britain even though we were totally outnumbered at the ratio of approximately 9 to 1. Adolf Hitler was now trying to break our spirit and morale in retaliation for the Normandy landings with a burst of vengeance weapons which were succeeding in badly damaging the City of London and its population. I didn't think he had a chance of winning the war with this new weapon because he was six days too late. If he had attacked with it prior to the Normandy landings I thought the balance of the war might have been different. The population of London and the South-East were already battle hardened from the Battle of Britain. He would not win this one since his forces were even then in retreat in Normandy under General Montgomery's and General Eisenhower's command. Victory for Hitler and his Generals, especially Field Marshal Rommel, seemed even more remote due to the lack of air cover over Normandy and northern France. The pilots of ADGB had been quite surprised that Hitler left the skies over northern France so weakly defended except for the gun batteries to protect his valuable launching pads. Perhaps seeing victory slipping away he had strengthened his defences by withdrawing the Luftwaffe back to Germany. It had amazed us that throughout our Diver Patrols over northern France and Caen not one of us had seen a German aeroplane. You would have thought that Hitler would have given adequate air cover to both these prized possessions, his new vengeance weapons, the V1 and V2. Where he got the resources from to manufacture such large quantities of tanks and planes was a mystery to all. The main worry we had was that Hitler had ordered the production of his new jet fighter, the Me 262. This aircraft, if completed before the Allied Forces in Normandy could gain a strong foothold in France and Germany, could have a devastating effect both in the air and on the ground. We had heard that the new Me 262 was on the production line. The problem with the vengeance weapons was that they were too late to prevent the Allied forces advancing into Normandy, all they were doing was demoralising the population of London and destroying their homes, but they had had this before in the early 1940s. The only trouble now was that they didn't get as much warning as they did in the Battle of Britain. Adolf Hitler's greatest mistake was not to invade us when we were at our weakest point, but instead he took on the mighty Red Army which saved us from occupation by the German Army. I believed Hitler was frightened of the English Channel since he was not a swimmer himself because he was afraid of water, and considering the number of countries he had invaded and had been successful – not one of these countries was separated by water.

With the introduction of the new Tempest 5, in support of the Mosquito, we did have at least some opposition to this new German threat, the Me 262. If it had been launched into combat three months prior to the Normandy landings, the outcome of the war might have been far less certain.

The weakness lay with Adolf Hitler and the German High Command. The one good idea which came from them to avoid the Allied bombing by the 8th Air Force was to move the launching sites from day to day rather than keep them in one place. This caused great problems for our bomb aimers who would target an area in northern France prior to taking off from Britain, only to find that when they got there, there wasn't a site to be bombed.

So the vengeance weapon bombing went on and the ADGB

did what they could to prevent these expendable aircraft from reaching their targets with the best weapons we had. The population of the City of London, who had seen it all before, was again being badly hit. Anderson and communal concrete shelters were built underground to give some protection against this accurate, heavy bombing. However, no matter how hard the V1 Flying Bomb attacked London and the South-East, the local people who were affected by these attacks kept going magnificently day by day.

At 1900 hours all aircrews of 629, 322 and 96 Squadrons ambled to their aircraft at the dispersal points, already tired from the hectic morning's flying. Soon the light would be fading and we would be spotting the orange exhaust flames of the V1 Flying Bomb, rather than looking for a missile half the size of the Spitfire XIV.

We all carried out cockpit checks and began to taxi out onto the bumpy grass airfield. The Squadron Commander told us we would take off in threes as normal procedure. I let go the brakes, slowly pushed the boost lever until it reached full position and the Spitfire bounded forward at a great rate swinging slightly to starboard as we gathered speed. We thundered down the runway at full throttle as straight as a die before climbing steeply into the open sky in the direction of Folkestone. I flicked up the lever operating the undercarriage hydraulics and felt the wheels thud into their wing bays. This often gave you such a jolt up your spine you didn't know whether to lift up from your seat or remain seated and take the bumps. The plane dropped a little as I raised the flaps but she soon recovered when I reduced the boost and eased her propeller into a coarse pitch. Before I could check all my instruments, especially my altitude gauge, I had climbed to 6,000 feet where I pulled her up into a horizontal line; she roared, whirled and screamed, but apart from that she was a lovely aeroplane to fly and I would be proud to be able to tell my grandchildren that I had flown a Spitfire.

Orders came over the R/T to drop our altitude to Angels

Five hoping that by reducing our height we would see the Fieseler Fi-103 Flying Bomb exhaust flames if there were any. We had been told by Doctor Brown at his first lecture that at twilight and especially in darkness we would see the exhaust flames for miles.

As we approached the French coast at the Pas de Calais it was soon apparent that Hitler's reprisal bombs had already been launched, with more to come, from the message we received over the R/T from the Wing Controller. All of a sudden below us we could see a number of orange exhaust flames flying in a straight line towards London. Paul suggested there were at least twenty if not more and the Squadron Commander ordered normal procedures for a large number of bombs. He suggested we do as we had practised, increase our height to about 3,000 feet above the Flying Bombs and then dive onto them until we equalled or reached their nominal speed. I decided to fly to 4,000 feet and see how the Squadron got on with their first attack. I saw Spitfires and Doodlebugs intermingled everywhere. Our aircraft could be seen firing at short range and fireball explosions lit the night sky. I could see a few V1s getting through our fighter defences but then they became the prime targets of the gun batteries on the North Downs.

Blue Section Leader came over the R/T to say another wave of V1s had been sighted just leaving their launching sites, so we all did a 180-degree turn and flew back to support Blue Section in their attack on the new sightings. It seemed for me from the day's report that FlakGruppe Criel was launching approximately 200 pilotless aeroplanes per day of which 50 per cent got through to London. It was a shame 91 Squadron, who were the experts at this game, were not here to support us because they had stood down for the evening. No wonder Intelligence had told us that 370 missiles would be damaged or shot down in the first month of the vengeance attack.

I decided that since I was getting low on fuel I would have a go at one myself. A V1 bomb was flying directly into my gunsight, outside the safety range, so I opened my firing button but as soon as I pressed it, nothing happened. I

141

panicked a bit, but had to dive quickly before I was one of Squadron Leader Mitchell's statistics. Luckily, I had a few yards to spare. The advantage of this form of combat compared to the old was that peace and tranquillity surrounded you as soon as you passed a target because they could not retaliate. The only problem you had was whether another fighter had attacked it or the gun batteries had hit it.

After checking Red Section was still intact I told them to return to base since we were now beyond our fuel range. By this time the aerodrome was in complete darkness with only a small green light on the caravan at the end of the runway. There was the odd light or two coming from the hangars and buildings, but in the main we had to land in darkness. I hated to think what would happen if we had mist or fog which was normal for June on top of the darkness. I supposed I would lower my undercarriage, close my eyes and hope for the best.

At the dispersal, Andrew was there on his crutches to greet me, trying to hold hands with Cynthia Woodhams. Approaching out of the dark was Chris Mitchell. 'Good show, chaps,' he said, 'you certainly made an impression with the gun and balloon crews in the South-East and thanks to you the London crews had a reasonably peaceful night.'

I told him that the gun crews should not be stationed on the North Downs but actually on the coast, since that would give us a more well-defined area of attack than the present arrangements, and also they would be more effective. Furthermore we could have another fighter force attacking the Flying Bombs between the gun defences on the coast and the balloon barrage surrounding London. He thought this was a very good idea and would put it to the Station Commander in the morning. Squadron Leader Mitchell said that he had always thought the guns on the North Downs were too far back from the main direction of attack and would cause fatalities amongst the population in that area.

With that I reported my findings to the Intelligence Officer, including my report to Squadron Leader Mitchell, had a quick shower, a few pints with Andrew and the boys, and since

I couldn't keep my eyes open any longer, I dropped onto my bed worn out physically and mentally.

15

At 0700 hours sharp, the Air Officer Commanding's chauffeur collected Andrew and me from the Guardroom. Andrew was busy cleaning the brass clips on his white belt and I was polishing the sheath of my sword. En route the Air Officer Commanding was collected with his wife from his huge house on the attractive Downs of Sussex. At 0900 hours we waited for Barbara to turn up so that we could all go through the large black gates of Buckingham Palace together. With the AOC twiddling his thumbs and looking a nervous wreck, Barbara eventually turned up. She seemed as radiant as ever, and not at all uptight. I introduced her to the AOC and my friend Andrew with his crutches and she carefully climbed into the black limousine and sat beside me. She leaned towards me and gave me a gentle kiss. I was impressed with her beautiful outfit which was a tightly fitted, navy-blue two-piece suit under which she wore a white blouse. The knee-length skirt had a little kick-out pleat at the back and the outfit was made complete with matching full-brimmed hat and white ribbon around the brim. I also noticed she was wearing in her breast pocket a dainty, white lace handkerchief and had managed to obtain high-heeled shoes, a navy-blue shoulder bag and gloves. She wore my blue sapphire engagement ring with two white diamonds enclosed on each side, her gold watch and pearl earrings to match the necklace. Her Chanel No. 5 filled the inside of the limousine so that the AOC asked for the window to be opened! Once she saw Andrew's left leg in plaster she asked him if she could sign it after the ceremony.

He said, 'Of course, my dear, you can sign your name all over me if you like!' Hearing this the AOC coughed nervously and we linked our arms together as we hadn't seen each other since I was posted to RAF Hambridge.

'Your DFC ribbon doesn't look straight to me,' the AOC's wife said.

'Well, Cynthia did it for me,' I replied. 'She's his girlfriend,' pointing to Andrew. After this she dropped the subject. The AOC then introduced his wife Margaret to Barbara and I thought it was a wonderful gesture when she stood up, kissed Barbara on the cheek and welcomed her to the party. The AOC said that we all had the day off to celebrate this important occasion, and we had to report back to Hambridge at 0900 hours the next day. I immediately wondered what I was going to do with Andrew. He had no girlfriend with him, only two crutches. Barbara suggested we take him with us to the Café Royale for lunch, but I wasn't so keen on that since I wanted to be alone with her. However I thought we could leave the decision making until after the Investiture.

As we approached the entrance to Buckingham Palace with its black wrought-iron gates tinted with gold at the top, we saw how well the King of England was guarded in his vulnerable position as Head of State. There were two Scots Guardsmen dressed in battledress and wearing their bearskins, which I thought looked ridiculous. Bearskins are always associated with scarlet tunics. Still, this was wartime and dress had to be changed according to the requirements of the War Office. The soldiers' rifles were at the stand-easy position. The senior guardsman controlled the movements of both the guards on duty, tapping his rifle butt to the ground to attract the attention of the other guard. We learnt that three taps by the senior guardsman, followed by a pause of two or three seconds, meant that the other guardsmen brought their rifles to the shoulder arms position. The next signal from the senior guardsman brought them to the present arms position, with the palms of their hands banging against the rifle. As soon as they noticed the pennant flying on the AOC's staff car, the senior guardsman nodded his head and both guardsmen turned inwards to face each other while the AOC quickly returned their salute before the police inspector approached the driver's window to inspect our invitations to the Investiture.

We all alighted from the staff car with Barbara holding on to her hat as she stepped down onto the forecourt. She put her arm around mine but as my sword was in the way she changed sides making it more comfortable for both of us. We noticed Margaret had done the same with her husband and looking behind us we saw with satisfaction that one of the ushers was helping Andrew by stabilising his steps towards the reception area.

When we reached the Great Hall, we found well-manned cloakrooms where we could leave an unnecessary clothing items before being separated. Barbara and Margaret were guided up the stairs by ushers towards the Crimson Ballroom where they were shown to their seats to wait for the Investiture to commence whilst being entertained by a light orchestra in the gallery above the entrance to the Ballroom which played a series of musical scores to suit all tastes.

The music also gave the atmosphere in the Ballroom a touch of relaxation, because on this momentous and magnificent occasion guests were extremely nervous and often overwhelmed by their surroundings.

The Air Officer Commanding, Andrew and myself were ushered into the Picture Gallery where the long walls were covered with priceless pictures going back over generations of Royalty and an official from the Central Chancery gave those of us receiving medals a pin to wear. At approximately 1040 hours the Comptroller of the Lord Chamberlain's Office entered the Picture Gallery from the Green Drawing Room where he had just been through the procedure for seven people receiving Knighthoods.

The Comptroller gave us a short briefing on what was expected of us in front of the King and we were put in a straight line in order of merit and told to stay in this order throughout the Investiture. We were then led via the Silk Tapestry Room and the East Gallery through the back of the

Ballroom and into a side Annexe. When your name was called out by the Lord Chamberlain you entered the Ballroom from the Annexe where the King stood on a dais. At this point my heartbeat doubled, my knees were knocking like drumsticks and my emotions were out of control. I bowed and took one pace forward to the edge of the dais where the King pinned the Distinguished Flying Cross on my left lapel. He asked me how air defence against the V1 Flying Bomb was going and I replied cautiously that progress was slow at this early stage against the new vengeance weapon because of its excessively high speed and the difficulty of attacking it. He wished my Squadron luck, then shook my hand which was a sign to depart. I took one pace back, bowed, turned right and departed from the Ballroom via the opposite entrance to the one I had entered. My medal was then unhooked from the pin extracted from my lapel and my medal placed in a box and handed back to me. I was shown back into the Ballroom by an usher and sat next to my Air Officer Commanding awaiting the arrival of Flight Sergeant Andrew Matthews having received from His Majesty his Distinguished Flying Medal.

After about one hour the King completed the award ceremony for about 130 recipients from the three major Services, the Merchant Navy and civilian services. The King stood to attention while the National Anthem was played before departing with his officials from the Ballroom. The Yeoman of the Guard, who had stood to attention behind His Majesty throughout the Investiture, followed him to the exit of the Ballroom looking magnificent in their uniforms which were first designed in 1425. Once all the officials had left the Ballroom we were allowed to join our guests and with Andrew lagging behind on his crutches, we joined up with Barbara and Margaret who were seated in the third row from the front.

The AOC decided to leave us, shook hands with Barbara and wished us all a happy day. Andrew, Barbara and myself had a group photograph taken by a professional photo-grapher in the quadrangle before departing for the tradesmen's entrance at the back of the Palace in order to get to the famous pub at the rear called The Bag of Nails. It had been a moving and emotional two hours attending the Investiture, a magnificent spectacle which Barbara and I would never forget for the rest of our lives.

We went by taxi from the pub to the Café Royale where the three of us were shown to our reserved table by the immaculately dressed Head Waiter.

There we enjoyed the wonderful five-course dinner in the relaxed atmosphere of other people's conversation and easy listening music played by a large orchestra sitting a few yards from us on a platform covered in a beautiful light blue Wilton carpet.

After ordering another bottle of Moet champagne, Andrew suddenly raised his crystal glass to Barbara and said, 'You know, Donald's a conspicuously gallant pilot. They only give the award he received this morning as a reward for the highest achievement in the Royal Air Force. He agonises over the deaths of his friends and colleagues. As a Flight Sergeant, I'm justly proud that he treats me personally as a close friend. He's an excellent leader, and we all admire him for his tenacity, courage and modesty.' He paused for a while and holding Barbara's hand whilst having a drink with the other, he said, 'When I baled out he did not hesitate to risk his own life until I was safely down. You're a very beautiful young lady and if I were you I would not hesitate to marry him while you've got the chance.' With that he asked us to raise our glasses as a toast to each other before sitting down again more comfortably in his chair to finish his glass of champagne.

Barbara stood up and said, 'I would be most proud, Andrew, if you would be my friend – that delightful speech you've just made makes me feel justly proud of both of you. I'm sure you make a good team together and I hope and pray you both come home safely from every sortie you fly.' With that she walked round to Andrew's chair, put her arm around him and gave him a tender kiss. I thought it was a wonderful gesture on her part to accept Andrew as she did and was justly proud of her actions.

She and I got onto the dance floor, which was polished to

148

perfection, and had a slow waltz together. Her slim waist without her jacket on emphasised her full bosom as she pressed her shapely body against mine as we danced to the beat of the orchestra. Andrew beckoned us over to the table where he asked my permission to leave since his leg was now giving him some concern. I asked Barbara to chat to him a minute while I rang the MT section, told them who I was and that I had an injured pilot with me who needed transport back to Hambridge. I told them this request was approved by the Air Officer Commanding ADGB and it was approved without argument. On returning to my seat I found Andrew resting his left leg on a stool provided by one of the waiters. I ordered him to sit there until transport arrived from Hambridge to pick him up and he agreed to do so as his leg was giving him a lot of pain. Barbara and he embraced and she kissed him goodbye. I told him I would see him the next day and with that, after tipping the Head Waiter, we departed from the Café Royale and made our way by foot to the Cumberland Hotel where I had booked a double room for the night.

With Barbara putting her arm in mine we enjoyed walking through the busy London streets where shoppers were patiently queuing up for their daily groceries for their families. British people have great fortitude and patience when waiting in long queues to purchase their food and clothes according to the number of ration coupons they had. We in the Armed Forces had no sense of direct rationing like the civilian population had. For the basic food items the soldier had no idea how many points were needed, but he could get by with charm and wearing a uniform. It was a lovely feeling to comfort Barbara as we relaxed in the lovely June air on our way to the hotel after sitting down for so long in the morning and then during our superb lunch at the Café Royale. As we got nearer to the hotel we laughed and made rude jokes about some of my colleagues we had seen in the morning. Barbara said one Army Captain had odd coloured socks on and obviously did not know until he bowed to the

King. The ladies in the audience thought this highly amusing, and had a little chuckle between themselves when they saw the embarrassing position he was in standing motionless in front of the Sovereign. As we walked through London with its colourful, open-ended parks, we could feel relaxed again after such a stressful morning at Buckingham Palace. She kept holding her wide-brimmed hat as gusts of wind tried to remove it from her head and clutched her shoulder bag which held the medal I had received that morning from the King.

We danced and frolicked about like two young teenagers going off to school until I was suddenly alerted by a very familiar noise in the sky behind us. Although only faint at first, it began to grow in volume until I realised that it was the eerie, ugly, pulsating sound of the pulse jet of a V1. As it got closer to us the renowned exhaust explosions of its motor became more pronounced, and the pilotless monoplane came into sight over the horizon with its yellow-flamed exhaust behind it. I told Barbara to take her hat off, and the reason why. I think she felt for some time I was disturbed by something in the sky and now she knew it. People started to take precautions as policemen's whistles began to blow. Some decided to watch while others, especially the elderly, took cover in Underground stations. The population had just begun to get used to Adolf Hitler's new vengeance weapon, the V1 Flying Bomb, or as Londoner's now called it, the Doodlebug. Barbara held me tightly, almost stopping the flow of blood through my arm and I could feel the tension building up in her body as the sound of the missile began to get louder and louder. I asked her whether she would like to join those people going underground or stay up in the fresh air and see the show. 'If I'm going to die like a true Welshwoman then we will both die together. Somehow, Donald, I would like that,' she said and squeezed my hand still harder.

I told her that if the pulse-jet exhaust explosions stopped we had just 12 seconds to take cover or fall flat on the ground. The flying bomb flew on for just a few more moments before the engine cut out, there was complete silence as it dived straight

150

down in the distance and there was an horrific explosion. I pushed Barbara roughly to the grass and as silence returned I gave her my hand and pulled her up. 'That was a bloody hard push, darling. Are you trying to kill me off before we get married?' she said. At the mention of this oblique proposal I held her in my arms and kissed her bright red lips as romantically as I could.

'Well, you've not said yes,' I murmured as she brushed her suit with her hairbrush.

'I'll marry you, darling, you're the salt of the earth,' and with that I hugged her tightly and shouted so that all could hear, 'Yes, my darling. Shall we do it tonight?'

'Of course we can't – my father wouldn't like that even though he likes you.'

On entering the Cumberland Hotel we booked in at reception in the name of Flight Lieutenant Hamilton. 'Your double room is ready, sir. Room number Two-One-Two. The bellboy will take your bags,' the burly, middle-aged receptionist said.

'We've only got two light overnight bags so I'll look after them myself, thank you,' I replied.

'Congratulations on your award, sir, at Buckingham Palace today; your wife must be very proud of you,' he said as he gave me the keys to our room.

I joined Barbara in the lounge bar where standing on a small lounge table were two glasses of brandy. 'How did you get these?' I asked as I faced Barbara full of admiration. With several waiters saying 'Hello' and other compliments I guessed she came here quite often. I knew her father frequently visited the hotel after work, possibly each day, because his office was close by and I knew he liked his soft drinks.

'What a day, Barbara, a day we shall never forget. I know I shall not forget meeting the King, the heroes of the day and being with you and Andrew.'

'Well, Donald, I have some room in my stomach for a nice

steak or a Dover sole this evening,' she said as she sidled up against me.

'I was very pleased with you in your appreciation of Andrew's speech at lunchtime. He would have been delighted with what you had said to him. He likes you a lot and is always asking after you at the Squadron.'

'Has he got a girlfriend, Donald?' Barbara enquired as she sat closer to me on the sofa with her eyes half shut.

'Yes, he has. A nice young WAAF called Cynthia Woodhams. She's the Squadron Leader's secretary and is very loyal and dependable. She admires the way that Squadron Leader Mitchell runs the Squadron. He's a very good friend of mine and often relies on me to solve his problems when he gets het up.'

'Well, darling, I don't know about you, but I'm off for some sleep and you look tired as well. I suggest we go up to our room and have a late afternoon nap.'

With that we sipped up our brandies and galloped upstairs to the second floor, where our room was right at the end. When Barbara turned the key and opened the door I picked her up in my arms. By God, she was heavy, so heavy in fact that I had to run to the bed otherwise I would have dropped her. We both took our jackets off and she kindly hung them up in our own respective mirrored wardrobes. In a few minutes I had fallen asleep.

Early that evening I was awakened by this warm body stroking my hair and kissing my lips. 'Dinner time, darling,' she said, as she stripped off her clothes, put a towel around her and ran to the shower room. I soon followed and we made love in the lovely warm water of the shower. I had never done this before but it was most exhilarating, to say the least. We left the shower to dress, unfortunately I had to put on my Officer's No. 1 uniform, while Barbara changed into a low-cut, red silk gown which suited her admirably. The complexion of her skin and colour of her hair perfectly matched her dress. Her soft voice and penetrating charm mesmerised me – she had blossomed into a mature woman since I had been away at Hambridge. She wore the same jewellery as she had at Buckingham Palace except that she also wore the golden bracelet, that I had given her earlier, on her right wrist.

After an excellent dinner we danced the traditional dances of the waltz, foxtrot, tango, quickstep and the new dance introduced by Edmundo Ross, called the cha-cha-cha. Although we found this difficult at first, we soon learnt to enjoy it.

After a lot of dancing we decided to say farewell to the ballroom and made our way up to Room 212 where we undressed and made love on the king-sized double bed. We then just lay there covering each other until we went off to sleep.

The next thing I knew was Barbara shaking me from head to foot, pouring cold water onto my face. 'What's going on, Barbara?' I mumbled as I tried to bring my thoughts to order after a heavy night's drinking. She came and lay beside me in her underclothes and gave me a tender kiss.

'Some of us, Donald, have to go to work today, not like you who just fly around in your Spitfire a few hours a week.'

'You must be joking,' I said to her as I pulled her into my arms and hugged her. With that she got dressed in the previous day's suit, brushed her hair, made up her face, checked her shoulder bag and closed it.

'What about your medal?' she asked as she held it in her hand.

'Do me a favour, Barbara, could you keep it at home in a safe place until I get home next, when I shall put it in a bank safe deposit box together with my citation.'

'I must be off now, darling, otherwise I'm going to be late for work. Ring me when you can, although I know it might be difficult being confined to barracks,' she said, then went on, 'I love you very much, darling, you're all I've got in life, so do take care of yourself. My mother thinks the world of you and I know that one day she'd like us to be married.' She then picked up her shoulder bag, hat and coat, kissed me goodbye and left the room. Feeling a deep sense of emptiness, I showered, breakfasted, paid the bill and left the Cumberland Hotel with very many happy memories.

I arrived back at Hambridge a bit late but in good spirits. All the crews came up to me to offer their congratulations and as soon as I had recovered I made my way to Squadron Leader Mitchell's office. 'Had a nice day, young man? All right for some having a day off, but I expect that later in life this may be the most important appointment you've ever made. I congratulate you on your award, and I've put you up for promotion to Squadron Leader because I think it's about time you had your own squadron.'

I thanked him profusely and asked, 'Have you seen Andrew?' Chris replied by saying that Andrew had to go back into hospital because he was in so much discomfort from his broken ankle. Cynthia had seen him last night, and he'd said how much he'd enjoyed being with Barbara and what a lucky man I was in having her as a girlfriend.

16

A few days after my Buckingham Palace Investiture I was summoned with 629 Squadron Commander to ADGB Headquarters. We had no idea why we were ordered to meet the Air Officer Commanding ADGB, but we arrived on time wearing our Number One best blue. We also took with us, in case they were needed, papers and records concerning the effectiveness of the Squadron in the defence against the V1 Flying Bomb in Diver Patrols, plus the demise of pilots and the response of replacements. Since we did not know the purpose of the meeting, we were well prepared for the majority of questions which might be put to us. The AOC was accommodated in a large house in Doodlebug Alley and we were invited by his personal assistant to wait in the waiting room.

After a few minutes we were invited in and were joined by two Army staff officers. One was General Pile commanding the Army ground forces attached to the ADGB, the other officer holding the rank of Major we guessed as being his personal assistant or a specialist in gunnery or observation.

'Good morning, gentlemen,' the AOC said as we all saluted. He stood up from the very large, highly polished, mahogany table and asked us to be seated. On the wall behind him was a very large map of northern France and the south coast of England, including the City of London. The map had marked on it numerous launching sites of the vengeance weapon and the various flight paths to London.

Adjacent to this was a diagram showing the number of launches per day, their success rate on targets in London and the achievements of all the defence units including fighters, ack-ack guns and the balloon barrage around the perimeter of London. We all sat in silence looking at this very large map which was also well illuminated.

'Gentlemen, I've called this meeting to discuss what we can do to tighten our defences since the Prime Minister is very concerned about the success rate the Führer is having with vengeance weapons reaching London and the Home Counties. It's all causing serious damage to domestic homes and industrial buildings with a high mortality rate amongst the population, especially in London.' The AOC went on by giving statistical facts from his other chart about Operation Crossbow so far, stating that about 200 Flying Bombs had penetrated our defences since the first launch on 13 June 1944. From reports issued by Intelligence, 101 missiles were shot down over Sussex and Kent during the first week after the commencement of the sighting of the first V1. This averaged 20 shot down per day.

He stood up and took a blackboard pointer to his map, saying that fresh ideas were required now we knew the Flying Bomb's performance since its launch on 13 June. These ideas were required to improve the effectiveness of our present defences and with his pointer on the map he explained that firstly the fighters of ADGB and the ack-ack gunners under the command of General Pile did not have enough air space to fire at their targets; secondly, and even more importantly the pilots were experiencing far too many fatalities from our own guns; and thirdly, the gunners were hesitant when our own fighters were in their target zone.

He concluded by saying we must sort these problems out as soon as possible since the Prime Minister was concerned not only about our heavy losses, but also that too many Flying Bombs were reaching their targets. We needed closer communication between all arms, the fighters, the gunners and the balloonists. We all knew at the meeting how the population of London was being demoralised by the damage to domestic and commercial buildings due not only to the precision of the V1s, but also to the insufficient warning the

156

capital was being given when coming under attack.

There was complete silence in the room as the AOC sat down in his chair and wiped his brow with a beautiful silk handkerchief. There were mutterings about coffee as there was no sign of coffee cups, however, this was a very serious meeting we were attending, especially with the news of the Führer's successes over London. The silence was broken by Squadron Leader Mitchell whose request to the Chairman of the meeting to put his point of view was accepted. He said he had been thinking of the problems which were brought to his attention by pilots of 629 Squadron. After careful consideration he posed similar questions to the Hambridge Wing with the approval of the Station Commander. Flight Lieutenant Donald Hamilton DFC had come up with one solution to increase the effectiveness of our defences.

The AOC then invited me to propose my plan to the meeting and gave me his pointer in case I needed it. I stepped up to his large map on the wall and explained to my distinguished audience that if we could move General Pile's ack-ack guns nearer the south coast than at present on the North Downs, this would give the fighter squadrons of ADGB two chances of attacking this lethal weapon, compared to the one we had at present. This would give the fighters the opportunity of attacking the missile soon after launching over the Channel and away from the gun belt, and the second chance would be to attack them behind the gun belt down Doodlebug Alley and before the barrage balloon defence on the outer perimeter of London. I continued by saying that this would give a much more effective area for the ack-ack gunners to work in and a better line of sight.

Having completed my synopsis of the current situation and my personal views for new developments I sat down. Squadron Leader Mitchell whispered in my left ear, 'Well done, my lad. Nicely put.' General Pile then stood up and taking the pointer from me walked over to the same map on the wall. He told the meeting he had similar thoughts about moving up the ack-ack gun belt because of the advantages that I had already given. He said the gunners could be more effective than hitherto if the guns were sited on the coast where they would have an uninterrupted field of view. They would also have a better chance of hearing the Doodlebugs and be more effective in shooting them down. The Royal Observer Corps could improve their detection rate by increasing the number of observation posts. He concluded that the fighters would have more freedom over the Channel, especially if they could attack the missile soon after launch when it settled down to its predetermined height and speed.

After a break for coffee we all returned to the conference table where it was unanimously agreed that General Pile should consider moving the gun belt from the North Downs to the coast, a mammoth task, to say the least, but he was quite prepared to consider the idea seriously. He said it would be an immense task to perform and possibly the most important move of the war. He continued by saying that a large number of heavy, medium and light guns would have to be moved, plus ammunition, accommodation and personnel and commented that it would be better to move this gigantic task force by road instead of rail due to obvious advantages. He asked for vehicles of all types and shapes to be made available to him if so required and everyone agreed to give him their full support.

When the AOC asked him how many days he would need to complete the operation the Major stood up and unflinchingly said, 'Two days, sir,' in a positive voice, going on to explain that the operation could be successfully accomplished by the middle of July. Plans had already been drawn up to bring down extra artillery from the north and west of England. The Major then sat down. General Pile then stood up and said that he had already discussed the plan with the Prime Minister on his own behalf, and that Mr Winston Churchill was pushing him hard to complete the operation not later than 13 July 1944. Although the AOC was not at all pleased with not being informed beforehand of the meeting with the Prime Minister he reluctantly accepted it. The operation would be carried out at a weekend in July. The United States Army would have to be considered since they were providing the British Army with their own new light ack-ack guns.

As the AOC called the meeting to a close he wished on behalf of those attending the meeting good luck to General Pile and his staff in the gigantic task ahead of them. He then asked Squadron Leader Mitchell and myself to stay behind after the meeting closed. When the Army personnel had left, the AOC asked Squadron Leader Mitchell if he would like to join his staff at Headquarters with the acting rank of Wing Commander. The purpose of the post would be to act as a direct liaison officer between the reports coming in from Maidstone from the ROC and the fighter squadrons under his command. This would speed up communication immensely and get the fighters airborne much quicker than at present. Mitch, although taken aback by the appointment and without any warning was a bit reluctant to agree to it because he felt his main duty was towards 629 Squadron which he had formed and trained efficiently since January 1944. He asked the AOC who would take over the command of 629 Squadron. The AOC immediately replied. 'You're looking straight at him,' smiling as he said so and picking up my personal file. He continued by saying this was unusual for a deputy to take over the command of his own squadron, but that this was an exception in that I was a very exceptional leader and pilot and had been involved in Operation Crossbow since nearly the start of it. He continued by saying that I knew a great deal about the Operation and it would be a difficult situation to bring in somebody new without the experience of either Operation Crossbow or Diver Patrols.

Mitch then smiled and said he would accept his new post at ADGB Headquarters whereupon the AOC stood up, turned to me and said, 'Hamilton, I'm very pleased to hand you over Six-Two-Nine Squadron with the acting rank of Squadron Leader with effect from the first of July nineteen forty-four.' He concluded that after completion of Operation Crossbow I would have to be posted to another squadron and I agreed to do so.

We both thanked the AOC for his time, saluted smartly in a

jubilant mood and left his office. We called at the nearest pub on our way back to base at Hambridge and celebrated with a large Scotch. It certainly went down well since we were very thirsty after a long meeting and the excitement at its conclusion over our promotions.

I rang Barbara from the pub and she was delighted with the news. 'Darling, that's wonderful,' she whooped down the telephone. 'Does that mean more money?'

'Yes,' I replied, 'now we can get married on my next leave and as a Squadron Leader I get accommodation as well, so you can't refuse me when I propose to you on my next leave.'

There was a hesitant silence, and then she said, 'I'll think seriously about it although I have my job to consider at the bank.'

'Forget that now as I'll be getting a substantial rise in pay with accommodation which will look after both of us comfortably. There's no excuse now to not marrying me, is there?' I waited intently for her answer.

She replied, 'I love you, darling, but you'll have to ask my father first.' I said that I would ask him by letter that night to which she replied, 'Do it as soon as possible. I love you, darling, take care. Happy landings,' then we were cut off abruptly.

We both had another Scotch before setting off to our base at Hambridge. On arrival there the good news had filtered through to the Station Commander and to the members of 629 Squadron. Everywhere there were congratulations at our promotions, not only from the Corporal at the gate, but even the Adjutant as we approached the Station Commander's office. On entering his office he was excited about our promotions saying that he was sorry to lose Mitch, but was pleased that I was taking over the Squadron, with his full approval. He said that the AOC had telephoned him, and the promotions were immediate as he wanted Mitch up at HQ the next day. We all then had a fair measure of whisky before leaving his office and returning to our rightful place at 629 Squadron's dispersal. There, all the members of the

Squadron were waving and cheering at us on our arrival. They were thrilled at the news but sad at losing their mentor and favourite Squadron Commander. Some of them had been with him since its formation and were very proud to have served under him. He was friendly, his expertise both on the ground and in the air was unparalleled and his leadership unequalled. He was a master at getting the best out of his men without being rank conscious. I had a tremendous act to follow and would have a tough job equalling his attributes and successes. Undoubtedly the Squadron was going to lose one of the finest leaders in the ADGB. However, the lads knew me well enough to accept me, and they all agreed they would rather have me than a stranger in the Squadron from another Command. In fact, some agreed that although I was young for the job, I had the experience and potential to lead them in our new task of defending the country against this new weapon.

After celebrating and seeing off Wing Commander Mitchell to his new post I returned to the Squadron office where I began to get conversant with the paperwork which goes with the task of being in command of a first-line squadron. After sorting out the rubbish from the real, answering the in-tray correspondence and making Cynthia my personal secretary, I called an immediate meeting with all members of the Squadron.

At a very brief meeting held outside on a bright sunny morning, I said that I intended that the ideals born within the Squadron would continue, and the high standard of discipline set by our previous Commander. I told them the Air Officer Commanding thought highly of us as a Squadron and that I meant that to continue while I was in command.

When I returned to my office, I asked Cynthia to type a letter to Barbara's father asking him if I could marry his charming daughter on my next leave. I knew I should have handwritten it, but since my handwriting was illegible, I thought the next best thing was to have it typed.

I also wrote a letter to Barbara telling her I was deeply in

161

love with her and wanted to marry her at the earliest opportunity and have a family as soon as possible. After sealing the envelope, I left it in my locked top drawer and told Cynthia it was there in case I failed to return from any sortie. She quietly understood, but was saddened that I had come to that conclusion which, with a lifespan of three weeks, all fighter pilots had to face when they took off at dawn most mornings.

When I got to the Officers' Mess, I received a telephone call from Barrie to say that he had been given the command of a new squadron in 11 Group with the full rank of Squadron Leader. I was pleased with his promotion, thanked him for his call and wished him the best of luck. He said that when he got settled he would organise a get-together. I told him I was hoping to marry Barbara on my next leave subject to her father's consent and hoped he would be best man. He was delighted with the prospect since he was wandering from one WAAF to another.

Andrew, who still had a plaster cast around his left ankle, organised a party in the Sergeants' Mess, so after a skinful of beer, and asking Cynthia to sew on my third thin stripe on my flying suit and battledress, I went off for a long sleep.

The next morning, with a dreadful hangover from the effects of the night before, I asked Flight Sergeant Devlin to call a meeting of all members of the Squadron to Hangar Number 3. Except for crews on emergency stand-by, I asked him for all personnel to attend whether sober or otherwise, since I knew that members of the Squadron had had a hectic night's drinking the previous night.

I commenced the meeting by informing all crew members that changes at Higher Command had been made by the AOC the previous day. The most important item on the agenda was that Wing Commander Mitchell had been posted to Command Headquarters for the purpose of liaising with General Pile and his gunners in order to improve communication between gunners and fighters and to reduce the fatality rate of our own fighter pilots attacking the V1s.

After informing the men of Mitch's departure I could see some glum faces especially on those of the Squadron who had been with him since its formation in January 1944. I tried to cheer them up by saying it was a great step forward for him and he was delighted with his appointment. However, I also told them he was reluctant to leave them, but the AOC had given him no choice since he was the best man for the job at hand.

I continued that the next subject was absolutely top secret and should not be talked about either in the bar or in their messes. I did not give them the new destination of the gun positions, but I told them they were being moved from the North Downs to a position which would not only give the gunners, the ROC and the fighter pilots more efficiency but that there would be closer liaison so that the fatalities of our own pilots would be reduced, and also the gunners would be more accurate. For the pilots' information I told them the new gun positions would be in place by 13 July. Further details about their actual locations would be given to them 24 hours after we had confirmation that they were ready for the Doodlebugs. I also informed them that the barrage balloon network was being strengthened by bringing more in from the north and west of England. It was important to tell the pilots of the Squadron that the chances of being shot down by our own defences would diminish once the ack-ack gunners and balloon defences were not only strengthened but moved to their new positions. The gunners would definitely have a better arc of fire, whilst the pilots would have two chances of attacking the ugly black missiles. I asked if there were any questions from the floor and straight away Flight Lieutenant McKinnon, leader of Green Section, asked whether the ack-ack guns would stop firing once they had seen a friendly fighter in pursuit of a Flying Bomb. I replied that this was a very difficult question to answer, that I did not know the answer but would come back to him when I had enquired at ADGB Headquarters. I told him to use his common sense and if either his section or himself was in imminent danger to

163

break away from the attack as up to now the gunners had a satisfactory record of success.

It was my own personal opinion that we should attack the vengeance weapon as far out to sea as possible. The weapon was very vulnerable as soon as it reached its predetermined height since it was slower then because of its heavier fuel load. As it approached London it had been recorded that some of the Doodlebugs had reached 440 miles per hour, whereas its initial speed at level flight was only 300 to 340 miles per hour.

I explained quite clearly to the pilots that there was a very thin line between attack and breakaway with the new communication set-up. I told them not to be martyrs, I needed live pilots with their machines, not dead ones. Spitfire XIVs were in short supply due to the new Griffon 65 engines and we still had to rely on our Allies flying new Tempests and Mustangs.

I concluded the meeting by saying everything was being done to improve safety and the risk of them being shot down by friendly forces was being reduced. My final words to the pilots was to keep above 4,000 feet when they sighted the bomb and keep a minimum distance of 200 yards when attacking it. Then I closed the meeting. As the pilots left I gave them a report including drawings of a pilot from 91 Squadron at West Malling who on two occasions had attacked a V1 but had run out of ammunition. He had decided to gain height once more, dive onto it to gain speed and fly along beside it. On doing so, he then tipped his port wing upwards. This upset the missile gyroscopes which governed the air supply to the rudder and elevator with the result that the Doodlebug turned over onto its back and fell to the ground. There was great enthusiasm as the pilots left the meeting to go to their respective tents and I had the impression that they liked the idea pioneered by the pilot of 91 Squadron, but I had my reservations about two wings touching together – it seemed to me a suicidal idea.

Flight Sergeant Devlin distributed information not only on the black paint being on the port wing of the attacking Spitfire to prove that it had come into contact with the pilotless plane, but also on the new modifications being carried out to improve the speed in level flight of the Spitfire XIV. Basically, the Griffon engine was now developing 2,000 horsepower, and the new Spitfire XIVs had a single fin and rudder. Also, they had elliptical front wings to give them more speed and higher octane fuel was being used.

I told my number one that we would be taking off at 1130 hours now that ADGB was providing 24-hour coverage per day. When I got to my office, I told Cynthia to type a memo to all ground and air personnel that we were still on Red Alert, all leave was cancelled and no telephone calls were to be made outside without my personal permission. These calls, if approved, had to be made on my own office telephone. I also told them in the memo that we were expected to fly up to four sorties a day now that the Wehrmacht was sending up to 200 Flying Bombs a day towards London. I strongly recommended that drinking should be kept to a minimum and party time should be limited as much as possible due to the demands now being put on us.

At 1115 hours, all pilots assembled in the briefing room. After weather reports and Flight Sergeant Devlin's seven hundred reports on the condition of each aircraft, we were informed we had nine complete first-line aircraft with two on stand-by. This was a great achievement and I asked all pilots to show their appreciation for all the work he had done with his loyal ground crews by a round of applause. This included our replacement for Pilot Officer Adrian Dalgleish, namely Sergeant Philip Tremeer from 610 Squadron West Malling.

We took off at exactly 1130 hours into the brilliant sunlight with some of us having our new Griffon engines on full boost. We climbed to 7,000 feet into the lovely azure sky. The cloud base was high so that we would have a clear, unrestricted view of the enemy if they came our way. We made for the Pas de Calais area which the Germans called Zone Interdite since they divided occupied France into two zones.

This was the area where the Wehrmacht had concentrated to bomb London, However, before we sighted the Pas de Calais region, several Doodlebugs in a salvo of six were sighted flying in a straight line approximately one mile apart. We estimated from our own speed that they were travelling at about 340 miles per hour. I called up Blue Section to attack on sight and break away from the Squadron. I could see out of my starboard window their immediate breakaway to attack while Red and Yellow sections stayed on station.

We stayed at 7,000 feet so that if we saw further salvos of Flying Bombs, we were in the correct position to attack. The height and speed of this very small mini-wing projectile, compared to the size of the Spitfire, gave great concern to the ack-ack gunners on the south coast of England. We had to attack and shoot them down well before the pilotless plane came within maximum range of the gun belt.

During the day the Royal Observer Corps, which did an excellent job sighting the missiles, guided friendly fighters behind the gun belt by firing rockets known as 'Snow Flakes'. The ROC on the fringe of the balloon barrage fired red rockets to warn off any pursuing friendly fighters, but over the English Channel we had no guidance except whatever information we received from Control, and our own instincts. If we were lucky enough, and that only happened occasionally, we got information from ships of the Royal Navy out in the Channel and the ROC stationed on the south coast. These observers would send their information to a control centre at Maidstone whose task it was to get it to us via our controllers at ADGB.

The fighters of 629 Squadron, under a high cloud base and a lovely blue sky, cruised at 7,000 feet over the northern coast of France looking for more robots. We could not go too near the Wehrmacht launching sites as the defensive gunfire was intensive. Since the flak would be heavy and I did not want to take any chances of our Spitfires being hit I ordered the Squadron to climb to 9,000 feet. Although this additional height gave us extra safety, we lost those vital seconds when sighting the V1s.

Suddenly over the R/T Flight Sergeant Windross shouted, 'Diver, Diver, Angels Six below us.' I focused on another salvo of cigar-shaped missiles travelling in their parallel lines which looked dreadfully small from where we were. To both Red and Yellow sections I shouted, 'Tally Ho, bandits approximately Angels Six below us travelling at about three-four-zero miles per hour. Attack before gun belt and good luck.' The first pilot to break away was Sergeant Philip Tremeer, our new recruit, in a steep dive followed by Windross. One moment I saw Philip lining up for an attack behind a missile, the next thing I saw was that the black mini wings and long fuselage were breaking apart and falling rapidly into the sea. I was a bit concerned because for one moment I could not see Philip's Spitfire then suddenly he climbed steeply away to regain his station.

I saw Paul nosedive onto his ugly target with flame pouring out from the pulse jet engine mounted above its fuselage. He had gained enough speed to be in position to fire his 20 mm cannon at it. The next moment I was flying near the edge of an orange fireball which burnt my port wingtip. It wasn't until I was a few hundred feet below the explosion that I noticed Paul flying only a few feet above the millpond of the English Channel. I was pleased to see him because when he fired I thought he was well within the danger zone of 200 yards in attack. We both climbed up together to our station to join Adrian at 7,000 feet. The debris of the explosion was scattered widely and the vibration of that one ton of high explosive had been felt by all of us especially Paul in the attacking aircraft.

While I was keeping cover for the remainder, Red and Yellow Sections were going about their business of attacking the remaining V1s in sight. I could not help but wonder what Adolf Hitler had said to his Chiefs of Staff in Berlin when he announced that no British fighter could overtake the V1, with the result that they could not be shot down. If he could only see what we were doing to his mighty special prize, he might retract his words to the German people. Our technique was working for we had learnt at a very early stage that if we attacked from above and built up sufficient speed to catch a

Doodlebug, an Allied pilot could shoot one down with a series of three second bursts of 20 mm cannon and a bit of luck. This theory might sound easy but it was very difficult in practice because the missile presented the attacking pilot with a very small target.

What was very disappointing on these Diver Patrols was the lack of combat with your adversary, which was just an enemy that flew in a straight line with one ton of explosive warhead heading for London or the Home Counties. You could not match your flying skills with a Doodlebug since it had no pilot to pit his combat skills against you. It was very boring for our pilots, but it had to be done to the best of our ability as these one-ton missiles posed such a serious threat to the population of England and the outcome of the Second World War. At night however, it was an entirely different ball game as it was much easier to identify the Doodlebug by its glowing orange tail jet, which could often be seen a long way off, subject to visibility.

Because there was not a set pattern of launching by the Wehrmacht the squadrons of the Air Defence of Great Britain had to operate 30 to 40 fighter aircraft in the air day and night which put immense pressure on both ground and air crews. Because the salvos of V1 weapons were being launched at random the attacking pilots often became strained and tired. It was therefore doubly important for them to stay alert which wasn't easy under the circumstances we were flying in. If there was heavy cloud then the Wehrmacht launchings increased because they knew it would be difficult for our defence system to spot them. Their success rate thus increased in bad weather.

Suddenly on my port side, a few thousand feet below me, I spotted a single black missile. It was travelling very fast but I dived down from 7,000 feet to 2,800 feet, lined up my gunsight and keeping a separation distance of 300 yards I opened fire with a three-second gun burst before steeply diving away. Seconds later I felt a violent vibration in my cockpit and as I did a 180-degree turn I saw that the Doodlebug was on fire as it turned on its back and fell into the sea. As we had been flying for some time and our fuel gauges were telling us to go home I ordered the Squadron to return to base.

After the usual debriefing with the Intelligence Officers, we learnt that we had shot down five V1s with two probables. Paul was the highest scorer for the morning's operation with two confirmed victories. He was very lucky with one of them with his tail being badly burnt from the explosion of one of the pulse-jet missiles, but luckily for him it did not affect his rudder or elevator. Philip also had a narrow escape and returned to base with his fuselage blistered.

I put Yellow and Blue sections on Alert for the next Diver Patrol while I rested Red Section and handed over the Squadron to Flight Lieutenant Neil McKinnon for the next patrol.

After a few drinks with Philip and Paul with Andrew tagging along with his plastered leg I went over to the Squadron office to write my patrol report and a recommendation for Flight Sergeant Windross to be offered a short service commission as soon as possible since I wanted him to be the new Red Section Leader. I checked the serviceability of the aircraft for the next day with Flight Sergeant Devlin repairing the airframe damage of the two Spitfires from that morning's battles.

On completing my morning's report I was summoned by telephone to see the Station Commander without delay. After knocking on the Station Commander's door, he shouted for me to come in. I entered, stood to attention, saluted and was asked to sit down on a well-worn upholstered chair opposite his large desk.

'Squadron Leader Hamilton, nice to see you and congratulations once again on your promotion to take over Six-Two-Nine Squadron. I'm extremely pleased with the way you conduct yourself and mix with your lower ranks which is an example to some of our officers. At RAF Hambridge we are all very proud of your leadership and airmanship. You are an example to all officers on this station. I feel you've admirably taken Wing Commander Mitchell's place and your men are very pleased since they did not want a stranger in their midst. If Hitler had thought about his attack three months ago, I think the strategy of the war could have been changed drastically for us. London could have been wiped out and the Normandy landings threatened.' He then took a solid silver cigarette case off his desk and offered me one. 'Of course, Hamilton, I forgot you don't smoke. Wise man. This unfortunately is one of my vices which sadly goes with the pressure of the job.' He carried on speaking about how unusual it was for a newly-promoted Squadron Leader to remain within his own Squadron. 'But I put it to Group that you were irreplaceable as you had the right knowledge and expertise so that I was allowed to retain you in your present capacity as leader of Six-Two-Nine Squadron. You're also a specialist in Operation Crossbow and the Air Officer Commanding was very impressed with your lecture at the recent meeting at Air Staff Headquarters. They wanted you to go to Eleven Group which is not directly involved in Operation Crossbow but I told them in no uncertain terms that it would be a great loss to ADGB if you left the Squadron. As I told you on your return from the meeting, after the completion of Operation Crossbow, you will eventually be leaving ADGB for your own Squadron with the full rank of Squadron Leader.

'Further, Hamilton, I want you to fly me up to RAF Bovingdon in Hertfordshire this afternoon for a meeting at Fighter Command's Headquarters at Stanmore, Middlesex. I want you to wait and bring me back about eighteen-thirty to nineteen-thirty hours. I've borrowed an Anson which I know you're certified to fly. Could I please ask you to take the two WAAF office girls with us as they've worked extremely hard this year and I think it would be good for their morale to give them a cross-country ride. It'll be all right, Hamilton, but don't broadcast it otherwise we shall have all the WAAFs asking for joyrides, especially my PA, Louisa Jefferson.'

While the Station Commander was in a good mood, I asked him if on our return flight we could go down a few feet and fly over my fiancée's house at New Malden. 'It's on our flight path to avoid the London barrage balloon network and the north gun belt on the North Downs,' I said and could see he was smiling at my suggestion.

'I hope you're not going to throw out a wedding present on a parachute?'

'Oh no, sir, just circle at about three hundred feet subject to the height of the trees.'

'Three hundred feet, Hamilton, a bit close isn't it?'

'No, sir, it's within safety limits. If the cloud base is higher, I can take her a bit higher if you wish.'

'It's a bit illegal, Hamilton, isn't it, especially with those guns and the barrage balloon network about.'

'Knowing the flight patterns of the Doodlebug, the time we arrive over New Malden should be a quiet period for the gunners since the enemy usually have a lull between nineteen and twenty hundred hours.'

'All right, Hamilton, but if anybody asks me, it's on your head.' Then he asked, 'I hope she's worth it?'

'Yes, sir, she's definitely worth it.'

'Is she pretty?'

'Yes, sir, she's a lovely girl. We hope, with your blessing, we can get married later this year on my next leave. Maybe, sir, you could meet her,' I replied.

'You'd better use my telephone here as I don't want the station to know what's going on tonight. Also, tell your fiancée we don't want to be chasing rainbows with all these Doodlebugs, guns firing and balloons about, although it would be great fun if we saw a Doodlebug while flying over New Malden, wouldn't it, Hamilton, and tip it over?' I quickly replied by saying that the Anson is not a fighter aircraft but a communications aircraft. 'Oh, well, it was a nice idea.'

'Yes, sir, but that would be impossible. I shall have enough to do as it is.'

The Station Commander said, 'You'd better get on the telephone. Take-off fourteen-thirty hours.'

I sat in his chair and dialled directly Barbara's telephone number at work. Luckily, she answered my call. 'Hello, darling, Donald here, how are you?'

171

'Pretty busy,' she replied. I told her the plan that I had been through with the Station Commander and that I would be flying over her house that evening in a twin-engined Anson between the hours of 1830 and 1900 hours. There was complete silence for a moment and then I said, 'Are you still there, darling?'

'Yes, I'm listening, dear. I love you and am always thinking about you in the dangerous job you're doing.'

I replied by telling her that since the visibility would not be good she should stand on a chair or box so that I could see her. 'I'll do two complete circuits in a clockwise direction, then fly straight over the road at 300 feet, subject to weather conditions at the time of arrival. I will be there, darling, take care. I love you.' Then we were cut off.

I left the Station Commander's office elated at being able to fly over Barbara's house, with the chance of seeing her. I thought 100 feet too risky, so I decided on 150 to 200 feet depending on the light and the tall trees I often used to walk under when taking Barbara home on one of our nights out together. Then, I thought if I flew parallel to the hill, instead of across it, we would be a lot safer. As I entered the Squadron office, I told the girls, Cynthia and Rosemary, the flight plan for the evening. They were highly delighted at being given the chance to go in the air. There were so many ground personnel who were not given the opportunity to fly, I personally felt the Royal Air Force let them down in a way because they well deserved the opportunity to do so.

I told them each to take a brown paper bag and two flasks of coffee and some sandwiches as we may have a late night out. 'You have ten minutes to get into that Anson parked over there in that dispersal.'

'Yes, sir,' Cynthia said ecstatically, and with that rushed to get the necessary food and drink. I left the office to go to the Operations Room to log my flight plan and find out how the weather would be over the Home Counties during our trip.

At 1430 hours we took off into a lovely blue sky with only the odd patch of cloud about. The Anson seemed heavy to control compared to the Spitfire but it was enjoyable to have a co-pilot and passengers on board. I could hear the two WAAFs singing their heads off as we climbed steadily into the sun. I thought it would be a great time to sunbathe on the beaches below but that was impossible since they were sealed off from the public. We climbed to 7,500 feet keeping a steady course. I did not want the girls to be afraid since it was the first flight for both of them and I kept this height in order to avoid the Flying Bombs and our own ack-ack fire which I might attract over the North Downs. In case the girls felt ill I had brought along a silver flask of brandy which my father gave me on my twenty-first birthday. The sun was still bright from the morning's sortie, so it was ideal weather conditions to fly in. The Anson felt like an old tank when using the rudder, otherwise she was quite a delight to fly. Her main role was one of communication and dropping secret agents into France. I suppose you could compare her to a miniature Wellington designed by Barnes Wallis. She was well liked by pilots flying her since she was stable and had a very good safety record. However, once trimmed she was stable to fly. We made our way to our destination at Bovingdon, a United States air force base a few miles from Hemel Hempstead, Hertfordshire. The Eighth American Air Force used the base as a training ground for aircrews manning Flying Fortresses before going operational over Europe.

In order to avoid the gun belt between East Grinstead and Maidstone I flew south of East Grinstead, over the cathedral city of Guildford, on to the industrial town of Slough and then over the stockbroker belt of Beaconsfield where my sister and brother-in-law managed a petrol station. I called up Bovingdon's control tower in order to let them know my co-ordinates and request their local frequency. This was answered in a broad Texan accent. They told me once I flew over the Chiltern town of Chesham I was to fly north 3 miles to Hemel Hempstead where I had to circle in a clockwise direction to await landing instructions from the local control.

It was a magnificent sight as we approached the airfield. The small villages on the fringe of the Chilterns were a spectacle in themselves with the undulating hills surrounding them. The runway sat on a plateau, was very long and was concrete which made a change from Hambridge which was all grass. Since I would have plenty of runway to spare on landing, I brought the Anson down very carefully in case my passengers at the back were worried and landed safely within the outer boundary which was the main Hemel Hempstead to Chesham Road. After coming to a halt I awaited local control instructions before proceeding on to their visitors' reception area.

The Station Commander was met by the American Station Commander in his jeep flying the United States flag. I was told to be ready to take off at 1830 to 1900 hours. The girls and I had the freedom of the base or we could do as we liked, so we decided to go outside the camp and visit the lovely village of Bovingdon, where a few months earlier Barbara and I had stayed the weekend when my uncle gave me his Standard 10 saloon car. I told the girls that Barbara and I had stayed at the High Croft Hotel, so it was agreed we should visit the old hotel and have a meal.

When we arrived we were greeted with the same professionalism as before. The receptionist remembered me and was delighted I was still flying and had returned with two WAAF guests. She said, 'You certainly like looking after the ladies.' I told her that we had just flown our Station Commander into Bovingdon and the two WAAFs in uniform were administrative personnel who helped me run my squadron. I told her we only had time for a meal since we were due back at the American air base by 1815 hours. I also told her that the girls had never flown before so that this was a real treat from the monotony of office work and that they deserved the opportunity to fly. She ordered free drinks for us, which was very kind of her, to show her gratitude to regular customers and showed us to a table in the lounge. The decor had not changed since Barbara and I spent that delightful weekend there a few months earlier, the memories of which

174

will always be with me.

We told the lady that due to our tight schedule we would like our meal served as soon as possible. I showed the girls the real red leather-bound hotel register with the famous names of Hollywood film stars such as Clark Gable and James Stewart. The girls' eyes lit up like watching a Guy Fawkes display when they saw the famous film stars who had stayed at or visited the famous hotel on the edge of the Chiltern Hills. Cynthia also noticed the names of Flying Officer and Mrs Hamilton in the register! 'Yes,' I said, 'that's when we stayed here for the weekend. It was just by chance that we found this lovely hotel while we were exploring the countryside in Hertfordshire.'

Cynthia said, 'Do you think any stars from Hollywood will be in here tonight?'

'No telling,' I replied, 'but since we have to leave here by eighteen hundred hours, my guess is that you won't see them. I suggest you go and ask the owner what is their usual time to visit the hotel.' This Cynthia did without hesitation, but she returned to our table with a gloomy face which said it all.

I told the girls that the hotel was heavily booked by American families whose husbands and boyfriends were serving at the base. Since it was a very small hotel close to the base, its accommodation was in great demand. Barbara and I had been lucky at the time of our arrival because one American family had just cancelled their booking. I explained to the girls that the Americans liked to organise regular visits by their husbands and boyfriends, which was not something we encouraged in the Royal Air Force. The pilots and aircrew had to arrange their own accommodation for their wives and families so that in the majority of cases the fiancées and wives were usually left behind in their own homes.

While we were waiting for the head waiter to show us to our table the girls wandered around looking intently at the pictures on the walls of the many famous celebrities who had visited the hotel over the years, especially those in the period 1939 to date. Eventually the head waiter approached me and said, 'Ah, Flying Officer Hamilton, good to see you again, sir,' as he led the three of us to our table. Cynthia very discreetly

175

told him that I was now a Squadron Leader leading 629 Squadron. The head waiter immediately approached me, apologised and congratulated me on my rapid promotion. I accepted his apologies and we got on with our meal since we were all very hungry.

After the meal we said our farewells and made our way down the country lane to our Anson at the American air base at Bovingdon. After doing my routine checks on the airframe, undercarriage, rudder, ailerons and elevator, and checking with the American gasline man that he had refuelled my aircraft, we awaited the arrival of our Station Commander. In the meantime I told the girls of my plan to fly over Barbara's house in New Malden on our return flight. They were delighted about the possibility of seeing her, even if it was only for a few moments. Eventually, the Station Commander arrived, and we took off into the setting sun on time at 1830 hours.

Staying mainly to the same route as we came on the outward journey, I flew at 6,000 feet due south to Windsor, and then east to Kingston upon Thames. Following the 213 bus route, which I knew so well after seeing Barbara home regularly, I arrived over New Malden where I circled at 3,500 feet to avoid the activity of other aircraft. Seeing no other air activity, I dropped the Anson to 1,500 feet and circled New Malden once more, taking extreme care of the high ground surrounding Coobe Hill. As we came over the hill the Station Commander yelled from the co-pilot seat, 'There they are, Donald, fifty degrees due west of us.' He seemed more excited than I was as I told the girls in the back to look west where the Morgan family and all their neighbours had gathered. I then dropped to 600 feet where I saw Barbara, her family and the whole bloody street which had turned out to see us. The road was a mass of people and flags flying as if it was a celebration to end the war. I circled once again and brought the nose of the aircraft into line with their road so that I could have a straight run over it at near stalling speed. I let my undercarriage down to reduce speed while over the road which consisted of very expensive detached houses owned by stockbrokers and

176

merchant bankers from the City.

I managed to get a glimpse of Barbara and her family before raising my undercarriage and putting on full boost to climb away steeply up to 6,000 feet. My main concern now after the excitement was the barrage balloon network which guarded the City of London so I climbed to 7,000 feet where I knew I would be safe and returned to Royal Air Force Hambridge. Rosemary and Cynthia both came forward to the flight cabin and said how wonderful it had been to see all the people below.

On arrival at base the Station Commander invited me to his office where he offered me a large whisky. 'Good flight that, Hamilton. I enjoyed it immensely. You kept away from those trees at Coobe Hill remarkably well considering we were so low. I think after your drink you'd better use my telephone and ring your fiancée and tell her you've arrived safely back at base.'

'Yes, thank you, sir,' I said as I hurriedly finished my drink and dialled Barbara's number. She came on the phone quickly as though she knew I would be calling. She said, 'Although I couldn't actually see you, I really felt your presence up there. I thought you were going to land on the road when you put your undercarriage down. It was great to see you fly. You make it look so easy. Was Cynthia on board? I could see some people waving white handkerchiefs behind you in the fuselage.'

'Yes,' I said, 'both the office girls were on board and the Station Commander was in the co-pilot's seat. I'm glad you enjoyed it, darling. I love you. Must go now. Will write soon. Bye for now,' and I put the receiver down.

On the way to the Squadron Office I met Andrew, Philip and Paul. 'Where the hell have you been? We've been looking all over for you for a game of cricket,' Andrew said inquisitively.

I replied, 'If you'd gone to the Ops Room you'd have known where I've been, taking the Station Commander on a cross-country run.' I also told them that I flew over Barbara's house with my undercarriage down.

Philip replied, 'You bloody fool – at low altitude? You could have killed them all including your audience.' After telling them that the Station Commander enjoyed it and that I'd had a real whisky in his office, we all went off to the bar to celebrate my successful sortie of the evening.

17

The next morning I received a message to report to the Station Commander's office with my two colleagues from Red Section of 629 Squadron – Sergeant Philip Tremeer and Flight Sergeant Paul Windross. When we arrived Wing Commander Ian Thraves was already there with him, several notes and maps in his hand, which were too bulky for him to hold easily.

'Good morning, gentlemen,' the Station Commander said, as we saluted in turn, 'please sit down.' As was his custom the CO offered us all a cigarette, which we refused, before lighting one for himself and settling down behind his large desk.

'Well, chaps, what I'm about to say is absolutely top secret and on no account must any of this information leak out.' We all agreed to comply with his order. 'Tomorrow, I have a very important sortie for you all to fly which has got to succeed. We must now defend our shores against another of Adolf Hitler's vengeance weapons, the Vergeltunswaffe Zwei, or V2 rocket, which is being manufactured at Usedom in northern Germany. Although the American Eighth Airforce Bomber Group have been hitting the underground concrete bunkers in daylight, at present due to the thickness of the concrete walls, the heavy flak and Luftwaffe fighter cover defending it, they've had heavy losses in trying to destroy it.'

He continued by standing up and walking up and down his office, smoking heavily and saying that the Chief of the Air Staff had decided that, due to the heavy losses incurred trying to bomb Usedom, we would go for their launching sites in Germany where the lethal V2 rockets were being launched.

He said we had just had news from local agents in Germany that a V2 rocket launching site had been built at Euskirchen, about 15 miles south-west of Bonn.

Whilst stomping up and down his office to relieve the pressure on his mind, the Station Commander said, 'The Chief of Staff has asked me, with the aid of Wing Commander Thraves, to organise one single attack on the rocket site, with a Mosquito Type Six from Four-One-Eight Squadron based at Middle Wallop. This aircraft will arrive this afternoon. The pilot's name is Brian Aston-Martin, the only son of Lionel Aston-Martin, the designer of the first Aston-Martin car at Brooklands, Surrey in the late Thirties. He is, in fact, the cousin of your Squadron Leader, Donald Hamilton. He'll stay the night here and will be loaded and bombed up by his own ground crew who are now on their way. Now that I've given you the outline of the op, code-named Operation Rocket, I'll hand you over to Wing Commander Thraves for further details.' The Station Commander sat down and lit up another Senior Service cigarette.

Wing Commander Ian Thraves then pinned up a large map of the South Coast of England, Belgium and Germany with colours pinpointing where evasive action should be taken against Luftwaffe fighters and heavy flak. He continued by saying we were going to escort the Mosquito which would not only bomb the rocket site at Euskirchen but also take as many photographs as it could. The aircraft would have its radar and electronics equipment removed in order that it could carry a full bomb load plus PR equipment.

'Your job, gentlemen, will be to draw off the heavy gun and machine-gun fire while he concentrates on dropping his bomb load and taking the necessary photographs. I suggest two of you from Red Section attack the flak positions at right angles to each other while he continues his specific job. This will confuse the gunners and give the Mozzie a chance of succeeding.

'I also suggest you examine the route detailed in your flight plan and take it with you. I further suggest you ensure you have in your Mae West some German, Dutch and Belgian money. Finally I must tell you that this is one of the most dangerous missions you may have to undertake, so I wish you all the best of luck under Squadron Leader Hamilton in destroying or trying to destroy this first V2 rocket site.' With that the Wing Commander gave us each a copy of our flight plan and sat down.

The Station Commander then said, 'Donald, your cousin has arrived, and I'd be grateful if you would go and meet him at your Squadron's dispersal at the end of this meeting. Secondly, just before you go, I have in my hand an urgent message which has just come in from the Chief of Staff of ADGB over the threat of the new Messerschmitt ME Two-Six-Two which has been seen occasionally over Germany.

'The message requests that everyone should take every opportunity of obtaining any information whatsoever about this twin-engined turbo jet aircraft. Intelligence reports are weak and infrequent over the details of another one of Adolf Hitler's new weapons. This is of great importance and from any sightings of it you must report as much information as you can on Germany's first jet aircraft. Believe you me, if this jet aircraft becomes operational, not only could it outspeed, outmanoeuvre and shoot down any Allied aircraft with its tremendous firepower, but it would give the Luftwaffe air supremacy just like the early days of the war.

'It's been reported through German propaganda forecast, that this new jet fighter has the speed, manoeuvrability and firepower to create very serious problems for the Allied Air Forces. The German fighter ace Adolf Galland has piloted one of the prototypes and is supposed to have said that it's a beautiful plane to fly and that all German aircraft factories should stop making conventional aircraft and switch to manufacturing it. However, because Adolf Hitler was determined to make this versatile new plane into a bomber, and not a fighter, as was originally intended, various technical problems have subsequently put its operational date back by several months.

'I enclose all known information in this envelope and am now going to give you the strictest instruction to memorise it and burn it before you take off tomorrow morning at oh-five-hundred hours. That's all, gentlemen, and good luck.'

With that we all got up, put our caps on, saluted and marched towards the Station Commander's door. 'Oh, Donald, good luck for tomorrow,' he said as he sat down at his desk.

'Thank you, sir,' I replied as I shut the door behind me. When we got back to the dispersal, a young Flying Officer and his Flight Lieutenant Navigator were sitting with Cynthia having a cup of coffee in the Squadron Office.

'Good to see you, Brian, after all these years,' I said. 'How are you?'

'I'm fine, Donald,' he replied. 'Did you know your Uncle Lionel has just died working on his latest Aston-Martin model?'

'No, I didn't, Brian, I'm indeed very sorry to hear the news. Give Auntie Katherine my deepest condolences and love when you next speak. You must both come to my wedding,' I said.

'Wedding, what wedding?' Brian replied as he sipped his hot coffee.

'I am going to marry Barbara on my next leave in August, if she will have me.'

'That's great news, Donald. I congratulate you, also the good news of your rapid promotion to Squadron Leader and your award of the DFC. Well done.'

I invited them all into my office and said, 'Coffee for all please, Cynthia,' as I looked at her beautifully shaped legs.

When we were all comfortably seated, I introduced my cousin and his navigator to Red Section. They all shook hands and sat down as Cynthia in the meantime brought in coffee in china mugs. 'Well, gentlemen, we all know what we have to do tomorrow at Euskirchen, south of Bonn. I suggest we take off at oh-five-hundred hours so that we have the element of surprise in our favour as I don't want us to wake up those Luftwaffe fighter pilots too early around Maastricht, Valkenburg, Gutesloh and Cologne. Flying Officer Aston-Martin will get bombed up at oh-three-hundred hours so we should all be ready to take off on time.

182

'I suggest that due to the speed of the Mozzie, Brian should lead the attack since he has a little more horsepower under his cowling than we do. Paul will cover his portside wing, I will cover his starboard. Philip will fly above us at seven thousand feet in case we have a gaggle of Me One-Oh-Nines trailing us.' Everyone nodded their agreement.

I continued, 'The only way we're going to be successful on this op is to let Brian make a straight run onto his target while Paul and I cause a diversion by firing at the flak emplacements. We'll do this at forty-five degrees to the Mozzie, but Paul and I will be ninety degrees to each other. In this way the diversion should be effective enough for the Mozzie to carry out its precision bombing on the target site. Paul and I will attack the gun positions and cause havoc for the German gunners twenty seconds after the Mozzie starts its bombing runs.' They all agreed after I'd run through the plan on the old school blackboard with the thinnest piece of chalk you could ever imagine. Any schoolmaster would have thrown it in the bin!

'After our attack I suggest we return over Duren but take a northerly course through Holland to keep away from the heavy flak around Maastricht and Aachen. Once we get into the flatlands of Holland we should be well away from the Luftwaffe and the flak.

'Well, gentlemen, that is all except for a very special treat.' I then unlocked the drawer containing Barbara's letter, her rose, my DFC medal and a bottle of real malt whisky. Paul went out and asked Cynthia to bring in five glasses, water and lemonade. Within minutes these had arrived and I poured a double Scotch for everybody because I had a gut feeling about this mission. I told them that morning tea would be at 0330 hours the next day, breakfast at 0400 and to be in the Operations Room by not later than 0430 hours. They all thanked me for the drink, saluted and dispersed. Rosemary had already made arrangements for accommodation for our two guest flyers so I asked Andrew and Cynthia to come in and have a drink with me before I started my paperwork. They both came in, saluted and sat down whilst I poured out their drinks.

'Andrew,' I said, 'if I fail to return tomorrow, I want you to take this letter to Barbara personally in New Malden.' With that tears began to trickle slowly down Cynthia's rosy cheeks so I offered her my handkerchief and told her to get a grip of herself. Andrew promised to deliver my letter and I went on, 'Andrew, I've confirmed with the Chief of ADGB and the Station Commander that your Combat Commission has been approved with effect from today.' They were both delighted with the news. Personally, as the Squadron Commander, I considered that he richly deserved his commission. I shook hands with them both, Cynthia embraced me and kissed me lightly on the cheek and Andrew squeezed me like a wrestler. With that they left my office. As soon as the door was closed I put my telephone on 'secret' and telephoned Barbara who straight away answered my call.

'Hello, darling, it's me, Donald. I've only a few minutes but I must talk to you now,' I said in a sombre voice.

'Yes, it's me, darling, what are you doing ringing me at this time of day? Are you coming home tonight?' she said excitedly.

'No, darling, I'm afraid I can't as I have an important mission tomorrow.' With that I could hear her deep breathing on the telephone line. 'All I want to say is that I love you very dearly and I will always love you. I want you to marry me in August. I've written to your father. Will you please marry me?'

She replied, 'Yes, darling, in August. I've already spoken to Mummy and Daddy and they're delighted', and then there was silence.

'Darling, if I fail to return from my mission tomorrow it is not to say that I shall not be coming back. I love you very dearly. Remember the happy memories we've shared recently. They will always be with you.' With that I could hear her voice rapidly changing. 'Please remember me as I am. I know I've put you on a pedestal, but you were my first and only true love, which throughout my life I shall cherish. Be a good girl, be brave and I will ring you at lunchtime tomorrow. My cousin Brian is flying with us.'

I could hear her voice becoming more and more despondent as she replied, 'I understand, my darling, and I'll be thinking of you tomorrow; please come back to me, you're all I have in the world. God bless you, I love you so dearly and wear your engagement ring with affection and pride. Goodbye, darling,' and she blew kisses down the phone which I put down slowly. I felt gutted, and was beginning to feel very nervous about our next mission but was pleased that I'd made the call to her to warn her of the dangers we would face in the morning.

After another Scotch, I put the bottle with Barbara's letter, my medal and a letter of introduction for Andrew, although he'd met Barbara at the Buckingham Palace Investiture. I then locked the drawer, gave the key to Cynthia, completed my daily reports and left some typing for her. She was still in tears and I hated seeing her so upset, but that's how it is in wartime. She was not only an excellent secretary, but also a trusted friend.

The steward woke me on the dot of 0330 hours with a nice cup of tea, laid out my flying gear, got the hot water ready to shave and polished my boots.

I put several foreign currencies which Barbara had previously obtained from the bank into my Mae West. These included French francs, Belgian francs, Dutch guilders and German Deutschmarks. I pocketed my map of the operation and after the steward had left the roon I went to my drawer and for the first time in the war I put my Colt 45 revolver and ammunition in my waistband holder which my mother had sewn for me on my first leave. I checked the compass in my second button, and with that I left my room via the Mess for breakfast before going on to the Operations Room where I met up with the rest of the team.

After a final briefing we boarded our aircraft which the ground crew had prepared and let the Mozzie take off first because of her high rate of climb. The Mozzie, as the Mosquito was called, was a terrific aircraft and made an immeasurable impact on the enemy. It was first designed in the late thirties at Hatfield, Hertfordshire, however it took the Air Ministry years before they accepted it after seeing the prototype fly in November 1940. The Chiefs of Staff thought it was a great aeroplane which the Royal Air Force badly needed, both as a fighter and a bomber. It was based on Barnes Wallis's Wellington bomber airframe, was built mainly of wood and the airframe was a sandwich of a low density core bonded on each side to load-bearing skins. It was driven by two Rolls Royce Merlin engines with paddle blade props and it had a range of approximately 1,860 miles due to fuel being stored in its belly plus wing drop tanks. Its speed fully laden was approximately 320 miles per hour with a top speed of 425 mph, while its ceiling height of 36,000 feet outweighed that of the Messerschmitt.

The Mozzie was extremely fast and manoeuvrable and flew over England and Europe with impunity. It had a crew of two and its armament was impressive with cannon, machine-guns and bombs. One famous raid was the attack the Mosquito made on the prison at Amiens in France which liberated many resistance workers who escaped through its shattered walls.

Once the Mozzie was airborne, Red Section took off on a beautiful sunlit July morning. The sun was just rising above the horizon giving me an inherent feeling of confidence and inspiration as we headed out over the English Channel although I was hoping there would be cloud cover for us over the target area.

We flew at 250 feet to avoid radar detection, crossed the enemy coast at Ostend and flew on to Bruges, Mederin, and turned slightly east at Maastricht where we knew there were enemy fighter squadrons and heavy flak positions. Crossing the German border at Valkenburg we made for the town of Duren where we turned south-east to the rocket site at Euskirchen.

Over the R/T I ordered Philip to climb to 7,000 feet and monitor the air above us while Paul and I aligned ourselves behind the Mosquito in order to give its navigator, Flight Lieutenant Wilson, 20 seconds to line up his target on the rocket launching site and drop his bomb load. As we approached the site heavy flak started coming up at us from all around. I ordered Paul over the R/T to take up our planned positions so as to confuse the enemy – while the Mozzie by now was almost over the target. As I dived away to make a right angle and come in to attack the flak positions, I could see a huge orange glow below us seconds after the Mosquito dropped her bomb load and was climbing up to 3,000 feet. As ordered in the flight plan Paul and I let go with cannon and machine-gun fire at the heavily guarded rocket base. Suddenly, out of the bright blue sky, the Mozzie did a straight run with all its cannons blasting at the enemy flak positions before climbing back to its planned position of 30,000 feet. Paul and I dived once more, strafing the remaining storage tanks and buildings situated on the rocket launching site before climbing up to join the Mozzie which was in level flight at her predetermined height and on the way home.

Calling Philip as Bronco 2 to re-form, I could see he was diving to a low altitude from east to west firing at the site before joining us on our way home to base in England. Since the Mozzie could outspeed us now she had released her bomb load I ordered Brian to head for home independently and the Mozzie quickly climbed to her ceiling height of 36,000 feet to evade any Luftwaffe fighters which might be hanging about. 'Wilco, Bronco Leader,' Brian answered and that was the last time I saw my cousin.

The three Spitfire XIVs from 629 Squadron dropped lower and flew east of Duren to avoid the high ground at Hurtgenwald. We followed the River Ruhr over Hücklehoven where we saw slag heaps from the coal mines and tracked west into Holland. We flew over Dutch flatlands, passing the junction of two rivers, the Zuid Willemsvaan and the Wessem, both busy with barge traffic on its way to Maastricht. We then crossed the main road from Eindhoven to Roermond and it was at Leende that Paul called me over the R/T to say he had spotted a long convoy of large German trucks travelling south and carrying German soldiers, heavy tanks and fuel. I told Paul we should have enough fuel and ammunition to attack and he quickly agreed after confirming his own fuel and ammunition state. I ordered Red Section to attack the convoy singly at 30-second intervals. Philip made his initial run in and all hell was let loose as it immediately became apparent that this convoy was of some importance to the German army – the lorries were heavily protected by light guns and machine-guns.

Weaving in and out of the flak on his approach Philip opened fire on the forward trucks setting fire to several of them. German soldiers were abandoning their trucks like passengers from a sinking ship as they jumped off the sides into the dykes adjacent to the road. Several trucks had opened up their canopies and were firing at us from machine-guns mounted on pedestals.

Paul went in next at a very low altitude, strafing the machine-guns and luckily hit the rear lorries which must have been loaded with fuel. Within seconds a mushroom cloud of orange fire, followed by thick black smoke, funnelled up at us into the bright blue sky.

As I circled the convoy, the German gunners were so accurate it was too dangerous to stay around. I dived to a low altitude, firing on the remaining vehicles and after completing my pass I climbed steeply to get well clear. As I turned my head to look behind me all I could see was orange fire, black smoke and burning vehicles with German soldiers lying injured or dead in the road.

But as I climbed away, my engine spluttered, coughed and misfired. I started to lose power slowly and I soon realised I had an engine failure. I could see small flames flickering out of my engine and onto my windscreen and the cockpit was getting unbearably hot and uncomfortable, so I decided to take my bearings and carry out my ditching drills as practised at Royal Air Force Rednal. Below me, as I circled, was Dutch flatland, with a lake large enough to land in so I decided to aim for it now that the flames were getting stronger and fiercer and I was really losing engine power drastically by the second.

Calling on May Day frequency I told Broncos 1 and 2 that I was ditching and gave them my co-ordinates. I heard a faint reply from Paul saying that they'd been attacked by several Me 109s. I wished them good luck still calling out 'May Day, May Day' over the R/T. As I concentrated on ditching my stricken Spitfire the fire in the engine was so intense that it cracked my windscreen with the black smoke getting thicker and more dense in my cockpit as the seconds ticked by. I quickly adjusted my Mae West, tightened my seat straps and opened the top of the cockpit leaving my port side door closed. Reducing speed I checked my undercarriage was up and gently steered my plane into the lake which appeared to be about three or four miles in length. On impact there was one almighty explosion with steam evaporating all over the engine and cockpit.

Quickly I undid my seat straps, opened the port side door, grabbed hold of the very hot cockpit frame and climbed out onto the port wing. Luckily the plane was still afloat. Taking no chances, I inflated my Mae West, held my Colt 45 with its ammunition above me and slid into the cold water of the lake. Within seconds of leaving the Spitfire, the weight of the engine tipped the nose of the plane downwards into the water and she sank peacefully straight away leaving no trace of an oil slick. I swam as fast as I could away from the aeroplane to avoid being sucked down as the Spitfire sank to the bottom of the lake.

With my Mae West inflated and my leather sheepskin-lined flying jacket keeping me tolerably warm I swam to the side of the lake where there were some large reeds, and decided to hide in them as they were dense, tall and gave good cover. It was then I noticed that my right hand and arm up to my elbow were badly burnt. It became increasingly painful but I thought if I kept putting it into the water it would cool the skin down – just as they had taught me at the Advanced School of Training.

I kept very quiet and still in case there were German soldiers out looking for me. In any case I was hoping that Paul and Philip had received my May Day message and would come over at low level to search for me, but unfortunately there was no sign of either of them. My legs were absolutely freezing and the pain in my right arm was becoming unbearable.

On the other side of the reeds there were marshes and flatland which led to a canal. Since there seemed to be no activity about, I struggled out, dashed like hell across a field and jumped into the canal. On resurfacing I saw a number of large barges which I guessed were about 100 feet or more in length. I decided to swim to the first one where I clung to the guy ropes, which were fastened to an anchor post, whilst still remaining in the water. After several minutes a woman came up to the stern of one of the barges with a large basket of washing. Swimming along the side of the vessel, and not meaning to frighten her, I whispered, '*Ik spreekt geen Nederlands?*' in a very poor Dutch accent. She did not hear me at first, so I repeated it again in a louder voice. This time she turned around but could not see me as I was in the water. When I shouted a third time she realised the voice was coming from the canal, so she came to the edge of the barge and said, '*Ga weg,*' in an amazing soft voice. I repeated, '*Spreekt u Engells/ Frans/Duits?*' She replied by saying she was Dutch and spoke a little English. Knowing she could speak a little English was very encouraging, so I told her I was a Major in the Royal Air Force and had crashed in the lake on the other side of the flatlands. As soon as she realised I was an English airman she hauled me aboard with a rope tied around my waist and greeted me with a smile.

She quickly got me out of sight by leading me downstairs to her beautifully clean galley in the stern of the barge. The woman, who must have been in her late twenties, sat me down on a chair at the table in the saloon. I told her that I had a severely burnt right hand and forearm. She asked me where I had crashed and I showed her on my map which was soaking wet. I told her the lake was on a plateau east of here on the other side of the marsh. She replied in broken English, 'Ah, that's Lake Peel De Veluwe.' She quickly went over to the galley door, which gave me a fright as I knew my revolver was possibly wet, as well as my ammunition which I had in my Mae West. However my nerves were settled when she brought out a large pair of scissors and started cutting away the right sleeve of my leather jacket. As soon as she saw the blackened

190

skin she said, 'You must see a doctor at once; the nearest from here is a surgery in Thorn, several kilometres from her. We must wait for my husband to come. There are many Germans in the area because we are near the Belgian and German borders.'

I asked politely, 'Is there any possibility of a hot drink or a bowl of hot soup?' as I had not eaten since 0400 hours. She went over to the sink, put the kettle on and brought over a large bowl of cold water with calamine lotion in it.

'Put your arm in this bowl for a few moments while I get you a bowl of soup.' While she was preparing my food she said her name was Miep Van Driel and her husband's name was Jan who belonged to the Dutch Resistance Movement. In the past he had helped several Allied airmen pass through Holland.

I asked her where her husband was now and she replied in broken English, 'At the frontier booking office registering the barge and crew. He has also gone shopping. We use bicycles around here, although they are in very short supply, as our main transport.'

She was very pleasant to talk to, with her white blouse showing her shapely breasts and a thick, black belt separating her blouse from her straight black skirt. She was very attractive even though she was heavily built with strong shoulders. Her facial skin and forearms were tanned by the outdoor life she led supporting her husband, her hair was auburn and her eyes were grey. I noticed that her forehead was heavily lined, rather unusual for such a young age. I was extremely relieved she spoke a little English since I could speak very little Dutch. Their coal hold in the bow of the barge was empty as they were on their way to Maastricht to fill up for the German Army in northern Holland. She had a mature mind and I guessed she did all the organising around the barge. She had a lovely smile like Barbara's.

After finishing my hot meal she told me to go to the stern, have a shower, change into Jan's spare clothing and hide in the engine room until he arrived home. In the meantime she would burn my clothing, keeping my watch, money, compass

191

and gun belt in her blanket box. She explained that the Germans often checked the barges for materials and identities of the crew aboard. They were strict on the curfew at 1900 hours. No barge or people could move after that time, otherwise they could be shot. I asked her where we were now, and she replied, *'Hoe Heet de ze Plaats.'* Also you are on the *Zuid Willemsvaam.'* I said in my poor Dutch, *'Doet de boot Thorn aan?'* (does the barge call at Thorn?). She replied, 'Yes, and we must get there in time to get you to the doctor's surgery before curfew, otherwise you are in grave danger of being captured without official papers or permits.'

After bathing my burnt hand and forearm we let the arm dry naturally and she covered it lightly with a dry bandage. I showed her my identity disc, Barbara's photograph and my revolver which I was now drying with towels and rags Miep had supplied me with. She said that I looked a real Dutchman in Jan's boatman's working clothes although they were slightly big around the chest and waist and she would shorten the length of the trousers as Jan was 6 feet tall against my 5 feet 8 inches. After talking to Miep I felt more relaxed as I sat studying my map while she began preparing the vegetables for their evening meal.

18

I must have gone to sleep on the floor in the engine room because the next thing I knew I was abruptly awakened by a heavy blow to my left shoulder. When my eyes had focused and my brain had begun to function, I realised that standing over me was a heavily built man, about six feet tall, with a flat black-peaked cap on. In his large tanned right hand he held my Colt 45 handgun which was about three inches from my perspiring forehead.

I realised I was trapped and lay motionless, as I did not know whether I was being threatened by a loaded revolver, or one which had no bullets in its chamber. The florid-faced, bearded gentleman did not introduce himself, so I did not know whether he was friend or foe. I decided to take no chances and lay perfectly still on the beautifully clean engine room floor until Miep arrived. I guessed he was either her husband or a friend, or maybe he was a Gestapo agent disguised as a Dutch seaman. What I did know was he posed a serious threat to me and to my escape plans back to England to rejoin my Squadron at Royal Air Force Hambridge. What worried me most was that Miep was nowhere to be seen.

'*Ik Kom Uit Engeland,*' I said in broken Dutch as he stood absolutely still above me. With no reply from him I repeated, '*Ich Flieger* from England.'

At last, after taking off his hat as a sign of friendship he replied, '*Ik Spreek een bee je Engeland,*' and he stepped backwards a few feet away from my exhausted body.

I replied, '*Begript U Mij?*' in a loud voice because I was getting agitated by my revolver still pointing directly at my forehead.

'Ja,' he said politely. In very slow English I asked him politely, to point the gun downwards towards the floor and also if I could sit up as I found my back was aching after lying motionless for some time. He said softly, *'Ja.'*

I replied, *'dat is heel vriendelijk,'* as I stood up, had a long stretch and completed my physical exercise by clasping my arms behind my head.

'Mag Ik u even wat vragen?'

The heavily tanned man, who looked to be in his early thirties, said as he stepped further backwards, *'Ja,'* in his native accent.

Suddenly, to my great relief Miep arrived with two jugs of piping hot coffee, which she gently laid down on the polished brass table adjacent to the steam engine. After greeting her down in that hot, unventilated compartment, which was small considering the size of the engine, I asked her quietly if she would tell her husband Jan to put my handgun down as it was still making me nervous and agitated. She replied hesitantly that she would ask Jan to put the gun down. As soon as she spoke he slowly put it in his waistband. She told him I was an English pilot who had crashed on the flatlands not far from here and also that I had behaved impeccably since I had arrived. 'He desperately needs medical attention for his badly burnt right hand and forearm.'

With that Jan put out his right hand as a gesture of goodwill and said, *'Graag Ge Daian,'* as at last a smile broke out on his rough lined face.

I replied, *'Spreekt U Engels?'* as I stood face to face with him.

'Ja, Ik Spreek een beetje Engels.'

I then asked him, *'Ik Wil Naar Thorn toe schen de Dokter,'* in the best Dutch I knew. The language was awfully difficult – no wonder they call it 'Double Dutch' in England.

Miep took hold of my right hand very gently and opened up the first round of bandage which she had so carefully administered earlier in the day. Jan replied in broken English, 'By God, he needs a doctor urgently, Miep,' and for the first time I saw an expression on his face which was almost of

194

concern. 'Miep, we must get up steam at once and get him to the nearest doctor at the surgery at Thorn. We will go by barge and then cycle to Thorn; in that way we can shorten his chances of capture by the Occupying Forces as the cycle ride is not too long from our anchorage at Thorn. I shall have to go ahead of him on the bicycle, keeping the usual distance of one hundred metres, with the doctor's guide between us. I can then go ahead and forewarn the doctor that we have a patient for him.'

With that he started the engine of the barge and ordered Miep to release the anchor ropes. He told me to stay where I was until he returned which I agreed to do as I realised for the first time I was amongst friends I could trust. I had been told in Blighty that the Dutch were a hard-headed race, but their resistance to the Krauts was second to none.

Within a few minutes, we were moving off and gathering speed. Jan invited me up to the galley while Miep was at the helm, with the big barge moving powerfully along the canal. He invited me to sit down and offered me a large tot of Asbach brandy for which I thanked him. 'That's a very serious burn you have there Major, and we must get to the doctor at Thorn before curfew commences at seven. With a bit of luck we should make it with Miep at the helm. She is an excellent bargee. We often get visits from the Germans so, as long as we do not get interrupted by them or the Gestapo, we should make it with a few minutes to spare. If you are on the streets after curfew, they will shoot you on sight.' This message sent cold chills down my spine. At first hand I was realising what bastards the Germans were.

I asked him if I could have my handgun back and he gently withdrew it from his waistband, as if it was loaded, and handed it to me. 'It's not loaded,' he smiled. He then showed me what the Gestapo had done a year earlier when they put a sharp knife through his right leg whilst interrogating him over the escape of an American Colonel attached to the Eighth Air Force in England. Jan had met him on the eastern plains of Holland while he was on the run from an air raid over Cologne in Germany. He explained he had helped several

Allied airmen pass through Holland and was a leading member of the local Dutch Resistance group based at Thorn where I was heading for medical treatment.

Feeling trapped, lonely and with no friends was a devastating feeling for Allied aircrew after being shot down. Since arriving on board the barge and especially having met Miep's husband, I felt that the Dutch people, although very helpful when they discovered you were a genuine Allied airman, were a hard race. They seemed to run their underground movement efficiently and took as many precautions as they could to protect themselves from false information and German infiltrators. Within the past few hours they had impressed me with their precautions, because not only was my life at stake, but more importantly their lives were in danger from the Nazis. We had been taught by a Dutchman at a seminar in England that if we walked or cycled in Holland, or in any of the occupied countries, we should let our guides walk, or cycle, a hundred metres ahead in order to give us ample warning if there was anything wrong.

I felt grateful that I had met such a conscientious couple who were prepared to give their lives for my freedom. I wondered what would have happened if we had been occupied by the Nazis in June 1940, when we were so vulnerable, and if Jan had been the airman shot down and I was the bargee on the Grand Union Canal at Hemel Hempstead. Would I be acting the same as Miep and Jan? It was a very difficult question to answer. We in the United Kingdom had never been occupied. Jan and Miep had been governed by the German occupying forces for four years and so there was a tremendous difference between us. They had been occupied twice in under three decades by the same enemy through no fault of their own and had suffered much since 1940. Many thousands of their people had been killed and the damage to Rotterdam in particular was indescribable as Jan explained to me how they had suffered under the Germans since their occupation in 1940.

Nevertheless I was wary of my hosts. Frequently the Gestapo had acted as owners of barges of this type, and so far, except for their apparent sincerity, I had no proof they either owned or rented the barge. Jan came over to me while I was deep in thought and said, 'I am sorry I frightened you down there in the engine room, but we have to be so careful. When we have decided that you are an Allied airman, we try to help as best we can but our resources are low and our security unsatisfactory. We can't, for obvious reasons, take on the whole German Army or even the German occupying forces in Holland, but we do try to disrupt them at frequent intervals and make a nuisance of ourselves as often as possible. The United Kingdom, from London, gives us regular orders and we try to carry them out to the best of our ability. We attack trains carrying German troops and equipment and also supply convoys, which daily pass this route, since the German High Command are now pulling first-line troops back to their native country.

'However, you should understand that we take the same risks of imprisonment as you do. On the other hand to strike a balance between friend and foe, we bring them coal, give them cigarettes and chocolate and our famous lager. Some Germans we befriend in order to maintain a bond between us so that we can get chaps like you back to England for you to fight again against the common enemy. Generally, those whom we have befriended treat us fairly well, but we must always remember that they are our enemy and I have no doubt that I would not hesitate to shoot any one of them if the need arose. I have been lucky up to now and Miep and I are still free and well. But the slightest hiccup in our operations could leave us in a very serious position. We trust no one, not even our friends. In that way we stay alive.

'It is the Gestapo, in their plain black leather coats, or in their black uniforms with the prominent black swastika armband on their left arm, who threaten the families of Holland most.' He warned me not to underestimate them.

'They are evil, clever and threatening to us and to you. They have a habit of asking you for a light or for some trivial information, but behind their questioning there is always a motive. So be very careful what you say. The less you say the

197

better for all of us. When we get you to the surgery at Thorn we must get your badly injured arm and hand treated. Then we must get some identification papers for you professing you to be a Dutch seaman bringing in coal for the German Army and also, I suggest, a permit, so that you work on call, as an electrician, at the German coal mine at Hücklehoven, which is not far over the border in Germany. In that way we can get you medically treated for your arm and you can go to and fro without risk, as you please. You speak quite good German and a little Dutch which will help you immensely if you are questioned.

'I suggest your name be Mijnheer Jos de Boer from now on. Doctor Chenneviere, a New Zealander, who is one of our main activists, will have better ideas about your future. You are in very capable hands, young man. She is a widow, whose late husband was a Captain in the French Army and was killed defending Paris. Her uncle Doctor Coen de Bruin is the owner of the practice. When her husband was killed, Doctor Chenneviere fled to Holland since she was trapped in Paris and could not escape to England as was her intention. She is a devoted doctor and we think highly of her, both as a person and for her medical abilities. She is also a specialist in obstetrics and gynaecology and delivers babies at the German hospital in Wassenburg, a few miles across the Dutch-German border. With her free pass between borders she can do wonders for us, especially with drugs and highly confidential German information which patients under her care inadvertently give her. Also she is friendly with a senior Luftwaffe airman, who gives us vital information on the Luftwaffe's strength, squadron movements and their daily operational sorties which we pass on to London by a transmitter sited behind the surgery in the Abbey at Thorn.

'Another task Doctor Sylvie Chenneviere has to do by direct orders from Heinrich Himmler is to deliver babies through his horrifying Lebenborn scheme, that is to produce an Aryan race untainted with any alien or Jewish blood. Himmler's scheme in 1937 was to produce a non-Jewish population of

198

Germans with blue eyes and blond hair, who would not only rule the occupied countries of Europe, but would also make up the balance of the German population which was expected to fall due to heavy casualties in the Second World War. Women of all ages were taken from as far afield as Poland and accommodated in "Baby Farms". Here they were well fed and comfortably housed and forced to produce babies by genetic selection to create a master race of Aryan people which would be German, and ruled over by Himmler.'

Jan continued, 'They used selected SS officers and senior officers of the Luftwaffe and the German Army. Himmler, who was Head of the SS and the Gestapo, told the German people that he intended to take German blood from any source that he could. To inaugurate his "Baby Farms" he commandeered hospitals throughout the occupied countries, espcially Poland. Doctor Chenneviere, an experienced obstetrician and gynaecologist, has just been ordered by the German High Command to be a consultant at the baby clinic just across the border at Wassenburg. She has been provided with the equivalent of a senior SS officer's pass, which gives her freedom beyond all expectations. It is a great asset to the local Dutch Resistance Movement since it gives us the freedom of movement after curfew time. Her pass from Himmler is invaluable to both you and me. However, it is not completely foolproof due to infiltrators and German agents. But that is the risk one takes on any exercise or military operation. Another important game which Doctor Sylvie plays is the one between gaining the trust and the confidence of the German High Command in the area and the amount of information she actually obtains from senior officers whom she befriends. She even found out about vital troop movements by rail and the Me 262 project. She also has a wealth of information on both the German vengeance weapons including the new sites in Belgium and Holland.'

As soon as I heard Jan mention both of these subjects, I asked him what he knew. He said although he had only seen the new jet fighter once, the Resistance Movement was correlating information at this time to send to London and they had a member of their group actually working as an engineer on the project. He said that Adolf Hitler had told the German nation that this new jet-propelled fighter would save Nazi Germany, turning defeat into victory, with the support of his vengeance weapons. He even told the German people that this new fighter would rule the skies over Europe once again. Jan continued, saying that they had seen it fly very low at high speed over the Maas River. I decided not to show too much interest so that I could hear other people's views, especially Dr Sylvie, before my report went back to London. I needed really to see the plane for myself in the sky, and to judge its manoeuvrability. Also, I needed to know more technical details about its maximum speed, ceiling height and weaponry.

Jan said, 'Once we have anchored at Thorn, I will get our Resistance courier, a twenty-three-year old musical student helping Doctor Chenneviere, to accompany you by bicycle to the Doctor's surgery at Thorn. She is a very pleasant girl, highly confident and with a sweet smile. However, she is very shy, but when she gains your trust and confidence you will find her to be a true friend. In the past she has endangered her own life for the sake of Allied airmen escaping through Holland. Even with her experience at such a young age you may think from her youthful appearance that she has not got the ability to carry out her orders from the Commander of the Resistance Movement, but believe you me, you are in safe hands, as her outstanding record shows. If captured she would rather die than betray us. She works as an assistant nurse at the Doctor's surgery. I shall cycle a hundred metres ahead of you both so that if there are any problems I can let you know.

'My courier, Anneke Van Rhoon, whose height is five feet, of slim build and a well-tanned body, will meet you here at the barge. The code name will be "Rose". She will wear black trousers, a black leather coat and a green beret. She has a scar on her face due to a major automobile accident. You can borrow Miep's bicycle and I would be grateful if you could leave it at the Doctor's when you have finished with it. The bicycle is not too stable, but with a bit of luck it will get you to your destination. Do not go too fast as frequently the chain comes off. In fact, if you get into trouble either with the bicycle or the Wehrmacht, tip your bicycle upside down and stand it on the handlebars. This will give a warning to Anneke that you are in danger. If this happens, you will be on your own. Otherwise she will constantly monitor your progress. She will only leave you if her life is in danger which is the general philosophy of the Movement. If a German approaches you while you have your bicycle upside down, curse in German or Dutch, preferably in German. If you feel confident that the danger is over, wipe it with the cloth in your basket to give the signal to Anneke that all is well. She will then proceed thirty metres ahead of you to the surgery at Thorn.

'When she gets to the house, she will cycle on but will take off her green beret when she is opposite the surgery. That's your signal to take yourself and the bicycle to the front door and ring the bell. The maid or man servant will answer the door. When you greet him or her say "Rose" and they will then know that I have sent you. Anneke will join you later. She will divert anybody following you by going to another address in Thorn. This is a safeguard we all have to undertake, since you do not know in this country who is following you. It could be Germans, the Quislings, the Collaborators or the implanted Gestapo. When you get into the surgery, you will be in good hands.'

Jan continued by saying, 'After an initial examination they will hide you in Thorn Abbey, which is only a short distance from the surgery. I expect they will have to treat you for many days or weeks with that arm of yours if you do not want to lose it.'

This statement of Jan's frightened me beyond belief. Barbara would not like that, making love to a one-arm bandit! Still, I was in their medical care in an occupied country where I had only Jan and Miep as trusted friends, who were taking great risks from the Gestapo and giving me all their kind attention which I deeply appreciated.

Jan's final words before we took off on our decrepit bicycles were that whatever I thought, I must do as they say, as their lives were at risk. He continued by saying that they had a proud record of getting Allied airmen back to their bases in England. 'Sometimes it takes weeks, sometimes months. You have got to be patient. You have to leave your future with us. Miep has already told me you want to get back home to marry your fiancée in August. With a bit of luck you might make it. But on no account can we, as a resistance movement, guarantee it. We know the Allied Armies have landed in Normandy, but there is nothing to say they are going to be here next month, or even next year. You have to be patient! Before we depart from the barge, here is a large brandy which will take the sting out of your pain for a while until we reach Thorn.'

'Yes,' I replied gratefully as I gulped it down in one go which burnt my throat. The pain in my arm was excrutiating. Jan then went on to say he would have to take my photograph at the surgery as time was getting short in order to beat the curfew at 7 p.m. This I agreed to since I wanted to get on my way as soon as possible and it was important at this stage to get my official documents as a bona fide resident and seaman. It would be suicidal to travel around Holland without them but we had to get to Thorn first. A nun who worked closely with Jan produced false documents to perfection because before she entered the House of God she was employed by the Dutch Civil Service in their Passport Office.

Jan said, 'Don't forget you are Jos de Boer, a Dutch seaman, and part time, you help the Germans as a qualified electrical engineer at their coal mine just across the border from Roermond, at Hücklehoven. For God's sake be on your guard. You have not met a German face to face; only from the air, so be careful what you say. The Germans are everywhere. If you are unfortunately stopped, stop instantly, otherwise they will shoot you. Speak out loudly in the best German voice you can. If you shout at them repeatedly they don't like it. If they persist, give them the lager and cigarettes I have put under a white cloth in the front basket on Miep's bicycle. Don't say anything unless you have to and if they question your bandaged arm, say that a steam valve blew on you in the engine room of the barge carrying coal for the Germans and you are on your way to Thorn to receive vital medical treatment. Keep cool and behave as a Dutch seaman on barges from Amsterdam to Maastricht. Miep has done a wonderful job in dressing you up as a Dutch seaman, so act like one. We must now go, Jos, otherwise we will not beat the curfew.' With that, after picking up my worldly possessions from Miep, including my revolver which had been strapped to my left ankle, I said my farewells to her. Instantly she embraced me, kissed me on the cheek and bade me good luck.

'Jan,' she said to her husband, 'I think he takes the part well in your Dutch seaman's clothes.'

Jan replied, 'He will do,' and with that we commenced our cycle ride to Thorn with our guide Anneke cycling between us.

Whilst I was cycling along the footpath on Miep's old bicycle, I wondered whether back home Cynthia had given Andrew my letter to Barbara to deliver to New Malden. With my May Day signal and being well overdue by now, the Wing Commander Flying would have sent my parents the dreaded and most common telegram of the war, 'missing presumed killed'. Jan, Anneke and I pedalled on uninterrupted on our way to Thorn. What Germans we did see, and there were many, were either chatting up the local girls or scrounging luxuries such as cigarettes, Dutch lager or home-grown tobacco. Eventually, just before curfew time, we arrived at the surgery at Thorn. Anneke indicated the house by taking off her green beret before going on to elude any Germans or collaborators who may have been following us. This was standard practice with the Resistance Movement.

The surgery was a very large Dutch house with white walls painted from basement to roof. The wooden windows desperately needed a coat of paint to prevent further deterioration. The house was white as most other houses were in this charming small town situated in the northern part of

Limburg, close to the Belgian border. Like us in the United Kingdom the street lamps were mainly supplied by gas.

As I pressed the doorbell below the brass plate which showed that not only was it Thorn surgery but also listed the names of the doctors. The heavy, wooden, glass-panelled door quickly opened and I was faced with a maid dressed in the usual attire. I said in a whispering voice the code name 'Rose' which Jan had given me on the barge. As soon as I said it the maid quickly ushered me into the surgery, closed the door and laid me down on the reclining examination table. In broken English she said, 'I'll go and hide your bicycle, and tell the nursing staff you are here.' As she turned towards the door she gave me a sweet smile and disappeared down the hallway. It was many minutes before Anneke entered the surgery in the bright, white starched uniform of a nurse. On her uniform were several badges showing her qualifications.

'Are you all right and comfortable?' she said with a nice smile. 'I am Jan's niece and I help here full-time, being a qualified nurse. I will get you a nice strong coffee as soon as I can.' As she undid the bandage to my right arm very gently, she showed her concern at the severity of my injury. Her slim fingers shook slightly and her sparkling hazel eyes lost their sparkle. She laid Miep's bandage in a sterilised chromium bowl and replaced it with a new one. 'I'll get the Doctor as soon as I can. They know you are here.'

She turned slowly and gave me a pleasant smile. She was very small in stature, about five feet tall, and her weight about eight stone as Jan had said. She wore no lipstick which I supposed was a luxury they could neither afford nor obtain. I thought how very attractive she was. Her strands of blonde hair hanging below her shoulders suited her weight and build but she seemed a very shy and private person.

Soon she came back with a piping hot jug of coffee on a silver tray and gently placed my injured arm on the arm rest attached to the bed. While trying to sip my coffee she was busily taking my pulse and temperature and making me more comfortable with more pillows so that I could recline in a

204

comfortable position. She then produced a chart asking me my date of birth, height and weight and hung it at the end of the bed, name – 'Jos de Boer', occupation – 'seaman'.

Going over to the other side of the surgery she sat down at the Doctor's table which was beautifully handmade from solid mahogany. Why, I thought, do Dutch people always build such heavy domestic or office furniture? Suddenly the silence was broken by the ringing of the black telephone situated on the Doctor's desk. Anneke answered it and after a short conversation in Dutch, she replaced the receiver on its cradle. 'I have to attend to another patient, Jos, so I will leave you in the good hands of the doctors. See you later.' She left, closing the surgery door behind her. Being left alone my thoughts began to wander. This was the first time I had been on my own since crashing into the lake. Being in a strange house seemed eerie, not knowing the occupants. I could not help thinking of home. I asked myself what I would be doing if I had been enjoying an evening with Andrew on his crutches and the lads from the Squadron. I only hoped Paul and Philip had escaped the gaggle of Messerschmitts. Then there was my darling Barbara, who by now must have received the bad news from my parents from the Wing Commander, all alone with her thoughts, wondering whether I was alive, a prisoner, or dead. Until I saw Jan I would not know the answers to these questions. I seemed to have lain there for hours on my own, but in fact it was only a few minutes, when I heard the rustle of steps outside the surgery which alerted my attention. Was it Anneke returning to look after me, or was it the Doctor I was expecting, or a German officer in need of medical attention? Since it was the major surgery for miles around, anybody could be visiting the Doctor's surgery. It could be friend or foe, and with that I withdrew my revolver from the holster strapped to my left leg and put it under my pillow just as a precaution. Many German officers popped into the surgery either on a social visit or requiring medical attention. It could even be a local Dutchman requiring help. On no account could I take chances since Anneke had left to attend to another patient. The door opened slowly, my heart beat faster and my legs turned to jelly from fear of the unknown. Until the panelled glass door opened my heart sank to my knees, but it was a beautiful woman in her late twenties wearing a starched white coat and with a stethoscope around her neck; my panic eased. As she closed the door I realised she was a doctor of some sort. She approached me as I relaxed and withdrew my left hand from the revolver which was lying beside me. She came closer to me and I could see that she had a thermometer, slimline torch, and a stainless steel pen clipped to her left outside pocket. Seeing the words 'Dr Chenneviere' on the name tag on her right lapel, I relaxed completely from the tension which had built up to unnecessary proportions when I first heard her footsteps down the hall. She introduced herself in a New Zealand accent as Dr Sylvie Chenneviere and asked me pointedly what my code name was. I replied by saying 'Rose'.

'Ah,' she replied, 'you must be Jan's friend; we've been waiting for you.'

'Yes,' I replied quietly. 'Actually I'm Squadron Leader Donald Hamilton of 629 Squadron based in England. I was shot down over the flatlands near Jan and Miep Van Driel this morning while I was strafing a military convoy near Someren.'

With that she smiled. 'Jan has given us all the information we need except he did not tell us you were decorated for gallentry by attacking the V1 launching sites in northern France. You're young to be a Squadron Leader?'

I answered, embarrassed. 'In wartime you die quickly and if you're in the right place at the right time you get promoted quickly. Remember, the life span of a Spitfire pilot is three weeks.'

'Is that so?' she said with surprise. 'Jan says you have a badly burnt hand and forearm so I suggest we remove Anneke's bandage and have a look at it.' With that she replaced my arm on an arm rest attached to the couch and proceeded to remove the dressing. When she had finished she quickly went over to a locked cabinet, withdrew a syringe and injected me with a small dose of morphine. 'This will help the pain. It's in short supply so I can only inject a certain amount for you. I steal it from the German hospital in Wassenburg when I am on duty there.'

The morphine soon eased the pain and I became a bit sleepy whilst I lay on the couch and I was physically exhausted from a long and hectic day. She said I had third degree burns which needed urgent attention by a plastic surgeon and that she would get Doctor Coen de Bruin, the owner of the practice, to have a look at them as soon as he had finished that evening. 'In the meantime I'll make you some more coffee.'

About thirty minutes later the surgery door suddenly opened and in came a white-coated doctor with frizzled fair hair, tinted on the sides with streaks of grey, followed by Dr Chenneviere. As he approached me he smiled, then put his right hand on my left shoulder. 'Pleased to meet you, Mr Hamilton. I am sorry for the delay in seeing you but I have been very busy this evening with a busy surgery. I have heard your case history from Doctor Sylvie here and Jan Van Driel, your coal barge captain. Well, Sylvie, shall we now have a look at his burnt arm?'

On closer examination, with his blue eyes scrutinising the damaged arm, he did not hesitate in a positive medical opinion. In a calm and collected voice he said that I needed urgent attention from a plastic surgeon. There were only two who came to mind, one was a German at Aachen, the other was Dutch and in Amsterdam. Since the latter was too far he decided to get the German surgeon to examine me. He then turned to Dr Sylvie and said, 'I will ring him this evening as soon as possible. Don't worry, Mr Hamilton, he's not a Nazi, but a genuine German.' Dr de Bruin put me at ease when he said he was a friend.

'If we can get you into the "Baby Farm" at Wassenburg, Doctor Sylvie will bring you back here to Thorn, since you must understand we cannot keep you as an in-patient at Wassenburg throughout the period of treatment. You can stay here tonight, but we shall have to move you to Thorn Abbey which is only a few minutes from here.' His decision was matter-of-fact and his bedside manner gave me confidence. After re-examination of my arm he said, 'Major, the nerves and muscles in your right arm are undamaged so you're extremely lucky considering the severity of your burns. Doctor Sylvie will give you something that will enable you to sleep comfortably. If you feel like it, I offer you our hospitality to join my friends in the lounge at a musical evening with Doctor Sylvie and Anneke. It will be good for you if you feel like attending as it will keep your mind off the pain.'

He told Doctor Sylvie that it was a good job that Miep did not put any tannic acid jelly on the burns. 'So I suggest you redress his arm and put it in a sling. Tomorrow we can consider taking off some of that loose skin if I see him after my surgery tomorrow morning.' With that he said he would see me the next day and left the surgery.

Doctor Sylvia dressed my arm, put it in a sling, washed my face and good hand and buttoned up my seaman's jacket. She said there should be no Germans at the recital, but said she could not of course guarantee it. 'Several senior SS officers and German officers often call in when they either want to socialise with us or hear music coming out of the house.'

She gave me a Dutch-English phrase book and said, 'I must now go and change for this evening. Doctor de Bruin has told me to feed you with eggs and ice cream to replenish the protein that you have lost.'

Within a few minutes she returned with a tray of food, including another jug of hot coffee, and told me, 'I am off now, Donald. I will come and collect you as soon as I can. I'll get Anneke to look in and see if you are all right. If a German officer comes in, try and act as though you have had an injection and act sleepy. Remember, although you have no Dutch papers yet, you're a Dutch seaman and you're wearing a Dutch seaman's clothes. If in difficulty, call out for a nurse or doctor. See you later.' She then closed the surgery door quietly and left me with my food and my thoughts.

I knew that the Germans had a reputation for defending their own borders fiercely when threatened on their own doorstep. With our experience of the First World War they fought more effectively in occupied territory near their own country than they did in faraway places like North Africa and Italy. I was particularly interested in the area of the rivers Rhine and Maas where a build-up of Allied and enemy forces would eventually become a major battlefield, making it a dangerous place to be in. Once Allied troops had entered the region they could open the door to the Rhineland. The region was therefore a threat to me in my escape plans and I must avoid it. It would be best for me to get into Germany to escape, which Jan had thought was dangerous. He had explained on the barge to me that all other Allied airmen had gone north rather than south in their bids for escape from Holland. As I thought hard about my plans to go via Germany Dr Sylvie entered the surgery. In a dazzling blue skirt and a low-cut blouse which was whiter than white, she asked me to join her and our host's friends in a musical evening. After putting the sling back on my right arm again and brushing my untidy hair with a sharp hairbrush she led me into the adjacent lounge.

The ceiling was very high and the room was spacious. A grand piano stood in a corner which, without looking too closely, I judged to be Steinway or a Bechstein. The room was furnished with solid dark furniture which had the hallmark of Dutch craftmanship. There was an air of affluence about the place with its highly polished floors and expensive antiques and pictures. I guessed the surgery, built in the late 18th century, had been handed down through generations of the de Bruin family, judging by the medical certificates hanging on the walls in the hallway and the surgery. The room was lit by electric light and a coal-fired stove in one corner of the room gave adequate heating. Several soft-backed armchairs with dark solid wood frames and arms were placed here and there. Dr Sylvie sat me furthest away from the stove so that the heat would not irritate the burns on my right hand and forearm which were well dressed so that I could wear one of Dr de Bruin's expensive shirts which matched my blue seaman's trousers provided by Miep earlier in the day on the barge.

209

We were joined by the Mayor of Thorn. He was a man of prominence, below average height, with a lean figure and the facial features of a man who had experienced stress, bereavement and responsibility during the occupation by the Nazis. His forehead was heavily lined and he had a pale face. A man of great integrity, I thought to myself, a man who gave all or nothing. He smoked an old English briar pipe, filled, I suspected, from home-grown Dutch tobacco.

We were also joined by his wife who had rosy cheeks and auburn hair brushed back loosely onto her shoulders. Dr Sylvie introduced me to other members of Dr de Bruin's family. His wife was tall and blonde but she spoke little English which surprised me being a prominent Doctor's wife. His two teenage daughters were very much like their mother, both blondes. What was most apparent was that no names were mentioned. I suppose this was a precaution Dr de Bruin had taken to protect his family. Although I had only been in his home a few hours he did not actually know who I was – this was yet to be confirmed from London when they sent their message about my arrival. At this point in time, I did not know whether Jan had got through to London or not which worried me a great deal, however, I had to be patient for I knew they had set times and frequencies for their transmissions.

As we all sat down, Dr Sylvie went over to the grand piano and commenced to play one of my favourite classical works, namely Chopin's Nocturnes. This reminded me instantly of Barbara and her family when, in the early stages of our courtship, we all went to London to the Royal Albert Hall. As Dr Sylvie played Anneke entered the room and showed Miep and Jan to their seats. Since I did not know they were coming, it was a great and heart-warming feeling to know they were there. They smiled accordingly as they settled down in their seats and I smiled courteously in return. Dr Sylvie played beautifully. Her long slim fingers touched the keyboard with elegance, sensitivity and precision. Anneke was by now standing beside her stool, turning the pages of her musical score, while Dr Sylvie concentrated on playing the piano.

Halfway through the score the lounge door opened quietly

and in came the maid Lisette, dressed in the usual attire of black and white, to offer us a glass of sherry or port. Finally, as Sylvie completed her recital we showed our appreciation in the usual way by clapping our hands, except for me with my injured right hand. Just at that moment we heard the roar of Lancasters flying low overhead on their way to bomb vital targets in Germany. Searchlights probed the dark sky as we all assembled outside, attracted by the noise. The sky was lit up with such intensity that I was reminded of many a Guy Fawkes's night in my home town of Richmond prior to the outbreak of war.

The maid, with the aid of a male servant, soon closed the outer wooden shutters and ushered us indoors. Dr de Bruin said it was going to be noisy and thought they would be going to Cologne or the vital oil refineries at Leipzig. The mayor said that it looked like another 1,000-bomber raid was imminent. Soon the ack-ack guns became more distinct and ominous with the result that you could feel the vibration through the floor of the Doctor's house. Anneke then amused us with a medley of Dutch tunes, which was both pleasant and entertaining.

My own thoughts started to wander nearer home. Had Jan sent the message to London to say I was safe? I also thought very consciously of Barbara. Had she received the official letter from the Station Commander that I was now presumed killed in action over southern Holland? I hoped that the Station Commander or Officer Commanding Flying would have telephoned her to explain the sad news. Here was I in the comfort of a prestigious group of doctors, their families and friends, while poor, dear Barbara was possibly all alone with her thoughts in her bedroom at the family home in New Malden, thoughts perhaps of shock, dismay and despair. Above all else the feeling of emptiness in her heart must have had the most profound effect on her. Except for being away at my station, we had never been separated before. We always had the usual telephone call to each other, or the odd letter. Now all we had was a transmitter from Thorn to tell her I was safe and in good hands and until she received that news via the

Station Commander, she had nothing but hope that I was alive and had been taken prisoner by the Nazis. This worried me tremendously. However it was in Jan's hands to get the message through to London that Bronco One was safe.

Since I could think of nothing else I went over to Jan to ask him quietly whether the message about me had been transmitted to London, He told me it would be going through this evening, could not give a time, but it was definitely going to be transmitted subject to radio contact being made. 'Thanks, Jan,' I replied happily. 'I'll be mighty relieved when it's received in London. I know you take incredible risks in sending these messages and am indeed very grateful to your operator.' I did not realise the operator was so near for he was situated in the tower in the Abbey of Thorn nearby, which was a 'safe house'. With that I returned to my seat and listened to the beautiful musical rhythm of Anneke playing. Finally Dr Sylvie and Anneke played a duet which they hoped to play at the next Thorn Festival a few weeks later.

I was now getting completely exhausted since I had been up since 0330 hours. The time was rapidly approaching to excuse myself from this enjoyable social gathering. I signalled to Dr Sylvie that I would like to leave and she nodded in acknowledgement as she finished her duet with Anneke. After accepting the appreciation of the distinguished company, she led me out of the warm room, but not until I had managed to pay my respects to everyone before my departure – I even kissed Miep on the cheek as a sign of my gratitude for the help she had given me during the day. She could so easily have handed me over to the Germans but she didn't.

Dr Sylvie gently took my good undamaged hand and with the lightest of touches, she led me upstairs to the top floor of the house where with the aid of a ladder we climbed up to the loft which had been prepared for my stay. There was a single flex of wire which supplied electricity to a small electric lamp with a switch cleverly incorporated into the wiring. The wooden floor was covered with straw and there was a blanket and pillow lying on it in case of need together with a tray of light food and a jug of water.

'I'm sorry I couldn't make this more comfortable for you, Major,' she said, 'but I have not had much time to myself today due to the hectic surgery hours I have had to do. At least the straw is dry and warm. Jan says you're only staying one night, but I have done the best I could with the resources available. It's too dangerous for the de Bruin family to accommodate you here so tomorrow you'll be moved to another house in the village. The Nazis and the German Army are always searching here, especially for escapees like you; but it's our prerogative to get you home to England so that you can fight the Germans again. We'll do all we can to help you. Many Dutch people, especially the farmers and peasants, have given their lives to help. All in this house are at very great risk of being imprisoned or shot for harbouring you.'

'I fully understand, Doctor, the enormous risks you are all taking on my behalf and I am indeed very grateful.'

She smiled sweetly and said, 'I've left you a very small amount of morphine for the night, but please do not use it unless you have to. It's in short supply. On no account must you open the loft hatch and lock it when I have gone. Only open it to three taps on the door. If you hear anything else, please disregard it. Proceed to the end of the loft and hide right at the end in the darkness. The Germans usually do not go further than the floorboards. At the end is a large blanket box in which you can hide, but please be very still and quiet.' She held my left hand tightly and kissed my cheek affectionately. 'You're a brave young man. Handsome, too. Highly decorated, Jan said. Are you?'

'Just decorated,' I replied.

With that she left the loft and on her way down she shouted, 'I'll be up in the morning to redress your arm with a fresh dressing.' She waved goodbye as I quietly closed the hatch and locked it thinking what a lovely person she was, so caring and interested in my wound which by now seemed more serious than when Miep first cut off the flying jacket covering my arm.

I was so tired that after drinking a large mug of water I lay down on the dry straw, pulled the blanket over my exhausted body and went off into a deep sleep.

The next morning, with my mind still sedated from the undisturbed sleep, I was awakened by three taps at the hatch door. When I opened it there was Dr Sylvie with my breakfast which included a piping hot jug of coffee plus a slice of bread. She said that she would bring a bowl of hot water to wash and shave with but under no circumstances was I to get the arm wet whilst I was washing. She asked me to go downstairs to the surgery at eight so that she could attend to my injury before her own surgery with the local people and the odd German officer that came in for minor ailments at nine.

When I arrived at the surgery she examined my arm and said that she would have to speak to Dr de Bruin about further treatment to avoid infection and she repeated that we needed a specialist in third-degree burns, either a Dutch surgeon or a German one. Of course this suggestion made me nervous and apprehensive. Until I had official papers making me a Dutch citizen, I could not possibly confront a German for the first time.

After a short discussion about Dr Sylvie's background, for I was intrigued by her being born in the lovely islands of New Zealand, we were interrupted by Dr de Bruin. Putting on his half-moon glasses, he said in English to both of us that my right arm was now black, wizened and clawed beyond all recognition. My forearm, although burnt, was not too bad since my sheepskin flying jacket had saved it to an extent. He continued by saying, 'Because he is in so much pain, you should subscribe morphine every four hours, if you can spare it – I know we are in very short supply. Once he has seen the surgeon, we may be able to obtain some morphine, or another painkiller, from him. If only more of your pilots wore goggles and gloves, quite a number of them would have been saved from serious burns. I know they're a hindrance in battle, especially when using gun sights, and are often discarded.' Turning to Dr Sylvie he asked, 'Did you feed him last night as I instructed?'

214

'Yes,' she replied cautiously. 'He had as much as I could muster.'

I thought I had not heard that word 'muster' since my training days at Royal Air Force Rednal.

'That's excellent,' Dr de Bruin commented. 'We had better get him more, if you can, Sylvie, before you depart for Wassenburg. I've arranged with the German specialist Doctor Gerhard Schmitt from Aachen to see him today. I suggest you do not arrive too early. Put him in your own consulting room at the hospital when you get there. This will keep him from the prying eyes of all those pregnant women and the German staff and also give you control over who sees him.' Dr de Bruin continued by saying, 'We will not touch his wound this morning but leave it to Doctor Schmitt when he examines him. I suggest that except for his revolver, ammunition and dog tag, we take everything off him which can be identified as British in case they search him thoroughly at the entrance gate. Jan has kindly produced his Dutch identity card and his permit as an Electrical Engineer to enter the German coal mine at Hücklehoven.

'As soon as your surgery is over Doctor Sylvie, you get off with our guest to the "Baby Farm" at Wassenburg, as it'll be near lunchtime and the number of guards on the gate there will be minimal.' With that he wished us 'Bon Voyage' and said he hoped to see me that evening. Dr Sylvie added that she would pick me up as soon as possible, but in the meantime I should go to my 'room' until she called. With that both doctors went one way down the long wood-panelled corridor and I went the other, to my room upstairs.

19

Although it seemed ages, Dr Sylvie knocked on the loft door within the hour. She was smartly dressed in her starched white housecoat with the stethoscope in her pocket. In her right hand was a wallet containing medical reports which she was taking with her to Wassenburg in Germany.

'Are you ready, Jos de Boer?' she called from the bottom of the ladder.

'*Ja,* Doctor,' I replied as I climbed down the ladder to a friendly kiss, so natural to Europeans, especially the French and Dutch. I checked I had my false identification papers and my Royal Air Force identity disc in the sole of my left boot which Jan had provided overnight. I left my other escape aids in the blanket box which I had locked at the far end of the loft. With Barbara's picture in my hat, I was ready to leave the surgery.

In a few minutes we were enjoying the comfortable ride that only a German Mercedes saloon could give. The air felt exhilarating after being cooped up in that loft especially as Sylvie had the soft leather hood down. The landscape from Thorn was flat and there were numerous dykes, windmills and canals, the latter forming an integral part of their irrigation system feeding the many farms growing colourful flowers and fresh tobacco. We followed the main road until we reached Roermond where the border posts were between Holland and Nazi Germany. It was a major crossing point between the occupied country of Holland and its invader.

When I saw the barrier, heavily guarded by armed German soldiers, I had no idea what to expect. With Dr Sylvie at the wheel of her large black saloon, a personal present from Heinrich Himmler himself, we moved forward gradually until we came to a halt at the barrier separating Holland and Germany. The senior officer of the German guard approached her with a smile, clicked his heels and saluted smartly. Although her sunroof was open she chose to wind down the driver's door window all of which appalled me beyond words. My knees started to knock together and my legs felt like jelly. This was the first time I had confronted the enemy face to face.

She took it all in her stride, her manner was calm and her speech measured. My mind was going through all sorts of questions – would the officer ask for my papers? Would they expect me to speak to them? Would they ask me to get out of the car? My heart was pounding and I could feel it through my chest. The scene felt like one of those movies where you don't know what is going to happen next and I did not have Barbara next to me to hold on to, as we used to at the Odeon cinema in Kingston-upon-Thames.

I lowered my head and stared down at the car floor. *'Guten morgen, Frau Doktor,'* said the senior guard, saluting.

'Guten morgen,' she replied hastily as she showed the officer her official SS pass. He grinned with approval at her highly honoured pass and returned it to her promptly.

'Have a good day, *Frau Doktor*,' he said as he saluted and beckoned the guards to open the massive, high-level, black iron gates. She put her special permit in her handbag and with me perspiring as though I had just come out of a sauna she drove off in the direction of Wassenburg. A few hundred yards up the road I said to Sylvie, 'Is it as easy as that?'

'Usually it is because of the frequency of my visits across the border. However, if there's an officer who is unknown to me, it can be a bit difficult. The pennant on the car and my SS pass from Himmler does wonders! They think I'm a senior SS agent,' she said as she quietly drove on. The landscape in Germany had now changed dramatically from flatlands to a mixture of undulating hills, coniferous forests and sycamore trees. It reminded me of when I was in my teens and my parents and I had travelled from Calais to Cognac in France where the scenery was similar.

Although we were in a German saloon car there was always the danger of being strafed by my own colleagues in the Royal Air Force. Away from the forests and trees the borders of the road were covered with golden wheatfields and red poppies were sprinkled here and there with accompanying blue cornflowers. We passed several German soldiers marching in groups of four, singing away to their heart's content as though the threat of an invasion to their own country was just a myth. Adolf Hitler had promised them that the new vengeance weapons, now being launched towards London, and their new jet fighter, the Me 262, would turn the victorious Normandy landings of the Allied forces under General Eisenhower into a catastrophe.

As Dr Sylvie drove past them they often whistled or waved to her. She was well-known in the district, especially on the road to Wassenburg. When in the air, we only saw the German swastika on the fuselage, and a pilot in the cockpit, to distinguish he was our enemy. We never knew who he was, whether he was a pure Nazi or a natural German-born flier, because we never came face to face with them. Here I was driving as close to them as ten feet, as though I was the Lord Mayor of London being driven by a chauffeur. It was the Nazi pennant flying on her near side wing which confirmed our importance.

All the time I had my Colt 45 at the ready with my box of ammunition in the sling supporting my damaged arm. There were Wehrmacht soldiers everywhere, strutting through the streets or marching in columns along the roadside. I said to Sylvie now that she was used to speaking on equal terms, 'Did you know that German officer at the Roermond barrier?'

'Yes, Jos, I know him personally, not only due to the frequency of my visits through there, but also I've met him socially at the Officers' Mess in Wassenburg, and as a house guest at the surgery. His name is Captain Johann Fritzell and he was decorated by Hitler with the Iron Cross at the fall of Paris in nineteen forty. Since he learned that my late husband, who was an officer in the French Army, was killed in the same battle, he has shown kindness and affection towards me. His family are having a dreadful time in Dresden where even now the Allies are bombing the city to a heap of rubble. Naturally he's worried about his wife and two children. He often comes to me confidentially to see if, through our resistance network, we can get some news of them. But up to now we've had no response. I think he fancies me in some way, but not intimately. He regards me solely as a trusted friend. However, it's not a two-way attraction. I use him to my advantage, to obtain information which I need, and that's that. He's often ordered to come to the hospital to be a donor for Himmler's Aryan Programme. So when I'm there I have coffee with him at the Hotel Goertz across the road in case I can get further information from him about troop movements etc.'

As she drove competently along I told her I had been frightened by the immediate danger at the border crossing, especially one as large as Roermond. 'Crossing with you just now made it look easy,' I said.

She replied, 'It is very difficult for the layman and usually very stressful. What makes it so easy for me, Jos, is that I hold one of the highest credentials you can have in an occupied country, that is, a travelling pass so that I can go where I please at any time of the day, signed by the Head of the SS and the Gestapo, Heinrich Himmler himself. So you, my lucky man, are travelling with authority. Without it I could not serve the Führer as an obstetrician and gynaecologist at his "Baby Farm" at Wassenburg. In case we get separated, you must try and contact Captain Johann Fritzell. I am sure he will help you in any way he can since he is not a Nazi, but a full-time ordinary German officer. In fact between you and me he cannot stand the Gestapo or the Nazi regime.

'To change the subject,' she said, 'tonight, on the return journey, we will go by the backroads to Thorn so that I can show you the colourful window boxes filled with the most beautiful petunias, red and white geraniums and pansies you have ever seen in your life! They are absolutely wonderful! Of course you may be drowsy or asleep by then after the minor

219

operation if you have it today. That will depend on the plastic surgeon who we hope will be coming to examine you this afternoon.'

As we approached the area of Etsburg, we drove through a beautiful, thick coniferous forest which gave us some protection from being spotted by low-flying Allied aircraft as we were in a German staff car flying a swastika pennant. On leaving the town of Birgelen and before entering Wassenburg we came down a steep hill which was open to aerial attack. Because we had no cover I asked Sylvie to step on it in case we were strafed. She did so and I was relieved when we arrived at the outskirts of Wassenburg where we had to turn left towards Wildenrath. The hospital we were going to visit was on a hillside in this pretty town near the Dutch border. It had several small shops and a lovely hotel named Goertz where Dr Sylvie knew the proprietor well. Being thirsty we stopped at the hotel for morning coffee, only to find that outside the entrance to the hotel were several German officers also drinking coffee. Dr Sylvie and the hotel manager were on good terms. In the past he had helped in the escape of Allied airmen and Dutch and Belgian Resistance workers who were on the run from the SS or the Gestapo.

She had changed her white coat for a lovely lightweight, grey, short coat, which matched her white blouse perfectly, whilst around her neck she wore an expensive gold chain which hung down to her bosom. On the left lapel of her jacket was pinned a solid silver parachutist's badge which I guessed could have been a gift from her late husband.

'You see those German officers over there, Jos, at the tables? Well, just walk the other side of me so I am nearest to them in case they want to talk. If they do, you go ahead and ask the hotel manager, Fritz, to find us a table at the end of the lounge, preferably near the window facing the entrance,' she said.

She was right. When we approached the entrance to the hotel, the German officers stood to attention, clicked their highly polished boots, and said, '*Heil Hitler.*'

'*Guten morgen, Frau Doktor,*' the senior officer said and shook her hand. He wanted to kiss her but she withdrew her hand so quickly that he did not have the chance. I took the opportunity to pass the group while all these formalities were going on and went into the entrance of the hotel before they had a chance to question me.

Proprietor Fritz saw me at once and showed me to a table. He must have guessed the situation by the way Dr Sylvie waved me into the hotel. I ordered, *'Zwei Kaffee mit Kuchen, danke,'* to Fritz as he hurried away to deliver the order. Eventually Dr Sylvie joined me at the far end of the comfortable lounge.

'Those bloody Germans. All they think about is sex. One cheeky officer tried to date me this evening. When I told him I was on Himmler's personal staff, and showed him my pass, he almost collapsed from shock. That'll teach him to ask, don't you think so, Jos?'

'Ja, Frau Doktor. Danke, gut,' I replied in near-perfect German in case anybody was listening. Within minutes of Sylvie sitting down the coffee arrived on a silver tray with a few biscuits.

'You'd better just have coffee, no biscuits, in case we operate this afternoon.'

'Ja, Frau Doktor, ich verstehe.' She looked with her sparkling eyes with surprise at my frequent responses in German. There was a sealed envelope on the tray containing a message to her. 'Please do not pay. On the hotel, and I suggest you do not stay too long' – signed Fritz.

With that we drank our coffee quickly and left by the side door so that we would avoid the unfriendly crowd outside which all the time was getting bigger. The first-class furnishings of the hotel reminded me of the lovely country hotel opposite the Eighth American Air Force base in Hertfordshire where Barbara and I had stayed.

We quickly got back in the car and left, soon arriving at the entrance to the hospital. It was not only heavily guarded by armed German troops but it also had a nine-foot brick wall giving it absolute privacy. The wall was topped with broken glass and covered with coiled barbed wire. As Dr Sylvie slowly approached the entrance she wound down her window. She

221

gave her SS pass to the German guard who examined it, clicked his heels and saluted.

'*Guten morgen, Frau Doktor. Wie geht es Ihnen?*' he smiled and took one step back to the rear.

Sylvie replied, '*Danke, gut.*' He quickly returned the SS pass and signalled to another guard to open the ten-feet high cast-iron gates under the ornate archway. Putting her precious document into her handbag she slowly and cautiously drove through the security barrier. As we drove up the long winding drive I found the scene in front of me most attractive. The gardens were well tended with magnificent flowerbeds and hedges complementing the vast lawns which gave the place a feeling of tranquillity and relaxation, a far cry from war. Because Himmler took pride in his own personal programme, the gardens were perfect; not a weed in sight, not a tree out of place.

As we approached the hospital itself you could see that a great deal of planning had gone into the architecture of the building. It was built mainly of stone and brick and the entrance was topped by two huge pillars of solid stone, reminding me of the entrance to the National Gallery in London. Contrasting this beautiful building was an embarrassing row of Nissen huts of corrugated sheets and no windows. There were signs everywhere, just like crossroads in London before the war, like 'Staff Entrance', 'Casualties' and 'Visitors'. One very large sign indicated 'Shelter'. All, of course, were in German.

As Dr Sylvie and I entered she had to report to the porter to sign the daily register. The porter bluntly asked her who I was and she replied, 'my patient'. She quickly turned away from him, took my good hand and led me down through a very poorly lit corridor to her consulting rooms at the end of the passageway. The entrance to her room seemed dark and unwelcoming for the colour scheme on the walls was most unattractive, a mixture of browns and greens. The corridor had a highly-polished wooden floor which looked similar to Richmond Ice Rink in Surrey. Natural light was lacking as there were few windows.

The majority of the wards on both sides were filled with patients who I guessed were pregnant women on Himmler's Aryan Programme, some in their early stages of pregnancy, some imminent. I found out later from Dr Sylvie that some came from as far afield as Poland, but mainly from Austria which was the birthplace of Hitler, Germany, Belgium, Holland and even Denmark. I wondered as I passed these wards full of pregnant women, at the work done there under Himmler's orders by Dr Sylvie and the other doctors to treat all these women. They were provided with all the comforts of home. Lavish decoration was obvious everywhere with expense no object in accommodating these women on the Aryan Programme. Everything they wanted they got. The scenic beauty overlooking Wassenburg was on a par with that of Windsor Castle, the only difference being that they had no view of the beautiful River Thames flowing past them.

Dr Sylvie ushered me into her consulting rooms at the end of the corridor and locked the door. After getting me to lie down on her adjustable couch, it was not long before there was a knock at her door. She quickly stepped forward and peeped through the inspection hole before opening the door. It was Dr Coen de Bruin and the German plastic surgeon, General Gerhard Schmitt. After the initial preliminaries, General Schmitt had a word with both doctors. He was a tall man dressed in a black civilian suit and a silver tie which matched his hair. He had large, slim hands with fingernails manicured to perfection. Except for the language he spoke you would have thought he had flown in straight from Harley Street, London. His bedside manner was pleasant.

Before the outbreak of the Second World War, Gerhard Schmitt had seen plastic surgery as an exacting art, the most rewarding of all in medicine. He was a bachelor and had lived with his devoted mother in Berlin. He had enjoyed his mother's cooking and a game of bridge in the evenings. He also liked classical music, opera and the occasional film, his favourite film stars being Humphrey Bogart and Vivien Leigh. Like his mother he liked reading and one of his favourite authors was our own Agatha Christie.

When war was declared he was called up by the German High Command to be part of the medical services of the Luftwaffe. Eventually he was sent to France and was stationed in Paris where he treated Luftwaffe pilots returning from the Battle of Britain. Eventually he was sent to Berlin, to his intense annoyance, to take charge of the Aryan Programme planned by the Führer and Himmler. He was promoted to General to give him the necessary authority to set up dozens of 'Baby Farms' throughout Europe. At the same time he was trying to encourage Hitler to open 'Burns Units' throughout Germany and the occupied countries in order to cope with the massive increase in burns cases, especially those associated with the Luftwaffe. General Schmitt saw plastic surgery as an exhilarating art and although difficult to administer to the patient, he discovered that the work was most gratifying. He found putting battle-traumatised pilots' faces and bodies together rewarding. His burns surgery in Berlin gained great respect. He had a partner in Colonel Karl Bohrer with whom he became lifelong friends. Himmler told him to share his workload between the 'Baby Farms' and plastic surgery units. Gerhard knew that the latter was his main interest but as the former was Hitler's idea, not his, he had no alternative but to work on both if he wanted to succeed with his pilot scheme in plastic surgery. Too many of his colleagues had either disappeared or had been shot defying the Führer or Himmler's orders. He had to report back regularly to Himmler in Berlin about the progress of the 'Baby Farms'. Himmler soon became paranoid about the slow development of his Aryan Programme due to the shortage of buildings and qualified staff. Hitler's vast scheme was impractical right from the start. He'd wanted 200,000 blue-eyed young Poles to be stolen, for an example, and an estimated 11,000 Aryan babies born in Nazi-occupied countries in SS 'Baby Farms'. World War II was a racial war, fuelled by Hitler's determination that Europe should be dominated by pure-blooded Germans. In 1935 Himmler had launched the 'Lebensborn Society'. The first word means 'fount of life', the aim being that the Third Reich would enjoy a constant flow of genetically impeccable children. The fathers were selected from the ranks of the SS whose Aryan credentials had been thoroughly checked as a condition of acceptance.

Gerhard Schmitt re-examined my arm and hand and after discussions between Dr de Bruin and himself they decided to operate. With a German staff nurse who had legs as beautiful as Betty Grable's, and Dr de Bruin acting as anaesthetist, the preparations for the operation began. The outline of the operation had been explained to me and I was given my pre-med injection. I was told it was one hundred and fiftieth of a grain of scopolamine to dry up your sinuses, throat and lungs. This was followed by another needle containing morphine and as I began to get drowsy I wondered how much more the surgeon had in store for me. Before going off to sleep I noticed Dr de Bruin with his anaesthetic trolley with tubes of piping protruding from it, several dials of different colours and large gas cylinders attached to the side of it. After hearing a few hissing noises, the world became a blank.

After the operation was over Dr Sylvie told me she had put an antiseptic swab over my burns. This was Evipan, which was actually invented in Germany. I also found out after I came to that Dr de Bruin had delicately mixed a proportion of nitrous oxide gas and oxygen in a mask which was placed over my face. The surgeon had then cut a thin graft of skin from my thigh with a Thiersch knife, like a paper-thin razor blade. He stitched the new skin onto my arm and hand, but not my fingers. That would come at a later date.

I was dreaming about Barbara and our cycle ride from New Malden to Brighton when the world of helpers and the horror of war became a reality – I was lying flat on my back on Sylvie's examination table in her consulting rooms. 'So you're awake?' said Dr Sylvie dryly. 'That wasn't too bad, was it?' After fully gathering my senses, I wasn't feeling so bad after all and thought I might get a whisky or a cup of tea. My mouth felt as though I'd been drinking port and brandy all night for I was dehydrated.

An hour later I felt much better. What a good job the 'Gasman', Dr de Bruin had done! Eventually when Sylvie was ready, they moved me on the trolley to her Mercedes. My arm seemed completely numb as they settled me sitting upright at the back of her car. The arm was completely bandaged and held in a sling.

On the return journey I must have fallen into a deep sleep and did not see Dr Sylvie's colourful window boxes which she had described earlier to me. The next thing I knew was that I was lying on her examination couch in the surgery at Thorn with Anneke looking straight into my eyes. 'Hello,' she said sweetly, 'I have got to check your pulse, blood pressure and temperature. Then you can go back to sleep.' Eventually I became fully conscious and asked her if I could have a nice cup of coffee. I must have gone off to sleep again because the next thing I knew was that my nose was being squeezed by Anneke. She had a hot jug of coffee on a tray with a plate piled high with bread and scrambled egg and a china mug with milk and sugar in it.

'Where the hell am I?' I asked in amazement.

'Jos, you are back with all of us at Thorn.' With a splash of cold water Anneke brought me back to my senses. Wiping my face with a clean towel I realised I had been dreaming again. That bloody Gasman, I said to myself.

Anneke said, 'You can sit up and have your supper,' and with that she raised the back of the bed so that I could eat comfortably. I ate my meal like a starving lion, but luckily nobody was watching. I was so hungry and realised that except for breakfast and a cup of coffee I had not eaten all day.

Dr Sylvie then entered the room smiling. 'How are you, Jos?' she asked as she took the tray from my bedside table.

'All right,' I said.

'No ill effects?' she asked.

'Except for a sore throat, I feel fine. Prefer to fly my Spitfire, or make love to Barbara, otherwise I feel fine.' With that, we both burst out laughing. 'What are you laughing about, Sylvie?' I asked jokingly.

She replied, 'Jos, the tension of the day is all over. I feel free! Looking after you is no joke when they're looking for an Allied pilot, and all the time you're in my care.'

I took her hand gently, put my arm around her and said, 'Thanks, Sylvie, I owe you and your team a debt of gratitude.'

'Thank you, Jos, it's nice to see that the Royal Air Force does send us over someone with a sense of humour, and handsome as well.' With that we laughed again, and embraced each other carefully as my arm was still in a sling.

I said to her, 'Dr Sylvie, have I still got my right arm?'

'Yes,' she said, 'except for a new covering of skin, your arm is OK, your nerves and your joints are intact. You're a very lucky young man indeed! With the right medical attention and skin grafts this should not upset your love or sex life with Barbara when you get home. Tell her from me that she's a lucky woman to have a fiancé like you, who treats women with the utmost respect and admires their femininity. For that, for all of us in the surgery at Thorn, we are truly grateful.' With that, she took my good left hand and slid it slowly down her left cheek. 'You are a gentleman, Jos, and we thank you.' Then she stepped back and sat by her desk. 'Dr Coen de Bruin has decided to keep you here for another night at the surgery because your blood pressure is still too high to let you loose on your own to the next "safe house". The safest room in this house is my bedroom and Dr de Bruin has decided you will sleep there this evening until alternative arrangements have been made.'

Dr Sylvie went on, 'As the room has only one bed, you, as our injured guest, will sleep in it.'

'Your bed?' I queried in surprise.

'Yes, Jos, my bed,' she repeated, and she helped me up the stairs to her bedroom on the first floor.

The room was very large indeed with dark brown furniture everywhere. Her desk was littered with medical reports and the odd X-ray was hanging on the wall. The photograph of her late husband was on her dressing table with pictures of her family in New Zealand, and her friendly Luftwaffe pilot.

The double bed was bigger than the standard British specification of six feet long and four feet six inches wide.

227

Probably, being metric, the bed was actually larger than it looked and was covered with a beautiful coloured duvet. Only the upper classes could afford such luxury. Even Barbara and her family did not have one.

'Where are you going to sleep, Doctor?' I asked as I sat on her luxurious bed. I had not felt such warmth since Barbara crept into my bed in New Malden on my transition to a front-line pilot way back earlier in the new year.

'On the sofa, by the door,' she replied confidently. 'If I am called out on a house call in the middle of the night, I shall not disturb you. If the Krauts come, then I shall be waiting for them in my pink dressing gown. That should frighten the bastards away, aye, Jos?' and she started to laugh out loud.

I remarked, 'I've never heard you swear before or even seen you smile like that. I like to see you relax, Dr Sylvie, it does you good. Your eyes are sparkling and you're relaxing. Now come over here and sit beside me.' She did so without hesitation and I put my good arm round her slim waist and kissed her passionately on the lips. She held me in her arms for a few seconds and then went over to complete making her bed.

'What a day, aye, Jos?' Still in my operating gown with rubber buttons at the rear, I got into bed. As soon as my head hit the lovely, silk pillow, I was out like a light.

When I awoke next morning I realised I was not alone – Sylvie was hugging me tightly. 'So you're awake then, Jos?' she said yawning gently.

'What are you doing here this time of the morning?' I said affectionately.

'You were shivering in the night, due I expect to the morphine, and since I couldn't find an extra blanket, I brought mine over and climbed in with you to keep you warm. I hope you don't mind,' she said softly, as she turned towards me. 'Are you surprised, Jos?' she said, beginning to close up the top button of her nightdress.

'No, not in the least. That Gasman must have given me a hell of a dose of morphine. I don't remember putting my head on the pillow. You could have seduced me and I wouldn't have known a thing about it.'

'Well, Jos, I was too tired to do that after the stress of taking you into Wassenburg.'

I replied, 'And I was too tired to feel passionate. I haven't slept with a lovely lady for months. I can't remember when Barbara and I last made love! Probably when I stayed with her parents' permission before joining my squadron and by the way, Sylvie, I'm still dressed in my operating gown.'

'Well, Jos,' she replied, 'Dr de Bruin decided not to move your right arm or sling unless we had to. Also you were so drowsy from the anaesthetic we decided to get you off to sleep as soon as possible. How about giving me a morning kiss before I get up and go and make coffee?'

'Who, me?' I said, absolutely flabbergasted.

'Well, Jos, I can't see or feel any other man in this bed,' she said as she pressed her warm body against me.

'Don't forget you're widowed, Sylvie, and I have a lovely and adoring fiancée at home waiting for me. You're a highly specialised doctor befriending a Royal Air Force Squadron Leader, or Major, as Jan likes to call me. Isn't this a bit intimate?' Before she could answer, I took my sling off my right arm and put my left arm around her and kissed her passionately. I could feel the warmth of her breasts penetrating right through my body.

With a big sigh, she lay on her back and relaxed. I guessed this might have been her first sexual experience since she had lost her husband in Paris. After kissing me lightly on the cheek, she got out of bed, put on her dressing gown and went downstairs to get us some breakfast. Soon she returned with a tray of food and drink. 'Make the best of it, Jos,' she said, 'it may be all you get until this evening.'

After breakfast, I pulled her back into bed, nightdress and all, and made love to her while the house was still peacefully quiet. 'God, Jos,' she said breathlessly, 'you squadron leaders don't waste any time, do you?'

'Who me, Sylvie?' I said as I lay exhausted on the bed. 'I felt that your need was as great as mine, you've been very kind to

229

me, and without you, I expect I would now have been captured by the Gestapo if it had not been for your courage, tenacity and self-preservation. I am indeed very grateful for what Anneke, Dr de Bruin and yourself have done. You've put your lives on the line for me and I will be truly grateful for the rest of my life.'

We kissed each other again before she slipped out of bed into the bathroom to shower and prepare herself for her day's work. She shouted from the shower room that if I did as I was told today, she might creep into my bed again tonight. 'It depends what that German surgeon has planned for you today. I expect he will examine your arm and leave the skin graft to heal before he does the next operation.'

When she had finished dressing she came and sat on the bed and said, 'On no account must you leave this room today until I return. Anneke will be up soon to look after you. Don't make a noise and don't open that door without the usual code.' With that she bent down, gave me a very passionate kiss and said goodbye. She locked the door behind her.

20

It was now mid-July and Dr Sylvie Chenneviere and I had made several visits for treatment to my damaged right arm and hand at Wassenburg Hospital. General Gerhard Schmitt gave up invaluable time and energy to treat my injury. Of all the medical staff he was undoubtedly the most vulnerable to risk being captured by the SS or the Gestapo. It was only by his very senior rank as General of the medical services in our region that he could have treated me without suspicion by the Gestapo. If he was caught there was only one punishment – death for him and maybe his whole family. Himmler never showed leniency to any of his senior staff.

We as Englishmen could never understand the speed and efficiency with which the Gestapo worked. He must have been a very courageous man to answer Dr de Bruin's request for help and he did it simply because of the rules of conduct doctors abide by. I found it extremely difficult to understand the situation since I was just a pilot and not a man that follows a professional code. I underwent several more operations with the same team of medical staff always present and the operating theatre always locked while I was in there.

At the end of the final operation for this stage the General said to me, 'It is now quite safe to travel so long as your bandages are replaced at least twice a week. As soon as you get to a safe port or ship, get them to have a look at your arm. Keep it dry and if you get an abnormal temperature seek medical advice as soon as you can. Now that we are losing the war, I hope when you get home you will put in a good word for me.'

231

'I certainly will, sir,' I replied. 'I owe you and your staff my lifelong gratitude for saving my arm and hand.'

'Next time, lad,' he said positively, 'wear your goggles and gloves,' and with that he said goodbye to me, wished me good luck and left.

In the meantime the Allied landings at Normandy were making slow progress due to the heavy resistance of German Panzer Divisions which had been moved from the Pas de Calais region where Hitler and his Intelligence Staff had decided the Allies would strike. It made the Allied forces under General Eisenhower stop in their tracks until re-inforcements arrived, until eventually the enemy gave ground. Later we learned through the Resistance network that General Montgomery had captured the key town of Caen. This was a strategic point in the advance of the Allied Armies. From the spasmodic information we were given we knew that the German Army fought harder when they were threatened than when they were in Russia.

On the night of my last operation with General Schmitt Sylvie suggested we should go out for a meal at the small country village of Wildenrath. This was just a few miles from Wassenburg, en route to Munchen Gladbach, a major town about 20 miles from Dusseldorf. So off we went through green fields and forests which I later learned were full of deep underground bunkers fed by twin track railway lines. With the threat of the Allied invasion in France, had they pulled back their V1 or V2 launching sites? Certainly the forest was too dense and too big to see anything from the air but was an ideal place for rockets. It was too far back into Germany for the V1 Flying Bomb with its range of 130 miles and the Germans would not have risked their own population at sites within their own territory.

We arrived at this lovely country restaurant called the 'Zur Post' which meant the First Bar. Inside was dimly lit with candlelight and the furnishings consisted of polished tables with uncomfortable chairs – it always seemed to me that

Germans preferred hard seats. German officers and their girlfriends were busy fraternising at the occupied tables and the restaurant seemed full. I said to Sylvie, 'Shall we go home?'

'No we're going to have dinner here, so stop worrying,' she said in an authoritative voice.

We eventually found a table where we could talk without being overheard. Light, entertaining music was being played from several misplaced speakers around the room, however, it was pleasant to listen to and it gave a romantic atmosphere, allowing the regulars to display their dancing skills, on the illuminated floor. We sat by the main door in case we had to make a quick exit. The atmosphere was very smoky and our eyes smarted from the thick smoke, mainly from the German officers' huge cigars.

The restaurant was divided into compartments. Heavy-duty pink glass panels separated the cubicles with an oil or paraffin lamp illuminating each area. The scene was very noisy, and sexy. Frau Sonia Heinmann, who was a trusted friend of Dr Sylvie, greeted her with great delight and obvious friendship. 'It's nice to see you again, *Frau Doktor.* Would you like your usual carafe of red wine? Your friend also?' She smiled and left the table. The meal was delicious culminating in a large glass filled with hot cherries and Kirsch, topped up with ice cream and rich cream. Although I was enjoying the meal I could not relax and my left hand was on my revolver for most of the time. I had no experience of how Germans socialised. They seemed to go on all night, while at home we used to call it a day by midnight. They did not start preparing dinner until at least 9 p.m. Most English people were either getting ready to go to bed or were in bed already.

The German officers' behaviour as they got more intoxicated seemed to embarrass Sylvie as the evening progressed. Eventually she decided to go after coffee. She thanked Frau Heinmann with a kiss on both cheeks and we left without delay.

After leaving Roermond we entered the flatlands of Holland and began to sing songs like 'Old Man River', 'Rule

233

Britannia' and some lovely songs from Sylvie's repertoire. She had a beautiful voice – no wonder that when she was studying classical music she was asked to sing in front of the Royal Family at the Opera House, Covent Garden. You could always tell when she was in the bathroom because the sound of her beautiful voice echoed throughout the house.

Suddenly she turned off the main road to Thorn, switched off the engine and pulled the handbrake on. She put her head back and took a deep sigh of relief. She just relaxed into a world of her own.

'What are we doing, Sylvie?' I said.

She replied without hesitation, 'I'm going to make love to you. You're leaving tomorrow, so this will be our last night together. I thought that since you're the only man I have loved since my husband died four years ago, I might as well make the most of it.' I was absolutely astounded by what she was saying. I knew she had a deep feeling for me, so I could understand her and her emotions and I was leaving the next day so could not blame her. I thought very carefully while I sat in the passenger seat about how Barbara would feel. I had never betrayed the trust between us and I felt guilty about our previous lovemaking. My feelings for Dr Sylvie were different – a strong affectionate friendship – whereas she needed the opportunity to make love to someone she found physically attractive and whom she liked immensely. She was aware of our imminent separation and knew that our lovemaking had no future.

We climbed into the rear of the car and made love until we could hear the birds singing. This was our signal to leave as it would soon be daylight. Sylvie said, 'Do you know, Jos, you're too gentle with women. When you get home, I know you may only have one arm, but you must work on your sexual relationships. If she is as shy about it as you are, then sexual satisfaction will not be achieved by either of you. A good open discussion between the pair of you would help.' And with that we drove back to Thorn with happy memories.

The next morning I was greeted by Dr Sylvie with the news that I was being moved within the hour to the next 'safe house' – the chapter house in the Abbey of Thorn.

A little later Dr Sylvie, dressed in a white blouse, grey skirt and with black high heeled shoes, accompanied me to the Abbey. As I left the surgery I thanked Mrs de Bruin and her staff for the wonderful hospitality they had shown me during my short stay.

Sylvie took me to the Benedictine Abbey (which had been closely associated with the history of Thorn since the year 925) which I learnt from her had become a secular house for noble ladies whose equivalent rank was that of a Princess of the Empire.

A few yards inside the Abbey I noticed the interior walls were whitewashed. From what I'd seen of Thorn all the painters went around the buildings with buckets of whitewash and huge paint brushes. Dr Sylvie led me through the library to the chapter house which was attached to the west wing of the Abbey. With the usual three-knock code on a heavy-duty wooden door, it was opened by Jan Van Dreil. He signalled us to enter, and Jan, before taking his seat around a dark brown table, introduced Dr de Bruin, sitting at the table to my left, and a young man called Stefan whom I had not seen before. A moment later one of the monks, dressed in a light brown robe, gave us each a cup of coffee and departed as quickly as he'd arrived.

Dr de Bruin called the meeting to order, thanked us all for coming and for being on time. We were here to discuss the request from British Intelligence for information on the new Me 262 German jet fighter and the new V-One launching sites in Holland and Belgium. They knew that I was in their company and requested that all available help be given to get me and the information back to London.

'Of the objectives which we have been given by London, we have three major items to discuss,' said Dr de Bruin. 'Number one is to obtain as much information as possible on the new launching sites of the V-One Flying Bomb in Holland and Belgium. Number two is to obtain as much information on the technicalities of the new and first German jet-propelled fighter, the Me Two-Six-Two. Number three is to find ways of delaying production of this new fighter as it poses such a serious threat to the Allied Air Forces over Western Europe. It's vital that Donald obtains as much information about the performance of this new jet fighter as soon as possible, since the British Government is worried that its specification may be higher than the first British jet-propelled fighter, the Vampire, which isn't yet off the production line.'

We all sat riveted, listening to Dr de Bruin. He went on, saying, 'In order for him to reach London as quickly as possible Donald has decided, with our help, to get to one of the German operational night fighter airfields flying Bf One-One-Ohs at Wahn, just outside Cologne, steal a fighter and fly back to England. If we can find a German airfield closer than Wahn, then we should go for that. As the advantages outweigh the disadvantages of this plan rather than going north and joining up with Allied ground forces in northern Holland, it would be best if we backed it, but personally I still believe it is highly dangerous, not only to us as members of the Dutch Resistance Forces, but also to Donald. However, he has got to get back to London, and he could go up and down to northern Holland as many times as he likes, and yet still be here weeks later.'

No one interrupted the Doctor as he carried on by saying, 'The one vital advantage Donald has in his plan is the element of surprise, the theft of a well-guarded German fighter at night. The Germans are sending many more troops up into the northern part of Holland to prevent the Allies from crossing the River Maas. I'm sure we can get him a German pilot's uniform and a passport and take him to Wahn so that he can fly a Bf One-One-Oh back to England. With the necessary maps, and a lot of luck, Donald could have a good chance of succeeding. There are several pilots from Wahn who visit the clinic, so we have plenty of choice in uniforms; also Doctor Sylvie is a friend of one of their most experienced Bf One-One-Oh fighter pilots, a Leutnant Dahn.' At this, Dr Sylvie looked around and smiled at everyone. Stefan raised his hand to the Chairman of the Committee and asked, 'Why don't we use Doctor Sylvie's friend?'

Jan interrupted, 'Isn't it too dangerous for Doctor Sylvie to use her friend? Surely if he goes missing, the SS, the Gestapo and even his own aircrew will immediately suspect her, for Leutnant Dahn will have certainly told his own crew that he befriends a doctor at the hospital?'

'Yes, I agree, Jan,' I said vehemently. 'But shouldn't we leave this decision to Sylvie; there are pros and cons in using Dahn. Firstly, Sylvie can track him down at anytime, as he often visits the hospital, or dates her. Secondly he has his own transport, a BMW motorbike and sidecar, and what's most important, which we should consider, is the time needed to change the photographs on the passport to mine. In other words, Sylvie will have to date him, let's say at the Zur Post, get him drunk and steal his identity card so that we'll have enough time to change the photographs and use our Gestapo stamp to validate it.'

Jan said, 'If Sylvie could get the passport to us early enough that evening, we could return it to her before she leaves the Zur Post. Usually she says goodbye to him at the restaurant in Wassenburg and he returns on his motorbike to Wahn; this is where the three of us should plan to kill him, between Wassenburg and Erkelen.'

'Great idea, Doctor de Bruin,' said Sylvie. 'I only have to die once, so it might as well be whilst trying to get Donald back to London, and I'd be happy in the knowledge that I've contributed something towards his vital mission.'

I stood up abruptly and said rather loudly, 'Sylvie, you can't afford to take that sort of chance at this stage of your life. Your friends are here, your future life should be here, so why give it all up for a "one armed bandit" and with a minimal chance of success? All of you kind folk here are risking your families' lives as well as your own.' I paused for a moment, 'Another important factor is that if we kill Leutnant Dahn, we are going to lose an informer from whom you have obtained invaluable information, and which no one else in this room could ever have achieved.'

Dr de Bruin asked, 'Jan, what do you think of this plan, and would it work?'

Jan replied, 'Well, it would certainly be easier to get the Major over to the UK with Doctor Sylvie's help, and I really can't see any other way,' Jan paused for a moment rubbing his chin. 'The only alternative is to steal a uniform from another pilot who visits the hospital, but the problem of the identity card is the most difficult part of the whole plan. It'll be easy to kill him and easy to take the motorbike so that Donald can proceed to Wahn in his new identity as a German pilot belonging to a night fighter squadron. And remember, it's most imperative throughout this operation that when we kill the Leutnant, we mustn't get any blood on his uniform, or the whole plan will have to be aborted.'

Jan, Stefan and Dr de Bruin put it to the committee that the best way to kill this Leutnant Dahn, or whatever pilot we chose, would be to string a steel wire cable across a road on his return route to Wahn, and the closer we did it to Wassenburg the more chance there would be of total success.

Dr de Bruin, on closing the meeting, asked, 'Why don't we all take this plan away with us, give it some serious thought and meet back here tomorrow morning at the same time? In the meantime Doctor Sylvie and I will take Squadron Leader Hamilton back to Wassenburg Hospital for further treatment on his injured arm. He should stay at the Abbey until they find him another safe house, which should be in the next few days.'

During the early part of that evening, as various ideas were turning over in my mind about my escape plan back to England, there was the coded knock at the chapter house door. The code was clear and decisive so I opened the door slowly and there stood Dr Sylvie in her white coat with her stethoscope around her neck. She looked absolutely exhausted, 'Can I come in for a few minutes?' she said wearily.

'Of course you can,' I replied, come and take a seat and I will get you a glass of homemade red wine.'

238

'That would be very much appreciated, Donald. I have had such a busy day.' I turned my back on her to close and lock the heavy chapter house door. Dr Sylvie chose one of the double wooden seats with loose cushions on them. She made herself comfortable, kicking her shoes off and putting her feet up and I gave her a glass of the Abbot's wine. The grapes had been grown in the grounds of the Abbey and processed in the Abbey basement. The occupants of the Abbey obviously drank limitless wine judging by the empty bottles in the disposal area. They must have drunk God's health on many occasions!

I said to Sylvie, 'You look absolutely exhausted,' as I looked at her and the glass of wine in her hand. The glasses were priceless, part of the possessions of the Abbey and were made of crystal, patterned on the outside with the logo of the Abbey of Thorn. I thought if I dropped one I would be in deep trouble with the Abbot.

'Yes, I'm very tired, Donald. I've had a very busy day,' she said sipping her wine slowly. 'How about you, lazing about here with your feet up and nothing to do?'

'That's not true, Sylvie. I've been developing my escape plans until I was bored thinking about them. I've especially been thinking about your involvement and the risks you're taking for me, just somebody passing by on their way home to England.'

'Well, what did you think of this morning's meeting?' she asked, putting her head on my left shoulder.

'I would be a lot happier if you were not involved at all. You're so vulnerable to this project. Everybody seems to know you befriend this pilot from Wahn. I expect even the German officers who frequently visit the Zur Post know of your friendship with Leutnant Dahn. The two major advantages you have are your SS pass and that you are an integrated and vital part of the administration of Himmler's "Baby Farm" at Wassenburg.'

'Well, dear,' she said with affection, 'I was involved up to my neck long before you came on the scene. So just another airman escaping from Holland back to England is just another job which has to be done. We have to give top priority to you because of your mission and the vital information which must reach London as soon as possible.' With that she shifted her legs and asked me to fill up her wineglass because it was empty. 'Listen Donald, when my husband died in the defence of Paris in 1940, I felt so lonely, depressed and let down by the French that it was not until I reached Thorn that I realised the best thing to do was get my priorities right and gain my revenge for the loss of somebody who was very dear to me. The only way I knew was by getting information from the Germans and passing it on to our Underground. If I'm put against the wall and shot at least I will have achieved something, if only in memory of my late husband. I am the only child of two very caring parents back in New Zealand. Otherwise I am widowed and do not have any family responsibilities, except my loyal parents.'

'What about your beloved Luftwaffe pilot?' I said smiling.

'Donald, he's a gentleman who is very kind to me and he shows me affection. He showers me with presents including food, which is vital to keep our Resistance group going, plus the vital information I get from him when it is requested. It's just a convenient friendship. You're not jealous are you, Donald?' she asked as she crossed her knees again.

'Who, me? Not in the slightest,' I replied as I put her glass down on the table and kissed her passionately.

'I think you're getting more daring each day. You'll be pulling my knickers off next,' she said coyly.

'I too am a gentleman, remember,' I grinned back at her.

'Although I think he's in love with me, he never shows it. It's the blind leading the blind, Donald. I lead him on, and he gives me the information I am after. Maybe the Allies are only round the corner, but I honestly believe if I asked him to take me to England he would. I think he wants to escape from the unholy mess his country is in and have a peaceful life in a free country.'

'Shall we ask him to fly us to the UK?' I asked jokingly.

'We can't, our plans could be in jeopardy. I don't trust the

240

Germans. Don't forget he believes even today that the Luftwaffe is the greatest air force in the world, despite their humiliating defeat in the Battle of Britain in 1940. His first love is flying, like yours. He detests the SS and the Gestapo and avoids any kind of conversation on concentration camps, especially those in Germany and in occupied countries like Poland. To me, although I think the German High Command are indescribable beasts, the average German in the rank and file is kind and considerate. They behave like us.' I poured out another glass of our host's wine. As I was filling my own glass Sylvie said, 'Should we be drinking the monks' wine?'

'Why not?' I said, laughing, 'they've got enough down in the cellars to fill a brewery!' Sylvie started to laugh and sing as the wine relaxed her enabling her to forget the hard day she had been through and especially the stress of having me around which must have added to her daily burdens.

'When you arrived, Donald,' she said, 'for the first time since my husband died, I felt wanted. Your trust and understanding has been reciprocated and you haven't taken advantage of me. You're so gentle, Donald, it's unbelievable. I'd have thought as a Squadron Leader, although only twenty-three, you'd be boisterous, harsh and possibly ruthless. But you're not, you're quite the opposite. You're certainly not like the other Allied airmen we have had to handle on their way through Holland.'

'I'm still worried about you, Sylvie, but I've learnt one thing, you're a very determined lady, and whatever I say or Doctor de Bruin says, you'll do your own thing anyway,' I replied.

'What I want to do is help you get back to England,' she said as she finished her second glass of wine. 'May I have another, Donald?'

'Sure, Sylvie, but don't you think the third glass will stop you going home?'

'Home where, Donald? I'm staying here!' she said.

'Here?' I said in complete amazement.

'Yes, here, Donald, unless you want me to turn you over to the Gestapo.'

I replied, 'No thanks, Sylvie. I would rather cuddle you than be beaten about the head with a rifle butt by a German soldier.'

'Here's to us,' she said, and we raised our glasses. 'My love for you is sincere. Any night could be our last night together, whether it be in the Abbey, the surgery or down an air raid shelter, so let's take the opportunity God has given us and enjoy it. If things go wrong with Barbara in England, will you promise to come back and see me here at Thorn in Holland when the war ends?'

'Sylvie, at this time in my life, Barbara is very important to me. I love her, cherish her and want to marry her. But war has a great effect on people's attitudes, affections and friendships. You've done an immense amount of work for me, getting me "safe houses", introducing me to your Resistance friends and obtaining the best possible treatment for the burns to my right hand and arm. If it wasn't for Jan, Miep and your local Underground movement, I could have been in Stalag Luft Three by now. I can't find words strong enough to show you all my appreciation.'

'Well, give me a kiss then, Donald, and hold me tightly.'

I stood up, went over to her seat, kissed her on the cheek and, holding her hand, said, 'After the war, which may take a few years yet, our attitudes, objectives and behaviour could have changed. Our appreciation for each other may grow stronger or weaker. But one thing is for sure, I personally owe you a deep sense of gratitude. Here is my home address in Richmond, Surrey, England and my parents' telephone number. As soon as you're liberated at Thorn by the advancing Allies, please write to me. If the war is still on, and I fly again, I'll fly over Thorn as many times as I can, depending on where I am at the time.' After slipping my note down her blouse she fell into a deep sleep.

I made up a makeshift bed for her and covered her over with a blanket as the chapter house was cold. Looking at her beautiful face while she was asleep, I thought what a lovely girl she was, a true professional, dedicated to medicine, curing people's illnesses and delivering babies, whatever their nationality and creed.

I made myself a bed on the floor, switched off the light and climbed into the hard bed. It had been a day of planning, stress and of emptiness in my heart. Tomorrow would be a day of planning both my escape and my destiny. With that I went off to sleep.

21

The next morning we all met at the chapter house. The sun was shining brightly through the lovely stained-glass window. Dr de Bruin opened the second meeting by first apologising for not formally introducing the new member of the committee, Stefan Miere. (This was normal practice with all Resistance meetings in case there were collaborators or enemy agents present.) 'Stefan is a leading Dutch Resistance leader,' said Dr de Bruin.

I looked at him. He was young, outgoing in his mannerisms, slimly built, with a drawn, narrow-jawed face and his hair was mousy as though it hadn't been washed for some time. He seemed undernourished which I expected was due to the ongoing problem of changing 'safe houses', since he was a prime target for the Germans. He spoke perfect English and we learnt later that prior to the war he had been a biology student at a college in Amsterdam. The more I spoke to him, the more I felt I could depend on him.

Dr de Bruin explained that he had now correlated all the ideas from members of the committee, and these were his proposals:

'Number One. Doctor Sylvie is to obtain Leutnant Dahn's identity card, the password to Wahn, and the take-off speed of a One-One-Oh. Further, to obtain any details, however small, of the German Me Two-Six-Two. Being an experienced pilot himself, I can't see Leutnant Dahn wanting to miss the chance of either hearing about it, or even seeing it. I suggest that you, Sylvie, start on your project straight after this meeting.' Dr de Bruin then sipped some ice-cold water.

Dr Sylvie replied, 'I'll do what I can without rocking the boat, the only worry I have is the question of take-off speed. Why would a doctor be asking such an aeronautical question and what reason do I give, Donald,' she said looking at me, 'for asking such a question?'

'That's difficult, Sylvie,' I replied after a few moments pondering the question. 'Couldn't you relate it to the effect the actual lift-off has on a pilot's blood pressure, or something along those lines?'

Dr Sylvie smiled at me and replied, 'Thanks Donald, you've given me something to work on. I'm sure I'll conjure up something.'

Dr de Bruin continued.

'Number Two. Jan and Stefan must make a dummy run in their coal lorry to Wahn. I want them to carry on with their usual deliveries to avoid suspicion, and whilst inside the camp obtain drawings, photographs, etcetera of sentry posts, machine-gun posts, crews' quarters and finally hangar positions. On your return home, pick a site where you're going to kill Leutnant Dahn. I've been studying the map, you'll need to choose a spot where you have plenty of cover, with forest on either side of the road. If you have to abort, you can hide in the forest, since that road is heavily patrolled by German armoured personnel carriers. I suggest between Wassenburg and Erklenz, the nearer to Wassenburg the better. The wire must be angled at least forty-five degrees across the road so that when Dahn hits it he's thrown sideways into one of the ditches. Newton's Law of Motion will make him do that.'

Everyone grinned at the mention of Newton's Law. We thought he was a Doctor of Medicine, not a Physicist. 'You must be fully armed with automatic weapons, side arms, grenades and heavy-duty torches. You might, while in the act of killing Dahn, meet up with a German patrol.

'Number Three. On a particular night, Jan is to arrange with Doctor Sylvie to pick up Dahn's identity card, get it processed by our friend at the Abbey and return it to Doctor Sylvie. She informs me that he often takes his jacket off while

245

dancing and hangs it on the back of his chair. This would be an excellent opportunity for Jan to sneak into the restaurant, steal the card and return it within the hour to its rightful place. Alternatively, Doctor Sylvie has suggested to me that when he visits the hospital and hands his clothes in to the Ward Sister, we take the golden opportunity of stealing his credentials since we can have the forger in the next room and it would be a lot quicker to process them this way.'

Dr de Bruin went on to explain the two main advantages to the latter plan, these being: '(a) There would be no direct suspicion of Doctor Sylvie if anything was to go wrong. (b) Time is saved by Jan not having to go back and forth from the Zur Post and Abbey. If he's caught with Dahn's credentials in his possession, he'll be in very serious trouble with the Gestapo.'

It was agreed unanimously that the hospital plan was undoubtedly the least risky and the best for everyone concerned.

'Number Four. Stefan is to obtain the steel wire. Also inform London that our plan is nearing completion. Once we have the necessary documentation we will, with the approval of Donald, give them a time and date to attack the hangars and out-buildings at Luftwaffe Wahn. We need this diversion to get onto the airfield and have cover to enable Donald enough time to take off from Wahn.

'Number Five. The disposal of Leutnant Dahn's body.'

Dr de Bruin said he had looked hard at this, one of the most important elements of the operation. 'If we bury him at the scene of the accident, it's going to take time. If we burn him, this could attract the attention of German night patrols. If we dump him in the River Ruhr or Maas, this is going to cause more risk and take time, and unless we weigh him down heavily enough he will float to the surface within three to four days. So I think the best idea is sitting on our doorstep. The crematorium is at Wassenburg Hospital. Here we have all the necessary equipment needed to burn his body with the babies we have to cremate daily. So I suggest Kees and I bring Leutnant Dahn's body back to the hospital, put him in the

246

morgue for a few hours and then burn him when we light the crematorium fires the next morning.'

We all thought this was a brilliant idea and applauded his plan. 'This means that Kees and I will follow the convoy on the night in question. Number Six. Donald will get into Dahn's uniform and with Sylvie's help dress up in German dispatch rider gear. He can do all this in Sylvie's car.' Dr Sylvie nodded in agreement.

'If the motorbike isn't damaged, he can ride it to Wahn with us. If it's damaged beyond repair, and since we can't burn or bury it, Jan will have to hide it in the forest and on returning from Wahn, dump it into one of the rivers. Donald, alias Leutnant Dahn, will then have to travel as a passenger in the coal lorry.'

This was agreed by everyone, since Dahn had flagged down Jan for a lift to Wahn in the past when his motorbike had broken down, and it shouldn't raise any suspicions to have him sitting in the front seat of Jan's coal lorry. Now that the preliminaries are over, this is the final plan for Squadron Leader Hamilton to escape from here back to "Dear Old Blighty". For those of you who don't know the London cockney saying, this means England.'

The chairman then gave a summary for the night in question:

'One. Doctor Sylvie will get Leutnant Dahn intoxicated, not too much so as to stop him riding his motorbike, but enough to make him oblivious of any dangers that might confront him on his way home to Wahn.

'Two. Jan and Stefan are to proceed to Wahn, one and a half hours before Dahn leaves the Zur Post. They lay the steel wire trap at an angle across the road, which should throw him off his motorbike and into a ditch.

'Three. Doctor Sylvie is to follow Dahn keeping about a mile behind him. She will be carrying all our weapons in case we meet a German patrol. If she's stopped on the way, her alibi is that she'd received a call from the Commandant's wife saying that her waters had broken, she thought that her baby was on the way and that any delay could be disastrous.

247

'Four. Kees and I will follow half a mile behind Sylvie. If we are stopped, I'm on night call.

'Five. When Dahn is riding his motorbike he will have the black cover with the little slit in it over his headlight, so he shouldn't see the wire across the road.' (This was a wartime regulation, which prevented light from shining up in the air.)

'Six. As soon as Dahn is thrown off his motorbike, Donald must check that he's dead, hopefully with a broken neck and no blood. And change out of his Dutch seaman's clothes and into the uniform of a Luftwaffe pilot. By that time Sylvie will have arrived and can help Donald with the dispatch rider's gear which will include helmet, goggles, heavy outer coat, black boots and gloves. And don't forget the black belt with the pistol and spare magazines on it. If the motorbike is serviceable we will use it. If not, then hide it, and Jan will deal with it later, by throwing it into one or other of the two rivers.

'Seven. Kees and I will put Dahn's body into my car, and bring it back to Wassenburg for cremation.

'Eight. The rest of the party will take a cross-country route, through Erklenz, Berheim, Kerpen and Efstadt. This way we will have partial cover through areas of forest to give us protection from marauding Allied aircraft. The Royal Air Force will attack at precisely the same time as the rest of the party arrive at the airfield, concentrating their attack on the defences and hangars.

'Well, that's the plan. I hope we can gather all the information needed in the next two days as we can't risk keeping Donald at the Abbey any longer than we have to.'

Dr de Bruin stood up and before leaving wished us luck in our various tasks. He warned us yet again about not leaving any written notes, here or anywhere else, but to burn them.

'Our aim is to get Squadron Leader Hamilton away to England in three days' time,' he said.

With that they all left except Sylvie and myself. She came across the room to me, put her hands on my cheeks and gently kissed me on the lips. She thanked me for not making any sexual advances towards her the previous evening when I had put her to bed in the chapter house. Then she asked me, 'Can you come to my room this evening after dinner?'

I replied happily, 'I'd love to.' We kissed again and she left.

Some time after the meeting Jan and I took a slow walk down through the streets separating the whitewashed houses, intending to have a nice cold lager at the restaurant. Jan had suggested that I leave my personal weapon in a locked drawer at the chapter house, just in case we were stopped by any of the frequent patrols. There were many heavily-armed German convoys going north to supply their own ground forces south of the River Maas. These patrols were everywhere now that the Allies had gained a foothold on Dutch territory.

It was a lovely day, the sun was very hot and the sky was clear with just a few clouds here and there. The houses had flowerpots full of geraniums hanging from the lintels of the windows. It was a beautiful setting for a photographer or artist to capture, in fact, the village of Thorn would make anyone from Devon feel very much at home. We eventually arrived at the restaurant and chose a table outside, as far away from the German officers as possible so that we could make a quick exit if necessary. Also we didn't know if Leutnant Dahn was amongst the officers as neither of us had seen him in a photograph or even in the flesh. In case I was stopped by the Gestapo or the SS, my cover story was that I was on my way to the coal mine at Hücklehoven as I was employed there as an electrician.

The waiter brought us a large silver jug of coffee, a small jug of hot milk and two beautifully glazed cups on a silver tray. I gazed around the village square. The scene was peaceful and quiet except for the noise of German troop movements. It was impossible to imagine that a war was going on just a few hundred miles away. Wherever I looked, whether on houses, public buildings or even noticeboards, large Gestapo posters were plastered everywhere warning the local residents that if they harboured enemy agents or spies they and their families would be shot immediately.

Jan and I were chatting generally about our families when all of a sudden the peace was shattered in the quiet village square by the heavy roar of armoured vehicles and trucks carrying German soldiers. They seemed to appear from nowhere with astonishing speed and efficiency and surrounded the café and nearby buildings like guards in a prison camp. Everyone was told to lie down in the road with their hands behind their backs. There were one or two rifle butts being stabbed into women's stomachs, followed by terrified screams, which ruined the peaceful atmosphere we had had a few minutes before.

We were eventually herded into trucks and taken to Gestapo Headquarters at Horst near Monchen-Gladbach. Luckily Jan and I were still together at this time, and we found ourselves in a 'holding cell' with a number of other people. Jan recognised one or two of the prisoners and quietly whispered to me, 'Your father was an IRA member and your mother is Dutch, born in Amsterdam. Your father, to evade capture, eventually brought his family over to Holland to your mother's house in Amsterdam. You're an only child. You went to school and college in Amsterdam where you qualified as an electrical engineer. You then joined me on the barge, and have been with me ever since. The Germans are desperately short of electrical engineers so they commandeered you to work at the coal mine at Hücklehoven on a part-time basis. In the meantime the Germans have allowed you to work as a barge man collecting coal from Maastricht to Amsterdam.' He paused before asking, 'Are you happy with your story?'

I replied, 'Yes, I am, thanks. You're quite an experienced storyteller. You should take up writing war stories after the war; you've seen enough to do so,' I laughed.

I had started to think of my cover story when I was at Thorn with an injured arm. The only thing that seemed sensible was that while I was cleaning the engine on the barge whilst it was still running, the steam valve blew off burning my right hand and arm. Jan had insisted that it be treated immediately in case of infection and pain. I therefore had to break my journey to Hücklehoven to obtain medical treatment. And since I was working for the Germans I was entitled to seek medical help and advice from German rather than civilian doctors at the hospital. I had chosen Thorn because it was the nearest treatment centre.

We were soon split up into small groups. My left wrist was handcuffed to a German soldier's right wrist. They couldn't handcuff my hands together because of the sling and bandages around my arm and hand. Also the fake pass from the German Medical Officer had excused me from heavy work because of my injury. Luckily they didn't remove the sling to check on my injuries after checking the pass.

The building echoed to the screams of the prisoners. The German soldier I was handcuffed to led me into a large room where a short, overweight officer in an impeccably tailored Gestapo uniform stood under the Führer's picture. The desk, which was highly polished, seemed as though it would befit a committee room rather than a German officer's working desk.

Two heavily armed guards flanked him on either side. A female secretary, smartly dressed in black leather trousers, white blouse and a black leather jacket sat to one side of the table and I immediately noticed that she was armed with a revolver, holstered on a thick black belt with a silver buckle. She had a pretty face with blue sparkling eyes. I imagined her dressed in a nice summer frock. She didn't wear any makeup or jewellery.

The name board on the table told me my interrogator's name was HAUPSTURMFÜHRER SCHMIT of the WAFFEN SS. He walked backwards and forwards behind his desk with my file in his hand. 'Good,' he retorted and I felt my heartbeat suddenly increase. I hope he didn't think I was a pilot or one of the Lancaster aircrew who had baled out near Augsburg earlier that morning.

Schmit said, 'The sooner you confess to being one of the

251

Lancaster crew members who baled out this morning, the better off you will be.' He carried on leafing through the pages of my file, but soon began to realise I wasn't either of those people he had originally thought I was.

Once I knew the heat was off me, I felt a feeling of great relief as if a great lump of concrete had been lifted off my head and my pulse rate generally came down to something resembling normal. On the other side of the corridor I could hear a young voice screaming. As time went on the noise got louder and louder. I heard Schmit tell his young secretary that they were pulling out fingernails one by one. What a ghastly sight it must have been, I thought. How could a human being inflict such torturous punishment on another human being?

My mind began to race again. I could have been the next one in there and I wondered briefly if it was Jan, but the voice didn't seem to match his, so again I felt relieved.

On his jacket, Schmit wore a red and white ribbon pinned at an angle of 45 degrees so that you could see the top of the ribbon but not the bottom. Whether it was a medal or a citation, one had to guess. The end of the ribbon was tucked inside the jacket. He opened my file again, put his glasses on, and I thought, well, what's my destiny?

Schmit carried on with the interrogation: Schmit – *'Was sind sie von Beruf?'* (What do you do?); Me – *'Ich bin ein arbeiter.'* (I am a worker); Schmit – *'Wo arbeiten sie?'* (Where do you work?); Me – *'Ich arbeite bei Hücklehoven.'* (I work at Hücklehoven); Schmit – *'Was sind sie von Beruf?'* (What do you do?) [second time of asking]; Me – *'Ich bin ein Elektriker.'* (I have a job as an electrician); Schmit – *'Wie heisst du?'* (What is your name?); Me – *'Mein Name ist Jos de Boer.'* (My name is Jos de Boer); Schmit – *'Wo kommen sie?'* (Where do you come from?); Me – *'Ich Komme aus Suden Ireland'* (I come from southern Ireland); Schmit – *'Ist dein Vater im IRA?'* (Is your father in the IRA?); Me – *'Ja.'* (Yes) Schmit – *'Wo ist dein Vater?'* (Where is your father?); Me – *'Er ist in Holland gestorben.'* (He died in Holland); Schmit – *'Was machen sie in Thorn?'* (What are you doing in Thorn?); Me – *'Ich arbeite für die Wehrmacht Hücklehoven.'* (I work for the German Army in

252

Hücklehoven). Schmit got up from his comfortable chair, walked up and down, lit a cigarette, put it in a black cigarette holder and in broken English, said, 'Say something in Dutch for me.' Schmit – *'Sprechen sie Dutch?'* (Do you speak Dutch?); Me – *'Mag ik u even wat vragen?'* (Excuse me, may I ask you a question?); Schmit – *'Ja bitte.'* (Yes, please); Me – *'Waar is de looked Schakelaar?'* (Where is the mains switch?). Schmit sat down, absolutely bemused by my question. Both guards looked up at the ceiling and down at the floor. The expressions on all their faces except that of Fraulein Helga Keller, the secretary, seemed totally puzzled.

All went quiet when Helga stood up, walked over to the door behind Schmit, fetched a chair and stood upon it to show Schmit what I had asked for. Helga – *'Das ist Schakelaar.'* (That is the mains switch). Helga returned to her seat.

'So you speak Dutch,' Schmit said as he walked towards her.

'I speak German, Dutch and a little English,' she replied.

'Very educated young lady,' Schmit said before he sat down at his desk. 'Has he been speaking true Dutch?'

'Oh yes, Herr Schmit, absolutely. No doubt about it.'

Schmit then looked closely at my papers, folded them back into my black leather permit holder, and handed them to me.

'Thank you for helping my country by getting coal from Maastricht to Amsterdam, and for being a good electrical engineer at one of our best coal mines at Hücklehoven.'

'You're very welcome, sir,' I replied, but I knew I must get away as soon as possible.

He told the guard to take off the handcuffs. The marks on my wrist were very red because of the metal rubbing against my skin. 'Would you please show our comrade to the main door, Fraulein Keller,' Schmit said courteously.

With that she got up, stretched her lovely slim body and opened the door for me. 'I'll walk with you to the main door; you won't find it by yourself.' She winked and gave me a piece of paper which I stuffed into my left trouser pocket. 'The officer has given you a permit to return to Thorn.' Quietly she said to me, 'I belong to the Dutch Resistance here at Monchen-Gladbach. I know Doctor de Bruin and I got Jan out before your interview with Schmit. He is waiting for you at the dentist's up the road, about two kilometres from here. Go there. If Jan isn't there, wait for him. I will see you straight after work. Good luck.'

'Thank you and take care,' I replied and walked out through the two big black iron gates as quickly as possible. I checked on the piece of paper she had given me. It was the address of the Dentist, Doctor Heinrich Muller. I put it inside my sling and briskly strode off to my new destination.

As I passed the Waffen SS guards I noticed the streets were full of wandering people carrying their bags of shopping and couldn't help but wonder how easy it had been to be free again. Was it a bit of luck? Had the Resistance been behind my release? Or were there going to be people shot for my release? When Schmit had said to Helga Keller that I could go, I couldn't believe what my ears were hearing.

If fate hadn't been kind to me since I landed in Holland a few weeks ago, it was certainly making up for it now. Why the Germans had let me go in that manner, I could only speculate. I tried to dismiss it from my mind as I was getting my bearings from Helga's map, my main objective now being to get to Dr Muller's dental surgery as soon as possible.

In the meantime I could hear the rumbling noise of gunfire. To me gunfire meant battle and battle meant death. Suddenly, out of the light blue sky flew a Mosquito with its machine-guns blazing away at the building I had just left. I thought to myself, that was a close shave! Did the Royal Air Force know I was coming out at this time, or was it coincidence? My question was soon to be answered. More Mosquitoes appeared as though it was a planned attack on the German HQ.

As the machine-gun fire became more intense, so more and more people added to the confusion. One huge explosion behind me lifted me off my feet. God, I thought, I hope Helga had gone to the surgery during her lunch hour. Black smoke mushroomed into the sky as bells of the so-called German

Army Fire Brigade began to sound in the distance. People with small children and load of belongings began running here and there. Some went into the underground shelters, others went down into their friends' shelters in frantic confusion. As I crossed the road a large hand slapped me on my left shoulder. Good God, I thought, what the hell was that? Amongst all the chaos there stood Jan, laughing, as I spun around.

'On your way to have your teeth out?' he said in German.

'Jan,' I said, 'follow me, but be quick about it.' We went from one side of the street to the other, looking for some kind of transport.

'I thought I had better collect you in case Helga couldn't bring you,' he said.

'I'm damn glad you did, with all this mêlée about us,' I replied.

'Good show, my boy,' he said, 'what more could you want? You've got your boys in blue blasting away above us, and people down here not knowing which way to go – great chance for an escape,' and he went on, 'we need to get to Doctor Muller's dental surgery now that I've found you. I told them I would be back within forty-five minutes if I found you.'

I asked Jan, 'How did the Royal Air Force know we were being released?'

'Ah, that's a secret,' he replied. 'When she left you, she ran back to the transmitter control room at the SS Headquarters, and sent a message to London informing them of the time of your escape,'

'Who, Helga?' I asked.

'Yes,' Jan replied, 'the only worry we had was how many Allied airmen we had in the building which was to be attacked.' I told him I had seen one in Schmit's building. 'Yes, you did, but Helga got him out to Stalag Luft Three this morning,' he replied.

'How many crashed, Jan?'

'Two at least, I believe, the boys are out looking for them now,' he replied.

As we turned the corner at the crossroads, a few hundred yards outside the village of Horst, we saw a lorry compound. In it were dozens of heavy-duty trucks, Kubels, tank carriers, lightweight vehicles like the Kubels and motorcycles and side cars which could accommodate three people. Due to the air raid, the guards had all gone, but of course the gates were locked. I managed to cut a hole in the poor quality wire and get into the compound where I selected a Kubel. (This is a four-wheeled, open-topped, lightweight vehicle used by senior officers as normal daily transport.) I found two wires under the dashboard, near the ignition switch, touched them together and the diesel engine fired up. Sweat was pouring from my forehead and down over my face.

Jan came running over with a 5-litre can of diesel. 'I've also pinched some thunderflashes,' he said. 'I've prised open the lock on the main entrance gates and removed the bar. The gates are now open.'

'You're a wonderful chap, Jan,' I said, 'I don't know what I'd do without you.' I checked the fuel gauge which showed nearly full and off we went as fast as we could to Thorn.

'What were you putting into their fuel tanks back there, Jan?' I asked inquisitively.

'Oh, that,' Jan replied. 'I was putting sugar lumps into as many of the tanks as possible.'

'Why?' I asked.

'Well by tomorrow morning, the dear old Obersturmführer in charge of the vehicles will have the shock of his life when none of them start,' Jan replied.

Once we had cleared the town the traffic thinned out but not for long, as we came across a vast convoy of German Army traffic travelling nose to tail. There were lorries, tanks, light-armoured vehicles, cars, a section of motorcyclists – every conceivable type of transport one could imagine, all going our way. The great German war machine was on the move, north-west to Holland. This gave us the opportunity of getting between two of the heavy armoured trucks without soldiers in them, giving us ample cover, keeping the Kubel as close as possible to them and hoping that the convoy was going to

Roermond. Although we were driving a German Kubel in Dutch clothes luck was with us for as we got to Erklenz they turned off the main road, leaving us to go straight on ahead into the peace of the night. This gave me the opportunity to see my favourite star, the North star. We soon arrived at the Zur Post and luckily for Jan and me Dr Sylvie was still with her boyfriend, Leutnant Dahn. This was a relief because we couldn't have got past the Roermond barrier in a German Kubel in Dutch civilian clothes. Jan decided to fetch Sylvie while I waited in the car.

Not many minutes passed when I saw Leutnant Dahn, Dr Sylvie and Jan appear at the entrance of the restaurant. Jan came across to me alone leaving Sylvie and her Luftwaffe friend to say their usual farewells. Soon we saw Leutnant Dahn, dressed in his motorcycle outfit, racing off in the direction of Wahn.

Dr Sylvie came running across to the Kubel, jumped in the passenger seat and kissed me tenderly. 'Oh, it's lovely to see you again, darling,' she said, as she kissed me again, holding my left hand. 'How are your right hand and arm, Donald?'

'Not too bad,' I replied, 'a bit sore and it itches like hell at night. We've been so busy that I'd forgotten that I had any injuries at all for a while.'

She looked around at the back seat area and asked, 'What have you got here, Donald.'

'In England we call it a cache. All these weapons were here when we pinched the Kubel,' I replied.

'What was it all for, do you think?' Sylvie asked.

'Since this vehicle was destined to go to Holland with a convoy, it must have been a supply truck.'

Jan was again doing his sugar lump trick. 'What's he doing?' asked Sylvie.

'Well, Jan said that if you put sugar lumps in the fuel tanks, by the morning the engines are disabled and won't start, which he finds great fun. So if you ever have any sugar lumps to spare, give them to Jan,' I replied.

'Yes, I'll do that, darling,' Sylvie said as she squeezed my hand. 'I've been so worried about you since you didn't return this afternoon. Doctor de Bruin cycled to Miep's barge but you weren't there,' Sylvie said. 'We then heard that you'd been captured at the restaurant in Thorn and had been taken to the Waffen SS Headquarters at Horst. Luckily Fraulein Helga Keller telephoned me a few minutes after the SS had compiled their list of prisoners.'

'God bless Helga,' I said, raising the bottle of beer which Jan had brought out of the restaurant when he went to collect Dr Sylvie. 'The walk to Thorn with Jan was quite an experience, Sylvie. These bloody Germans move like lightning. Dozens of them came in from all directions even as Jan and I sat at our table.'

Sylvie angrily said to me, 'You are careless, Donald. All of us here are risking our lives for your freedom and there you were taking a bloody walk through the streets of Thorn to have a drink. Next time I will crown you with a coffee pot with such force you will have a headache for days.'

I asked Jan to get us three more lagers as we were all very thirsty. 'What a day, Sylvie,' I said. 'The SS would frighten anybody to death; it was lucky your friend Helga was there. I couldn't understand how London found out when the first wave of Mosquitoes came over and started bombing the headquarters and surrounding buildings.'

After a few beers I drove the Kubel up to Wassenburg Hospital where we transferred the arms to the Mercedes and hid the Kubel in one of the disused garages. Sylvie then drove us back to the surgery at Thorn.

22

The next morning Sylvie woke me with a warm hug, kissing me on the lips in her lovely double bed, alone in the surgery at Thorn.

'I'm so exhausted after that escape from the SS at Horst, I could really do with a few hours lie in,' I said to Sylvie, as I awoke to the most important day of my life. Today, I thought, I might be killed, imprisoned, or be home in the early hours of tomorrow morning. One half of my mind was considering answers to the ever increasing questions feeding my brain. The other half was enjoying the warm embrace Sylvie was giving me, since this was to be our last day together.

'It's your own bloody fault you're so tired. Fancy going for a walk with Jan in broad daylight into Thorn to have a drink, both of you must have been mad! What did you think you were doing? Walking down Oxford Street in London to have a few beers? In reality you were walking into an ambush from the ever increasing number of German foot patrols in the area. I'm very annoyed with both of you, especially Jan, who should have known better,' she said, half turning away from me in the lovely warm bed while the birds sang a chorus outside the window.

'I'm deeply sorry, Sylvie. I promise not to leave my "safe house" again without a Dutch Resistance member with me,' I replied.

'I'll forgive you this time, darling, but next time I might even shoot you myself,' Sylvie said.

I turned her towards me and kissed her slim, beautiful body. 'You're a wonderful person, darling, and I love you,' I said, letting her go.

'Don't forget the two passwords I've got for you. The one to get you into Luftwaffe Wahn is *"Der Pfeil"*. The other is to get you onto the airfield perimeter, and that's *"Der blau vogel."* I've written the words down, remember them, then destroy this note,' Sylvie said as she handed it to me. 'Come on, it's Finals Day, or call it what you like. We have a lot to do,' she said as she kissed me and hopped out of bed. She showered, washed her hair and got dressed in a plain black skirt, a white blouse, which had three buttons in the top half, plus a collar which had a very attractive frill around the neck.

Sometime later I joined her for breakfast. Food was in short supply, but the full coffee pot compensated for the shortage.

At 0930 hours we joined the third meeting chaired by Dr de Bruin in the Abbey chapter house. In attendance were the usual members plus the monk who would be forging the identification papers at the hospital that afternoon. He opened the meeting by saying the Allies had now established a strong foothold in northern Holland while the V1 Flying Bombs were increasing by the day from their newly established launching sites. They were being moved frequently from the threat of attacks from the American 8th Air Force based in England. Dutch Resistance was doing the best it could under the circumstances to get information on the sites back to London.

Dr de Bruin then informed us of the two passwords to gain entry into Luftwaffe Wahn and the airfield. He said, 'Jan and Stefan have done an excellent job bringing photographs and drawings of the most important installations which we needed to get Squadron Leader Hamilton away with the Messerschmitt. Doctor Sylvie received information last night from Leutnant Dahn on the range, ceiling height, armament, cruising speed and stalling speed of the aircraft. She didn't get the take-off speed so it's up to Donald to use his own judgement on that score. We can't help him since he's the only pilot amongst us.

'It was agreed that Doctor Sylvie see Leutnant Dahn in the

hospital at four this afternoon, for his "sex session". Our friend, Piet van de Houst, will then get the identification papers completed and return them to the ward sister as soon as possible. Squadron Leader Hamilton will then have in his possession his complete set of identification papers and passwords. Any questions, ladies and gentlemen?' Dr de Bruin asked. There was complete silence.

'Well then, ladies and gentlemen, I suggest we disperse as soon as possible, and once again you must burn any paperwork before you leave this room. I would like to thank, on behalf of all of us, the efforts Stefan Miere has put into this operation,' he said as he sat down. We all applauded quietly and each of us either embraced or shook hands.

'I now close this third and final meeting, and wish you all God speed and good luck in tonight's operation. Further, I would like to thank Squadron Leader Donald Hamilton for being an excellent guest. I hope he gets back to England safely, taking with him so much vital information. We wish him every success and happiness in his marriage to his fiancée Barbara on his return.' He came over and embraced me saying, 'Good luck, son,' as he left the room.

After a few words with me, Sylvie left the room to start her morning surgery. Jan, Stefan and I got out the maps to absorb the information on the airfield installation, details of the route and the spot where we were to kill Leutnant Dahn.

Jan and I chatted for a long time on how I was going to fly an aeroplane which was unknown to me. What with no introduction and no familiarisation with night flying, this task did not thrill me, in fact, I was rather frightened at the prospect. But with all those Resistance workers giving me their support, and the high risks they were taking against the occupying forces, I had no choice but to fly the machine at all costs. I gave both Jan and Stefan their instructions for helping me to start the aircraft. Jan would have to stay on the ground at all times to support me in starting both engines. If we come under intense fire from the machine-gun posts, we would have to abandon the flight and escape in the coal lorry as best we could. London would be informed of our potential time of

261

take-off and would be attacking Luftwaffe Wahn at that time. At least, the Royal Air Force would not only make a diversion but would keep the Wehrmacht busy while we made our escape.

After Jan and Stefan had left, I sat down with my map of Europe, which included Holland, Belgium, and southern Germany where Luftwaffe Wahn was situated.

As I was preparing myself to leave with Jan and Stefan in the coal lorry, I saw Dr Sylvie, dressed as though she was going to an English film premiere, on her way to meet Leutnant Dahn at the restaurant Zur Post.

Jan dropped me off at the Zur Post later and I hid on the back seat of the Mercedes, while Jan and Stefan continued on their journey towards Erklenze to prepare the steel wire trap for Leutnant Dahn. It seemed a long time, waiting for Sylvie and her Luftwaffe pilot to appear at the entrance of the restaurant. I got cramp in my legs and chest as I lay there on the floor behind the driver's seat. But Sylvie timed her exit from the restaurant to perfection. It was dark and although there was cloud about the night was quite bright with a near full moon. I was too far away to hear what they were saying but I saw the German pilot embrace Sylvie, kiss her and salute. He then put on his motorcycle clothes which he had stored in the sidecar. With one kick the engine roared into life with a big plume of smoke from its exhaust. After putting on his lights, he waved her goodbye and off he raced in the direction of Erklenze, where Jan and Stefan were waiting.

Dr Sylvie rushed over to the Mercedes and after a few stretching exercises I sat in the passenger seat. Minutes later we followed Dahn's route, keeping well out of sight. We passed a few German motorised patrols, some of which were local while others were large enough to be on their way into northern Holland.

We arrived at the spot where the coal lorry was parked in the trees off the road. If it hadn't been for Stefan's flashlight, we would have driven right past them. Two hundred yards up the road was where they had set Dahn's trap, and it had

262

succeeded. When I went over with Stefan, Jan was pulling his body out of the ditch. His face had been badly damaged, and his neck was broken. He was dead! Jan said he had hit one of the trees when he was catapulted off his machine.

While Jan and Stefan were getting the motorcycle out of the ditch, I was swapping clothes with the dead Luftwaffe pilot. Once I had them on they were not a bad fit! His chest was slightly bigger than mine so his jacket hung a little loosely over my shoulders. I checked I had my identification papers in my top pocket and completed dressing, putting on the helmet, trench coat and boots and placing the goggles around the top of my helmet.

I went over to Sylvie, embraced her and thanked her for all the work she had done and for the love she had given me. 'I love you and if I don't marry Barbara I'll come over to Thorn as soon as I can after the war has ended.'

She held both her hands against my face and said, 'Goodbye, Donald. Good luck. It's been lovely knowing you,' and with that she kissed me before returning to the car.

Dr de Bruin and Kees arrived. They put Dahn's body into their car, along with my Dutch clothes, and set off for Wassenburg Hospital. By now Jan and Stefan had the motorcycle on the road. The front mudguard was bent, and so was the headlamp, but after a few minutes all the repairs had been done to the best of their ability. I prayed that the headlamp would work. When I kick-started the engine it fired first time and the lights came on. Jan said, 'Let's go.' I waited until they had backed the lorry onto the road, and we set off for Luftwaffe Wahn. I followed about a hundred yards behind with Sylvie close behind me. Her headlights were a help to me, enabling me to see the road more clearly.

As we approached the airfield we stopped about half a mile short of the main gates and within minutes of switching off our engines and lights the first wave of Mosquitoes arrived. Huge orange and yellow flames leapt into the sky after the first attack. They must have dropped their 500 lb bombs on the hangars, crew quarters and fuel dump; there was a huge explosion when that went up and we could feel the force of the explosion from where we were waiting. Jan switched on his lights, signalling it was time to go in. Sirens were going now all over the whole aerodrome as another wave of Mosquitoes came in machine-gunning the entrance gates and surrounding buildings.

By the time we arrived there was only one sentry left. He operated the barrier by hand, a brave man. He stopped Jan, checked his papers, lifted the barrier and let him through. As soon as he saw me he saluted and let me pass too. On seeing Dr Sylvie's Mercedes with her pennant flying he just waved her through. I stopped and looked behind me. She went straight to the Commandant's house while I went on up to the airfield. I gave the sentry my papers and password, he saluted then ran like hell as the Mosquitoes came in very low, strafing with their machine-guns again. God, I thought, I hope I don't get hit, and I sped through the gates onto the perimeter of the airfield. I rode to the final Messerschmitt at the end of the line up having collected some parachutes from the flying room of the only remaining hangar.

I was surprised to see Jan and Stefan were already there. 'What about the coal?' I asked Jan.

'Oh that, we've still got it; your boys were too hot for us to deliver so we made our way here.'

The Mosquitoes were still circling, blasting off their guns at treetop level. Stefan, with his torch, was sending a morse code message to every plane that came in sight. Jan helped me take off my motorcycle outfit but I kept the goggles, as they might come in handy. Out of the blue Dr Sylvie arrived at the scene. 'There weren't any German guards about. They took to the underground shelters when the Mosquitoes started their attack. They were certainly doing some damage,' she said.

She came over to me as I was just about to get into the cockpit. 'Can I come with you, Donald?' she said excitedly.

I replied, 'Are you sure you want to?'

'Yes,' she said, 'I want to come with you to England. I shall be safe there. One day the Gestapo are going to get me, my luck can't last, Donald.'

I kissed her and said, 'Of course you can come with me,' and I told her and Stefan to get a flying suit and a parachute each from the sidecar.

I then went over to Jan, embraced him and said, 'I owe you a great deal. Thank you for everything you've done. After the war I'll come back and visit Miep and yourself.' We embraced again.

'Go on, Donald. Get in that bloody plane and good luck,' he said. 'What's Sylvie doing here?'

'She's coming with us,' I replied.

He went over to her, held her tight, kissed her and said his farewells to her. 'We will miss you, Sylvie. Good luck.'

I then asked Jan and Stefan to find me an electrical starter and they went off to find a trolley ACC. In the meantime I kitted out Sylvie with her flying suit and parachute and looked around inside the aircraft for something to pad the three bucket seats. Luckily the last crew to use if had left their flying jackets behind which we used as best we could to make the seats more comfortable.

At last Jan and Stefan arrived with the trolley ACC which carried the large, heavy-duty accumulator to start the engines. Except for Jan, we got into the aircraft. Sylvie and Stefan settled themselves in and told me over the intercom that they were ready to go. I gave the signal to Jan to plug in the heavy-duty powerline from the trolley to the aircraft's electrical system. He gave me the thumbs up which indicated I could go ahead and start the engines so I set the controls for starting. I pressed the port engine button and the engine fired with a roar of satisfaction. I checked that the engine revolutions were building up on the port engine RPM gauge and the oil pressure was rising to its normal level. When the port engine generator warning light went out I pressed the button to start the starboard engine. After a couple of restarts she fired with tremendous thrust. As with the port engine, I checked the dials for the appropriate oil and revolutions. With both engines ticking over and the engine dials working satisfactorily, I signalled to Jan to unplug the trolley ACC from the aircraft.

While taxiing my way round to the take-off point, I did my take-off checks. This would save stopping so that I could move the German fighter straight into position and into the wind for take-off. As I came closer to the take-off point, I checked that the cylinder head temperatures of the two engines had reached normal levels.

As I moved into position I could see that the Mosquitoes were on target and doing their stuff. Seconds prior to releasing the brakes I told the crew over the intercom we were about to leave Germany. I then pushed the engine throttles forward and the wheels gradually gained speed over the bumpy grass runway. As we accelerated I pushed the two engine throttles forward as far as they would go to obtain maximum power for take-off. When we reached flying speed of 170 k.p.h. the wheels left the ground and I had to put slight back pressure on the control to achieve a positive rate of climb.

Once at a safe height I selected undercarriage up. The lights went from green to red and when fully retracted all the undercarriage lights went out. You could hear the whine of the wheels rising into their housing and a satisfying thump as they locked in. At last I was happier with the dials and controls of the aircraft so I called over the intercom to see if both my crew were all right. Sylvie said she was a bit nervous but was enjoying the excitement, which was more than I was struggling to fly a German aircraft.

With an empty sky under a half moon I began to wonder what was going to happen next as we were now some miles from the noise and destruction at Wahn caused by the Royal Air Force bombing raid. These minutes of quiet we had had since take-off were vital to us, but eventually our luck ran out. In a matter of seconds all hell was let loose as ground gun flashes appeared below and exploding shells began to appear all around us. One was so close that it shattered part of the aileron but luckily the aircraft had split ailerons. The exploding shells threw us about somewhat but at least we were still flying. Then the darkness ahead was lit up by searchlight beams probing the sky. I decided immediately to climb as steeply as I could to 15,000 ft which we reached in seven minutes. The Bf 110G was a powerful machine, although she was a bit heavy on the controls and her manoeuvrability was sluggish.

Although we couldn't escape the searchlights, we managed to escape a lot of the flak that was being thrown at us. The moonlight was an advantage flying over unknown territory and as we flew north east I picked up the landmark of the River Rhine. However as I didn't know how much fuel I had on board, I decided to leave the Rhine just west of Düsseldorf. We could see the Royal Air Force had heavily bombed the city from the fires they had left behind. Burning buildings and factories were still blazing over a large area and even smaller fires could be seen a few miles from the damaged city. Perhaps we had just missed one of Bomber Harris's thousand-bomber raids which by now were quite common at night over Germany.

I turned west to cross the border near Venio. As soon as I made my manoeuvre Stefan shouted down the intercom that we had company. It was a Me 109E, one of the most successful German fighters of the Second World War. I told Stefan to prepare his twin 7.9 mm machine-guns for action in case our friend had been notified of our existence. He circled us repeatedly, probably to read our registration number or what group we were attached to.

I selected my two forward 30 mm cannons and the two 20 mm cannons which were in the nose in case he became unfriendly. Since there was only one of them, I reckoned that perhaps he didn't know who we were otherwise I'd have had swarms of them around us. But caution had to be exercised as he could have been sent out knowing that one of their precious machines had been stolen from Wahn. I kept waving my wings and maintained course so as not to entice him into combat although I had enough armament in the nose of the aircraft to blast him out of the sky. The problem for me was that he knew my weaknesses, namely the twin 7.9 mm pivotal machine-gun at the rear and my poor manoeuvrability.

He was quite determined to be a nuisance to us but I decided not to play with him and kept on my original course and eventually he got bored with my antics and flew south towards Cologne. I was very relieved when he left us as it seemed he'd been monitoring us for long enough. I reduced height to 10,000 ft so that my crew could remove their oxygen masks, and also to preserve fuel. When we crossed the Dutch border just south of Venlo I was greatly relieved, since I knew the ground below very well. I told Sylvie where we were and that we were heading a few miles south of Eindhoven.

When we reached the inlet of Westerschelde I worked out that we had flown 200 miles. I was still worried whether I had drop tanks attached to the wings which some of these type of aircraft were fitted with and asked Sylvie to come forward with her torch. 'How exciting being up front with you, Donald. Look at all those dials. Jesus, how do you know what dial gives information about what?' she said bemused.

'You have certain indicators like height, fuel, artificial horizon, air speed, temperatures of the cylinder heads of the engines and so on. These are fundamental to all aircraft,' I replied quickly. 'Do me a favour with your torch and have a look around the cockpit and under or near my seat, and see if there are any levers of any kind, will you?' After looking around most of the cockpit she said she couldn't see what I was after. 'Thanks, Sylvie, on your way back to your seat, just look out of your windows either side, look under the wings and see if you can see any objects which look like cigar-shaped fuel tanks. There will be one under each wing if we have any on board.'

'Yes, dear,' she replied as she returned to her seat. After a few minutes she came over the intercom to say that the engines were in the way and she couldn't see anything cigar-shaped.

As we left the coast of Holland behind and started to cross the North Sea, I reduced height once again to 6,000 ft to conserve fuel. As I took a breather, wishing I had a bottle of Dutch lager at hand, I thought about the most hazardous part of the journey home now that we had got away from the danger zones over Germany and Holland. I wondered just how I was going to get to Royal Air Force Hambridge, with those heavily defended southern coastlines. Apart from a radio with

German frequencies on it, all we had on board which was very fortunate for us, was an Aldis lamp. Even that wouldn't save us from a high explosive shell or a marauding Spitfire pilot. I could fly north to Felixstowe and then down behind the two major gun belts, the problem being that I might not have enough fuel. My gauges were indicating well below half full now so I decided to reduce speed which would give me a bit more time to think and also reduce fuel consumption. I told the crew to put on the seat belts since we were now approaching the British and American defences on the English coast.

Over the intercom I asked Stefan to get the Aldis lamp ready and to make safe his twin machine-guns. 'We don't want any mishaps at this stage,' I told him.

'Yes, Captain,' he replied.

I switched on the German radar equipment which included a monitor on which you could adjust the brightness and a number of black circles appeared on the screen. The range of the equipment seemed to be 2.5 miles. I decided, after checking my remaining fuel, that I would head for Rye, as I knew that the ground defences weren't so concentrated there compared to Dover. I would then do a 45-degree north-east turn and fly south to Ashford. At least I would have a better chance of avoiding being hit by ack-ack on this route. I would then fly to Hambridge. Only one problem came to mind – our own night fighters of Spitfires, Mosquitoes and the new American Mustang, which was very fast.

I switched on the radio transmitter and twiddled the knobs. All I could get were various whistles and spurious responses. Just as I was struggling with all these problems I had another one on my hands, a radar blip on the outer edges of the screen. It had to be an aircraft of some sort. Immediately I told the crew that we had company. I didn't know what to expect as he was flying across my screen. This meant he was flying parallel with us and going our way, which told me it was one of ours returning to base in England. Eventually I saw him about 10 miles from Rye.

He swung his aircraft immediately towards us and in seconds he had damaged the outer edge and aileron of my port wing. I dived steeply to sea level and he followed me. Luckily with a light fuel load my plane's speed was faster than his. I told Stefan to flash him with the Aldis lamp to say we were friendly, and British, from 629 Squadron, and I reduced speed to demonstrate my friendliness. He flew alongside me and I repeatedly waggled my wings whilst slowing down to the lowest speed I dare without stalling. In daylight my attacker would have pointed his hand in the direction he wanted me to go, but this was night, and we pilots couldn't see each other. Stefan kept up his morse code on the lamp and eventually he got the message and flew straight in front of me. He was very close which I could also see from the radar blip on my monitor; he climbed to 3,000 ft and I followed. He took us straight over Folkestone and both of us dropped our landing gear down. After doing my landing checks I touched down at Royal Air Force Hambridge.

I manoeuvred the plane at the instructions given by the ground controller who was holding two lighted torches in his hands. After stopping at the requested pan on the far side of the airfield, I applied the brakes and switched off the engines. As I opened my cockpit the first person to shout at me was one of my 629 Squadron groundcrew, Corporal Jackson. I told him I would be down in a minute, and went back to tell Sylvie and Stefan to sit tight in their seats until I got back which might be a little while. On no account were they to leave the aircraft, for any person, of whatever rank. 'Tell them you're Squadron Leader Donald Hamilton's guests: you, Sylvie, are a naturalised New Zealander and Stefan, you're a leader in the Dutch Resistance. If they insist, tell them that if they remove you from these seats they will be personally answerable to me.' They were both happy with the situation when I had explained to them that by law they were both foreigners.

As I climbed from the aircraft I was surrounded by a huge gathering of trucks, fire engines, ambulances, jeeps and dozens of people, some from 629 Squadron, others from other squadrons of all ranks from caterers to administrators. It was a tremendous reception especially at that time of the morning.

Once away from the aeroplane I was greeted by the Station Commander, the Adjutant, Duty Officer and the Senior Air Traffic Controller. Running up into my arms was Cynthia from 629 Squadron Office. She embraced me so tightly that some of my sweat soaked into her uniform as she gave me a passionate kiss and said how pleased she was that I was home. She had telephoned my parents, Barbara and her parents, and my three sisters. After talking to the Station Commander and the Intelligence Officer it was agreed that my guests would be released into my custody. The first thing was for us all to go to the Officers' Mess, have a meal and a shower, and discuss formalities later.

There were great cheers and applause as Dr Sylvie and Stefan jumped down off the port wing of the plane. Corporal Jackson, who was a real gentleman, helped her off the wing as I introduced them both to the senior officers present and we all jumped into the Station Commander's jeep. He told the Adjutant to put a 24-hour guard on the plane.

As we arrived at the Officers' Mess Flying Officer Louisa Jefferson was waiting to greet me with a salute and a smile. 'Pleased to see you home,' she said jubilantly, 'I have arranged some tea, coffee and sandwiches as I didn't think you'd want a cooked breakfast at this hour.'

'Thank you, Miss Jefferson, and congratulations on your promotion,' I replied as I stood by her.

'Thank you, sir,' she said, 'your family and fiancée will be arriving around eleven. They're being flown up by Anson, having coffee and lunch and then they'll be flown back to Royal Air Force Bovingdon.'

'Could you find some accommodation for my guest Doctor Sylvie Chenneviere, who will be staying a few days as my guest?'

'Yes, sir, I'll do that immediately.'

'Put her as near to your room as possible,' I said.

'Yes, sir,' she answered as she went off to make arrangements with either the Mess Secretary or the Duty Officer.

I went over to the Intelligence Officer to talk to him about

Stefan and how he had saved my life. 'We'll have to put him in the guardroom for the night after he's eaten. I'll go over and talk to him; you'd better come with me,' I said.

'Yes, sir,' he said, following me over to Stefan who was at the bar drinking his favourite lager.

'Stefan,' I said, 'after you've eaten with us I'm afraid we shall have to put you in a Guardroom cell, just for the night. Then tomorrow we'll make arrangements for you to go to London and meet up with your friends. Is that all right?'

'Can I take a few beers in the cell?' he asked.

'I think we can overlook the rules this one night, eh, Jim? Especially as tomorrow I'm recommending him for an honorary award.'

Jim replied, 'Yes, OK, but not too many, we don't want any trouble in the Guardroom.'

'Of course, Jim, I understand. He's been up about twenty-seven hours, so I don't think it will be very long before he's asleep,' I replied.

Just then noises came into the anteroom and there were Pilot Officer Matthews and Philip Tremeer. We were all delighted to see each other and all embraced. Matt said, 'You look thin, Donald.'

I replied. 'So would you, living on bread and water for a few weeks.'

Matt went on, 'Glad to see you back.'

'Thanks,' I said.

'I see you've had your plaster off.'

'Oh that bloody thing, yes, it came off a while ago.'

'Now you can get a beer for Doctor Sylvie Chenneviere, and one for me,' and I introduced them both to Sylvie. I sat her down with Stefan at a table with upholstered chairs.

I heard Matt say, 'I don't know how Donald finds such attractive, professional-looking women. A doctor, eh? She won't be single long if I have anything to do with it.'

Philip said, 'Trust you to go for all the women who are pretty and slim.'

'That's my boy,' Matt replied as they walked away to the bar.

While we were all chatting about what had happened to the Squadron while I was away the Station Commander came over and shook hands with my guests. 'I'll see you in the morning, Donald. Could you be in my office at half nine?'

I stood up and said, 'Yes, sir.'

He stepped back, looked at my waist and said, 'I think you'd better hand that gun in to the armoury in the morning and get your batwoman to get you a replacement number one blue uniform, don't you think?'

Smiling back at him, I replied, 'Yes, sir.' We shook hands and said goodnight.

While the pilots and ground crew joined us for a real rave up, I could see that Sylvie was nodding off. It had been a long, hard, stressful day. I clutched her hand, said our farewells to the lads at the party and led her along the corridor towards the WAAF Officers' Mess. 'What lovely accommodation you have here, Donald, such beautiful paintings and furnishings, are all Officers' Messes the same?' she asked, putting her head on my shoulder. Then she turned her head, kissed me on my left cheek and said, 'No wonder you're a Squadron Leader, you're such a fine pilot and the boys back there think the world of you. You must be very thrilled at being home. You'll be seeing Barbara tomorrow while I'm making contact with my cousin in London, won't you?' With that she clasped my hand tighter but I didn't reply. Flying Officer Jefferson came along and took Sylvie to her quarters. Somebody was occupying my room, a Squadron Leader Negus who had taken over 629 Squadron as my replacement.

I just found another empty room, stripped off my German uniform, had a shower and went fast asleep in one of those standard Officers' Mess beds.

23

After a deep sleep, I woke up at 0830 hours. God, I thought to myself, I have to be in the boss's office at 0930 hours. Luckily I met Juliet in the corridor. She almost fainted when she saw me. 'Pleased to see you, sir, it's been a long time, hasn't it?' She gave me that beautiful smile of hers.

'Yes, Juliet. Can you find my number one blue or battledress, and get me a cup of tea? I have to be in the boss's office within the hour. Also tell my guest, Doctor Sylvie Chenneviere I will see her for coffee between ten-thirty and eleven-thirty in the ante-room where we were last night.'

'Yes, sir, I'll get on with that right away. Glad to see you back, sir.' She walked off quickly to help me get ready for my appointment. The boss was a stickler for timing, so I wouldn't be late. At 0930 hours I reported to the Adjutant's office to see the Station Commander. His door opened and he shouted, 'Come in, Donald.' I entered the room feeling rather tired and weary, saluted and was offered a seat in front of the boss's table. 'Nice to see you home, Donald. We had some anxious moments in the first few days when we didn't get any news of you. I'm afraid I had to send the usual telegram to your parents. But as it's procedure, I had to send it. Neither Matthews nor Tremeer actually saw you go down,' he said as he sat down.

'Yes, I know. I kept calling out May Day, but with no response. Still, as you will see in my report later I was lucky to land in a lake near a river with barges carrying coal from Maastricht to Amsterdam. I was also fortunate to find a young couple, who sheltered me on their barge until I got help from

274

the Dutch Resistance. They were wonderful to me. Without their help, I would be a prisoner of war by now.'

'Donald, could you submit your report as soon as possible. I suggest that as you can't write with your injured arm, you dictate it to Miss Jefferson in her office.' The boss then yawned his head off – he must have been as tired as we were after such a late night. He continued, 'As Miss Jefferson may have told you already, as soon as we had heard you had left the Dutch coast, we made contact with your parents and Miss Jefferson telephoned your fiancée. All associated relations, I believe five in all, will be arriving at eleven this morning by Anson from Bovingdon. I'll pick you up in my staff car at ten-fifty at the Mess. Is that OK, Donald?'

'Yes, sir,' I replied.

The Station Commander went on, 'I've arranged light refreshments for when they arrive in the ante-room, and lunch at one. I thought a good Sunday lunch would be appropriate for this occasion, at the end of which I'll give a welcoming speech to all those who attend. Some of your fellow pilots have been invited, including two major contributors from your ground crew, now Warrant Officer Devlin and Corporal Jackson. I think for this occasion we can break the rules and invite non-commissioned officers, don't you think?'

'Definitely,' I replied.

'Once you've completed your report, will you get Jefferson to bring it into me immediately? I want her to start typing on completion of your dictation.'

'Yes, sir, I'll do it now,' I replied.

'As soon as your report is typed, I've got to telex it to the Air Ministry, so you know how important your information is going to be.'

I stood to attention, put my cap on, and saluted with my left hand. I then closed the Station Commander's door and went into Louisa's office. When I had completed my dictation to Miss Jefferson, I was called back into the Station Commander's office. 'Donald,' Group Captain Walker said, 'I have some good news for you which is well deserved. Now that you can't fly on combat operations until your arm has healed, Air Officer Commanding ADGB has promoted you, with immediate effect. After treatment at the Plastic Unit at East Grinstead, and a spot of leave, you will be posted to Royal Air Force Hawkinge in the substantive rank of Squadron Leader, to offer your expertise on attacking the V1 Flying Bomb. In the meantime, and while being treated, you will still be under my command here at Hambridge. You can help me with all this unbelievable paperwork which hangs over my head each day.' He lit another cigarette, stood up and shook my good hand. 'Well done, Donald, you've been an inspiration to us all at Hambridge, and we wish you every success at Hawkinge.'

As he sat down I replied, 'It's been a privilege to serve under your command, and to lead such a fine bunch of lads at 629 Squadron. They've become my friends, all of them. I'm sorry to be losing their company and friendship. Could I make a request, sir?'

'Yes, of course,' he replied.

'I would like to take Corporal Cynthia Woodhams with me to Hawkinge, sir, as my secretary.'

'I don't see why not,' he replied. 'I'll have to talk to Squadron Leader Negus, your replacement, but I'm sure he won't mind.

'Thank you, sir,' I replied, and went back into Miss Jefferson's office before walking jubilantly back to the Officers' Mess.

I went into the library and there was Sylvie reading a book about London. 'You all right?' I asked with a sparkle in my eyes.

She kissed me and said, 'Where is Kensington in London? I have a cousin living there and would like you to take me there tomorrow if you have time.'

I replied, 'We'll have lunch at the Café Royale with Stefan, and find your cousin. Alternatively, you can be the guest of the Station Commander and stay here for a few days. Would you like that?'

'That would be lovely, Donald, but what about Barbara?'

'Well, I'm sure she won't mind a couple of days. I can always fly up to see her any evening.'

'That would be wonderful, Donald.' Changing the subject, she said, 'You know, you officers live in a palace compared to Luftwaffe pilots.'

'Yes, I know, but they worry more about gold braid epaulettes on their uniforms, rather than their accommodation.'

At 1030 hours the Station Commander's car arrived and off we went to meet the Anson twin-engined Communication Flight aircraft which had left Royal Air Force Bovingdon earlier. At 1100 hours the aircraft landed on the runway and was directed to the front of Air Traffic Control. Corporal Jackson stepped forward on a signal from the pilot and put chocks under both wheels. He then opened the rear door and placed a stepladder up to the opening, for the passengers to alight. First came my parents, followed by Barbara and her mother and we all embraced each other. It was quite an emotional scene. Barbara hung on to me tightly for some seconds before releasing me as tears began to roll down her colourless face. I gave her my handkerchief. She wore a green and black dress with a narrow belt around her waist, complemented by shiny, black high-heeled shoes and a dark green plain coat, open all the way down the front. She looked tired, gaunt and not at all well. Her hair was longer than usual and she seemed very nervous. Only her bright red lipstick and highly polished fingernails brightened her appearance. After welcoming her mother, they were ushered by the driver into the Station Commander's car while Barbara and I held hands in the back of the Land Rover.

In the ante-room at the Officers' Mess I introduced my guests from the Dutch Resistance and fellow pilots from 629 Squadron. Barbara went straight over to Matt with whom she had kept in touch while I had been in occupied Holland. He had also comforted her the evening I was reported as missing. She gave him a warm hug before returning to hold my hand while my mother never stopped talking to the Station Commander and my father quietly examined the Mess Hall and the priceless pictures hanging all round the ground floor rooms. He was especially interested in the portraits of some of the fighter aces stationed at Hambridge during the Battle of Britain.

I sat with Barbara and her mother. They wanted to know how my injured arm was and how I had escaped from occupied Holland. Barbara's mother was a charming woman who always treated me as an equal in the family circle. 'I'm so pleased you're home safely. For the first few days I had a hell of a job with Barbara as she was in shock at the possibility of you being killed in action. Once she heard from your sister, and the Pilot Officer that came up to see us, she just went to pieces. She kept all your lovely letters and photographs and read them over and over again. Eventually, I got her back to work, but she missed you terribly, Donald.'

'I missed her too, Mother. I love her very much.'

Mrs Devereaux held my hand and said, 'Donald, we're very proud of you. I hope you and Barbara can marry soon; she loves you and misses you terribly.' She released her grip on my good hand and I kissed her on the cheek as a sign of my affection.

Barbara came over to me and said, 'Could I have a word with you, Donald, dear, in a private room?'

'Of course,' I replied. I took her hand and led her to one of the writing rooms off the corridor leading to the main Mess Hall.

I sat her down at a writing table and went and locked the door. We both embraced warmly for quite a few seconds before she withdrew her lovely, shapely body.

'Donald, I have something to say to you which is going to hurt you deeply, but I can't prolong it any longer. I love you very much. I'm not very experienced with men, and I'm naive. You came along at the most important period of my life, I fell deeply in love with you. You're such a gentleman, it was unbelievable that I'd found a man so gentle with women. You put me on a pedestal, and this put great pressure on me to

278

abide by your rules. I began to worry that I couldn't match your ideals of behaviour, and basically sexless relationship. You're not forthcoming enough in an intimate relationship and I began to fear we would never have children. You would put your career first, and me second. The main problem, Donald, was we never saw much of each other throughout our courtship. Only once did we go on a long holiday, which was wonderful, on the Isle of Wight. I've been so lonely, due to the demands of the war on you, that in the end I couldn't cope any longer. We had a few hours here, a few hours there. I even had to go without you to choose my engagement ring.

'When your sister Beryl rang me to say you were missing presumed killed over occupied Holland, I just went to pieces. I was so lonely and distressed I felt a piece of my heart had left me. I cried for days. I wouldn't go to work. I just brooded around the house. My father wasn't any help at all. He didn't understand the sacrifices of war. One day you love someone, the next day you're alone in the world of conflict and tyranny.

'Eventually, after a few days, my mother made me go back to work, and after a while I met a plasterer from Paddington. My father was giving me hell at home so I went to stay with this man who I didn't love and have now left. Donald, I'm pregnant. It's not your baby, so you don't have to worry on that score.'

She came around from the other side of the table and held me. Tears were flowing fast down her bloodless face.

'Pregnant, Barbara? You can't be,' I said in anger and desperation, pacing up and down the room. 'I've been away only eight weeks, and you've gone and wiped out all that I've fought for in an occupied country, with Germans everywhere. And you've done this to me. I'm extremely hurt, Barbara. I loved you so very much, ever since we first met. I'll always love you until I die.

'I just don't know what to say. Without the help of those two Dutch people, I wouldn't be alive today, what with the infection in my arm, and the cat and mouse game I've had with the Germans.'

She came over to me, held my good hand and said, 'Darling

Donald, I'm so very sorry.' Her lacklustre eyes said everything.

'Are you going to marry this man?' I said sharply.

'No, I'm not. I've left him for good and I'm living with my cousin in East London. My father would have nothing to do with me. Two weeks after I left home he burnt all my clothes, our pictures and all your letters, which I had treasured. I've lost everything from the past we had together.'

'I'm so sorry to hear that, Barbara,' I said as I held her tightly. 'I still love you, you know. Now that I'm home, we could get married and I'll look after your baby as though it were my own.'

She replied earnestly, 'Donald, it won't work. I've been through all of this before. I'm breaking off our engagement.' She put her engagement ring and gold watch down on the polished desk. 'As you said to me once, Donald, war can make or break relationships. Well, I'm afraid this one is broken. I've been proud to know you. You're a wonderful and gifted person, and I still love you. My decision this morning may be the greatest mistake of my life. Only time will tell,' With that she dried her eyes and tidied her hair. We left the writing room hand in hand. At 1300 hours we went into the main dining room where a long, highly-polished table was decorated with the Officers' Mess silver, wineglasses and bright red serviettes. The Station Commander sat at the top of the table. I sat Barbara on my left and Sylvie on my right with, to her right, Stefan Miere. Around us sat the remainder of the guests from 629 Squadron, including my fellow pilots and some ground crew, namely, newly-promoted Warrant Officer Devlin and my reliable Corporals Jackson and Woodhams. Completing the guest list was Rosemary.

WAAFs in short, white, highly-starched jackets were in full attendance. After an excellent meal, the Station Commander stood up and commanded silence. He began by welcoming my own and Barbara's families. He also thanked Doctor Sylvie and Stefan Miere for getting me back to England and briefly outlined the task the Air Ministry had put on me while I had been with the Dutch Resistance in occupied Holland. He praised my courage and determination to complete my mission with the help of Dutch Resistance at Thorn. He also praised my unquestionable skill in bringing home to England a new German night fighter which, without training or familiarisation, I had flown home from Germany with consummate skill.

He paused as the Officers' Mess Manager interrupted him, giving him an unopened envelope. Looking down, he opened it up. Inside were two set of papers. Reading from the first he announced that Squadron Leader Donald Hamilton had been promoted.

He was interrupted by handclapping and whistles, especially from Matt. The Station Commander then asked for silence while he read out the following teletext from the Air Officer Commanding ADGB:

From the AOC ADGB. I have just received the following telegram from the Prime Minister, which says: Congratulations to Squadron Leader Donald Hamilton DFC for successfully completing his mission without due regard to his own personal safety and for showing courageous airmanship in piloting home an unfamiliar German night fighter. With immediate effect, the Air Force Commanding ADGB has promoted Acting Squadron Leader Hamilton DFC to the substantive rank of Squadron Leader. Also, His Majesty King George VI has awarded Squadron Leader Donald Hamilton DFC the award of the Air Force Cross; to Doctor Sylvie Chenneviere, the award of Member of the British Empire; to Mr Stefan Miere an honorary award of the Military Medal, for their outstanding contributions to this successful operation.

Signed,
Winston Spencer Churchill

The silence was broken by the raising of glasses, embraces and handshakes all round. Barbara's eyes sparkled. Sylvie was almost crying on Stefan's shoulder with joy. It certainly was a lot to try to take in, in one telegram.

Barbara hugged and kissed me, and said, 'Congratulations. You're now certainly a hero, as she kissed me warmly.

I held her right hand for quite some time, and whispered in her ear, 'I still love you.'

'Yes, Donald, I know,' she replied. Sylvie pressed my right knee. Stefan and I congratulated each other. I was glad he had got an award from our King as it was richly deserved.

The Station Commander then requested silence. 'Let us stand and raise our glasses to these gallant people.' And this they all did.

While all the celebrations were going on, I whispered to Sylvie, 'Will you marry me?' She turned to me, shocked and surprised.

'Yes, darling,' she replied, smiling.

'Next week?'

With utter amazement, she said, 'Yes.'

I asked Group Captain Walker if I could make an announcement. 'Yes, of course, Donald,' he replied. I picked up Sylvie's hand with my good hand, and led her to the top table adjacent to the Station Commander.

'Ladies and gentlemen. Firstly I would like to thank you all for giving me such a warm homecoming. It doesn't seem eight weeks since I took off with Matthews and Tremeer on a patrol over Holland. Without the co-operation of my two Dutch friends, I would not be standing here, so I'm very pleased they have been recognised by His Majesty, King George the Sixth with their very appropriate awards today. There was a third member of the group who we had to leave behind, namely Jan Van Driel. Without him, who was the anchor of our escape, we would have all been captured by the Gestapo. Also to the Squadron Leader commanding the Mosquito attack to divert the Germans at Wahn. We owe him and his pilots much gratitude. I'm sorry to leave the Squadron. I shall never forget your friendship and trust. I thank you all for your loyalty and devotion to duty. Finally, I would like to announce that Doctor Sylvie Chenneviere and I are getting married next week at Hambridge Church. Everyone here is welcome to attend. The reception, by kind permission of the Station Commander, will be held here in the Officers' Mess.'

Applause interrupted the short silence. I could see Matt was shocked by the announcement, since he was so close to Barbara and me. Everybody, including Barbara, came forward and offered their congratulations on our forthcoming marriage. Barbara warmly embraced Sylvie, and then came across to me. She hugged me and said, 'Donald, you've made a perfect choice. She is highly intelligent, like yourself, brave, and above all, charming. I wish you unlimited success, and I'm sure you will both be very happy. Each day of my life I will think of you. I still love you, but not enough to marry you. Mother is extremely disappointed in my letting you go, but the major factor was loneliness. Except for your sister, I got no support from your family. Your mother treated me unbearably, although I thought your father was a lovely gentleman, just like yourself. Good luck, Donald. Happy memories.' She then kissed me goodbye.

Matt called the assembly to attention. 'I would like, on behalf of the pilots and ground crew of the Squadron, to congratulate today, Donald's wedding to Doctor Sylvie Chenneviere, and his promotion to full Squadron Leader and the award of his Air Force Cross. I doubt whether we would have achieved such a high degree of success against the V1 without Donald's leadership. I also doubt whether we shall ever again have a friendlier commander on the ground, but in the air, a more ruthless one. We all wish Barbara every happiness in her new life, and we wish Donald and Sylvie a happy and long-lasting marriage. Can we now raise our glasses, and wish them God speed and everlasting happiness.'

Everyone stood up, toasted our health and sat down. The Station Commander then stood up and thanked everybody for attending. Our guests were asked to assemble in the foyer, as their cars were waiting to take them to the airfield. I collected the coats of our guests and, holding Sylvie's hand, ushered them into the waiting cars outside the Mess. Matt came over and kissed Barbara and her mother goodbye.

On arrival at the Air Traffic Control tower, where the Anson was waiting, I said goodbye to my parents, Barbara's mother, and finally Barbara. We kissed each other goodbye for the very last time. As they got on board the aircraft, Sylvie and I stood on the grass and watched the Anson taxi around the perimeter track of the airfield, and eventually take off on a very slow climb into the sunny blue sky. Sylvie and I stood there, waving goodbye long after they had gone. We hugged each other, and I kissed her, saying, 'Are you happy, darling?'

'Oh, yes, Donald, and I love you dearly,' she replied.

'You will be Doctor S. Hamilton next week.'

'Yes, I know.'

We held each other tightly and got into the car waiting to take us back to the Officers' Mess for a celebration drink with the lads of 629 Squadron.

SELECT BIBLIOGRAPHY

Allen, Dizzy, *Fighter Squadron,* William Kimber
Barker, Lt. Col. A.J. Bowyer, Chaz and Grant, William, *Classic Aircraft of WW2,* Bison Books
Bates, H.E., *Flying Bombs Over England,* Froglets
Bowyer, M.J.F., *The Battle of Britain,* Patrick Stephens
Deighton, Len, *Battle of Britain,* Book Club Associates
Gilbert, Adrian, *Waffen SS,* Guild Publishing
Godfrey, H.C., *Luck Thirteen,* Biddles
Guthrie, D., *Spitfire Squadron,* Robert Hale
Gunston, Bill, *Aircraft of WW2,* St Michael
Henry, C., and Miller, M., *Children of the SS,* Hutchinson
Johnson, J., *Wing Leader,* David and Charles
Longmade, N., *The Doodlebugs,* Hutchinson
Lucas, James, *Storming Eagles,* Guild Publishing
Ogley, Bob, *Doodlebugs and Rockets,* Froglets
Philpott, Bryan, *German Military Aircraft,* Park South Books
Pitt, Barnie, *The Military History of WW2,* Guild Publishing
Rolls, W.T., *Spitfire Attack,* William Kimber
Smith, D., *Spitfire into Battle,* John Murray
Vader, John, *Spitfire,* Pan/Ballantine
Young, R.A., *The Flying Bomb,* Ian Allan